PENGUIN BOOKS

BLACK ARROW

Parker, winner of a Shamus Award for the short story
_kitada's First Case," is the author of *The Dragon Scroll,*
Rashomon Gate, and *The Hell Screen* and lives in Virginia
Beach, Virginia.

BLACK ARROW

I. J. PARKER

PENGUIN BOOKS

PENGUIN BOOKS
Published by the Penguin Group
Penguin Group (USA) Inc., 375 Hudson Street, New York, New York 10014, U.S.A.
Penguin Group (Canada), 90 Eglinton Avenue East, Suite 700, Toronto, Ontario,
Canada M4P 2Y3 (a division of Pearson Penguin Canada Inc.)
Penguin Books Ltd, 80 Strand, London WC2R 0RL, England
Penguin Ireland, 25 St Stephen's Green,
Dublin 2, Ireland (a division of Penguin Books Ltd)
Penguin Group (Australia), 250 Camberwell Road, Camberwell,
Victoria 3124, Australia (a division of Pearson Australia Group Pty Ltd)
Penguin Books India Pvt Ltd, 11 Community Centre,
Panchsheel Park, New Delhi – 110 017, India
Penguin Group (NZ), cnr Airborne and Rosedale Roads, Albany,
Auckland 1310, New Zealand (a division of Pearson New Zealand Ltd)
Penguin Books (South Africa) (Pty) Ltd, 24 Sturdee Avenue,
Rosebank, Johannesburg 2196, South Africa

Penguin Books Ltd, Registered Offices:
80 Strand, London WC2R 0RL, England

First published in Penguin Books 2006

3 5 7 9 10 8 6 4

Publisher's Note
This is a work of fiction. Names, characters, places, and incidents either are the product
of the author's imagination or are used fictitiously, and any resemblance to actual persons, living or dead, business establishments, events, or locales is entirely coincidental.

LIBRARY OF CONGRESS CATALOGING IN PUBLICATION DATA
Parker, I. J. (Ingrid J.)
Black arrow / I. J. Parker.
p. cm.
ISBN 0 14 30.3561 4
1. Japan—History—Heian period, 794–1185—Fiction.
2. Nobility—Fiction. I. Title.
PS3616.A745B57 2006
813'.6—dc22   2006046558

Printed in the United States of America
Set in Minion

To my daughter Karin

ACKNOWLEDGMENTS

I am indebted to my readers, all writers themselves, who have offered advice, suggestions, and editorial comment on the early drafts of this novel. They are Jacqueline Falkenhan, John Rosenman, Richard Rowand, and Bob Stein. And, of course, my gratitude also extends to my editor, Ali Bothwell-Mancini, who saves me from embarrassing errors. Finally, as always, I'm deeply grateful to my agents, Jean Naggar and Jennifer Weltz, whose faith in me and whose tireless work and support mean everything.

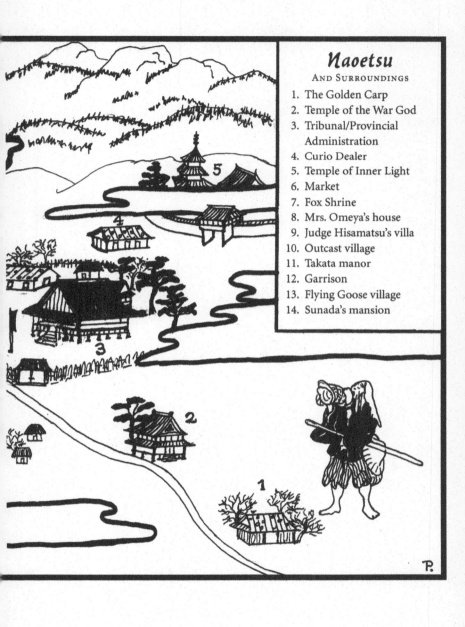

Naoetsu

AND SURROUNDINGS

CHARACTERS

MAIN CHARACTERS

Sugawara Akitada	Deputy governor of Echigo province
Tora, Hitomaro, Genba	His lieutenants
Seimei	His secretary
Tamako	His wife
Hamaya	Head clerk of the provincial administration
Yasakichi, Oyoshi	Two coroners
Chobei, Kaoru	Two sergeants of constables

CHARACTERS INVOLVED IN THE CASES

Uesugi Maro	The old lord of Takata castle, provincial chieftain, and high constable of Echigo

Uesugi Makio	His son and heir
Kaibara	Steward to the Uesugi family
Hideo	Servant to the old lord
Toneo	Hideo's grandson
Hokko	The abbot of the Buddhist temple
Takesuke	Commander of the provincial guard
Mrs. Sato	An innkeeper's widow
Kiyo	Her maid
Takagi, Okano, Umehara	Three travelers arrested for murder
Sunada	A wealthy merchant
Boshu	Sunada's agent
Hisamatsu	A judge
Mrs. Omeya	A widow
Goto	A fishmonger
Ogai	His brother, a deserter
Koichi	A porter

Also: Tradesmen, outcasts, servants, and constables

THE FATAL ARROW

ECHIGO PROVINCE, JAPAN:
LEAF-TURNING MONTH (SEPTEMBER), A.D. 981

The evening sun slanted through the branches of tall cedars and splashed across a bloodred maple on the other side of the clearing. From the valley below came sounds of horses and shouts of men.

A young woman emerged from the trees, leading a child—a boy, no more than three years old, in bright blue silk and with his hair childishly parted and tied into loops over his ears. The young woman was slender and beautiful, and dressed in a costly white silk gown embroidered about the hem and full sleeves with nodding golden grasses and purple chrysanthemums. Her long hair, which almost reached the hem of her dress, was fastened with a broad white silk ribbon below her shoulders.

In the middle of the clearing the child pulled free to chase a butterfly. The young woman called out anxiously, then laughed and ran after him.

From the thicket, Death watched the two with hot eyes, clasping the large bow with his left hand, while the right slowly reached over his shoulder to pull the long, black-feathered arrow from the quiver slung across his back.

The boy lost the butterfly and turned toward the woman, who sank to her knees and spread her arms wide to receive the child.

Death bared his teeth. He was close, his bow powerful, the arrow special. With luck it might take only the one shot. He placed it into its groove, pulled back firmly, and aimed.

With a shout of laughter the boy hurled himself into the waiting arms, and Death released the long steel-tipped missile. He watched as it found its mark just below the silken ribbon in the woman's black hair, heard the muffled blow clearly in the sudden silence, and watched as she fell forward, slowly, burying the small figure of the child beneath her. Heavy silken hair slipped aside, and a large red stain appeared on her white silk gown, spreading gradually from the black-feathered arrow like a crimson peony opening its petals in the snow.

Even the birds had fallen silent.

Death remained frozen for a few moments, watching, listening. But there was neither cry nor movement under the white silk, and he slowly lowered the bow.

The silence was broken by a small bird's voice, then by the humming of insects and distant shouts of the hunting party in the valley. Death quickly left the clearing.

ONE

THE OUTPOST

ECHIGO PROVINCE, JAPAN
GODS-ABSENT MONTH (NOVEMBER), A.D. 1015

*T*wo men armed with hunting bows rode single file down the steeply sloping track toward the dark huddle of buildings on the plain below. They hunched into heavy clothing against a sharp wind that swept across the black-and-gray landscape of rock, evergreens, and sere grasses. Below them the black roofs of the town were a blot in a wintry plain, and beyond the plain a pewter ocean stretched toward a distant line where it melted into the murky grayness of low clouds. A highway ran along the shore. Behind the horsemen rose mountains, their tops hidden in gray vapor.

The prospect was dismal.

Most of the town straggled along the black line of the highway, which looked not unlike a dead snake with a large rat bulging its middle. The rat bulge contained the tribunal and a small temple, surrounded by low, steep-roofed houses—the center of Naoetsu, capital of Echigo province.

This was the rough north country, won only recently from its barbaric inhabitants and not yet fully civilized. In the short summers, the plain between the mountains and the ocean was green with fields of rice, ramie, and beans, and the ocean dotted with fishing boats. Echigo was a fertile province, but now it prepared for the long winter, when a thick blanket of snow covered the land, and men and beasts lived like bears inside their homes until the snow melted in the spring.

The rider in front, a muscular man with a neatly trimmed graying beard and the sadness in his eyes that attracts women, looked out at the choppy sea and up at the roiling sky. The wind was bitterly cold. He called over his shoulder, "Looks like snow."

"Smells like it, too." His younger companion in the bearskin coat gave a shiver and pulled his handsome face back into his collar like a turtle. A string of birds dangled from either side of his shaggy pony's neck. "Nothing like we expected, is it, Hito?" His voice was muffled by the fur.

"Few things are. The master was sent here to set things right."

"It's another trap, I bet," grumbled the young man into his bearskin. His name was Tora, or "Tiger." He had chosen it years ago when his birth name had become a problem. Fifteen years Hitomaro's junior and from peasant stock, he had served their master longer and was closer to him. Hitomaro—Hito for short—had only joined them a few months ago in the capital, along with his friend Genba.

"How so?" asked Hitomaro.

"Reminds me of Kazusa. He was meant to fail there, too, but he was hot to succeed, sure it would make his career. They sent him on a wild goose chase, hoping he'd screw up. He gave 'em a black eye instead."

"This time his friends got him the assignment."

"Don't you believe it. This is much worse. They're letting him fill in for some prince who's taking his ease in the capital and raking in most of the income. Only this time they made sure they tied both the master's hands behind his back so he couldn't defend himself. And then they hobbled his feet so he couldn't get away. What gets me is he's all fired up again anyway."

"Then he'll succeed just like last time."

"With just the three of us? When the whole province is about to rise up in arms against him?"

"You don't know that. And we are four. You forgot Seimei."

"Amida, brother! That old man's never held a sword or a bow. Even her ladyship can at least ride a horse."

"Seimei is smart. Stop complaining, Tora, and let's move on. We'll have to cook the birds tonight."

"Heaven help us," muttered Tora. "I wish we could make Genba do it. He likes food."

Hitomaro, who had reached level ground, urged his horse into a trot. He called back, "Genba eats. He doesn't cook."

Tora followed. If the truth were known, he was by nature an optimist but he hid his confidence in hopes of impressing the older and more worldly wise Hitomaro with his experience.

On the outskirts of the city they encountered a disturbance at a mangy hostel called the Inn of the Golden Carp. The place was, despite its fancy name, a mere collection of low hovels, the sort that serves bad food in skimpy portions but generous helpings of vermin.

"Wonder what's going on there?" Tora's face emerged from his bearskin as if he smelled excitement.

Hitomaro spurred his horse, scattering the gaggle of people staring through the gate, and rode into the inn yard. Tora followed, and so did the spectators. A constable in a patched brown jacket and dirty trousers met them. "Nobody's allowed," he cried, waving his arms. "Disperse. By order of Judge Hisamatsu."

Hitomaro and Tora ignored him and dismounted. They tied their ponies to a post, but the constable drew his *jitte* and barred their way, swinging the two-pronged metal weapon at them.

"Hey! I said . . ."

Hitomaro growled, "Put that toothpick down and stand aside. By order of the governor." Sweeping the man out of his way, he stalked past him into the main hovel.

Tora slapped the constable's shoulder with a grin. "Didn't recognize us? Keep an eye on our birds, will you?" He pointed to the string of freshly killed quail and doves.

Inside, a dank stone-flagged passage led past the kitchen toward a large common room. An odor of dirt and garbage hung about the place. No point in removing shoes; the floors were either stone or dirt and could have used a sweeping out.

In the kitchen, a slovenly maid stood beside the hearth, sniveling into a corner of her skirt. Tora deplored the dirt but scanned with interest her shapely ankle and an immodest expanse of leg and thigh.

Hitomaro was already in the common room, another dirt-floored space with a central fire pit. The fire was out and the room empty except for Hitomaro and a stocky character in half armor.

They knew Chobei and he knew them. Chobei was the sergeant in charge of the tribunal's constables, and they were the newly appointed lieutenants in the governor's staff. Chobei was a local and theoretically under their command but did not see it that way. Relations were becoming strained, because Hitomaro and Tora had no plans to relinquish their authority. Never mind that they represented the entire governor's guard, they still outranked Chobei.

"This is a local matter," Chobei was saying, pushing out a

pugnacious chin. "Nothing to do with you. I've sent for the judge."

Hitomaro snapped, "Everything in this province concerns us. What happened here?"

"Just a simple robbery. Done by outsiders."

Tora raised his brows. "Outsiders? What do you mean?"

Chobei sneered, "I mean strangers. Not by our people."

"Ah." Hitomaro pretended interest. "And how do you know that?"

Chobei cast up his eyes. "It's an inn, isn't it? People who don't live here stay at inns. Strangers. Outsiders. Like you."

Tora growled in the back of his throat. Hitomaro gave him a warning look. "What about the owner?" he asked. "The maids? The staff? Any of them could be involved. Who was robbed and what was taken?"

The sergeant smirked unpleasantly. "If you must know, it's the owner who was robbed and all his gold was taken. Right out of his locked chest."

"I want to speak to him."

Chobei snorted. "Can't. They cut his throat."

"Look here, you useless piece of garbage," Tora exploded. He pushed Hitomaro aside to get his hands on the sergeant and teach him a lesson in manners.

Chobei backed off, yelling, "Be careful. I'm in charge here. The judge won't like you interfering in the execution of my duty. This is a serious crime."

Hitomaro held Tora back. "Carry on, Sergeant," he said. "We'll just take a look to make sure we report the matter correctly to his Excellency." Without waiting for an answer, he headed to the back of the inn. Tora scowled at Chobei and followed.

The dingy passage led to dingy rooms, all of them apparently empty. The last one seemed to be the owner's, and dirtier than the rest. Its floor was stamped earth, but in one corner was a wooden sleeping platform large enough for three people. Filthy blankets lay tumbled about the corpse of a fat elderly man. The man's torso and most of the blankets were soaked in blood. Beside him an empty wooden box rested on its side. It was the sort of box small shopkeepers keep their money in, with iron clasps and a lock. The lock had been forced.

Tora looked at the corpse. The dead man's mouth gaped above a gruesome wound in his throat. "Ugly old bastard," he muttered. "Looks like a toad snapping for flies."

"If he was asleep, it wouldn't take much strength to cut his throat with a sharp knife," remarked Hitomaro, looking around. "I don't see a knife, do you?"

"No. Wonder how much they got. Couldn't be a fortune in a place like this."

Chobei put in his head. "Satisfied?" he sneered. "Here's the judge."

Judge Hisamatsu bustled in as fast as short legs could carry a large paunch and thick layers of clothing. He had a round, clean-shaven face with pinched lips. The cold wind had given it some color, but he looked the sort of man who rarely spent time in the outdoors. At the moment he was irritated. "What's this then?" he demanded. "Can't you do anything yourself, Chobei?"

Chobei bowed. "A murder, your Honor. Nasty. I thought . . ." he began apologetically.

The judge stared at Tora and Hitomaro. "What are these people doing here? Get rid of them. Is that the victim?" He waddled to the platform, peered, and immediately turned away. "You might have warned me," he said, gulping air.

The unfairly chastised Chobei bowed humbly. "Very sorry, your Honor. I tried, but being kept by idle questions, I was unable to greet you. It won't happen again."

"See that it doesn't. Where's Yasakichi?"

"The coroner has been notified, your Honor."

The judge twitched impatiently. "Well, he should be here then. Must I do everything? What happened?"

"Murder and robbery, sir. The victim's name is Sato. The owner of the inn. His money box has been broken open and his gold is gone."

The judge glanced at the box. "Ah. You have arrested the killer?"

"Killers, your Honor. No, sir. Not yet. But they left only a few hours ago. On foot. I've sent a constable to the garrison with descriptions. The soldiers will bring them back shortly."

"Good. Anything else?"

"No, your Honor."

Hitomaro cleared his throat and stepped forward. "Your pardon, your Honor," he said, "but could we find out about those killers?"

The judge peered at him in the poor light. "Why? Who are you?"

Hitomaro saluted. "Lieutenant Hitomaro, sir. And this is Lieutenant Tora. In his Excellency's service."

Tora straightened up a fraction.

"What? What Excellency? I don't know you."

Tora gave another low growl, which was somehow appropriate for his bearskin and made the judge skip a step away from him.

"The governor, your Honor," Hitomaro said, keeping a straight face while kicking Tora in the ankle.

"The governor? Oh, you mean you're with the fellow from the capital? Sugawara?"

"Look here," Tora burst out, "you'd better keep a civil tongue—"

Hitomaro got a hard grip on Tora's arm. "His Honor probably hasn't been fully informed, Tora." Turning back to the judge, he said smoothly, "His Excellency, Lord Sugawara, has been duly appointed to take over the administration of this province. The imperial decree was read in front of the tribunal a week ago and a copy is posted on the notice board. I'm sure your Honor will wish to pay him a welcoming visit."

Judge Hisamatsu opened his mouth, thought better of it, and waved it aside. "Yes, well, we've been very busy. But I'm sure you won't be needed in this case."

"About the suspects," Hitomaro persisted. "Could we be told about them?"

Hisamatsu hesitated. "Well, it's not really your business, but I see no harm in it. Chobei?"

Chobei bowed. "There were three of them. Riffraff. The maid described them. They came separately, but left together before dawn today. When she got up, she found them gone and her master dead. Two of the men come from far away. A peddler by the name of Umehara and an unemployed actor called Okano. The other man claims to be a local peasant by the name of Takagi."

"There you are," said the judge to Hitomaro. "Now please go. Here is Dr. Yasakichi."

"Just a minute—" Tora started, but Hitomaro took his arm and pulled him out of the room. In the dim passage they moved aside for the coroner, dingy-robed and carrying a satchel.

Hitomaro released his companion when they were back in the drafty courtyard. "Look," he said, "you've got to control your temper better. We don't know what's what yet and you can't be making enemies before we even get to know these people. Remember what the master said."

Tora felt rebellious but nodded. "I guess you're right, brother. Did you smell that coroner? Not that I blame a man for having something to warm his belly in this weather." He gestured across the highway. "Since we didn't get much informa-

tion here, how about a cup of hot wine in that shack over
there?"

The "shack" was opposite the post station next door. A train
of pack horses was leaving, the grooms shouting and whipping
up the animals. Steam rose from their shaggy coats in the cold
air. Near the wineshop, a few hawkers had set up their stands.
Bundled up, they were selling straw boots and rain coats, rice
dumplings, and lanterns to travelers departing for the warmer
south before the snows came. The onlookers at the gate were
gone, no doubt beaten back by the constable.

Tora and Hitomaro crossed the street after the pack train. A
tattered bamboo blind with faded characters covered the door
of the wineshop. They lifted it and ducked in.

A thick miasma of smoke, oil fumes, and sour wine met
them. The light was dim because both tiny windows were covered with rags and blinds to keep out the frigid air. What little
light there was came from oil lamps attached to the walls and
from a glowing charcoal fire in the middle of the small room.
A handful of customers sat around the fire, and an ancient
woman, round as a dumpling, was pouring wine and carrying
on a conversation. An even older man, his thin frame bent almost double, bustled forward. Hitomaro and Tora decided to
stay away from the haze around the fire and sat on an empty
bench near the door. Leaning their bows against the wall, they
ordered a flask of hot wine.

"What did you make of that?" Tora asked, jerking his head
toward the Golden Carp.

Hitomaro looked thoughtful. "Lack of cooperation. Not
surprising, really. The judge wasn't too sure of himself, though,
or we wouldn't have had the time of day from them."

"I meant the murder."

Hitomaro chewed his lip. "Could be it happened that way."

"I don't think so."

"Oh?"

"A peddler, a peasant, and an actor agreeing to kill an inn-keeper on the road? They wouldn't agree to do anything together."

"How do we know that's what they are?"

"The maid said so."

"Maybe the maid lied."

Tora considered the maid until their wine came. Her shapely legs featured in his thoughts.

The old man set down the flask and two cups along with a plate of pickles. "Are the gentlemen new in town?" he asked, peering at them from watery eyes.

Tora tasted the wine. It was thick with sediment and sour. He put down his cup. "You guessed right, uncle. Looking for a place to stay. Someone told us the inn over there is cheap, but there's been a murder. We don't like places where they kill the guests." He held up the flask. "How about joining us in a cup?"

"Thank you, thank you!" The old man cast a furtive glance toward the old woman and produced a chipped cup from his sleeve. This Tora filled, and the old man drained it, smacking his lips and tucking the cup away again in the twinkling of an eye. "As for the Carp," he said with a toothless grin. "It's old Sato, the innkeeper, who was killed and the guests did it. Serves him right. The old skinflint puts up anything that crawls in off the road and has a few coppers. His poor wife's been trying to spruce up the place and bring in a better clientele." He cast a dubious glance at their rough clothes, his eyes lingering on Tora's bearskin.

Tora sampled the pickles and found them excellent, crisp and nicely spiced. He slipped off the bear skin and revealed a neat blue cloth jacket underneath.

The old man looked relieved. "It's been hard for that young woman," he said, "running a place with such a husband. Like an ant dragging an anchor."

Tora grinned. "Well, she's rid of the anchor now. Young, you say?"

The old man chortled. "Oh, my, yes. And a beauty! Old Sato didn't deserve the pretty thing, and that's the truth. But she knows it, so don't get your hopes up." He sighed. "Some men have all the luck." He cast another furtive look over his shoulder, started, and put a gnarled finger to his lips.

The old woman waddled up. She gave them a nod and told the old man, "I need some firewood if you want me to cook the rice and keep the wine warm. Somebody's got to do the work if we're to eat."

"Get it yourself. My wife," he said to Tora, rolling his eyes. "Can't stand to see a man rest. Ask her about the Carp. She knows everything."

Tora turned on the charm. "Lucky you. Your lady's not only fetching but well-informed. I bet she makes these delicious pickles herself."

The woman's round face widened into a broad smile nearly as toothless as her husband's. She sat down beside Tora. "A family recipe. Been making them all my life. So, where are you two from?"

"The capital," Hitomaro said, chewing a pickle. "We stopped across the street first. You know anything about the murder?"

She nodded. "It should suit the whore just fine," she said darkly.

Her husband bristled. "You've no right to call her that, woman."

Tora laughed. "If she's as beautiful as your husband says, I might court her myself—now that she's single again."

"Then you'd better watch out. That one's a fox," snapped the old woman.

"Horns grow on the head of a jealous woman," muttered her husband.

She punched his arm. "What do *you* know about such women?"

"Pay no attention to her, young man," the old man said, rubbing his arm. "Mrs. Sato was a good little wife. Dutiful daughter, too. Not many young girls let themselves get sold to a cranky old geezer like Sato."

Hitomaro put in, "I don't think she was home just now."

"She went to visit her sick mother yesterday," the old man said. "Maybe she's gone back." His wife gave a snort, and he glared at her. "A dutiful wife and daughter, I say, and a fine little manager, too. She'll do wonders for the place now that old Sato's dead."

"Hah!" said his wife and left.

Her husband stayed. "Sato was a terrible miser. He let the inn run down. Charged bums a few coppers for a place by the hearth and a bowl of beans or millet with wilted greens. His wife's been wanting a nicer place."

The fat little wife came rolling back with another plate of pickles. She said, "Guess what? One of the men's from Takata. He says the old lord's dying."

Her husband pursed his mouth. "Lord Maro? He's been dying for years. But I'd better lay in more wine anyway. If it's true, we'll be busy around here for the funeral." His face broke into a happy grin for a moment, then he said piously, "Lord Uesugi's the high constable. May he be reborn in paradise."

"If he's the high constable," Tora said, "he's had a good life already. Save paradise for us poor people."

"You wouldn't want to trade places with him," said the old man. "There's a curse on that clan."

"A curse?"

"Ah, terrible things happen to them. Take Lord Maro's older brother. He used to be a champion with the bow and could hit the eye of a rabbit at two hundred paces, but one day he killed his father's wife and her little son. Killed his own brother!"

"What happened to him?" Hitomaro asked.

"The angry ghosts ate him."

Tora's eyes widened. "Really?"

The old woman rolled her eyes and cried, "It's the truth. The ghosts of that poor young lady and her babe. He was never seen again."

Her husband scowled. "I'm telling the story." He turned back to Tora and Hitomaro. "Lord Maro's father was pretty old when he married again and had another son. I should be so lucky!" He gave his wife a meaningful look. This sent her into hoots of derisive laughter and she waddled back to her customers.

"So? Go on," Tora said.

"Well, they found the lady and her boy in the forest. Killed by the same arrow!" He leaned forward. "The older son's arrow. It went through both of them. Like two birds on a spit. Lord Maro's father had doted on them and it killed him." He paused and eyed the wine flask. "You're not drinking. Can I get you some more wine?"

They shook their heads. Tora said, "How about another cup for you?"

In a flash the cup reappeared from the old man's sleeve. Tora filled it, the old man gulped it down, tucked the cup away, and continued, "Well, Lord Maro succeeded his father, but he had no luck either. Only one of his children lived. That's Makio. But Makio's wife died young. They say she jumped off the upper gallery a few weeks after the wedding. He never married again. Then Lord Maro went out hunting and lost his mind. Came back raving mad. Locked himself away and never came out of his room again. They say there's crying and wailing day and night in that room. It'll be a blessing if he finally dies."

Tora gave a shudder. "Angry ghosts will drive a man mad."

The old man nodded. "Mind you, there'll be more trouble soon. It's the new governor. Makio will get rid of him, just like his father did the last one."

"What?" Tora and Hitomaro asked together.

"Hah! You don't believe me? Name of Oda. Came from the capital just like this one and wanted to run things. Broke his neck falling off a horse. They called it an accident." He snorted.

Hitomaro said, "It wasn't an accident?"

"His horse came home with an arrow in its ass."

Tora and Hitomaro exchanged glances, then Hitomaro got up and tossed some coins down. "That's foolish talk," he said harshly. "If someone raises a hand against a governor, the emperor sends an army to teach them proper respect."

"Well," the old man swept up the coins, "it'll make trouble all right. That's always the way in the end."

Outside, Tora asked, "You think there was any truth to that?"

"To what? The murdered governor? Or this Makio's plans for us?"

"Both."

"No idea. He had no reason to lie and he seemed rational enough—except for that ghost business. They say rumors are more honest than official welcomes. We'd better report it to the master."

But when they got back to the inn yard, Tora burst into a string of curses. His catch of birds had disappeared—all but one skinny dove which had been nailed to a pole with a knife. Stuck to the knife was a piece of paper with the words, "This will be you next time."

TWO

FIRST SNOW

The capital of Echigo province was not a planned city like Heian-kyo but had sprung up around an old fort that once guarded the northern highway along the shore of the Sea of Japan. The fort had long since been abandoned as the emperor's armies and independent warlords pushed the hostile Ezo people farther north into remote parts of neighboring Dewa province.

The remnants of the fort were now the tribunal and seat of the provincial government. It consisted mostly of a collection of dilapidated buildings, once barracks and stables for horses, which huddled inside a broken-down palisade.

The main hall occupied the center of the compound. It was the only raised timber building and contained the official reception areas and offices of the governor's staff. It also served as living quarters for the new deputy governor, Sugawara Akitada, and his young wife.

When Hitomaro and Tora returned, Akitada was sweeping

leaves and dirt from the floor of the reception hall. Before anyone could say anything, Hitomaro crossed the room to take the
broom from his young master's hand. "Allow me, sir," he said
and set about the chore efficiently.

"Thank you, Hito," said Akitada, "but I was almost done. It
looks much better, doesn't it?" He was trying to convince himself
but, judging by their faces, his lieutenants suppressed dismay.

"Looks fine, sir," said Tora stoutly. "A bit of oil will polish the
floor nicely and we can always drape some hangings over that
back wall." The back wall had lost half its boards to vandals.
Gaping holes revealed the room beyond.

Akitada nodded. "Excellent idea. Seimei is in the archives,
organizing the documents. It's very dusty work." He smiled a little. "He sent me away because I was wasting time reading everything I picked up. Did you have any luck?"

Tora grimaced. "We shot enough to feed us all for a week,
but some bastard stole our birds."

"Ah, I expect people are hungry. From what I have seen,
there is a lot of hardship here. The granaries are nearly empty."

"And now there's murder, as well," said Hitomaro. "We ran
into some trouble on the outskirts. An innkeeper. Killed by his
guests, it seems." He opened the door and swept the pile of dirt
out onto the veranda and from there into the courtyard below.
A cold wind caught part of it and blew it back. He muttered under his breath.

Akitada closed the door while Hitomaro wielded his broom
again. "Did you investigate?" Akitada asked.

"Couldn't. Chobei and the judge wouldn't have it. Their jurisdiction, they said."

Akitada opened the door again, and this time Hitomaro
managed to dispose of the dirt without mishap. He returned
quickly. It was as cold inside the hall as in the open but at least
there was no wind. He and Tora looked at each other.

"You were polite, I hope," Akitada said to Tora.

Tora flushed. "They're bastards, sir, and they're out to get us." He told Akitada what the old man in the wineshop had said and showed him the crudely written note that had been attached to the dove. He added, "And I don't like the way they're handling the murder. They're going after three men—an actor, a peddler, and a farmer. I got the notion that they were convenient scapegoats. Can they get away with that?"

"Of course not," Akitada said firmly. "They may arrest suspects if the circumstances warrant it, but there is the judge, after all. He will investigate the evidence. If he is not satisfied, he will have the suspects released. In any case, trials are public. You can't simply find people guilty of murder without having convincing proof."

"I don't like that Judge Hisamatsu, sir. Can't you check into it? Or let me and Hito do it?"

"No. Let the proper authorities do their work."

Hitomaro and Tora exchanged glances again. Hitomaro said, "It looks like people here don't like their governors, and our constables are poorly trained and uncooperative. They claim to be busy with other chores every time I ask them to assemble for drill."

"And," added Tora, "the lazy bastards refuse to help us clean up the place. We even have to feed our own horses. Is it true that one of the governors got murdered?"

Akitada frowned. "A foolish tale. Do the best you can with the constables. We should be able to get more done very soon. I am to meet some of the local dignitaries at Takata."

"Oh," cried Tora, "you haven't heard then? There's talk in town that the old lord is dying."

Akitada raised his brows. "It must be more rumor. His son would have canceled the banquet if it were true. No, I must go, but you can come with me, Tora, so get ready."

As Akitada walked down a narrow, dark corridor, he had to pause for another wave of nausea to pass before entering their private room. He reflected bitterly that the long-awaited invitation from the younger Uesugi was spoiled by this cursed bout of illness, caused, he suspected, by the tribunal cook, either through ineptitude or by intent. Though he had managed to hide his fears from the others, he knew that the local people looked upon him as their enemy. Poison? No, not that. They would not dare raise a hand against a duly appointed official from the capital. With a shiver, he pushed open the door.

His wife, a slender, pretty young woman in a rose-colored, quilted silk coat over full deep-red trousers, was arranging his formal robe over a bamboo stand. Gray smoke curled up in a thin spiral from a censer nearby and filled the air with the exotic scent of sandalwood.

Akitada said peevishly, "I wish you wouldn't bother! These border warlords are hardly going to be impressed by a perfumed gown."

Tamako gave him a searching glance and said, "I think you do Uesugi an injustice. The family has money and they have for generations sent their sons to the capital to be educated." After a moment she added, "I hope there is no reason to suspect them of disloyalty. Perhaps you should postpone this visit."

Akitada growled, "Nonsense," and went to a cushion near a brazier full of glowing charcoal.

Lowering his tall frame gingerly, he watched his wife's graceful movements as she placed the censer under the bamboo stand and used her fan to direct the scent of incense toward the garment. He held his chilled fingers over the glowing coals. "It is clouding up," he said, his heavy eyebrows glowering. "The chances are excellent that I will get a good soaking on the way. The very idea, wearing a perfumed silk robe for a ten-mile ride across rough roads in this kind of weather."

"You can put your straw raincoat over it. Or better still, why don't you let Tora take your regrets and stay here with me?"

She laid down her fan, came to him and knelt, placing a cool hand against his forehead. "At least you are not feverish," she said. "Are you still feeling ill?"

Akitada shifted away irritably. "It is nothing."

He thought: And I must go. Unless I can get Uesugi to support me, I am wasted here. He clenched his fists. In the week since his arrival he had met with sullen stares from the people in the streets, and with lack of cooperation and outright insubordination from what passed as his staff at the tribunal. Not that there was much of it, for the entire paperwork of the province seemed to be in the hands of one senior clerk and two frightened youngsters. And in the jail and constabulary matters were even worse. Never had he seen a more depraved looking gang of cutthroats than his tribunal constables and their brutish sergeant, while the few prisoners in their filthy cells looked starved and bore the marks of cruel beatings.

To add insult to injury, the provincial guard, commanded by the haughty Captain Takesuke, seemed to take its orders from Takata. The old Lord Uesugi was the provincial high constable. Evidently his authority also extended to legal matters, for since Akitada's arrival not a single man or woman had come to the tribunal to lay charges or ask for adjudication of a case. He sighed deeply.

"What is wrong?" his wife asked.

"It may be," he said heavily, "that we should not have come here. Nothing has gone right. The tribunal is practically a ruin, the provincial granaries are almost empty, and the people are sullen to the point of disrespect. We have yet to receive a single welcome."

She got up to return to her work. "It is true that this is a strange place, but you were eager to leave the capital. Remember how unhappy you were with your work and how cruelly the minister used you? If only winter were not so near." Her voice trailed off uncertainly.

Akitada was suddenly ashamed of having taken out his ill humor on his wife. "Tamako, are you sorry you came?" he asked anxiously. "This is called the snow country, you know. They say we will be snowed in for six months and rarely see daylight because the snow covers the whole house. And we don't even have a house. How will you pass your time?"

She gave him a smile. "We can make this place livable and we will be together."

Akitada looked about at the handsome screens and movable hangings and at the large lacquer chests holding their bedding and clothes. But he was worried about other matters. "There are no women's quarters here. And the men are not only hostile and rebellious, but uncouth. Your maid may be raped within a week. I should never have brought either of you."

There was a brief silence. Then Tamako said in a brittle voice, "If you don't want me here, I will go back. Then at least I shall be of some use to your mother and sisters."

They both knew they were too far from the capital and he could not send her home, but he refused to acknowledge his defeat. Instead he changed the subject. "Today there were more dispatches from the north. The Ezo have attacked on several fronts, and our troops are fighting as far south as Tagajo. It made me wonder why the younger Uesugi does not join them. After all, their local reputation rests solely on their military ability to protect this province."

"I expect the old lord is worse. The women in the kitchen say he cannot last much longer. Do you think the Ezo will push as far south as this?"

"No. Our soldiers are staunch fighters. Besides, the snow will make the roads impassable. No doubt that is the reason for all the unrest. The Ezo are trying to improve their positions before retiring into their winter camps."

There was a scratching sound at the door and it slid open. A soberly dressed elderly man with a thin white mustache and chin beard entered and bowed.

Tamako cried, "Seimei, I am very glad to see you. Your master insists on riding to Takata tonight in spite of his indisposition. Can you make him one of your soothing teas?"

"Gladly." The old man looked up eagerly. "But your ladyship flatters my poor skills. Are you still nauseated, sir?" He came closer and studied Akitada's face. "Is there a bloated feeling in your belly? Or angry dragon sounds in the bowels? What about your stool? Any sign of flux? Or flatulence?"

Akitada growled, "For heaven's sake, leave me alone, both of you! No, Seimei, I don't want any tea." He got up. "Tamako, you can send for me when you are done. I need some fresh air and will be on the veranda!" He stalked from the room.

The tribunal hall was raised several feet above ground. In warmer climes and in the summer months this construction assured cooling air circulation, but here it meant that the icy air seeped mercilessly through the wooden floors. Akitada walked along the veranda under the deep eaves and looked across the open courtyard toward the smaller outbuildings that served as the kitchen, storehouse, stable, constabulary, and jail. All of it looked depressingly derelict.

A cold gust of air tore at his robe and flapped one of his wide sleeves into his face. He shivered, but breathed in deeply, trying to settle his stomach. Dusk would be early because of the weather. Stepping to the railing, Akitada glanced up at ominous clouds scurrying across a leaden sky. The wind rushed through the bare trees in the courtyard, sweeping before it red and brown leaves. Some danced across the wooden boards under his feet and gathered in drifts against the walls of the building.

Beyond the tribunal palisade stretched more bare trees and dark thatched roofs. Somewhere in the gray distance lay the ocean. Akitada turned a corner and looked at the mountains, which already wore white patches of snow. Winter came early in Echigo.

When he and Tamako had traveled north, the woods had reminded them of pieces of brocade, the maple leaves weaving glowing designs against the deep green of the pines. They had taken their meals by the side of the road, and remarked on the beauty of the country.

But then the weather had turned dismal and the winds bitterly cold. No wonder Echigo was a place where the emperors used to send their political enemies. And now they had sent him and Tamako to this godforsaken place.

Akitada closed his eyes against the dreary grayness, stubbornly blocking such thoughts from his mind. It was this confounded bellyache. At his age, being appointed deputy governor, even if it was just a provisional appointment with limited powers and even more limited salary, was an extraordinary piece of luck. Here he could make a name for himself and prove his worth.

He gulped more air and wondered how he would get through the banquet tonight. Any reluctance to sample the offered dishes would be interpreted as an insult. Perhaps it was wiser to stay home. No! He must find out how things stood. He could not go on this way. Conditions in the tribunal were intolerable. He wanted to replace the entire staff, but where to find loyal men in this hostile city? Why was everyone against him?

A horrible sound—like the distant wailing of a lost soul, culminating in the bellowing of an angry bull—tore at his ear drums. He jumped, looked about wildly, and rushed around the corner.

There, just below the rear veranda, stood a very strange

creature. For a moment, Akitada thought he was a ghost, the ghost of an old man with long, unbound white hair and a large white beard blowing crazily in the wind.

When the old man saw Akitada, he slowly lowered a big conch shell from his lips. He was dressed in short, dark cotton trousers and a full-sleeved blouse of black and white checks with strange tassels hanging about his neck, and he stood motionless and silent, supporting himself on a carved staff. He stared fixedly at Akitada.

"What in the Buddha's name do you think you are doing, blowing that thing here?" Akitada demanded in a shaking voice. "This is the tribunal and you're trespassing. Get away from here or I'll call the constables."

Without taking his sharp black eyes off Akitada, the old man slowly hooked the conch shell to his belt and stepped a little closer. Akitada, irritated by this latest example of disrespect, glared back. He was amazed at the darkness of the old man's skin, blackened rather than bronzed by exposure and all the more startling for the contrast with the silver-white mane and beard. His eyes fell to the man's legs, naked from the knees down to his bare feet, and as dark and leathery as his face.

In this cold.

A hungry beggar. Suddenly shame overwhelmed Akitada's anger. "Forgive me," he said to the old man, bowing slightly. "How rude of me. I have not been feeling very well and you startled me. It is cold outside and I am sure you have not eaten. You are welcome here, but I have nothing to offer you. If you will go across the courtyard, you will find the kitchen." He pointed. "Tell them that the governor said to fill your bowl until you have had enough and to find you a warm place to sleep."

The beggar, inclining his head slightly, like a haughty nobleman, turned away. A strange piece of fur, attached to his belt in the back, flapped as he melted into the dusk.

Behind Akitada, a door opened with a creak, and Tora asked, "What was that cursed noise?"

Akitada turned. Tora, in his shaggy bearskin, reminded him of one of the northern barbarians. "Do you plan to wear that pelt tonight?" he asked irritably. "You look like a wild animal."

Seimei appeared behind the young man. "Her ladyship says your clothes are ready, sir. And she wonders about the strange sound a moment ago."

"Thank you, Seimei. It was an old beggar blowing a conch shell. A peculiar way of asking for alms, but perhaps he is a mute. I sent him to the kitchen for food and lodging. Try to find him some straw boots, Seimei. The poor old fellow was barefoot in this weather."

Tora asked, "Was he wearing a checked blouse and carrying a tall staff?"

"Yes. You know him?"

"Not really, sir, but you've just met a *yamabushi*. They're holy men that live in the mountains and pray to the Buddha by standing naked under a waterfall in the middle of winter."

"Then they must be mad," Akitada said impatiently and headed for his quarters. "Come along."

Tamako greeted Tora with a smile. Of her husband's three lieutenants, he was the only one admitted to their private quarters. Though Tora had been an army deserter when his path crossed Akitada's, there was a strong bond of mutual obligation between them. They owed their lives to each other. And Tora's loyalty to his master extended also to his young wife and the rest of the Sugawara family in the capital. Even Akitada's mother, the ill-tempered old dowager, had been softened by his cheerful willingness to be of service to her.

Tora sat down near the door and watched as Akitada, with his wife's help, dressed for the visit to Takata.

"What do you hear from Genba?" Akitada asked, slipping out of his robes and handing them to his wife.

"He's settled in nicely. Has a room above a rice-cake baker's and all the rice cakes he can eat. His landlord's besotted with wrestling. He wants to enter Genba in the regional matches."

"Good," Akitada said, his voice muffled by a silk undershirt he was slipping into. "The baker may win back his investment. After all, Genba used to be a wrestling master." He emerged from the shirt and reached for a pair of voluminous white trousers made of stiffened silk. "I am glad the local people accept him. They respect wrestlers. Soon we will find out about the strange mood in town."

Akitada had reason to trust his three lieutenants. They had proven their loyalty. In return he had offered Genba and Hitomaro employment though they were fugitives from murder charges in their home provinces. Genba had killed in self-defense when two provincial constables had been ordered to assassinate him because his lord's son had had a fatal accident during a wrestling bout. And Hitomaro had avenged his young wife who had committed suicide after being raped by his neighbor.

Justice was not always evenhanded.

Akitada frowned and said, "I hope you and Hitomaro are careful when you visit Genba?"

"We change into old clothes and leave by the back. Genba doesn't have much to report yet, except that people are scared of a draft for the northern front."

Akitada sat down to slip on a clean pair of white socks and tie the legs of his trousers securely below his knees. He shook his head. "Doubtful. That trouble should be over as soon as the snows come. By the by, how does the weather look to you? Rain, do you think?" Back on his feet again, he accepted, one by one, several light silk robes in shades of blue and topped these off with a finely patterned dark blue brocade vest.

"It smells like snow. You should have a fur cloak like mine. Neither rain, nor snow, nor wind can get through this." Tora stroked the rough fur lovingly.

"No, thank you." Akitada sat down again and took the round silver mirror his wife handed him to adjust the formal black silk hat over his topknot. He sniffed the air. "The warmer that bearskin gets, the more it reeks," he said.

Returning the mirror to Tamako, Akitada stood up and reached for the silver-gray formal gown with its rich pattern of intertwined pine branches. Tamako helped him put it on and adjusted it lovingly. He smiled at her. "I feel like Prince Genji, who made all the ladies swoon with the fragrance of his robes. Are you not worried about sending your husband among the beauties at Takata?"

"I thought it was Tora who needed watching with the ladies." She glanced at the bearskin coat and added with a twinkle in her eyes, "Though perhaps not tonight."

Seimei came in, carrying a straw rain cape. "Everything is ready, sir. The horses are waiting."

"We'd better be on our way." Akitada sat down to put a pair of leather boots over his black silk slippers. Before leaving, he turned to Tamako, who was folding away his discarded clothing, and said, "Don't wait up for me, my dear. I shall be late."

"Return safely!" She made him a formal bow, and turned away quickly to hide her anxiety.

In the courtyard, a pair of constables stood beside four horses. The constables were in uniform and armed with bows and arrows. One had a banner announcing Akitada's rank as governor.

Akitada felt something cold touch his face and cast an uneasy glance at the rapidly darkening sky as he mounted his horse. White spots danced before the dark shapes of the build-ings. Snow. Seimei extended the straw cape and Akitada flung it about his shoulders awkwardly, fastening it across his chest. The wind tore at his headdress, and he tightened its cords. Already a fine dusting of snow covered the horse's mane. He nodded to the others, and they set out into the approaching storm.

THREE

TAKATA

They rode against an icy head wind that drove needle-sharp sleet into their faces, and Akitada's nausea faded. His mind was occupied with the disquieting gossip about his host's murderous intentions toward him. It came from the lowest source, but at the moment he had nothing else to go on, and the Uesugi had not been welcoming so far. Besides, everything that had happened so far in Echigo supported such ugly rumors.

The small village of Takata huddled at the foot of a steep hill which dominated the surrounding plain. The land for miles around belonged to the Uesugi family, as did the village. On the very top of the hill, the curving roofs of the family compound rose sharply against the darkening skies. The Uesugi manor was a stronghold that hovered above the plain like a huge hawk perched on a rock, its wings spread in readiness for its prey.

A troop of soldiers, in full battle gear and carrying pennants bearing the Uesugi crest, awaited them on the road outside the town. Their officer dismounted and approached stiff-faced and stiff-legged, bowed, and announced that the governor's party would be escorted the rest of the way.

This reception felt more like an arrest than an honor, but Akitada was intrigued in spite of the unpromising appearance of things. This was his first experience with warlords.

"You know," he said to Tora as they rode up the narrow paved road from the village, "the placement of this residence makes it far more impregnable than the miserable wooden palisades we have been building around forts in the plains. A remarkably good idea!" He looked back and saw that the hill controlled the post road to the north. "In fact," he added, "nobody approaches without being seen or passes without their permission."

"It feels like a bad place," Tora grumbled, looking up at rock and stone foundations and precipitous walls. "I'll be glad when we turn our backs on it. Remember that curse." He shuddered. "I bet the hall is full of those angry ghosts."

The first gateway, surmounted by a watch tower, came into view, and the road suddenly narrowed between rock outcroppings on both sides. They had to ride single-file. It would be easy to defend this gate. Any attacking army would be squeezed through the eye of a needle and deprived of its striking force. Akitada looked at the walls. The sheer drop below the foundations made it impossible to use ladders. And the walls were crowned with wooden galleries that had loopholes cut into them. Beyond, the steep roofs of many halls rose against the murky gray skies.

They passed through the gate, traversed several courtyards terraced into the mountainside, and came to a halt before the main hall. Here another honor guard of mounted warriors was lined up behind a middle-aged man in a handsome black-and-white-patterned silk robe. He stood alone, legs wide and arms folded across his broad chest.

When they had dismounted, he approached and bowed. "This humble one is Kaibara Danjo, steward to the Lord of Takata," he announced loudly. "I bid your Excellency welcome."

Akitada nodded and stretched his sore limbs. Then he removed his straw raincoat and handed it to Tora, who kept scanning the courtyard nervously. Firmly suppressing his own mounting sense of foreboding, Akitada glanced up at the double-storied block of wood and plaster which rose windowless for twenty feet before its projecting wooden balconies began.

Dismissing Tora and the others, Akitada nodded to Kaibara. "Lead the way."

A narrow doorway gave access to an equally narrow winding stairway, stone at first, then wood. At the top, a servant helped Akitada remove his boots. The steward Kaibara also removed his shoes and donned a pair of brocade slippers. Akitada noted the gray in his hair and close-trimmed beard, though the steward's movements were those of a much younger, and well-trained, soldier. They entered a large gallery, its walls covered with weapons and armor. Here Uesugi Makio, son and heir to the ailing lord of Takata, awaited them.

As a warlord, Makio was a distinct disappointment. A short man in his fifties, with thinning gray hair, mustache, and chin beard, he looked more like a self-satisfied civil servant. At one time perhaps well-muscled, he had become heavy, and his eyes were mere slits between rolls of fat. Perhaps his paunch or the stiff brown brocade robe prevented him from bowing more deeply. He murmured the formal phrases of greeting.

Akitada disliked him instantly, but much depended on his goodwill, and so he made an effort. "Ah, Uesugi," he said genially. "A great pleasure to meet you at last. I hope I'm not late. The weather is turning and the wind was against us all the way."

"Not at all. Your Excellency is most punctual. I apologize for the dreadful inconvenience of traveling so far only to be offered rough country fare in crude surroundings."

The usual polite formula, delivered mechanically. Akitada tried again. "On the contrary, I have looked forward to this visit. You have a magnificent home." It certainly made for a telling contrast with the tribunal accommodations. "And I congratulate you on the ingenuity of the fortifications. You need not fear enemy attacks."

For some reason, Uesugi stiffened further. "Your Excellency is too kind. Fortunately our defenses have never been tested. If you will step this way, the other guests are waiting to meet you."

Akitada sighed. It promised to be a difficult evening.

They entered a large room which would not have shamed an imperial prince. Heavy timbers supported it and crisscrossed its ceiling. Three of the walls were sliding screens painted with mountain landscapes and hunting scenes. The fourth consisted of shuttered doors. Akitada guessed that the doors led to the gallery he had seen from below. At the moment they were almost hidden by the woven reed curtains with large crimson silk tassels that surrounded a seating area in the center of the room.

Cushions lay on thick matting there, candles and oil lamps were placed around, and large bronze braziers filled with glowing charcoal heated the area.

Five men stood together in a small group. Four were strangers to Akitada. The fifth he recognized as the commandant of the garrison. Captain Takesuke, in his late twenties like Akitada, was not in uniform tonight. The others were an old monk; a very handsome, tall man in his forties; a short, fat man in his fifties; and another short, elderly, and very ugly individual. They approached and bowed as Uesugi made the introductions.

The cleric in the black robe and brocade stole was Hokko, abbot of the city's large Buddhist temple. Akitada disliked Buddhism and avoided its clergy whenever he could. Now he was forced to apologize, with some embarrassment, for not having paid this man a courtesy visit yet. He was rewarded with a smile and a pleasant invitation.

Takesuke, who had mainly impressed Akitada with his standoffish manner on their last encounter, was, if anything, even cooler tonight. They nodded warily to each other. Uesugi smiled and clapped the captain on the shoulder. "My friend can be relied upon to keep the peace in the city," he said to Akitada. "You may leave matters safely in his hands."

What matters? Was Uesugi suggesting that he, as acting governor, could not or should not maintain law and order in his own province? Akitada was also unpleasantly surprised by the apparent friendly relations between the warlord and the commander of the military guard. As a rule there was jealous competition between such men.

The handsome man was Sunada. Since he was wearing a sumptuous dark silk gown and had a very refined manner, Akitada was startled when Uesugi introduced him as a merchant. Sunada bowed very deeply and murmured something about being honored.

The other three men Uesugi summed up dismissively with a wave of his stubby hand: "Oyoshi's the pharmacist, Hisamatsu's the judge, and you've already met Kaibara."

So the ugly old man was a pharmacist, and the pudgy fellow the judge. The pharmacist was of no interest to Akitada, but the judge was another matter. He must be the one Tora and Hitomaro had had the run-in with earlier that day. That suggested a certain hostility toward the new administration. Akitada, who had placed first in law at the university and served in the Ministry of Justice in the capital, intended to take a personal interest in legal matters here.

But for the moment, he said politely, "I have been looking

forward to meeting the local notables," then took his place on a cushion next to his host.

The others seated themselves on either side by some pre-arranged system of protocol which placed the most important closest to Akitada and Uesugi. It put the abbot on Akitada's left, and Captain Takesuke on Uesugi's right. Sunada and Oyoshi sat farthest away. Uesugi clapped his hands, and four handsome serving women in softly colored silk gowns entered to pour wine into gold-speckled lacquer cups and to place these and pickled vegetables in small gilded bowls on the elegant lacquer trays before each guest.

Time for more compliments. Akitada leaned toward his host. "You spoil your guests, Uesugi. The entertainment prom-ises to be most impressive."

"Thank you, Excellency, but the test of a banquet is the food and wine. I'm afraid that you will find our rough fare a sad dis-appointment after the capital."

Akitada made a polite disclaimer. He inspected the food, which soon appeared in a rapid succession of pretty bowls and plates. His nausea had subsided, but he sampled cautiously. The prevailing taste seemed to be of some tongue-burning spice. "Excellent," he told Uesugi. "Spicier than the food at home but very flavorful. And the wine is superb." It served to put out the fire in his mouth and throat.

The stiff courtesies to his host over, Akitada turned to the guests, who were a curiously ill-assorted group. By cautious questioning he discovered that the merchant Sunada was a wholesaler with connections along the northern circuit and an intimate knowledge of shipping along the coast. He reconsid-ered his earlier judgment. Such a man had experience and could be very useful to a new governor. Unless, of course, he was al-ready useful to his enemies.

The judge was a disappointment. Akitada's inquiries about

local crime met with a pedantic lecture on the advantages of instituting the harsh Chinese system of punishment. Akitada was a staunch Confucianist himself, but he knew that Japanese customs and conditions were quite different from those in China, and that anyone who applied Chinese precepts too rigidly knew little about legal history. In any case, it was the periodic release of violent criminals from jails, whenever the emperor felt like having an amnesty, that caused problems, not the lack of executions or mutilations. Under the Chinese system, a judge had to watch as his sentence was carried out, and Akitada wondered at Hisamatsu's interest in the various torturous methods of killing a man or woman. He seemed to take inordinate pleasure in detailing their finer points.

Akitada tugged at his collar and shifted a little. He was getting hot. The wine, the spicy food, and the proximity of a large brazier at his back made perspiration bead his face and neck.

The pharmacist, who apparently also was a physician, puzzled him. What was he doing here? A small, ugly, and almost hunchbacked man, he had lively black eyes which kept watching Akitada in a penetrating and searching manner. He decided that Oyoshi was present because he was the Uesugi family's doctor and there was illness in the house.

Reminded by this of an oversight, Akitada turned to his host. "How is your honorable father these days? I was very sorry to hear he is not well."

"Your Excellency is most kind. My father's poor health is the reason I have not left for the frontier. My place is in battle, defending his Majesty's territories against the northern barbarians, but how can a dutiful son leave his father's bedside when he fears for his life?"

Uesugi did not look the eager soldier, nor the doting son, but Akitada said, "I am sorry to hear his condition is so serious. Can nothing be done?"

"My father is in his eightieth year. At his age decline must be expected."

A brief silence fell. Then Oyoshi said, "I shall be more than happy to look in on your honorable father now, if you wish, sir. Luckily I have brought my medicines with me."

"Under no circumstance," Uesugi snapped. "My father is already asleep." Seeing Akitada's astonishment at this rudeness, he flushed and added more quietly, "Besides, you are my guest tonight, Oyoshi. Enjoy your food and wine!"

Oyoshi bowed and turned his attention back to his tray.

They had done justice to three courses already, broiled salmon, stewed abalone, and a vegetable dish containing slices of bean curd, all of it highly spiced, when Akitada became aware of a peculiar gurgling discomfort in his belly. Recalling Seimei's questions, he wondered if he would finish his dinner without disgracing himself. He dabbed at his streaming face with a sleeve and sighed inwardly. He had rarely been this uncomfortable.

His host leaned toward him. "Will your Excellency be sending any dispatches to the capital before the snows close the roads?" he asked.

"Certainly. I report on a regular basis," Akitada said, momentarily distracted from his troubles by the intense interest in Uesugi's face.

Uesugi laughed and some of the others joined in. "Oh, my dear sir. Nothing happens here on a regular basis once the snows come, least of all dispatches or mail. The roads will be impassable until the beginning of summer. We will be completely cut off from the capital. If your Excellency plans to send a messenger, it had better be soon. Takesuke has some good men. I ask because the matter of my confirmation as high constable of the province is overdue."

So that was it! The real reason for this invitation: Makio

Uesugi wanted that appointment shifted from his ailing father to himself. To save the expense of large standing armies in distant and unsafe provinces, the government had taken to appointing high constables from among local noblemen and landowners, and had given them the power to collect taxes and enforce laws by using their own retainers. Makio Uesugi's father had held this position, and now his son aspired to it. It conveyed upon the holder not only power, but almost certain wealth, as a good portion of the collected taxes found its way, legally or otherwise, into a high constable's coffers.

Akitada was on principle opposed to the practice because it gave too much power to local men and diminished the authority of the governors. He certainly had no intention of acceding in the present case. Now he said evasively, "I shall give your request serious thought. If the weather conditions are indeed as you say, I must make my recommendations as soon as possible. Still, the province seems very peaceable. There has been amazingly little legal business since I arrived."

A flash of anger passed over the other man's face, but he merely bowed.

Takesuke said, "A person like yourself, Excellency, newly arrived from the capital, will not yet have an idea of local conditions. I am certain that I speak for General Uesugi as well as myself when I offer your Excellency my full assistance in military matters."

Before Akitada could ruminate on Takesuke's insistence of pushing his guard on him, Uesugi returned to his own topic. "The office of high constable has been in Uesugi hands for generations," he pointed out. "Without assigning blame to the many talented gentlemen from the capital who have served as governors here, serious matters have, as a rule, had to be resolved by the high constable. Our honorable governors from the capital have been most grateful to be relieved of onerous and dangerous duties."

Kaibara, flushed with wine, gave a short bark of laughter. "And how! Most of them saw no need to spend the long winters here. They paid extended visits to friends and relatives in more temperate provinces. Some never came back."

Perhaps this was the official version of what had happened to at least two previous governors who seemed to have disappeared in the middle of their tenure here. The thinly veiled suggestion that he, too, belonged to this type of corrupt official made Akitada angry. And the exchange had reminded him of the state of the provincial granary.

"I meant to ask you about recent rice harvests," he said to his host. "I am told they were good, yet the granary seems nearly empty."

Uesugi raised his brows. "Don't tell me you have not been informed. The granary, as I am sure you noticed, is in very poor condition. We have been storing the provincial rice privately for a number of years now. As custodians of provincial taxes, we have borne the expense ourselves. Kaibara, make a note to send a full accounting to the tribunal."

It was a very undesirable state of affairs, but Akitada had to accept it and thank Uesugi.

A sudden, painful cramping in his belly brought new perspiration to his face. Then the nausea was back, and he felt violently ill. With a muttered excuse, he stumbled up.

A servant came quickly and led him out into the gallery. Cold air blew in through the latticed openings and cooled Akitada's moist face, but he silently cursed his treacherous stomach, the slowness of the servant, and the long way to the privy.

There he purged his body of everything he had eaten and drunk and emerged shivering and weak-kneed into a blast of air from an open shutter. The servant was waiting patiently, but Akitada needed to clear his head and drive away the remnants of sickness. He stepped up to the opening and looked out over the rocky and wooded terrain below the residence. Snow had already turned the world into an ink painting. Bluish black, the night brooded over broad sweeps of white. In the distance, where the drifting snow obscured hills and forests, light and darkness faded into mysterious grays. Carried by gusts of wind, thin flakes danced past Akitada's eyes, and a thick coating of white covered the sill. There was a terrible, deathly beauty about the scene.

With an effort, Akitada shook off his morbid mood and breathed in deeply. He gathered a little snow to cool his face, and when he felt better, he leaned out to get an idea of where he was.

To his right, the building ended at a corner and he saw a part of a courtyard below. To his left, the gallery continued, its dark wood sharply traced against the snowy roofline. It terminated in a pavilion, its curving roof white against the night sky. Golden lamplight escaped from the pavilion's shutters, making it seem to float in the blue darkness like a magical lantern. The picture was unexpectedly romantic, and Akitada imagined for a moment that Uesugi kept a lover there.

Behind him the servant cleared his throat. Poor man. No doubt he was freezing. Akitada closed the shutter and returned to the gathering, determined to assert his authority. He found that the conversation had turned to magic.

The captain was in the middle of a tale about one of his men who claimed he had been seduced by a fox spirit in the shape of a woman. He had succumbed to a strange illness. Neither medicines nor a priest's prayers could cure him until someone sent for one of the mountain priests to exorcise the evil spirit. The mountain priest brought with him a female medium who had chanted her spells and caused the fox spirit to leave the soldier and slip into the old woman's body where it had cursed and complained bitterly before finally departing.

Akitada, who disapproved of such superstitions, thought this an appropriate opening to address the abbot beside him. "You must be troubled by unholy practices among the natives, Reverence," he said.

But Hokko shook his head. "You misunderstand, Excellency. It is not another faith. The *yamabushi* practice both Buddhism and exorcism. Sometimes they use a female to aid them. The priests are skilled healers who look after the mountain people very well and may be said to tread in the Buddha's footsteps more sincerely than many a learned disciple of the holy Saicho himself."

Akitada was still coping with astonishment at this testimonial to unorthodox practices, when the pharmacist leaned forward to say earnestly, "It's true. Some of their medical skills surpass anything I know, your Excellency. They gather medicinal herbs and roots in remote areas of the mountains and have, to my own knowledge, cured patients I gave up for lost. His Reverence and I have made every effort to communicate with these *yamabushi,* but they are extremely shy and secretive, and the local people protect their privacy."

Uesugi listened with every sign of impatience. "Nonsense, Oyoshi. They're a pack of outlaws! Those you are pleased to call *yamabushi* are nothing but *hinin* and escaped criminals. It is absurd to discuss them in polite society."

Hinin. Outcasts. Akitada knew that Echigo had many of these, descendants of Ezo prisoners of war and of Japanese exiled for various crimes. Outcasts were not permitted to live or work in ordinary people's houses. They lived in their own villages, and came into the cities only for menial, dirty, and taboo jobs like cutting wood, tanning leather, sweeping streets, cleaning stables, and burying the dead. But he did not like Uesugi's high-handed manner.

"All the people in this province interest me," he said sharply, "and most particularly those who seem to stand outside the law. We also have such people living near the capital. Many of them perform useful trades, and they maintain order among themselves by electing headmen and elders. In any case, since I am sworn to uphold law and order in this province, I am much indebted to his Reverence and Dr. Oyoshi for the information about local customs. As you and your steward reminded me earlier, I have much to learn about local matters, and I intend to do so to the best of my ability."

After a moment's uncomfortable silence, Uesugi muttered, "Very laudable, I am sure," and changed the subject by waving to one of the maids. "Here, girl. Fill his Excellency's cup! And your Excellency must try these pickled plums. They are delicious."

"I should be careful with the plums, Excellency," Oyoshi said quickly, "unless you have a strong stomach." Seeing the angry look on his host's face, he added, "They are said to test a warrior's stamina."

"In that case," Akitada said, "I am greatly flattered, but will pass. I am afraid I am a scholar rather than a soldier."

Uesugi exchanged a glance with the captain. An awkward silence descended on the party. Akitada was less nauseated but he was afraid to eat or drink anything else. He knew that he had failed in his efforts to bring Uesugi to his side and wished himself elsewhere. As he looked around the gathering, he noticed that Kaibara had left. Kaibara's neighbor, the merchant Sunada, met his glance and smiled. His teeth were almost as good as Tora's.

"Mr. Sunada," Akitada responded, "I take it you are very well informed about the local merchants and their guilds. I would be grateful if I could call on you sometime in the future."

Sunada looked startled. He glanced at Uesugi before bowing. "Certainly, your Excellency. I'm deeply honored. Anything I can do. You need only send for me. I live in Flying Goose village near the harbor."

"Thank you. That is most kind of you." Akitada's throat was parched and he could not rid himself of the sour taste in his mouth. Besides, the heat from the brazier was worse. He wished for cool water, but having none, he drank deeply from his cup. The wine produced an unpleasantly feverish feeling, and he pulled impatiently at the neck of his gown. The silk of his under-robe clung to his skin. He brushed new perspiration from his forehead and cheek. To add to his discomfort, he could feel more painful cramps starting in his belly. Shifting uncomfortably, he found Oyoshi's sharp eyes on him.

To forestall a question, Akitada said, "You mentioned the *yamabushi* earlier. It so happens I had a visit from one this afternoon. I took him for a beggar."

Oyoshi was surprised. "A *yamabushi* in the tribunal? What did he look like?" The abbot also looked up with interest.

"He was a very old man with long white hair and beard, but quite healthy and strong for his age. He was barefoot in this cold."

The pharmacist and Abbot Hokko exchanged a glance. Oyoshi said, "You have been honored by the master himself, Excellency. He never comes down from his mountain for ordinary visits."

Akitada made a face. "Oh dear, and I sent him to the kitchen for something to eat and a place to sleep."

"I expect he was pleased," the abbot said with a chuckle. "Should he still be there in the morning, would you send for me? I am very eager to speak to him."

"The man will hardly wait around to be arrested," the judge snapped. "I expect he has good reason to hide on his mountain. Half of those people are hiding from the authorities. He is probably a criminal or a traitor. I wonder that he slipped past the constables."

This caused a heated debate between the abbot and Hisamatsu, during which Akitada was forced to rush off down the drafty gallery again.

When he emerged from the convenience this time, he felt physically and mentally drained and stood for a moment, leaning against the wall. He wondered if his food or wine had been tampered with. The same servant, who had followed him with a lantern, was squatting on the cold wood floor, watching him. Outside the wind whistled past the shutters. Suddenly there was a brief distant sound, something between a shriek and a wail, borne on a gust of wind and snatched away again. Akitada and the servant both straightened up to listen.

Akitada strode to the shutter and threw it open. The snow was still blowing outside, but there was no sign of life in the white landscape below or in the courtyard. In the corner pavilion a shadow moved across the lighted shutter. Perhaps someone else had been startled by the sound.

The servant looked frightened. "Come away, sir. They say the ghosts of the dead cry for justice."

More superstition. "Nonsense," said Akitada. "It was probably some animal. A wolf or an owl." But he recalled Tora's tale about the Uesugi family. With a shiver he closed the shutter.

When he returned to his seat, his host had disappeared. Akitada was uneasily aware that his repeated absences had caused curious glances from the guests. To cover his embarrassment, Akitada asked the judge about criminal activity in the province and got another dreary lecture on the need for harsher penalties. When Uesugi returned soon after, he looked tense and preoccupied. "The snow is getting worse," he announced, "and the road to Naoetsu may become impassable. I hope you will all honor my house by spending the night."

Akitada was seized by outright panic at this idea and rose abruptly. "Thank you, no. This has been a lavish entertainment and most pleasant company, but I must not impose on your hospitality any longer," he said. "Urgent duties await me back in the city."

A general bustle ensued. Most of the others also made their good-byes, intending to join Akitada's cortege on the journey back to the city.

Uesugi made only the barest of protests to the sudden exodus. He accepted Akitada's formal thanks, his face devoid of expression, but his small eyes glittered and moved about strangely in the flickering light. Perhaps it was Akitada's illness, but suddenly Uesugi appeared menacing, and the shadows in the corners of the great hall seemed alive with danger.

Akitada knew his escape into the snowy night was craven and irrational, and a fitting end to the most unpleasant and unproductive evening he had ever spent. He was filled with foreboding.

FOUR

THE THREE PRISONERS

𝒯hree days after the visit to Takata, on a clear and cold morning, the tribunal's dilapidated buildings huddled inside the
broken-down palisade and looked more depressing than usual
with patches of dirty snow in piles and corners. The brief snowfall had changed to watery sleet, then back to snow, and to sleet
again during the past days.

When Akitada stepped out on the veranda, he saw that the
main gate was still closed even though the sun was up and it
was well into the day. Tora and Hitomaro were below, shouting
for the constables who trotted out reluctantly, some still chewing their morning rations. The creaking gate finally opened—
somewhat pointlessly, since no one waited outside and access to
the tribunal could be gained anywhere a man wished to kick
down a few rotten timbers in the fence.

Akitada descended the steps into the courtyard and looked
sourly at the ragged line of constables drawn up for inspection,

their breath steaming in the cold air. Hitomaro was in full armor and exhibited stiff military bearing. When he saw Akitada, he gave a shout, and the ragtag constables in their mostly unmatched garb fell to their knees and bowed their heads to the ground. From their sullen expressions, Akitada gathered that Hitomaro was about to put them through a drill.

Their headman, Chobei, lounged against the gate, his arms crossed and a mocking grin on his coarse face.

The insolence of the brute! Akitada could feel his blood rise and lost his temper. Glaring at Chobei, Akitada snapped, "Make that dog kneel, Lieutenant."

Hitomaro shouted an order, then drew his sword and approached the headman. Chobei stared stupidly, his grin fading slowly. For a moment it looked as though he would ignore the order, but then he went to his knees, placing his hands on the icy patch of gravel before him.

Tora, also armed, walked across till he towered over the kneeling man. "Head down!" he ordered. Chobei started up with a curse. Tora drew his sword and brought its flat side down on the man's bare head. With a cry of pain, Chobei assumed the proper position.

"Pity you didn't bother with mittens and a warm coat this morning, Sergeant," Tora said conversationally. "My guess is that your hands will freeze to the gravel in less time than it takes to fill your prisoners' water bowls. And you won't budge till you're ready to crawl all the way to his Excellency to apologize for your lack of manners."

Akitada already regretted the incident but could not take back his words without losing face. "See to it that he remains until he has learned proper respect!" he snapped. Then he strode back to the main hall.

This building was in better repair than the others, but it was large and extremely drafty. In the chilly front area, the public part of the building, his senior clerk, a sober, middle-aged man, waited.

"The documents about rice storage are on your desk, sir. They seem accurate."

"Ah. Is there any new business, Hamaya?" Akitada asked, as they passed through to the quiet archives where two shivering junior clerks were shuffling papers. Akitada was headed for a corner room under the eaves that he had made into his private office.

"Nothing, Excellency," said the thin Hamaya, hurrying after him.

In his office, Akitada removed his quilted coat. Hamaya received it respectfully and waited as Akitada sat down at the low desk.

"I don't understand it," Akitada muttered, rubbing his chilled hands over the charcoal brazier filled with a few glowing pieces of coal. "The notices have been posted for days. A province of this size must have a tremendous backlog of civil cases. My predecessor not only departed without explaining the empty granary, but he left unfinished business."

The clerk still stood, clutching Akitada's clothing. "Under the circumstances, I suppose," he ventured, "it is a good thing, sir. Only two of the clerks have reported for duty."

Akitada rubbed his belly morosely. He still suffered from occasional bouts of cramping and had refused breakfast as well as another dose of Seimei's bitter brew. Now his stomach grumbled also. And he still felt ashamed of his outburst in the courtyard. By losing his temper he was playing into the hands of enemies who apparently manipulated both the tribunal staff and the local people. Since his visit to Takata, Akitada thought he understood the reasons for his difficulties.

Now he looked at his clerk. "Tell me, Hamaya, are you and the other clerks afraid to come to work here?"

Hamaya hesitated, then said, "I believe that the two youngsters outside have great need of their salary because their families are very poor. As for me, I have no family and need not fear anybody."

Akitada clenched his fists. "This is intolerable!" he muttered. He thought for a moment, then said, "Tell my lieutenants to report when they are free. I know you and Seimei are still organizing the archives, but have one of your clerks make a search for information about the outcasts and their dealings with the Uesugi family."

He spent the next hour as he had for the past week, reading reports left by his predecessors. Some of these were woefully sketchy and tended to cover up the fact that the incumbent had been unable to cope with matters. A pattern began to emerge. Of the four types of major reports each governor or his representative had to dispatch to the capital every year, three showed adequate levels of productivity for the province. These were prepared carefully and signed off on by the governor. The fourth report, called the court report, was a different matter. It indicated the condition of the provincial administration, both of its buildings and supplies and of its staff. These reports listed woeful shortages, were poorly written and prepared, and liberally laced with complaints by the incumbents. They pointed to inadequate staffing, insufficient funds, lack of labor, and lack of grain delivery to the provincial granary. The specific details were better than the conditions Akitada had found, but they explained to some extent why governors and their representatives had eventually absented themselves from the provincial capital. The tribunal was "uninhabitable" and the staff "nonexistent," one recent official had written.

The documents Uesugi had provided to account for rice collection and storage were as neat and careful as the earlier three. They specified what amounts were stored locally and what had been shipped north as provisions for the fighting troops.

The difference between the court report and the others, as Hamaya had explained, was that anything involving the collection of rice and tribute was in the hands of the high constable. The appointed officials had simply approved documents prepared elsewhere.

It was an appalling situation. Akitada was effectively without the authority he needed to govern.

When Tora and Hitomaro reported, he said, "Sit down! The day for registering civil suits is past. I fully expected a stack of depositions by now, yet not even a single case has been filed. Since human beings cannot live together for a whole year without disagreeing, we must assume that the people have been instructed not to file their claims with this court."

"But why worry?" asked Tora. "It's less work."

Hitomaro shot him an impatient look. "Think, Tora. If there's no work for him, our master will be recalled."

"Exactly," said Akitada. "Someone wants to be rid of us, and everything points to the Uesugi."

Tora thought about it. His face darkened. "What if we don't leave?"

Hitomaro grunted. "What? Five of us against hundreds of Uesugi warriors and thousands of locals? And the provincial guard are not exactly our friends either."

The five were, of course, all male and included, besides Akitada and his three lieutenants, the aged Seimei. Akitada said, "I'm glad you understand our position." Unlike Tora, who was the son of a farmer, Hitomaro belonged to provincial gentry and was therefore better educated and quicker to see political intrigue. "Since, as you remind us, we are without military support, we must find allies as quickly as possible. We need the support of the local people and must try to win their trust. That is why I wish we had court cases. They attract the curious, and we might gain a bit of respect among the townspeople that way."

Hitomaro scratched his short beard. "There is always the case of the innkeeper's murder. They brought in the suspects last night. Chobei and his men have been questioning them all night and say they have confessions. You could hear the case instead of Judge Hisamatsu."

"I have to show cause to do that." An uncomfortable silence fell. Akitada's stomach growled noisily.

Tora and Hitomaro exchanged glances. Tora said, "I bet they beat those confessions out of them, sir."

Akitada shifted in his seat. Constables customarily flogged prisoners to encourage confessions. By law, a confession was necessary for conviction of a crime, but these confessions had come very promptly, and the questioning might have been rather too efficient. He frowned and said unhappily, "I suppose I could take a look at the documents. Tora, go get the transcripts of the interrogation!"

Tora returned with a fistful of loose papers and a grin on his face. "That threw them into a proper tizzy. Didn't want to turn them over. Said they were for the judge's eyes only. I had to use a bit of pressure."

Akitada noted his bruised knuckle but said nothing. Instead he took the papers and sorted through the badly written pages of questions and answers. They did not take long to read. Akitada laid down the last page with a sigh. His lieutenants looked at him expectantly.

"I'm afraid the evidence is solid. There are witnesses who have identified two of the men as belonging to a notorious gang which has been robbing inns up and down the northern road. The one called Takagi had the bloody knife still on him when he was caught. He is from this province." Akitada paused. "And the other two, Okano and Umehara, have signed confessions."

Tora and Hitomaro said simultaneously, "But, sir—" and broke off. Tora nodded to Hitomaro. Hitomaro said, "If you will permit, sir, Tora and I'll have a look at the prisoners."

"No. I don't want to give that judge any more reason to complain that I have been interfering in his affairs. Just return the transcripts with my thanks."

They exchanged glances again. Hitomaro bit his lip. "Tora and I heard screams during the night. It sounded like torture. The prison is part of the tribunal. What goes on there falls under our jurisdiction."

Akitada thought about the brutish Chobei and his men. "Very well. But make it an inspection rather than an investigation."

◆

They returned quickly. Hitomaro was grim-faced, and Tora barely suppressed his outrage.

"The inhuman bastards nearly killed them," he snarled the moment he entered. "There's no way those poor devils could have done it. I'll never believe it. You've got to investigate, sir. It's just common decency."

Akitada looked at Hitomaro.

"Tora is right, sir. If you would take a look at Umehara and Okano, you'd see that they could not possibly be robbers. A mouse would send them scurrying. Those confessions were beaten out of them. We've seen their backs."

Akitada still hesitated. Uncooperative defendants often got a taste of the "green bamboo," but both Tora and Hitomaro knew that. "Hmm," he said. "What about the third man? The one with the knife."

"He looks worse than the others. And he never confessed. They got tired of beating him."

Tora said, "They'll kill him, poor brute."

"Hisamatsu has already released the body for cremation. Tell me again what you found at the inn."

They did. Tora laid much emphasis on Chobei's officious behavior and the judge's lack of interest in the case.

Akitada sighed. "Very well. Bring the prisoners to me one at a time. And tell Hamaya to come in and take notes."

◆

The first to arrive was Umehara. He was in his fifties, a skinny fellow with a large runny nose and a continuous shiver. When told that he was before the governor, he crouched on his knees and trembled so badly he could hardly support himself. His eyes were red, either from his cold or from weeping.

Akitada saw that the man was on the point of physical collapse. "Get him a cup of warm wine, Tora," he said. "Have you had your morning meal, Umehara?"

The prisoner gaped at him. Someone had knocked some of his teeth out recently and his gums still bled a little. Akitada repeated his question and got a shake of the head in answer.

"Can you speak?"

"Yes." It was a croak, like an old man's, hoarse and quavery. "I don't think I could swallow food." He received the brimming cup of wine with trembling hands and drank, then asked timidly, "Is there good news? Have they found the real killer?"

Akitada raised his brows. "No. According to the documents you have confessed to the murder of the innkeeper."

Tears rose to the man's eyes. He trembled again. "Will there be more beatings?"

"No, but it does not look good for you." Akitada watched

him sink back dejectedly and added, "I wanted to hear your story myself. From your deposition I see that you arrived in town two days before the murder. What made you choose this particular inn?"

Umehara recited hopelessly, "I always stay at Sato's. It's cheap. I sell weaving supplies. In my line of work, you can't afford to spend your income on high living." He paused. "But it was different this time."

"How so?"

"Old Sato was sickly, and his new wife didn't want to be bothered with commercial travelers. When I got there, she was angry with him for giving me a lower rate. He walked away, and she told me to sleep on the kitchen floor or pay extra."

"And you slept in the kitchen?"

The man nodded.

"And the murder happened during the night?"

"Not that night. The one after."

"Very well. What happened the next day?"

"The next morning the wife left. The maid was supposed to take care of her sick master and the guests. The girl had a cold and did as little as possible."

"Yet you stayed for another night?"

The wine must have given the prisoner some of his strength back because he spoke more easily now. "I didn't mean to, but I needed a new backpack. I paid a fellow twenty coppers for one. He cheated me. There was a hole in it. But I didn't know that and left it at the inn while I went to call on a customer in the city. I didn't get back till evening rice. Too late to leave by then."

"I see. What about your companions?"

Umehara looked uneasy. "They're strangers."

"They arrived after you?"

"The actor must've come late the first night. I found him

there in the kitchen when I woke up. People like that keep late hours. And Takagi came the next day after I'd left to take care of my business."

"What about the two pieces of gold they found on you?"

His eyes widened with fear. "They were mine. I swear it." He nearly wept again and looked at Akitada beseechingly. "I don't like to carry loose coins, so I always change my coppers into gold. I tried to tell the constables, but they said I was lying. Your Honor, I swear I'm innocent. Buddha's my witness."

"Hmm. So during the night of the murder you slept on the kitchen floor with your two companions?"

Umehara nodded, sniffed, and wiped his nose on his sleeve.

"They were, as you said, strangers to you, yet you were not afraid that they might steal your gold?"

Again Umehara became evasive. "They looked decent enough. Just hardworking fellows like me."

Akitada raised his brows, but only asked, "Did they get up during the night?"

"I don't know. I sleep like the dead."

An unfortunate remark, but Umehara apparently was not aware of it.

"So now we come to the morning after the murder. Why did you all leave the inn together before anyone was up?"

"We knew there wouldn't be any food in the morning and wanted to make an early start." He shook his head. "I could've made good money. So many customers still to visit in the northern part of the province. A lot of orders, what with winter coming. Why, I could have earned at least another gold piece. And now my money's gone—and I've lost my customers, too."

Akitada nodded to Hitomaro, who helped Umehara up and led him from the room. Akitada winced when he saw the blood stains on the back of the man's jacket.

Tora said, "You see what I mean? That dried plum hasn't got the willpower to say 'boo' to a mouse. He'd never have the get-up to kill someone."

"It does not take much strength to slit the throat of a sick old man," said Akitada. "A woman could do it."

Hamaya looked up from his notes. "Besides, there were three of them."

"The other two are worse."

"Really? You intrigue me." Akitada rubbed his stomach. "I grant you," he muttered, "it's strange that a man who faces a sentence for murder should worry about his business losses."

Tora snorted. "If you think *him* strange, just wait."

The next person teetered in on tall wooden sandals. For a moment, Akitada wondered if he was looking at a woman in man's garb. His visitor moved with painful, mincing steps and waving arms. Small and pudgy, he or she was dressed in a flamboyant silk robe and had a red silk scarf around the head. Though much younger than Umehara, the smooth, round-cheeked face made it difficult to guess age or gender. The creature collapsed in a heap in front of Akitada, raised tearful eyes and cried in a childishly high voice, "Oh, blessed Kannon, protect Okano! He cannot bear any more. He is dying!" and burst into noisy sobs.

"Who is this?" Akitada asked, astonished. "Where is Okano?"

"That's Okano." Tora grinned.

Hitomaro added, "He says he's a 'theatrical performer' from Otsu, between engagements and on his way to visit relatives in the mountains when he was arrested."

Okano howled pitifully. Akitada thought he detected a trace of perfume among the stench of blood and sweat.

"Is he badly injured?"

Hitomaro shrugged. "He got a beating. I'd say a bit less than Umehara."

Okano wailed.

"I see. More wine, Tora." Akitada shifted uncomfortably. He did not know how to deal with a weeping man, and this one was hysterical. A renewed cramping in his belly provided the excuse. "I'll be back in a moment. Get him calmed down."

When he returned, Okano was sitting up and smiling coyly at a scowling Hitomaro.

"I thank the Buddha for this kind officer," the actor told Akitada. "He is the first person who has shown some feeling for poor Okano. I have been beaten and starved, humiliated and almost frozen to death in your jail, and all for no reason."

"Not quite without reason," Akitada said dryly. "You spent the night in a place where a murder was committed, left under cover of dark with two companions, one of whom was found in possession of the murder weapon, and you carried on your person a share of the gold taken from the victim."

"Oh!" Okano's eyes filled with tears again. "But I explained that. The two pieces of gold I had with me are mine, a farewell gift from a fan."

Akitada pursed his lips. "A rich tip indeed! What is this benefactor's name and where does he live?"

The actor drew himself up proudly. "I cannot tell. It is a matter of honor."

"Don't be ridiculous," Akitada said coldly. "If it was a legitimate gift, there can be no harm in your telling me his name."

"No! Never! Such a thing is never done. It is not possible between gentlemen. Here! You may torture me again, but I will not reveal my friend's name." He pulled open his robe and slipped it off his round pale shoulders. Angry red welts caked with blood marked his chubby chest. "Go ahead," he wept. "Kill me!"

Akitada felt nauseated by the sight and the weeping. He snapped, "Stop making scenes and put your clothes back on!"

Okano obeyed, casting a glance over his shoulder at Hitomaro, who looked away quickly.

"Why did you confess, if you did not do it?" Akitada demanded.

"I was afraid they would kill me."

"You arrived very late during the night before the murder?"

"Yes. Some gentlemen in a wine house asked me to perform the dance of the River Fairy, and my effort was so well received that I ended up entertaining a crowd." He smirked.

Tora made an uncouth noise, and Hitomaro coughed. Akitada frowned at them and asked, "Why did you not continue your journey the next day?"

"It turned cold and I had no warm clothes. Since my audience was generous the night before, I decided to do some shopping and continue the day after. I bought a lovely quilted jacket. A very becoming color and pattern. White cherry blossoms on blue waves. But those animals took it away along with my gold."

"Did you see the innkeeper while you were at the inn?"

"Only the wife, in the morning. She was leaving for a trip to the country. Just like a woman. Her husband's ill, and she's off." He turned down the corners of his mouth and shook his head.

"What did you think of Umehara and Takagi?"

"Not my types. The old fellow was already asleep when I arrived, and he left before I got up. The farmer came after I went out. I didn't really talk to them till evening."

"Don't evade the question! Did you trust them? Do you think them capable of murder?"

"How would I know? They seemed all right, a bit rough, especially that farmer." Okano gave an exaggerated shudder.

"Would you have noticed, if one of your companions got up during the night? Perhaps to relieve himself?"

"Oh yes. I don't sleep well, and the maid was snoring in her cubicle. They didn't get up. It is too dreadful that we were the only guests. Someone arrived in the afternoon just after I got back from my shopping. I was having my bath. They made a great clatter in the entry, but I expect whoever it was didn't like the place and left again."

"Very well. You may go. If you recall anything useful, get word to Lieutenant Hitomaro."

"With the greatest pleasure." Okano rolled his eyes at the muscular Hitomaro and tittered. On the way out, he made a show of stumbling and grasped Hitomaro's arm, but he found his hand quickly removed.

When the door had closed behind them, Tora burst out laughing. "Hitomaro's finally made a conquest." He swished across the room and fluted in falsetto, "'With the greatest pleasure.'"

Akitada watched him sourly. "Okano's another one who worries more about trivia than his life. But his accounting for the gold is as unbelievable as Umehara's trust in total strangers."

Tora stopped prancing. "Maybe not. In the capital, rich men take actors for lovers, and when they get tired of them, they pay them off. If they don't, the bum-boys haunt their doorstep. Okano's getting a bit past it as a pretty boy, so he could be telling the truth."

"He is thirty-one according to the record, Excellency," offered Hamaya. "And he is, of course, an outcast. By law, he was not permitted to sleep at the inn. I expect that's why they shaved his head."

"They shaved his head? I suppose that explains the red scarf," Akitada said. "Make a note to look into the matter. I do not approve of wanton cruelty toward those who cannot defend themselves."

Hitomaro returned with the last man, the young farmer who had carried the bloodstained murder weapon among his belongings.

Unlike the other two, he walked in with a firm step, wearing nothing but a loincloth and a shirt of rough hemp which left bare his thick muscular thighs and legs and revealed a good deal of barrellike chest. With his low forehead and vacant look he reminded Akitada more of a docile beast than a man. Hitomaro had to push him down into a kneeling position, where it became obvious that the back of his shirt was soaked in fresh blood.

"Takagi, sir," said Hitomaro. "Son of the headman of Matsuhama village in the mountains."

The young man grinned and nodded.

"Let me see his back," Akitada said.

Tora and Hitomaro turned the prisoner around and lifted the crimson cloth. Akitada recoiled. This man's back was one huge open wound. It seemed impossible that a mere flogging could have done so much damage. Or that he should still be able to walk upright or kneel.

"Has he been seen by a doctor?"

Hitomaro answered. "No. They just got through with him an hour ago. He never confessed, but they ran out of bamboo canes and complained of muscle cramps. Chobei told them to take a rest and continue later."

"Tell them I forbid it. And have a doctor sent for."

They repositioned Takagi and covered his back again. The peasant submitted passively, staring around the room with a vacant expression.

Akitada leaned forward. "Takagi, look at me. Where did you get the gold you had?"

"Three pieces of gold." Takagi nodded proudly, holding up three fingers. "The soldiers took the gold. I got to have it back. It belongs to the village."

"What do you mean?"

"It's for the bowls and the oxen. My father said, 'Takagi, go sell our bowls in the markets of Shinano province where they have much gold, and sell the oxen, too. Then we don't have to feed them in the winter when they are no good to us.' And so I go and I bring home three gold pieces." He held up the three fingers again.

Akitada nodded. "A good plan. How many oxen did you take?"

"Two. To carry the bowls."

"So you were on your way home. Why did you stop at the inn so early in the day?"

"Tired. I walk and walk, and then I rest and walk again. Sometimes I rest at night, sometimes in the day."

"So you went to sleep at the inn as soon as you got there? Did you sleep all day?"

Takagi looked puzzled. "I wake up hungry. I ask for food, but no food. The girl is with the mistress. So I go to the market and buy noodles. For a copper. The coppers are mine to keep. The gold belongs to the village. Will you give it back? I have to go home."

"What time was it when you saw the mistress?"

He leaned his head back and studied the ceiling. His plain face contorted with the effort, but he finally said, "Don't know."

"Where was her husband?"

The face became blank. "Husband?"

"How did you get the knife?"

He began to frown deeply again, then smiled. "I know. The knife was from the kitchen."

"How do you know?"

Takagi frowned again and scratched his head. "A nice big one." He held his hands apart about a foot. "The girl is cutting a big radish with a little bit of a knife for our dinner. The big knife is better for big radish."

"So!" Akitada slammed his fist on his writing table, "Confess! You liked the big knife so well you stole it. And that night you started looking for something else to steal and found the innkeeper ill in his room. You killed him, took his money, sharing it with the other two so they would keep quiet, and the three of you made your escape. And you kept the nice large knife for a souvenir." He straightened up and added coldly, "Confess now, and the law will be merciful."

Takagi looked dully at him, shaking his head from side to side. "Stealing is wrong. Demons bite off your hands." He held out his big, work-scarred paws. "See? I didn't steal."

"Then how did the knife get in your bundle?"

Takagi looked blank again.

"What did you do with your bundle at the inn?"

"The girl said to put it in the kitchen. When I walk, I carry it on a stick over my shoulder."

"Did you take it to the market with you?"

"No. The maid said to leave it behind the rice basket."

"Weren't you afraid someone might take your gold pieces?"

Takagi laughed out loud. "No gold in bundle. Oh no. Father said, 'Put gold inside scarf and tie it around your waist.'" He patted his middle and remembered his loss. "Three pieces of gold. Will you give them back?"

Akitada stared hard at the farmer and then waved to Hitomaro to take him away. "I wonder," he muttered to Tora. "Someone must have seen these three in the market. They're memorable enough."

"And how! I don't know about the other two, but it looks bad for Takagi. He's not too bright. The fool admitted that he saw the knife and liked it."

"True, that was not very bright, but it gives his story a certain convincing ring. And remember, of the three he is the only one who did not confess. You were right. Not one of the three is the criminal type. Umehara seems just what he claims to be, a middle-aged traveling salesman. Any number of locals may be able to testify to his character. Perhaps the magistrate will make an effort to verify his story, and that of the others, but I'm beginning to have my doubts. The actor Okano is afraid of his own shadow, and the peasant is slow-witted enough to believe that demons punish people for crimes. I cannot imagine who accepted that ridiculous tale that they are members of a gang." He sighed. "I am convinced. We must check into the case." Giving Tora a quizzical look, he added, "I expect you are just the man to talk to the maid at the inn."

Tora jumped up eagerly.

"Not so fast. You haven't shown much diplomacy so far, and I am very reluctant to interfere with a properly appointed judge in the execution of his duty. Only the thought of having this kind of abuse going on makes me intervene. Be very careful about what you say or do."

Before Tora could depart, Hitomaro came in to announce a visitor. The new arrival was a warrior in full armor bearing the Uesugi crest. He had a strip of white cotton tied about his helmet.

"A messenger from Takata, sir," Hitomaro said unnecessarily.

Akitada looked at the white cotton band and sat up. "Speak," he told the man.

The warrior knelt and bowed snappily. "This humble person announces the death of the great Lord of Takata, Uesugi Maro, High Constable of Echigo, Barbarian-Subduing General, and head of his clan. May the Buddha guide his soul to paradise."

The news was not unexpected, and Akitada made a suitably pious response, adding, "Tell his son, the new lord, that I shall express my condolences formally and in person."

When the messenger had left, Akitada looked at his lieutenants. "This changes everything. We must not lose any more time. I want both of you to go out immediately. You, Tora, will ask questions in the market and go to the inn to talk to the maid. I have decided to investigate the handling of criminal cases.

The official reason will be suspicion of negligence by the court. Judge Hisamatsu will have to explain the abuse of suspects among other things.

"Hitomaro, it is time to contact Genba again. After that I want you to check on the outcasts. The younger Uesugi has an irrational hatred for them. I want to know why. You must both be quick and discreet and report back as soon as possible."

They left, and Akitada went in search of his wife. While he would never admit such a thing to her, he found great comfort in her good sense and loving care.

FIVE

THE GOLDEN CARP

𝕿ora and Hitomaro slipped out of the tribunal by removing some loose boards from the back palisade and stepping into a weed-choked alley. Dressed in the rough, quilted cotton jackets and short pants of laborers, they walked to the market, a collection of shops crammed together under the deep overhanging eaves of the houses that lined the main street. Here they parted company.

Tora headed toward the outskirts of town to Sato's inn. He raised his eyebrows at a large new sign above its open gate. A gilded fish sported on it, and the words "Golden Carp" and "Mrs. Sato, Proprietress" were executed in elegant lettering. As the old couple had predicted, the new management planned to cater to a better type of guest. With old Sato barely dispatched to the judge of the underworld, Tora thought such haste a little unseemly.

As he pondered what this might mean, a lanky youth came

through the gate and began to sweep. Tora strolled across the street. The youth stopped what he was doing and stared at him.

"You're a good worker," Tora commented. "Your boss is a lucky man. If you play your cards right, he'll invite you to marry his daughter some day and, before you know it, you'll be the boss yourself."

The youth spat. "Hah! My boss is a woman," he said.

"Even better. Marry her. Never mind if she's a bit long in the tooth, you'll be all the more precious to her."

"Shows what you know!" snapped the youth and kicked the last chunk of horse dung into the road before disappearing into the inn's stable.

Tora looked after him. Apparently the beautiful widow had not endeared herself to her staff. He crossed the yard of the Golden Carp and, since no one else was about, he walked into the inn.

Today the hallway was scrupulously clean. In the kitchen, he found his objective. She was scrubbing vegetables with a vicious fury.

He leaned against the door frame and whistled softly. The maid swung around. When she saw Tora, her eyes widened and she dropped her radish. He stroked his mustache and let his eyes travel appreciatively over her tall, sturdy frame. Her scowl changed to a smile. She was a plain-faced girl and her teeth were crooked, but Tora could make even pretty girls forget the simplest prudence. And he distinctly recalled the shapely limbs under her dirty skirt.

"Well-met, pretty flower," he said with a bow. "How is it that you do this dirty work when you ought to save your charms to greet the guests?"

She put on a tragic look. "I'm just the kitchen maid. Somebody's got to do the work around here now that we've become fancy, with a cook and singsong girls to serve to the guests." She eyed Tora's patched clothes. "I hate to tell you, but if you're hoping to spend the night, it costs a fortune and you don't look like a rich man."

"Ah." Tora made a face, but he knew that old clothes did little to hide his strong physique and flexed his shoulders.

"It's a great pity," she said, watching him. "If it were up to me . . ." She dimpled.

Tora smiled back. "The old man across the street warned me, but I thought I'd look in anyway. Where is everybody?"

She jerked her head toward the back of the house. "One of the guests is sick and the mistress is wetting herself for fear it'll hurt her business."

"Didn't someone just die here? This must be a pretty unhealthy place."

"Shh! Not so loud." The girl peered down the hall. "It's all right. She's still in his room. We're not supposed to talk about it. It's her husband that died and he was murdered. But she's had an exorcism, so you needn't fear. That's why she's so upset about the sick one. She was all for dumping him in the temple grounds during the night to let the monks tend to him, but that might get back to the authorities, so she sent for the doctor."

"And here I am, at your service," announced a reedy voice from the hall. A small gray-haired man stood in the passage, carrying a bamboo case and peering at them with sharp black eyes under grizzled eyebrows. He looked a bit like an old monkey, thought Tora.

"Well, Kiyo, where's the patient?"

"This way, Dr. Oyoshi. The mistress is with him." The maid wiped her hands on her apron, and led the way down the dark hall. Tora, who was curious about her mistress, followed.

In one of the rooms a small group of people stood around a gasping figure under a quilt. Three handsome girls with painted faces and colorful robes, the lanky youth from the yard, and the landlady all stared down at the sick man. So did the doctor and the maid when they joined the group.

Tora gaped at the landlady.

The widow Sato was still in her early twenties, with a dainty figure in a dark blue silk gown, shining hair neatly pinned, skin like pale ivory, and eyes that were almond-shaped and luminous. She was a beauty. At the moment, however, she looked very angry. "So you finally get here, Oyoshi," she cried to the doctor. "Do something. This person refuses to leave. He claims he's too ill. Hah! He wants free lodging, that's all. Everybody is trying to take advantage of a single woman. Look him over and then make him get out. The rest of you, back to work!"

She whisked out of the room without glancing at Tora, who had retreated into the shadows, hoping she would take him for the doctor's assistant. He watched her trip lightly down the corridor, then turned his attention back to the scene in the room.

The doctor knelt on the floor beside the shivering figure and pulled back the quilt. The sick man's face was white and wet with perspiration. His eyes were glassy and his mouth slack. His breath came and went in shuddering gasps. Middle-aged and gray-haired, he looked ordinary except that an old injury had taken a small piece from one of his large earlobes.

Oyoshi spoke to him softly, but got no response. He felt the patient's forehead, peered into his mouth, and then parted the man's gown to lay his ear against the heaving chest. A rattling cough racked the patient, and a thin dribble of blood appeared at the corner of his mouth. The doctor covered him up again and rose with a sigh.

"He's much too ill to be moved," he said, pulling Kiyo aside. "I'll give you some medicine to ease him a bit, but it does not look good. The end is near, I'm afraid."

One of the painted girls said with a shudder, "The mistress won't like it. Can't we take him to the monks?"

The doctor looked shocked. "Certainly not. I won't allow you to put the poor soul through that, and I'll tell your mistress so."

"Tell me what?" The widow appeared in the doorway. "Why isn't he up yet? I tell you, he cannot stay. He has no money left, and I don't run a charity hospital. Besides, nobody will spend the night in a house where there's a sick person. We learned that well enough when Sato was ill. Oh, that this should come to plague me now when the old lord's funeral will fill all the inns and hostels for miles around!" She stamped her dainty foot in frustration.

The doctor said in a low but firm voice, "This man is not able to speak or stand, Mrs. Sato, let alone travel. He must remain where he is. Believe me, it won't be long. I'll leave some medicine and give you a note certifying that he does not have smallpox or any other infectious disease."

The beauty flushed and cried, "Tell me, since you are so high and mighty about the matter, who will pay for his lodging and nursing? He's nothing but a vagabond. He has no money. I've looked. And who will pay for all your treatments, pray? Surely you don't expect me to come up with the money?"

The doctor said coldly, "I do not expect anything but common courtesy from you, madam."

She tossed her head and went back into her room. The doctor returned to the kitchen with Kiyo and Tora. There he sat down and opened his case. Taking out writing materials and rubbing his ink stone with a few drops of water supplied by Kiyo, he dashed off a note. Then he poured several powders into a paper, twisted it, and said, "Make an infusion of this with boiling water and try to get half a cupful down him every two hours. And keep him warm! A brazier of coals day and night." He closed his case and fished around in his sleeve. "Here's some money for the coals. Send for me if I'm needed. And give the note to your mistress!"

Tora followed the doctor out into the courtyard. "Sir?" he called, holding out some coins. "I'd like to pay for the poor fellow's treatment."

The doctor stopped and peered up at him from under grizzled brows. "Ah. It's you. I didn't recognize you before." He took the money. "Very kind of you. How is your master feeling? Still troubled by those cramps?"

Tora's jaw sagged.

"Are you incognito then, my dear fellow? Well, there's no one about just now. I wondered because his Excellency had all the symptoms of acute intestinal distress at Takata. You are one of his lieutenants, aren't you? I've seen you about and, if I'm not much mistaken, that was you under all those animal skins that night?"

Tora grinned weakly. "Your eyes are sharper than mine, sir. You're right, and my master still suffers a little from the same complaint."

"Say no more." Oyoshi set down his box and rummaged in it. "Here you are. My own recipe! Powdered oyster shell and ground bark of the cherry tree, mixed with the dried leaves of chamomile and some powdered rhubarb root, along with a bit of honey to hold it all together. Have him dissolve each pill in a little hot wine and take it with every meal. Can you remember that?"

Tora nodded and tucked the small package away. "What do I owe you for this?"

"Let your master settle with me if the medicine works."

Tora thanked him, then said, "You seem to know these people. Did you see the innkeeper after he died?"

Dr. Oyoshi nodded and smiled. "Ah, I thought that was why you were here. Is your master looking into the matter then?"

"Uh . . ."

"Never mind. I treated old Sato when he was ill. Chronic

chest pains. Wasn't getting any better, but should've lasted at least another year. Imagine my surprise, when I found him with his throat slit! The maid, Kiyo, sent for me. The lady of the house was away—visiting her family, I'm told. What is it that you want to know?"

"Anything you can tell me about the death."

"I see. Groping in the dark. Well, I don't think I can help you. He died during the evening or night and did not do it himself. When I saw him he was stone cold and stiff. The maid threw a fit. Nothing unusual in that. The constables eventually showed up and asked a few foolish questions. That, too, was as usual."

"If the three travelers hadn't stayed here, who would you think would've done such a thing? His widow's young and handsome, and he was an old geezer. There could've been all sorts of mischief."

The doctor raised his grizzled eyebrows. "You didn't like the beautiful Mrs. Sato? Too bossy? Been listening to gossip? Well, apart from the fact that she was not here and could not have done it herself, I've never heard anything against her. I expect the widow's only problem is too much *yang*."

"Yang? Who's he?" Tora asked suspiciously.

The doctor smiled and patted Tora's arm. "Well, there is *yin*, the yielding female principle, and *yang*, the aggressive male force. All of us have a bit of the opposite force in us, which is a good thing, for a female without a little *yang* can't manage her husband's home. Mrs. Sato simply has more *yang* than most. Mr. Sato had the opposite failing. Unfortunately, such an imbalance in a woman seems to make other women hostile toward her. Much like hens in the farmyard, they all gang up on her. As they say, a good deed won't even pass the gate, but slander travels a thousand leagues."

Tora's forehead creased as he pondered that. "I see, and I also see that she probably led her husband by the nose. Even with all that *yang* stuff, she's through and through female. And I know about that."

The doctor laughed. "Maybe so, maybe so. Farewell, my friend."

Tora returned to the kitchen where the maid was preparing the medicine. She greeted him with a big smile. "You're back! Give me a moment to tend to the sick man and we'll talk."

Tora moved closer and ran a finger down her cheek. She giggled. He blew in her ear and murmured, "I'd rather see you after work, sweetheart. When it's more private. By the way, I'm Hiroshi."

She put down her ladle and turned a flushed face toward him. "Oh, yes, Hiroshi. You'll be back? Truly?"

Tora grinned and nodded. When her eyes began to shine, she looked almost handsome, though he wished she wouldn't bare those crooked teeth which reminded him a little of fangs. Her sturdy, buxom body, at any rate, promised a vigorous encounter, and Tora felt magnanimous.

She said eagerly, "I sleep in the storeroom behind the kitchen. Come after the hour of the boar. There's a door next to the rain barrel."

The sharp voice of her mistress sounded from the passage. Tora pulled her close and, fondling a plump breast, murmured, "I can't wait," and departed.

◆

He spent the rest of the day in the market, chatting with merchants about the three prisoners and consuming a modest meal of stuffed rice dumplings before returning to the Golden Carp well after dark. The gate stood invitingly open for late guests, and a dim paper lantern was lit near the door. But Tora headed for the darkness in back of the inn.

When he opened the rickety door next to the rain barrel

into pitch blackness, a pair of sturdy arms seized him. Jerked forward, he overbalanced and tumbled, flailing wildly, into a soft nest of bedding and warm female flesh.

She gasped at his sudden weight, then giggled. "What took you so long?"

He chuckled and explored with his hands. She choked on a little scream when his cold hands found her soft, warm belly. "You might've warned me," Tora murmured into her ear, his hands busily investigating and approving large breasts, firmly muscled thighs, and a smooth bottom.

She gasped again, and tugged impatiently at his sash. "Oh, Hiroshi. I've been waiting so-o long," she moaned.

Tora had planned to spend a little time getting acquainted and picking up some firsthand information about the murder before proceeding to more personal matters, but clearly the young woman had her mind on other things—and who was he to teach her modesty?

Sometime later, when they lay contentedly side by side, he asked, "Why would a nice girl like you work for a mean woman like that?"

She sat up. He could feel her staring down at him in the dark. "You don't admire her?" she asked in a tone of surprise and disbelief. "Why not? All the men are mad about her."

"I hope my taste is better than theirs," Tora said primly.

She lay back and snuggled into the crook of his arm. "She's a bitch all right. An ungrateful bitch. But he deserved her. After all I did for the old bastard for years, he had to go marry her. He was a fool about that woman. Would you believe, he'd make me ask the fishmonger for free fish bones to make soup, but whenever she wanted a new gown, he'd give her the money and more. How that man spoiled her! And she'd be gone all day, leaving me to do all the work. I was always taking care of him. Even the day he got killed. She went off to visit her family—or so she said—leaving me alone with her sick old man and the inn to look after. And now she's got it all and I'm still the kitchen drudge. It's so unfair." She pounded her fists into the bedding. Tora patted her shoulder and made soothing noises.

"Well," he said after a moment, "she's hired those girls and the new cook. You've got a lot less work, I bet. And more time for me." He gave her a little squeeze.

She giggled and rolled on top of him. "You're right. I'm not tired," she whispered, biting his ear and pressing her breasts against him.

Tora gave an inward sigh and stroked her buttocks. Their lovemaking had been good, but now he wanted to get on with his job. Still, there was no reason an experienced man couldn't do both. "I guess your mistress paid him back with a bit of this at night," he said, pulling her down on himself, "and he thought it a good bargain."

"Oh, no," she gasped, moving energetically, "she wouldn't have him . . . and he, fool that he was . . . doted on her anyway."

"Maybe she has a lover." The girl was so agile, Tora was having difficulty concentrating on his questions.

"Mmm! . . . I like you."

"You're not bad yourself, my girl!" He grunted and forced his mind back on business. "I suppose she could've paid to have the old man killed."

She stopped moving abruptly. For a moment she said nothing, then, "I thought she didn't like those three. Made them sleep on the kitchen floor and said it was good enough for such rubbish. But it's true, they did do her a big favor. Never mind. The dirty old bastard deserved what he got." She sounded venomous when she said that, and started moving again, furiously, mumbling, "Bastard . . . mmm . . . aah!" She collapsed on top of Tora with a sigh. "That woman doesn't know how lucky she is! I tell you, she owes me!" she muttered, as they rolled apart.

Tora frowned in the dark. Kiyo had some unexpected attitudes toward her employers. He wondered about the widow. "Well, did she have a lover?" he asked again.

"She's a cold fish, though she acts the slut with those weird eyes of hers, and men like that. No, making money and buying clothes for herself is all she's interested in."

"That night Sato was killed, did you hear anything?" Tora asked, pulling the quilt over their sweat-covered bodies.

"Not me. I had a bad cold. Took some of the old man's medicine with a little hot wine and slept like a bear. I'm glad they didn't slit my throat, too. Would've been easy enough. Say, what is this? Let's talk about us!"

Tora pulled her close. "I was thinking about you, all alone with those killers in the house," he whispered in her ear.

She cuddled. "You know, I could really go for a man like you! And not just in bed. Do you like me?"

"What do you think?"

"Want to do it again?" She propped herself on an elbow, and tickled his ear.

Tora almost yelped. "Look, Kiyo, a girl shouldn't ask a man. It's forward. A man likes to be in control of these situations."

She flopped back down. "Well, if you really want to know, my cold was horrible. What with the medicine, and feeling that awful, I couldn't cook dinner that night and forgot all about old Sato. I did feel bad about it the next morning and, seeing that the three guests had already left, I made him a special soup, with bits of mushrooms and a handful of rice and some bean paste. He used to like that before the bitch moved in. And there he was, blood all over, the room in a mess, and his money box lying there empty!"

"I bet that shook you up," Tora muttered, his mind in turmoil. One moment she cursed the old geezer and the next . . . an unpleasant thought took hold of him. He moved away from her abruptly and sat up. "Wonder what time it is. I'd better go."

She yawned. "You can stay the night, Hiroshi. Maybe after a rest you'll want to do it again?"

"No!" He was up, straightening his clothes hurriedly. "I can't."

"Why not?"

Tora paused at the door. "I forgot something I have to do." Then he took to his heels as if a demon were after him.

SIX

THE OUTCASTS

*A*fter parting from Tora, Hitomaro continued on the main road for a while, then turned off in the direction of the coast and harbor. He passed among dwellings and shops of ramie weavers, smiths, rope twisters, broom makers, and soothsayers. The houses gradually became smaller and shabbier, their inhabitants now laborers or porters. At the point where the narrow street turned into an open dirt road through barren fields, and the last straggling outskirts of Naoetsu merged with the first scattered dwellings of Flying Goose village, stood a small shack. Its dilapidated sign promised fresh seafood.

Hitomaro lifted the worn curtain that served as a door and ducked into the dimly lit interior. Steamy heat met him and the powerful smell of fish frying in hot oil. On a wooden platform a small group of men sat around a hissing and bubbling cauldron, presided over by a red-faced, sweating cook with a blue-checked rag tied about his head. He was stirring the kettle and watching in a fatherly fashion over his chattering customers.

A huge man, a mountain of flesh and muscle, rose from the group and greeted Hitomaro in a booming voice. The firelight cast a red glow on his shaven head and round, smiling face. "Throw in some more abalone, Yaji," he told the cook. "And the rest of you, make room." He waved Hitomaro over. "Come and eat, brother. We're planning our strategy for the match."

Hitomaro grinned at Genba, nodded to his supporters, and settled himself on the platform. He knew only Genba's landlord, the rice-cake baker, a stringy middle-aged fellow in a faded, patched cotton gown. The others matched him in age and also looked like small tradesmen.

"May your opponents eat the dirt at your feet, Genba," Hitomaro said. "Allow me to pay for the next round of wine."

A storm of protest arose: Both Genba and his friend were their guests and they would be deeply hurt if not allowed to treat them.

The food was as fresh as the sign had promised. Since Genba's disguise had such unexpected benefits, Hitomaro accepted graciously a share of the excellent fried abalone and very decent wine, listening with only half an ear to their discussion of odds, weights, and the physical attributes of various competitors. When someone mentioned outcasts, his interest perked.

"Totally ruined, I tell you," the man said. "One year district champion, the next a nobody. And all because of a *hinin* woman. Those outcast women are witches. You beware of those foxes, Genba. Go to regular prostitutes."

"I abstain from sexual activity while in training," Genba said piously. He smacked his lips and held up his empty bowl for a refill. Genba had put on considerable weight since their days of hardship when there was a price on their heads. Hitomaro was convinced that those years of near starvation had made Genba prefer the pleasures of food to those of the bedchamber.

"Well, I'm not a wrestler," he said, "and I'm not afraid of any woman so long as she's a looker and good at her job. Are they really so special?"

The short man shook his head doubtfully. "Oh, they're very handsome and know some clever tricks, but I for one don't want to chance it."

The cook chortled, "You're just henpecked, Kenzo."

"That's right. Your old woman won't let you out of her sight," agreed another man. "Seven brats in eight years!" he told Hitomaro. "He hasn't got the time or the money, let alone the strength to tangle with one of the mountain beauties. If you're game, go past the shrine behind the market. The brothels are back there. You knock on a door and talk to one of the aunties; she'll fix you up with an outcast girl. But it'll cost you. A hundred coppers for a top girl." Seeing smirks on the faces of the others, he added, "Or so I'm told."

"A hundred coppers!" The little baker was outraged. "If you have a hundred coppers, invest them in your friend here! Women aren't worth it."

"Tell that to Sunada! They say he's a regular at Mrs. Omeya's. And he's got more money than anybody around here."

"Yeah, but he's a crook. Honest people can't make a decent living anymore," grumbled the baker. "The price they charge for their rotten rice flour!"

A blast of cold air blew in and a gruff voice demanded, "What was that, you little bastard?" A burly man with an ugly red scar across one cheek had flung aside the door curtain. Now he crossed the room in a few big strides, jerked the baker upright, and smashed a fist into his face before his companions could catch their breaths. "That'll teach you not to tell lies about your betters," he said, dropping his victim like a dirty rag.

"What the devil—?" Genba shot up with an agility surprising in so large a man, and Hitomaro followed. But the small room suddenly filled with other burly, sunburned, scowling men.

"Please, no fighting, Master Boshu!" squeaked the cook, dropping his ladle. "Master Genba here is an important contender in the great match. Mr. Sunada would not like it if you made trouble for him."

The scarred man looked Genba up and down and growled, "The new contender, eh? I heard about you. You keep bad company. Nobody calls Mr. Sunada names and gets away with it around here. We all work for him. Half the families in Flying Goose village do. He looks after his people, and we look after him. So watch your step if you want to stay healthy." With a jerk of the head to his companions, he turned and left, his grinning followers filing out behind him.

The baker sat up with a moan. He was pressing a blood-soaked sleeve to his mouth.

Hitomaro looked at him. "I'll have a word with that piece of dung!" he snarled and went after the intruders.

Outside he pushed past Boshu's companions and grabbed him by the shoulder. Swinging him round, he said, "Not so fast, bastard. I'm not a wrestler and I don't mind teaching bullies a lesson. You probably broke that little guy's jaw. He's half your size and twice your age. That makes you a coward."

There was a low growl from the others, and heavily breathing men pressed around him. Boshu's face purpled until the scar flamed against his dark skin, but he shrugged off Hitomaro's hand. "Not here," he ground out. "You heard the cook. Mr. Sunada doesn't like public fights. But we'll meet again." He brought his brutish face close to Hitomaro's. "I'll know how to find you, asshole. Not here and now, but soon. You won't forget this day." He bared yellow teeth in an unpleasant grin and strode away toward the harbor. His band of toughs barred the way until Boshu had gained some distance, then followed him.

Hitomaro looked after them with a frown. When he returned to the restaurant, Genba and the others were gathered about the baker, muttering angrily.

Genba said, "His jaw's all right, but he bit his tongue and lost two teeth."

"Who was that bastard?"

The cook looked apologetic. "Boshu is Sunada's manager. They're regulars here. I wish I'd seen him come in."

"Sunada's the richest man in this part of the country. Can't blame a man for defending his master," said Genba peaceably.

Hitomaro exchanged a glance with him, then poured the baker a cup of wine. He said, "I'd better be on my way before they decide to come back and make more trouble."

Genba nodded. "I'll walk out with you."

Outside the road was empty. A salt-laden gust of icy wind hit their faces. In the distance they could hear the roar of the ocean. Flying Goose village, a small huddle of low brown buildings gathered about a larger compound, marked the distant harbor. The square sails of several big ships and the masts of many small fishing boats rocked uneasily in a choppy gray sea. The horizon was lost in a milky haze.

Hitomaro said, "The bastard wouldn't fight. Strange, when you think about it. There were enough of them. I don't like it. It's a good thing nobody knows who you really are. Find out what you can about this Sunada."

Genba nodded.

"Last night the old warlord died. Our master thinks his son is the one who's plotting against us. Are you sure the local people aren't hostile toward us?"

"They're good people. You saw what they're like. This wrestling match is about the only thing they have to look forward to. Their sons are sent to war with the Ezo, and taxes have made them poor. They work too hard to have time for plotting."

Hitomaro said, "Tora's working on a murder case, but you and I are to report anything that will help the master get control. I'm off to become acquainted with the *hinin* women."

Genba raised his brows. "Better you than me, brother. Not my kind of training. Come to think of it, it's not much in your line either. Tora should make that sacrifice." He chortled.

Hitomaro did not smile. "Well, I have no choice. It's a good way to get information. If you have some more news, we'll meet at the shrine near the hour of the boar. I'm to report to the master tonight."

Genba nodded and ducked back inside.

Walking quickly back to the market, Hitomaro dodged the muffled housewives with their baskets near the vegetable stalls, found the pharmacy, and turned down a narrow alley. The deep eaves of adjoining houses almost met overhead. He had been told that the city streets would become tunnels underneath mountains of snow, but at the moment he saw gray sky above. The small Shinto shrine in the next block lay deserted under its pines. He passed it and found another street of small, tidy houses.

Hitomaro hardly knew what to expect of the local pleasure quarter, but it was not this quiet line of modest houses behind bamboo fences. Neither garish banners nor paper lanterns marked this street as special. There were no painted women calling from windows, nor male touts running up and down the street looking for customers. And for music there was only the solitary sound of a single lute. He passed a fan and comb shop without customers and saw only one other person on the street but reminded himself that it was still early in the day, and that the scene would surely change at night. The lute music seemed to come from the largest house in the middle of the block. At the end of the street, he recognized a wineshop by its painted door curtain and decided that this was as good a place as any to ask about outcast women.

The prospect was unnerving to Hitomaro, who had, since his brief and tragic marriage, steadfastly avoided female company of any sort.

He had almost reached the large house, when the music stopped. As he looked, the door opened and a slender young woman in a cream-colored silk gown appeared. She carried a lute wrapped in a brocade cover and was speaking over her shoulder to a middle-aged, sharp-nosed female in black. Fascinated, Hitomaro stopped. The young woman passed something to the older one and turned to leave.

When he saw her face, he gasped, "Mitsu?"

The young woman paused. She looked him over carefully, smiling a little, while Hitomaro hid his shaking hands and stammered, "Forgive me. I thought for a moment . . ." He faltered, as his eyes traced her features and his heart nearly burst with mingled grief and joy.

She laughed softly, hiding her mouth with her sleeve, and he was lost. Just so had his young wife laughed up at him. Mitsu, who had hanged herself after their neighbor had raped her. The face of her beautiful look-alike receded into a fog of black despair.

"I hope she is pretty," the young woman murmured with a sidelong glance. "She is a lucky person to have so handsome an admirer."

With an effort Hitomaro came back to the present. He realized that this woman was flirting with him in public, and since she was very beautiful and had come from a house of assignation, he decided she must be one of the famous *hinin* courtesans. Perhaps she had entertained a customer and passed the auntie her fee before going home. The old woman still stood in the door, watching them, her head cocked and her pointed nose twitching.

He turned his eyes back to the enchanting girl. "Yes, she was beautiful," he said, his voice shaking a little, "as beautiful as you. Could I . . . would you allow me to . . ." He flushed at his awkwardness and pulled a string of coppers from his sleeve. Seeing her eyebrows rise, he delved into his sleeve again and came up with a silver bar. "Is this enough?" he asked, extending it to her.

She looked at the silver and started to laugh. "Naughty man," she murmured. "If you wish an introduction, you must ask permission of my aunt, Mrs. Omeya." She nodded toward the older woman, bowed, and walked away quickly.

Ah, so that's the way to do the business, Hitomaro thought and turned to the auntie. "How much and when should I return?"

Old Sharpnose stared after the young woman. Her mouth twitched. Then she snatched the silver out of Hitomaro's hand. "This will do, and come back tomorrow, same time." She slipped back into the house and slammed the door in his face.

"Wait! What's her name?" Too late; the old one was gone and so was the only woman who had set his blood racing in years. He stood for another moment, a bemused smile on his face, and then walked off toward the wineshop at the end of the road. Suddenly he felt like drinking.

The wineshop was no more than a single room. Two walls on either side were lined with low wooden seating platforms, the third with large wine barrels, a rack of shelves holding earthenware cups, and another curtained doorway. It was empty, but an oil lamp flickered on a sake barrel, and the straw mats on the platforms were reasonably clean. Hitomaro sat down and shouted, "Oy!"

A young woman appeared through the doorway. She was small and pert and had unusually curly hair and snapping black eyes which lingered on Hitomaro after the first glance, but Hitomaro's mind was on a pale goddess he hoped to hold in his arms the next day. It had been too long. To think that such a perfect creature was a prostitute—an outcast who sold her body to any man with money.

Absentmindedly he ordered the wine, then remembered that his report was due tonight and that he might not be able to return tomorrow.

The waitress brought a flask and cup just as he hit his head with the palm of his hand and cried, "I'm a fool!"

She giggled. "Not at all, sir. The wine is excellent here."

"Oh. Sorry. It's just that I forgot something I have to do." Taking notice of her for the first time, he blurted out, "I like your hair. I've never seen hair curl like that. What do you do to it?"

Her smile froze. "Nothing. I was born with it. And I don't like it when people make fun of me."

He was bewildered. "No, I really like it. It's very attractive. But I guess they used to tease you in school."

"School? Hardly. I'm an outcast. An untouchable."

Hitomaro greeted that with pleased surprise. "Oh? Are you really? Well, that explains it. I was told all outcast women are beautiful. I see it's true."

There was a pause, then she asked, "You're not from here?" When he shook his head, she said bitterly, "Most people think of us as animals. They only treat our women decently when they want their bodies. Untouchable! Pah! They can't get enough of touching us in bed." Her voice shook with anger.

Hitomaro was sorry and said so.

She tossed her head. "Don't be! We make them pay."

Remembering the silver bar, he said awkwardly, "Let me buy you dinner tonight." Seeing her flush, he added quickly, "No strings attached. I'd like to make up for mentioning your hair."

She chuckled at that. "I was wrong about you. I tell you

what. You can be *my* guest. I'm Yasuko. We have a beautiful salmon at home, and if you don't mind eating with outcasts, I can promise you a fine meal."

Hitomaro accepted eagerly. Before he left the wineshop, he got directions to her village. The intervening hours he passed talking to market vendors about the three convicts.

◆

Shortly after sunset he was walking rapidly along the country road in the gathering dusk. He carried a gift of rice cakes stuffed with sweet bean paste, and felt a general sense of satisfaction with his day. His master would be especially pleased to hear that he had already made friends with two of the *hinin*.

Because Hitomaro was preoccupied with the genealogy that had produced two such extraordinary women as his curly-haired hostess and the pale goddess he had met earlier, he was unprepared for an ambush.

At a bend in the narrow road, near a stand of pines sur-rounding a small shrine to the fox spirit, a band of rough men, their faces covered with black cloth below their eyes, fell upon him with cudgels and staffs. Dropping his packages, he went into a defensive stance, ducking and fending off the blows, but he was unarmed and badly outnumbered. He took them for a band of robbers at first, but since he was wearing old clothes, they could hardly have expected to enrich themselves.

When he realized who they were, he fought back with re-newed fury though he was at a disadvantage against so many cudgels, wielded with such expertise. At first they struck at his arms and legs and his lower back. He landed a few kicks to a groin or two and put his fist into a few faces, but then a well-placed hit to the side of his head sent him reeling. Flashes of red-hot pain exploded behind his eyes and his knees buckled. He collapsed in the roadway.

When he came to he was still lying down. Every part of his body hurt, but mostly his head. He tried to push the pain aside to concentrate on where he was. Odd sounds of rummaging and murmuring meant he was among people, and he opened his eyes a slit. He seemed to be lying on a dirt floor, looking up at an opening in a strange conical roof. Firelight flickered across beams and rafters that were tied together with vines. Nets, woven from sedge and holding various household goods, hung suspended from them. The flickering light and a certain warmth on one side of his body told him that he lay next to a fire. Its smoke spiraled up toward a patch of starry sky.

He turned his head painfully and verified that the fire was contained in a sunken pit. Beyond he saw dim shapes—people—seated or standing in the outer gloom that the firelight did not reach. He grunted experimentally, and one of the shapes approached and became Yasuko, the waitress from the wineshop.

"Oh, it's you," he mumbled. "I don't remember getting here." He grimaced and felt his scalp gingerly, wincing again at the sharp pain in his shoulder and arm. He noticed blood on his hand and sleeve, and his hand looked bruised and swollen. Memory returned suddenly, and he jerked upright with a string of bloodcurdling curses.

"Lie down!" instructed a deep, commanding voice. Hitomaro obeyed because pain and a sudden dizziness made the room spin crazily. When his head cleared, he looked up at an old man with a silken mane of white hair and a long beard. The old man was bending over him to apply a cool and fragrant compress to his head. Hitomaro sighed with relief and closed his eyes again.

Then Yasuko began to wash the blood from his hands and face and he looked at her. She smiled. "You are in good hands," she said. "The master himself was visiting our village when Kaoru brought you home."

She was very gentle with him. Hitomaro murmured, "Oh. Much obliged. I was waylaid near a fox shrine." When she was done, he raised himself again, more carefully, and looked around. "I had some rice dumplings I meant to give you, but I must've dropped them when those bastards jumped me. At first, I thought it was a hell of a thing to do to a fellow for a few dumplings . . . Who's Kaoru?"

"I am." Slim and muscular, the young man wore the traditional garb of a woodsman. Like Hitomaro, he had a short beard and mustache but his hair was long and loose. He came closer and looked down at Hitomaro. "I doubt it was the dumplings," he said. "Those men were set on giving you a beating, maybe even killing you. It was hard to get their attention." He smiled, his teeth very white against the brown skin.

Hitomaro smiled back, painfully since his lip was split and swollen. "No, it wasn't the dumplings. You're the one who brought me here?" he asked. "Thanks, friend. I won't forget the favor. How did you manage it by yourself?"

"Oh, I was not alone." Kaoru smiled again, and, reaching for a large, beautifully made bow, said, "Meet my assistant, Dragon Flash." He whistled softly, "And my best friend, White Bear." A large, shaggy white dog appeared. The dog leaned against the woodsman's leg and looked down at Hitomaro. Yawning largely, he revealed a set of ferocious teeth, then let his tongue loll out to give Hitomaro a friendly greeting.

"You managed to incapacitate two of them. I wounded four," the woodsman said. "White Bear savaged the legs and buttocks of four more, and the rest decided to run for it, carrying off their wounded. There were twelve altogether, I think."

"You have made a bad enemy," remarked the old man to Hitomaro, as he came to change the compress on his head. "Perhaps you would rather not tell us your name under the circumstances. You are among friends here. We know all about keeping secrets and we often give refuge to those in trouble with the authorities."

"The authorities?" Hitomaro looked shocked. "Good heavens! Those bastards were scum. They were the hired thugs of a fellow called Sunada. We had a small disagreement earlier in the day after one of them roughed up a friend of a friend."

The old man sighed. "Sunada's men? In this place, authority is not always in official hands, so watch yourself, my son." Turning to Yasuko, he said, "He will stay here overnight. A very light supper, and a solid breakfast, and he should do well enough. Now I must check on my other patient."

"No!" Hitomaro began to scramble up again, but the white-beard placed a surprisingly strong hand against his chest and forced him back. "You don't understand," Hitomaro pleaded. "I have to return to the city tonight. I'm meeting a friend."

"Why?" Just that word, but the inflection expressed surprise rather than curiosity, as if in the larger scheme of things nothing mattered but Hitomaro's health.

"Well . . ." Hitomaro hedged, then said, "Never mind."

The old man nodded. "You will stay." His tone left no room for argument.

Yasuko accompanied the healer to the door and bade him farewell with many deep bows. When she returned, Hitomaro said, "You have strange doctors here. He was a *yamabushi*, wasn't he?"

She smiled. "Not just any *yamabushi*. The master himself. He lives in the mountains in a cave and only visits to tend the sick and dying. He's a great man, a saint."

"I admit that compress of his is very soothing. Who's his other patient?"

"Oh, that one!" She sniffed. "An army deserter came here to hide. He showed his gratitude by raping one of our girls. There was a fight after that. We should've known from his broken teeth that he was bully. I think someone broke his arm."

"Why do you hide criminals?"

"They aren't always criminals. Some just don't get along with the authorities. The master insists we take in anyone who's in trouble. He says in a world without justice, every man deserves a second chance. It's a rule that can't be broken. Most of those who came to us have been grateful. I'll get your dinner now."

After she left, an old crone sidled up and sat down next to Hitomaro. She stared fixedly at his bandaged head and muttered under her breath.

Her glittering eyes made him nervous. "What's that, Grandmother?" he asked.

Suddenly she bent over him so closely that he flinched away from her foul breath. "Are you afraid, my handsome lord?" She cackled crazily, rocking back and forth. "Blood. Red blood and white snow. Ah, the pretty flower and the pretty bud." She leaned over him again. A thin thread of saliva drooled from her toothless gums. She hissed, "The dead will have their due, my lord. Where will you hide then? In your grave?" She doubled over with a wild shriek of laughter.

"Quiet, Grandmother!" Kaoru reached down and helped her up. "Time for your supper and bed."

The crone clung to him, whimpering now. "Make him go away. Make him go away." Kaoru made soothing noises and took her to the far corner of the house, where he bedded her down and gently wrapped a blanket around her. Yasuko took her a bowl of food, and Kaoru returned to Hitomaro.

"Grandmother is a shamaness," he said. "Such women suffer great mental strain in their work. She's been having spells of confusion for the past year, and today has been an especially bad day for her. I hope you will forgive her."

"Of course, but what the devil was she talking about? What blood? Which dead?"

"She doesn't know what she is saying. She's old and weak and gets confused."

Hitomaro said nothing. He had begun to wonder why this outcast woodcutter spoke like an educated man.

Yasuko brought a bamboo tray with fragrant pink chunks of fish nestled in green cabbage leaves. "She's calm now," she told Kaoru. "The fit started when she heard someone talk about the old lord's death. I put your food next to her bed, Kaoru. Please sit with her for a little." Turning to Hitomaro, she said, "I promised you salmon, and here it is." She knelt beside him and selected a tempting piece with the chopsticks. Proffering it, she added, "You mustn't be greedy though! The master said you are to eat lightly, and I mean to make sure you behave."

She looked so charming with her face rosy in the firelight, that a man might well forget his manners. Hitomaro enjoyed the experience of being fed, and not only because the fish was delicious and he was hungry. He swallowed and thanked her, then asked, "Why would your grandmother be upset by old Uesugi's death?"

"Otakushi is Kaoru's grandmother. She used to visit Takata manor just as her mother did before her. They both had the gift of foretelling the future. It's dangerous work. Otakushi's mother once almost lost her life. She foretold that one of the lord's sons would kill his brother."

Kaoru appeared beside her, eyes blazing with anger. "Yasuko. Come."

She looked up, startled. Gathering the tray with shaking hands, she told Hitomaro, "You must rest now," and scurried away.

SEVEN

FLUTE PLAY

*I*n the gray predawn hour of the following morning, Akitada sat hunched over his desk, reading documents from the provincial archives. From time to time his eyes moved to a twist of paper and a scrap with some childish scrawls on it, and he muttered to himself.

Hamaya put his head in the door. "Did you wish for anything, your Excellency?"

"No, no! Just . . . you might glance outside and see if either of my lieutenants is about."

Hamaya disappeared. Akitada shivered, took a sip from his teacup and made a face. The tea was cold already, and no wonder in this chilly place. If he could only shake this trouble in his belly, he might have more energy, ideas, solutions. The gods knew he needed them. Neither Tora nor Hitomaro had seen fit to make their reports last night as instructed. He had waited for hours. When he had finally gone to the room he shared with his wife, she had been fast asleep. Not wanting to disturb her, he had ended up spending the night in his office, hardly closing an eye, chilled to the bone by the icy drafts coming from the doors and through the walls.

Then, this morning, on his desk, he had found the mysterious twist of paper on top of one of Tora's illegible notes. The paper contained some mud-colored bits smelling vaguely of dried grass and resembling rabbit dung.

The door opened. Hamaya said, "Lieutenant Tora is just . . ."

"Sorry, sir," Tora mumbled, slinking past the clerk and dropping onto the mat across from Akitada. He looked uncharacteristically glum and sounded apologetic. "You were asleep when I got back, so I waited in the stable. I guess I dozed off. That fool of a constable had orders to tell me the minute you were up."

Akitada said nothing but looked disapprovingly at the pieces of straw clinging to his lieutenant's hair and clothes. Tora fidgeted, discovered the straw, and muttered another apology, adding, "I hope Dr. Oyoshi's medicine worked, sir." His eyes were on the twist of paper.

"Dr. Oyoshi?" Akitada's heavy brows rose. "This illegible scrawl is about some medicine sent by him?" he asked sarcastically. "From what I could make out, I thought your nephew's business was ailing, and he decided to write poems in praise of constipation."

"Oh." Tora's face reddened. He reached for the note. "I guess I got some of the characters mixed up. The fact is, I had a shocking night."

Akitada's stomach hurt, and Tora's problems were not his. He snapped, "Well, well? What did the doctor say about the medicine?"

"Oh. Can you imagine, he recognized me right away and knew all about your loose bowels? He must have the eyes of a cloud dragon!"

"Medicine!" Akitada bellowed. "What am I to do with these pellets?"

Tora looked hurt. "You take one in some hot wine three times a day."

"Hamaya!"

The clerk put his head in the door. "Excellency?"

"Some hot wine. Quick!"

"Well, as I was saying . . ." Tora tried to continue his report.

"Wait!" Akitada scowled ferociously, and Tora sank into glum silence.

After the wine arrived and he had taken his first dose, Akitada sighed and remarked more peaceably, "It was good of you to stop by the doctor's place and ask for these. I am sorry I snapped at you. What shock did you have?"

Tora did not meet his eyes. "Uh . . . I didn't exactly . . . that is, the doctor recognized me at the Golden Carp and asked about your, uh . . . and gave me the pills. I offered to pay him, but he said not to unless they work. The fact is, he was calling on a patient at the inn. Mrs. Sato wanted to get rid of a sick guest, but the doctor forbade it. She was very angry. She said sick guests are bad for her business, and this one also had no money. When the doctor left, I ran after him to pay for the poor fellow's medicine. That's when . . ."

Akitada held up a hand. "Wait! If you were at the Golden Carp, you may as well start your report at the beginning. What did you find out in the market?"

Tora shifted miserably. "A little. There was one fellow who thought he'd changed money for Takagi or someone like him, but he wasn't sure about the day. Two men remembered Okano's act in the wineshop." He sighed deeply. "There's not much point in checking out those guys. I know they didn't do it."

"And how do you know that?" Akitada asked, astonished.

Tora swallowed. "I . . . the maid and I, uh, last night. I

thought it was a good way to get some information. Amida, I shouldn't have touched her. She did it, sir! She killed the old man. I bet the bitch slits men's throats regularly. Start digging behind her kitchen and no telling what you'll find. She gets 'em in her bed and then . . ."

"Tora!"

Tora stopped and looked at him blearily.

"Did she admit to the murder?"

"Not in so many words. But I knew. I put the clues together, just like you do, and they added up." Tora raised a finger and counted off, "One, she hates her mistress, but not because she works her too hard or pays her too little. Oh, no! She hates her because old Sato married a pretty young thing and doted on her. Two, Kiyo—that's the maid's name—used to take *care* of Sato. If you know what I mean." Tora glowered.

"Are you sure?"

"Oh, yes," Tora said bitterly. "She's one of those females who can't get enough of it. I guess even an old geezer would do for her."

"Hmm. Why are you so upset?"

Tora looked at Akitada. "It's disgusting—like I slept with a leper."

"You think she killed her employer? Why?"

"She hated him. You should've heard her. She went on taking 'care' of him after his marriage because the wife wasn't interested, but it was the wife he gave the money to, the wife he talked about in bed as if she were some kind of goddess. Well, one day, while the wife was visiting her parents, she got fed up and took her revenge and his gold. I bet Kiyo figured the money was hers—for services rendered. She must've done it that afternoon, while the three guests were at the market. Nobody saw or heard old Sato after midday. And remember, she used her own kitchen knife. Takagi saw it in the kitchen in the morning, but in the evening, when they were back from the market, it was gone, and she was slicing radish with a little knife. So you see? She had the motive *and* the opportunity."

Akitada nodded. "Those are very good points."

Somewhat consoled, Tora concluded, "There's one more point, and it clinches the matter. After those three fools went to sleep, she slipped back into the kitchen and put the bloody knife in Takagi's bundle. Who else could've done that?"

"Hmm." Akitada thought, pulling his earlobe and pursing his lips. "It seems to me you supposed a lot of things. What did she actually say?"

"What I just told you. How she took care of him all those years, and the wife didn't, and how the wife got everything she wanted and was ungrateful."

"But that is hardly a murder confession, is it?"

Tora looked confused. "But . . . you should have been there, sir. It would have turned your stomach, she was so full of hate. It had to be her." He shuddered. "I slept with a murderess."

"Well, let it be a lesson to you not to sleep with every girl you run into. You have made an interesting case against that maid, but for the moment we do not have enough evidence to arrest her. Where is Hitomaro?"

"He hasn't come in? That's not like Hito. I'll go look for him."

"No." Akitada pushed the documents aside irritably. "We don't have the time. While you and Hitomaro were out, I have been checking the records. We have a bigger problem than that murder. For three generations now, the Uesugi have ruled this province as their personal domain. During that time they resisted every effort by the government to bring Echigo in line with the *Taiho* and *Yoro* law codes. No wonder Judge Hisamatsu runs his court to please the lords of Takata and himself. No wonder the three travelers are being made scapegoats. I expect miscarriage of justice has been the order of the day. And no wonder everybody wishes to be rid of me."

"Let them try!" Tora said belligerently.

Akitada gave him a long look. "Think, Tora. We have no real power. We don't even have the support of the military guard, and there is no police force. On five separate occasions the imperial government has dispatched trained police officers from the capital with instructions to set up a local force. The Uesugi sent them all back, claiming that a high constable and a judge were all that is needed. In consequence, the local people take their orders from Takata and ignore us."

"Why didn't the other governors object?"

"Apparently they were bribed or threatened into acquiescence."

Tora's mind returned to another matter. He frowned. "Something must've happened to Hitomaro."

"Hitomaro can handle himself." Akitada reached for a document roll and called, "Hamaya."

When the clerk came in, Akitada handed him the documents. "Here, take a look at these. They have been tampered with. Names have been erased and a whole section has been removed. The affair concerns the late lord's older brother. I want to know what happened."

The clerk received the roll with a bow, studied the pertinent sections carefully, and nodded. "Yes, your Excellency is quite right. It was before my time, of course, but I think there was a scandal of sorts. The son in question was repudiated by his father. Changing the documents is quite legal. It is a father's right to have the son's name expunged from official family records for serious crimes against family."

Akitada glowered. "Not on documents in my administration. What happened?"

"I know very little, sir. The family has a history of tragedy.

Very brutal times back then. I believe there was a double murder in the women's quarters. One of the concubines and her child were slain. I don't know whether that has anything to do with the son."

"Hmm. See what you can find out."

The clerk bowed and left.

Akitada pulled his earlobe again. "If they have covered up a crime, we may be able to establish some authority. I think I shall request another police chief from the capital and set up a regular force by next spring."

"That'll be a relief," Tora grunted. "Those lazy, ignorant dogs of constables and that bastard Chobei are hardly my idea of efficient law enforcement."

"You can stop worrying about Chobei," said a voice from the doorway. Hitomaro, his face swollen and bruised, walked in with a smile. "I've found us a replacement."

"Amida, what happened to you?" Tora gasped.

Hitomaro lowered himself cautiously to the floor. "Sunada's thugs set a trap for me. I just got back. And I missed Genba last night."

Akitada sat up. "Sunada? The merchant? I met the man at Takata."

Hitomaro told him about the argument outside the restaurant.

Akitada listened glumly. "More bad news," he commented. "I was hoping to use him to win the local merchants over, but the situation you describe does not promise well. I won't countenance gangster tactics."

"The three of us can easily settle that account and teach the merchant a lesson at the same time," Tora said.

"Not yet. An open confrontation will drive Sunada into the Uesugi camp, and so far, if I don't miss my guess, Uesugi is reluctant to deal with him. Are you well enough to work, Hitomaro?"

"Fit for anything, sir. The soreness will wear off. And you?"

"Much better, I think. That pill seems to be working. A good thing. Tomorrow I have to attend the old lord's funeral. And, since the town will be full of people, I plan to hear the case of the innkeeper's murder the day after."

Hitomaro said, "We'd better post notices right away. And Tora can drill the constables in their duties. I suppose we'll have to use Chobei a while longer, sir?"

"Yes, I'm afraid so. Who is this replacement?"

"One of the outcasts, sir. His name is Kaoru. He's been working as a woodsman or woodcutter, but he saved my life when those thugs jumped me. There were twelve of them . . ."

"Twelve, against one unarmed man?" Tora cried. "The filthy cowards!"

"Yes. They had cudgels and I passed out pretty quickly. I doubt I'd be here, if Kaoru hadn't stepped in with some first-rate archery and his dog."

"I look forward to meeting him," said Akitada, suppressing some qualms. "But first, let's hear what you found out. What about the three prisoners?"

"I found a couple of witnesses who will swear that Umehara and Okano did precisely what they said they did, but nobody except for a soup vendor remembers the half-wit."

"That is good enough. Arrange to have them testify. What did Genba have to say?"

"The local people don't trust the Uesugi, but they submit as long as they can carry on with their business or farms. There's a lot of concern about Uesugi drafting young men to serve in the border wars, and some think money is being extorted from families to exempt their sons. That seems to be all."

"It may be useful. I'll have Hamaya look into it. Did you learn anything from the outcasts?"

Hitomaro smiled. "Yes, sir. After talking to Genba, I managed to get myself invited to the outcast village. They had a *yamabushi* there who tended to my wounds and scrapes. I spent the night."

Akitada clapped his hands. "Well done! I was told they normally keep to themselves."

"Their women are known for their beauty and sexual skills, so I went to the amusement quarter first." Hitomaro blushed. "The waitress in a wineshop there was *hinin* and invited me home for dinner."

Tora burst out laughing. "Only you would go to the amusement quarter and end up with a free dinner, Hito."

Hitomaro frowned at him. "It was the easiest way to get to know those people," he said defensively. "And I did stop at a house of assignation first. It catered to private customers."

"Please get to the point!" Akitada had a sinking feeling that he was about to be treated to another tale of debauch. "What about the outcasts? Whom do they obey?"

Hitomaro looked relieved. "No one. They are very poor, sir. They grow a few vegetables in their gardens and work the usual dirty jobs in town for a few coppers. But some of the women sell their bodies and bring good earnings home to their families. I got the feeling they are close-knit. The only ones they take instruction from are the *yamabushi*. I was patched up by the master *yamabushi* himself."

Akitada sat up. "Really? The master? An old man with a very long white beard and long hair?"

"You've met him, sir? Very impressive. Amazing how educated those mountain priests are. He spoke as well as anyone I ever met, sir. And so does Kaoru, now I think of it."

Akitada raised his brows. "A well-spoken woodcutter? You surprise me. And the *yamabushi* speaks, does he? What did he have to say?"

"He thought I was a fugitive looking for sanctuary. It seems he has told the outcasts to take in anyone who's in trouble with the law. That could account for Uesugi's hatred of them. They had some toothless deserter hiding there who assaulted one of their women and got his arm broken for it. They don't want him, but the *yamabushi* protects him."

Akitada's brows contracted in an angry scowl. "Things have gone far in this godforsaken province. Not only am I prevented from upholding the law, but there is a conspiracy afoot to harbor criminals right under our nose." He fell into a gloomy abstraction. "Worse and worse!" he muttered. "The Uesugi govern, the merchants are gangster bosses, and outcasts hide all those criminals who are not already protected by the other two factions. Where does that leave us?"

"Out in the cold," quipped Tora, opening a shutter and peering up at the sky. A blast of freezing air blew in.

"Close that," Akitada snapped, "and pay attention!"

"Things may not be as hopeless as they seem, sir," Hitomaro said. "I think the outcasts are fighting the Uesugi in their own way. And I've found them very decent people. They not only took care of me, but they also tend to a madwoman there. Spooky creature. She's Kaoru's grandmother and a soothsayer. She kept looking at me and babbling about blood and murder."

Akitada said grudgingly, "Well, we are in their debt for helping you, in any case."

"And none of the small tradesmen will have anything to do with Sunada."

Akitada sighed. "Yes, that is good. I must be patient."

"What about Kaoru, sir?" Hitomaro asked.

"When he comes, bring him to me. At least he's not likely to be working for Uesugi. If he is moderately intelligent and does not help our prisoners to escape, you may train him to replace that rascal Chobei. Now you had both better get on with preparations for our first court session."

"Sir?" Hitomaro avoided Akitada's eyes. "May I have a few hours off this afternoon? It, er, concerns the outcasts."

Akitada opened his mouth to ask for details but, thinking better of it, he nodded. His lieutenants left.

As soon as they were gone, Seimei came in. He gave Akitada an anxious look and asked, "How about a nice cup of herbal tea, sir? I know you don't like the taste, but I found some honey."

"No need, Seimei. I feel much better, but if you are free, there is some work."

For the next hour they drafted the notices to be posted around town, set the clerks to work copying them, prepared a list of witnesses Akitada wanted called, and wrote instructions about the arrangements for the hearing. When they were done, Seimei left to get matters organized.

At midday one of the junior clerks brought Akitada a bowl of rice gruel and some pickled vegetables. He ate hungrily and took another of Oyoshi's pills with the wine. For the first time in days his stomach felt pleasantly full, and a general sensation of well-being pervaded his body.

After his meal, he just sat quietly, savoring the return of his health. He found he was once again looking forward to the challenges ahead. Now that he had begun to take action, he felt confident of establishing control over the province. The hearing on Sato's murder would be the first step. He would show the local people how things were supposed to be done. And Uesugi was little more than a silly, posturing border lord. Only the distance from the capital and the venality of past governors had kept him in power. His good times were over.

Into this euphoria walked Judge Hisamatsu. Announced by Hamaya, he entered, bowed stiffly, and took the seat offered by Akitada.

"Your visit is very welcome," Akitada said with a smile. "I

have wanted to greet you officially, Hisamatsu. As you may have heard, my own background is also in law. May I ask when you attended the university?"

Hisamatsu, who had been glowering, gulped. "Ah, quite a few years ago, Excellency. I don't believe we could have met," he said frostily.

"No, perhaps not. Do you recall the names of any of your law professors?"

Hisamatsu waved this away. "Names. What are names? But I shall never forget their teachings. Their wisdom is with me every day."

"Ah, no doubt you studied under Ogata, then."

Hisamatsu hesitated just a fraction, then said, "Of course. What a legal scholar!"

Satisfied that Hisamatsu had not attended the imperial university, which had never had anyone by the name Ogata teaching there, Akitada relaxed. "This province seems backward in many ways. No doubt there is much lawlessness and you are kept very busy."

Hisamatsu gave a small laugh. "Oh, yes. Very busy. I earn my salary many times over."

Akitada nodded and looked thoughtful. "I was afraid of that. I, on the other hand, seem to have few cases to occupy my time."

Too late Hisamatsu saw the trap. "Oh, I am perfectly capable of handling the caseload, Excellency. And that brings me to the matter I wished to discuss."

Akitada faked surprise. "Forgive me. I misunderstood your purpose. I thought this was merely a courtesy visit."

Hisamatsu flushed. "Yes, yes. That, and, well, it has come to my attention—just today, as a matter of fact—that your Excellency has taken an interest in a minor case of mine."

"I cannot imagine what you mean."

"The murder of a local innkeeper?"

Akitada chuckled. "I see. You were joking. A minor case? Very funny. Well, actually, it looked interesting to me. Complicated. I rather enjoy complicated cases, don't you?"

Hisamatsu blustered, "Your pardon, Excellency, but you must have been misinformed. The case is very simple and straightforward. We have the culprits in jail. They have confessed. All that is left is for me to pronounce sentence."

"Ah, Hisamatsu, I thought perhaps you had jumped to conclusions there. A good thing I checked into it. We can't have a miscarriage of justice at the beginning of my tenure here, you know. How would it look? The people have a right to be reassured that they can place their trust in their new governor."

Hisamatsu was becoming angry. "Miscarriage of justice? I fail to see how you can charge such a thing. Confessions, Excellency. We got confessions. Really, I do not understand what all the fuss is about. It will be very much better if you just let the law take its course."

"Better for whom, Hisamatsu?"

"Why, for everyone. Justice must be served. The victim demands it. The widow demands it. The people of this province demand it."

"What about the accused? You have arrested three men. Shall they be given justice? No, no, Hisamatsu. In this case due process has not been served. Only two of the men have confessed, and then after the most brutal beatings. I myself have seen their wounds. I trust you are familiar with the regulations pertaining to torture of prisoners?"

Hisamatsu looked startled. "If those constables have exceeded their duty, I shall certainly have them punished." He paused. "But this will make no difference, for the accused will repeat their confessions in my court. The evidence is clear."

"Possibly Okano and Umehara will do so. They are as timid as mice. But Takagi will not confess. In any case, you are not ready to hear the case. You have yet to check the three men's testimony."

"Check what?" yelped Hisamatsu. "They confessed. They had the gold and the knife. And Takagi is retarded. You don't expect a brute like that to cooperate right away?"

"The law states that you must have confessions to find men guilty."

"Trust me, Takagi will confess."

Akitada said dryly, "Yes, I suppose you will find a way. But your way is not mine. And I will investigate the case myself."

Hisamatsu's high color changed to purple. "What? You can't do that. There's no precedent. It's . . . it's not legal."

"I fear, Hisamatsu, that I have a better notion of the law than you. In the future, confine yourself to really minor cases and make certain that transcripts of all your findings are submitted to me before judgment."

Hisamatsu shot up. "That is insulting. I serve under the high constable."

Akitada looked up at him and shook his head sadly. "The high constable has died—or hadn't you heard? And I have no intention of appointing another until I am convinced that this province is loyal to his Majesty. I'm afraid you're stuck with me."

Hisamatsu made a choking sound, bowed, and left.

Akitada smiled and got up. He stretched and walked to a small carved chest. After rummaging in it, he pulled out a narrow brocade case and a notebook and carried them back to his desk. Undoing the silk cord of the brocade case, he lovingly removed a plain bamboo flute and turned it in his hand. He had not played since the capital. For some reason neither his wife nor any one else in his household had shown much interest in flute music. A pity.

He really felt extraordinarily well after his meeting with Hisamatsu. The man had folded quickly when faced with firm authority. The present troubles would soon be past.

He lifted the flute to his lips and blew experimentally.

Ah! The fullness of its sound! His heart lifted. He opened the notebook and studied a page. Perhaps he would begin with a passage from "Cicadas in the Pine Trees."

Halfway through the first scale, the door flew open and Hamaya burst in, his two assistants peering wide-eyed over his shoulders. Akitada lowered his flute. Their expressions changed from shock to intense embarrassment.

"Yes?"

Hamaya turned to the other two and motioned them away. To Akitada he said with a bow, "Forgive the intrusion, sir, but the sound was so unexpected that we thought . . . we were afraid . . . please forgive the interruption."

"I was only playing my flute," Akitada explained, holding it up. "The song is called 'Cicadas in the Pine Trees.' Here, if you listen carefully, you can distinguish the cicada's cry." He lifted the flute and produced a series of shrill squeaks and grating rasps.

"Indeed, sir," stammered Hamaya, "it does sound something like, that is, just like . . . I must return to work." Bowing again, he retreated and closed the door softly.

Akitada stared after him. Curious. It was almost as if they had never heard flute music before. He shook his head. What a godforsaken province this was! Well, they would soon learn to appreciate it. He returned to his practice.

◆

In the private rooms, Tamako was sipping tea with Seimei. He had reported that her husband seemed quite well again, much to her relief because she knew he had not come to bed the night before. Now they heard the squeal of the flute and looked at each other. Tamako smiled.

"Oh, I am so glad. He *is* better. Was it something you gave him?"

Seimei frowned. "No. He has not taken any of my infusions. He can be very stubborn. Against unreason even the Buddha cannot prevail."

◆

Outside, Tora and Hitomaro, on their way from the constables' barracks, stopped and looked at each other.

"He's started again," said Tora in a tone of horror. "It's that devil's instrument. People will say he's mad. As if we didn't have enough trouble. I wish he'd left the cursed thing in the capital."

Hitomaro, who was in an unusually good mood, laughed. "Don't complain, brother. It means he's feeling better." He looked up at the sun. "I must go, but I should be back for the evening rice."

Tora watched him stride out the gate. Something was up with Hito. He had never seen him so excited. Or so concerned with his appearance. One would almost swear he was on his way to meet a girl.

◆

Several hours after Akitada had wrapped up his flute again and returned to his paperwork, he was startled by the loud clanging of the bell outside the tribunal gate. This was meant to be rung by persons who wished to lay a complaint against someone or report a crime. Finally! He sat up in anticipation.

Hamaya showed in three people. "Mr. Oshima and his wife, sir, and their daughter, Mrs. Sato," he announced, looking unhappy. "Mrs. Sato is the widow of the slain innkeeper."

The elderly couple in their neat cotton gowns knelt and

bowed their heads to the mats. The young woman lifted her veil, then followed their example more slowly and gracefully. Akitada tried not to stare. She was quite beautiful and wore silk, very inappropriate for the widow of a mere innkeeper. But his primary reaction was disappointment. No new case after all. Still, at least these people acknowledged his authority.

"You may sit up," he told them, "and inform me of your business."

The parents settled themselves on their knees and cleared their throats. They cast uneasy glances at Akitada's official brocade robe, at the elegant lacquer writing set and the document stacks on the desk, and at the thick, silk-trimmed floor mats— Akitada's own property, which his wife had insisted on installing when she saw his office.

"Don't be afraid," Akitada said pleasantly. "I am glad you came and will do my best to help you."

The old man murmured, "It's our daughter, your Honor. She says that her husband's death must be avenged because she's troubled by his spirit."

Astonished, Akitada asked, "The dead man's ghost appears to her?"

"My husband's ghost resides in our inn," said the widow in a surprisingly firm voice. "He's everywhere, in all the dark corners. I live in fear that one of the guests will see him. And at night he hovers over me as I lie on my mat. Sometimes I hear his blood dripping. I have not slept since he died." She touched a sleeve to her eyes.

"But surely you should call an exorcist."

"Of course I did that. It was no use."

Akitada frowned. "I don't see how I can be helpful."

The widow's chin came up and her eyes flashed. "Where am I to find justice, if not from the law? And is not the tribunal the place where we have our wrongs redressed? Ghosts walk only when murder goes unpunished."

Akitada thought her manner lacking in respect and humility, but he only remarked, "I assure you, madam, I am giving your case my personal attention. The day after tomorrow I shall preside over a public hearing of the matter. You would have been notified shortly."

"A hearing?" she cried, a flush staining her porcelainlike complexion. "What good is a hearing? The criminals have confessed and must be sentenced."

The old lady gave a frightened cry. She scooted a little closer to Akitada's desk and bowed deeply. "Please forgive my daughter's bad manners," she murmured. "It is her grief and worry speaking. We came to town for a visit and saw the notices. It is merely to ask about them that we came, your Honor."

Akitada opened his mouth, but Mrs. Sato was quicker. "No!" she cried. "I have no more patience. I want justice now. And since I'm not getting it, I am filing a complaint."

Akitada's mouth snapped shut. He locked eyes with the widow. She did not lower hers, and he read a challenge in her set face which told him negotiations were futile. Suddenly there was no doubt in his mind that this was the beginning of a well-planned campaign. "Very well," he said coldly. "It is your right to do so. See my clerk. But you will all three attend the hearing anyway."

EIGHT

MOURNING THE DEAD

Clouds of incense drifted between the massive pillars, obscuring the carved and gilded ceiling beams and putting a haze over the black robes of the monks and the dark clothing of the mourners. The sweet smell overwhelmed the senses, and the hum of sutra chanting, the clanging of gongs, and the chiming of cymbals floated on the air in gentle waves. The celebrants circled and spun in a graceful ritual dance, and Akitada's eyes closed and his fingers began to move in accompaniment on an imaginary flute.

Abbot Hokko, seated next to him, cleared his throat softly, and Akitada returned to reality, guiltily plunging his hands into his voluminous sleeves. The ceremony was drawing to its end, and not a moment too soon. Two hours of prayers, readings, and making reverent bows to the coffin of the late high constable, to the statue of the Buddha, and to Lord Makio, the chief mourner, were beginning to take their toll on Akitada who had been up most of the night preparing for the hearing.

He looked at the solitary, motionless figure of the new lord for a moment. Makio wore full armor, lacquered red and gold and laced with deep purple silk. He sat holding his black helmet with the gilded studs stiffly in front of him. His only concession to mourning was a white silk sash draped across his chest. He had not moved a muscle or changed his stern expression throughout the ceremony. Akitada knew that the wearing of the armor carried a message to himself. More important, his adversary was a man capable of great self-control. It would be a mistake to underestimate the new lord of Takata.

Akitada glanced at the long line of mourners from the Uesugi household. Some wore armor with the Uesugi crest prominently displayed and white mourning armbands, but the rest were in dark robes and the hempen jackets required for a funeral of the head of the clan. Their faces showed reverence or indifference, as the case might be, but no grief. The exception was a small boy at the end of the front row of male retainers and upper servants. His soft face was blotchy from weeping, and he sat sunken in despair, the stiff hemp enveloping him like a strange cocoon. A grandson? No, Makio had no children. Perhaps the old lord had befriended the child of a retainer and thus earned for himself the tears of affection none of the others were able to shed.

Akitada caught a quick movement out of the corner of his eye. A gray mouse had scurried from one of the pillars and ventured into the open space in front of the mourners. There it paused, twitching its nose. A half suppressed gurgle came from the child. He put a hand over his mouth, trying to stifle his laughter. Their eyes met and Akitada smiled, nodding at the mouse. To his delight, the boy lowered his hand and gave him a conspiratorial grin and a wink.

The ceremony ended and the mouse reconsidered and dashed back into its hole. The mourners filed out of the temple hall into the bright sunlight, where a carefully orchestrated cortege assembled to accompany the body of Lord Maro to its final resting place in the family tomb near Takata manor. The Uesugi held on to an old family tradition of burying their dead.

Akitada had already expressed his condolences to Makio before lending his official presence to the ceremony. He was not expected to attend the burial, but out of respect he could not rush off before the mourners.

He stood near the corner of the great temple hall and watched the milling crowd. A spirited black horse was led forward and Makio climbed onto its back—not without some difficulties, Akitada noted with secret satisfaction. It took three men to control the beast and lead it to its proper place in the line.

Someone tugged at his sleeve.

It was the small boy. He asked, "Is it true that you are the governor?"

"Yes. What can I do for you?"

"Will you help me find Grandfather?"

For a moment Akitada was confused. His heart contracted and he looked at the coffin which had been placed inside an elaborate palanquin and was being hoisted onto the shoulders of strong bearers. "Your grandfather?" he asked uncertainly.

"Grandfather did not come back from Lord Maro's room the night the great lord died. I looked everywhere and asked everybody. Nobody could tell me. Then Kaibara-*san* told me Grandfather had gone into the mountains to mourn his master. But Grandfather would have said good-bye to me."

The boy's eyes filled with tears and his lip quivered, but he controlled himself well. How old could he be, eight or nine? He looked frail, but his large mourning robe had something to do with that.

"What is your grandfather's name and position?"

"He's called Hideo, sir. He served the old lord. Grandfather was the only one to take care of him. Grandfather loved the great lord. He was very sad he was dying, but he would never, never have gone away without me. Please, sir, you must believe me." A sob escaped the boy.

Akitada bent down to put his arm around the narrow shoulders, but another arm intervened and snatched the boy up. Kaibara.

"Sorry, Excellency," said the Uesugi steward. "The youngster is a nuisance. I hope he has not troubled you?"

"Not at all, Kaibara. I am very fond of children," said Akitada with a smile—which slowly faded as he stood looking after them.

◆

Tora and Hitomaro looked surprised to be called to Akitada's office as soon as he returned from the funeral. Hitomaro's bruises had darkened, but he seemed otherwise fit again. Akitada had changed from his official court robe into a hunting coat and boots and told them to saddle three horses.

"Where are we going?" Tora asked.

"To Takata. Hurry. There isn't much time."

The sun was bright in the cold blue sky, and the earth beneath the horses' hooves so hard that they made good time. When they approached the stronghold, they caught sight of the tail end of the funeral cortege in the distance as it entered the village below.

"Come," Akitada called to his lieutenants. "Let's strike out across the fields. I want to have a look at the back of Uesugi's place. The woods will be our cover."

Tora and Hitomaro exchanged glances and felt for their swords.

Once they entered the trees, they had to slow their horses. Here the snow still lay in drifts and obscured pathways and fallen branches. In a short while they were lost.

"We'd better lead the horses, sir," Hitomaro said. "It'll be faster and safer."

Akitada agreed, and they moved forward cautiously, guessing at the direction and looking for a thinning of the trees.

Tora stumbled over a root and cursed. "You'd think there would be some roads or paths through this forest. We must be getting close."

"I expect in times of war, guards patrolled the area," Akitada said, "but the province has been peaceful for generations. I hope we don't come across any tracks."

This was too much for Tora, who had been bursting with curiosity since they left the city. "Why not? What's this all about?"

"Patience. Ah, I can see the sky over there. We must be coming out of the forest."

They emerged on the rugged edge of a deep ravine separating the forest from the steep hillside and saw above them the north side of Takata manor.

"Amida," breathed Tora. "That's steep. Only a spider could get up there, and it'd have to learn to fly across this ravine first."

"Do you see the roof jutting out over there?" Akitada pointed. "That is the north pavilion. I want to get close enough to see if anything has been tossed from the gallery above, but we will stay in the cover of the trees as long as possible."

Hitomaro said, "I doubt anybody's looking down. They'll all be at the interment, sir."

Akitada looked anxiously at the sky. It was clouding over. "I hope so," he muttered, "but we have lost too much time in the forest. Come on."

When they reached the area just below the north pavilion, they saw only heavy, undisturbed mounds of snow in the shade of the steep cliff, and the ravine was even wider here.

"I don't see a thing," Tora said. "Do you want us to climb down and find a way up the other side?" He did not sound enthusiastic.

Akitada hesitated, looking up at the sky again and studying the gallery above. There was no sign of movement.

He was just about to call off the search when there was a whirring sound followed by a sudden rush of something white among the trees behind them. They took immediate cover behind their horses, and loosened their swords.

A whistle sounded, and some branches cracked. Then silence.

"We are trapped here," muttered Akitada. "The ravine is behind us."

"And swords aren't much use against arrows," Hitomaro added. "If I'm not much mistaken, that was an arrow we heard."

They tried to keep their horses quiet and waited.

Suddenly the shrubbery near them parted and a fierce shaggy animal appeared, its ears laid back, and its nose slowly wrinkling up to reveal ferocious teeth. It growled and crouched. The horses backed nervously.

"A white wolf," Tora gasped. He drew his sword and fumbled for his amulet. Dropping the reins, he jumped forward.

"No, brother!" cried Hitomaro, snatching at the reins as Tora's horse reared. "It's a dog. It's White Bear." He called to the dog, then shouted, "Ho, Kaoru!" The dog raised its ears, then looked back over its shoulder.

They heard a shout from the forest, and then a tall young man dressed in furs appeared. He was carrying a longbow and a dead rabbit, and he grinned at Hitomaro. "It's you again, is it?" Taking in their defensive posture, he chuckled. "I see you were expecting hostilities, but it was just me shooting a rabbit." He held it up.

"This is Kaoru," said Hitomaro to Akitada.

Akitada nodded. "Yes, I gathered that. I am Sugawara Akitada, the governor, and this is Tora, my other lieutenant. We are grateful for the assistance you gave Hitomaro."

Kaoru's teeth flashed. Tossing back his long hair, he bowed. "It was nothing, Excellency. Are you lost?"

"Not really. I have reason to suspect that something was thrown from that gallery above, but there doesn't seem to be a way to get to the other side."

"Some object?" Kaoru stared at Akitada, then looked up at the pavilion. He muttered, "By the Buddha!" then said, "Follow me. I know a path."

They tied up their horses, leaving Kaoru's dog to guard them, and climbed down into the ravine. As Akitada picked his way among the loose rubble, he scrutinized the ground, following Kaoru, who had found a rough trail leading up the other side.

Once there, they moved slowly along the foot of the massive rocks, poking at the snow piles with their swords. Kaoru was slightly ahead when he suddenly stopped beside a small mound. Akitada compressed his lips. He joined him and bent to brush away the snow. Clothing appeared, stiffened by frost, and then the snow turned red, and there was a thin, aged hand, made rigid by death and the cold, with frozen blood caking the fingers and palm.

"Amida! A corpse!" gasped Tora. "Wonder how long it's been there."

"Since the night of the banquet," Akitada said, cleaning more blood-soaked snow away with Kaoru's help. The body belonged to an old man. His thin white hair was encrusted with ice and blood, as was the face except for patches of skin discolored by purplish-blue bruises. The eyes stared sightlessly at the sky above, and the mouth gaped in a permanent silent scream. His limbs lay at odd angles and the body had twisted unnaturally. A pool of blood had frozen to the earth under the corpse.

"It's old Hideo," said Kaoru, bowing his head. "Poor old man. He was the old lord's personal attendant."

Tora stared up the looming gallery above them, and said accusingly to Akitada, "You expected to find him, didn't you? Did he fall or jump?"

"Neither, I suspect, though we cannot be certain it wasn't an accident."

Tora frowned. "He could've jumped. If he was a faithful servant to the old man all his life, he might want to kill himself after his master died. It would bring honor to his family and makes more sense than an accident. He's lived here all his life. How could he tumble over that high balustrade?"

Kaoru fidgeted, and Akitada did not answer immediately. He cleaned off the old man's face with gentle fingers. The skin was broken and puffy about the jaw and cheekbones. And the bruising suggested a systematic beating rather than the sort of haphazard damage done by a fall. Akitada bent to inspect both hands. Bloody crystals had formed around the fingertips. He breathed on a thumb until the ice melted.

"Ah!" he murmured and removed a small sliver from under the fingernail.

"What is it?" Tora leaned forward curiously.

Akitada dabbed at the fragment with a bit of saliva. "Wood."

"What's it doing under his nails?" Tora bent closer. "There's blood under the other fingernails, too. Holy Amida! When I was a soldier, they caught a fellow spying. They drove bamboo slivers under the nails of his fingers and toes to make him talk. You think this poor guy's been tortured?"

Akitada straightened up, looking puzzled. "Perhaps, but not the way you think. The nails are broken and torn, and so is the skin of his fingers and palms. I believe he was questioned and beaten, but he hurt his hands when he was heaved over the balustrade and tried in vain to grasp at something. I wonder what he knew. And if he talked, and to whom."

They all stood and stared down at the contorted face of the dead man. There was terror in its expression, but also something else, stubbornness, even a sort of exultation.

"He didn't talk," said Hitomaro. "Not this one." He asked Akitada, "Do you think Makio did this?"

"Who knows? But we must leave him here. This is Uesugi territory. I have no jurisdiction in Takata."

Hitomaro and Tora protested, and Akitada raised a hand. "Wait. Perhaps there is a way." He turned to Kaoru, who had remained silent. He looked grim now, and the cheerful smile was gone.

"You knew and liked this man?" Akitada asked him.

Kaoru nodded.

"I believe he was murdered. If you want to see justice done, I will need your help."

"I want justice. What do you want me to do?"

"You would have to bring the body into the city, ring the bell outside the tribunal to report a crime, and later testify in a court hearing. Think before you agree, because the murderer may be someone close to the Lord of Takata and will almost certainly try to prevent this. He may even turn on your family. And I shall be unable to protect you or them."

The woodsman met his eyes. "I'm no friend to the Lord of Takata, and a man's life is useless unless he can be of service to his people."

"Good," said Akitada. "I am grateful for your help. But you will need a horse, and we cannot offer you one of ours."

"I can borrow one."

Akitada reached into his belt for some silver, but the woodsman held up a hand. "No money is needed among friends."

Akitada nodded. "Forgive me. Hitomaro tells me that you might be willing to serve as sergeant of constables?"

A strange, almost mocking smile passed over the young man's face, but he said quite humbly, "I would welcome the opportunity if you think me capable."

Akitada nodded. "Well, let's see how you handle your first assignment." He glanced up at the sky. "We must return now, but you had better start your journey after dark."

Kaoru bowed, and they parted. When they reached the other side of the ravine, Akitada looked back. The woodcutter had removed his fur vest and was laying it gently over the corpse's face before covering him again with snow.

When they reached their horses, the white dog wagged its tail, then perked up its ears and dashed off.

"Kaoru must've called him," Hitomaro said. "They say dogs have much finer hearing than men."

They had put some distance between themselves and Takata when Tora brought his horse up to Akitada's. "You could've told us from the start what we were looking for," he complained.

"I wasn't sure myself."

"But you knew where to look. I bet you knew whose body it was, too."

"I suspected."

"Well, it wasn't fair. Sometimes you ask a lot, sir."

Akitada felt a pang of guilt. "I am sorry," he said humbly. "I should have trusted you, Tora."

"I only mention it because we can help much better if we know what you're thinking. How did you know we would find the old man at the bottom of that wall?"

"You remember the night of the banquet? I had occasion to leave the company twice to use the convenience. On the first trip I glanced out of the gallery and saw the north pavilion. On my second visit I heard a scream from that direction. A servant heard it, too, but he said it was a wild animal in the woods, so I put it from my mind. Then, today, at Lord Maro's funeral, a small boy asked me to find his grandfather. He said his grandfather was the old lord's servant and did not return the night of his master's death. I could see the boy was sick with worry, but Kaibara, the Uesugi steward, snatched him away before I could ask questions. That was when I remembered the scream and decided to have a look."

"Poor kid," said Tora, shaking his head.

"What did you think of Kaoru?" Hitomaro asked, bringing his horse alongside.

"Very capable." Akitada frowned, then added, "But surely he is a man with secrets."

"Yes, I noticed that, too," Tora said. "Let him explain that fine bow! No outcast ever carried a weapon like that. It looks like those the young lords in the capital use for their archery contests. And like Hito said, he talks like one of us. Like he's been educated."

Akitada suppressed a smile. "You're right, Tora. That bow is unquestionably a special one. You're becoming a very good observer."

Tora glanced at Hitomaro to see the effect of this, then said importantly, "That's what made me suspicious, sir. He must be a thief and a liar. We shouldn't have trusted him."

"Wait a moment," cried Hitomaro angrily. "The man saved my life. And as for being a thief, I can tell you he's much too good at using that bow to have stolen it. He let me try it, but it takes a stronger and better arm than mine to bend it. Kaoru is very modest about his ability as an archer, but he's superb. He says he was taught by his grandfather when he was just four years old."

"Don't argue," Akitada said. "Remember, we need help badly. It is true that our new friend is not all he pretends to be, but the outcasts are at odds with the Uesugi and he did protect Hito-maro's life." Akitada paused as a vague memory crossed his mind. Someone else had said something similar recently. Something about pretending to be someone else, he thought, but he could not recall the details or the speaker.

"Sorry, brother," Tora apologized. "I tell you what. Let's wait up for your friend tonight and take him out for a nice late dinner at that good noodle restaurant. Make him feel welcome."

But Hitomaro said stiffly, "Not tonight. I'm busy."

NINE

A CORPSE AT THE
TRIBUNAL GATE

*T*here was another, heavier snowfall during the night. Akitada rose later than usual. As they had gone to bed, Tamako had expressed her first fears. She had talked about the bitter winter to come and the birth of their first child. Neither had touched on the dangerous situation in the province. He had lain awake for a long time after she went to sleep beside him. The thought of losing her terrified him far more than any personal danger. He finally slept, but woke late and, though he felt more optimistic, he spent some time considering how he might at least increase her comfort and safety in the tribunal.

Because his mind was preoccupied with domestic arrangements, he did not realize that a large, unruly crowd had gathered outside the tribunal gate until he crossed the courtyard on his way to see if Kaoru had delivered the corpse of the Takata servant. The gate was closed, quite against regulations at this late hour, and the hum of angry voices and shouts of "Keep back!" startled him.

Akitada's first thought was that something had gone terribly wrong with his plan. He blamed himself for not having waited up for Kaoru.

Changing direction, he tugged open the heavy gate. A constable tried to hold it from the other side, but desisted when he saw Akitada, who stepped through and gazed at a gathering of about a hundred people.

They looked back sullenly and muttered.

Off to one side, Hitomaro and three of the constables stood around something on the ground. Hitomaro, looking grim, came over quickly and saluted. With a glance at the crowd, he said in a low voice, "It's the body of a mendicant monk, sir. Someone left him here during the night. It must have happened after the hour of the rat, the last time the gate was used." He met Akitada's questioning glance and added, "Someone delivered another dead man late last night. It's raining corpses."

A harsh voice from the back of the crowd shouted, "Let's see you lazy officials do something for a change. Maybe we'll get a verdict on this one next year." The crowd guffawed.

Akitada walked over to look at the body and winced.

The monk in his ragged robe was thin to emaciation. Someone had smashed his face to a pulp and cut off his hands and feet.

Akitada made a quick and superficial examination. The corpse was quite cold, but rigor had passed. He found no other wounds, and it was impossible to tell if the mutilations had killed him. Without glancing at his jeering audience, Akitada said loudly, "Have the body taken inside and notify the coroner. Then send to Abbot Hokko to ask if he is missing one of his monks."

◆

A short while later Hitomaro joined him in his study. Akitada looked up from his paperwork.

"The abbot says everyone is accounted for, sir. We sent for Dr. Yasakichi, the coroner. He should be here any moment."

"Hmm. I gather your friend Kaoru carried out his assignment without problems?"

"Yes, sir. In the middle of the night. We put that corpse into the armory for the time being. Tora left with Kaoru afterward. We thought it safer not to alert the constables."

"Good. They won't like getting a new sergeant, and we don't need a mutiny before this afternoon's hearing."

"What about the dead monk, sir?"

"He was brought here and we will have to investigate it as murder. Since he is not a member of the local monastery, he must be an itinerant priest."

Hitomaro pulled a dirty piece of paper from his sleeve and placed it on Akitada's desk. "That was pinned to his robe when we found him."

It was a crudely scrawled poem with the title "A Curse on all Governors." Akitada read it aloud, his face tightening with anger.

>   *Their ignorance appalls the skies.*
>   *Their idleness confounds the seas.*
>   *They take away our rice,*
>   *And let killers roam at ease.*

"Well," he said bitterly, "that explains the hostile crowd." He crumpled up the paper in his hand. "This smacks of conspiracy to incite a popular insurrection against imperial authority." He rose and began to pace, muttering under his breath. After a few passes, he stopped and smoothed out the message again. "Look at this," he said. "The writing is rough and in the native style, but the verse is anything but illiterate. In fact, it is a translation of a poem by one of the Chinese political satirists, if I'm not mistaken. It is meant to look like the work of an ordinary person, but no commoner would know Chinese texts. We may be able to find out who is behind this."

"Whoever he is," said Hitomaro, with a grimace of distaste, "he's enough of a fanatic to kill some poor begging monk to make a point. What kind of people are these?"

Akitada shook his head. "We don't know if the monk was murdered, but certainly somebody has a warped mind. The mutilations prove that, if nothing else. It should be interesting to hear what the coroner has to say about it."

"What about Uesugi?"

"Warlords would not hesitate for a moment to kill, mutilate, or torture if it became expedient. But in this case I doubt it. The verse was written by someone here in the city. It is in reaction to the notices we just posted. Uesugi could not have known in time to set up an elaborate scheme, dead body and all, even if he had not been preoccupied with his father's funeral. I'm afraid someone else is acting independently but with the same purpose. I shall have another look at that corpse when the coroner arrives."

"He should be here by now, sir. I'm afraid that crowd will not leave. I ordered the constables out to guard the gate."

Akitada shook his head. "Like setting the cat to guard the fish. The sooner we come to grips with this situation, the better. I don't like such open defiance of authority. Let's go and see about that monk."

The mutilated corpse lay on a plank table in an empty jail cell. A short fat man was about to remove the dead man's tattered robe.

"Stop that!" Akitada said sharply. "Who are you?"

The man turned around and looked at Akitada from bleary eyes. He was dirty from head to toe: his hair greasy and matted, his gray gown stained, and his sandaled feet caked with mud. "Yasa . . . Yasakichi, the cor'ner," he mumbled, and a strong smell of sour wine and rotten teeth greeted their noses. "And who might you be, young man?"

Hitomaro growled, "Bow to the governor." When the man merely gaped, he pushed him to his knees.

"Ouch. Let go," the fat man whined, pulling away from Hitomaro's grip. "How was I to know? It's too early in the morning to see clearly."

"Let him be," Akitada said. "Get up, Dr. Yasakichi. Did you check the dead man's clothing carefully before removing it?"

"Well, no need, is there?" The coroner staggered to his feet. He tugged at his robe, which was coming apart across his belly, and shook his head as if to clear away the fog of drunkenness. "Mere rags. Obvious what killed him. Mut'lated, then bludgeoned to death. Vicious but common crime among vagrants. I was just about to look for other wounds, though it won't matter one way or 'nother. Anything you can see with your naked eye is 'nough to kill a man. I'll get a report ready."

"Hmm. What did you make of the rice husks on his robe and"—Akitada bent over the body and pointed at the mass of torn flesh and bone that had been a face—"in those wounds?"

"What? Ah. Wouldn't worry about 'em. Look at his rags. He's slept in all sorts of dirt."

Akitada glanced at the coroner's stained gown, but made no comment. He lifted the hem of the victim's ragged robe and looked at the thin legs and thighs. They were as pale-skinned and flabby as the frail arms. Stepping back, he gave the coroner a thoughtful look and said, "I think perhaps we'll dispense with your services in this instance. Hitomaro, send a constable for Dr. Oyoshi! And tell him it's urgent!"

"What?" The coroner swelled with outrage and his robe parted again. "This is *my* duty," he shouted. "Oyoshi's a mere pharmashist. You can't put a pill roller on important judish . . . legal matters like this! Why, he could comprom . . . ruin the whole case!"

Akitada eyed him coldly. "You are insubordinate. In fact, I believe you are drunk on duty. Consider yourself dismissed."

The coroner opened his mouth to argue, but Hitomaro took him by the arm and marched him out the door. When he returned, he said, "I think the fellow was drunk when he was at the Golden Carp. We both smelled wine on his breath as he passed us."

Akitada was bent over the body. "I would not be surprised," he muttered. Straightening up, he added, "Still, a slit throat is fairly simple to identify as cause of death. This, on the other hand, is no vagrant. With that pale skin on his arms and legs, he has spent his life indoors, and fully clothed. The muscles are also underdeveloped. An itinerant monk does a lot of walking. He should have muscles in those shanks."

"Yes, I see. What about the rice husks?" Hitomaro asked.

"The body was kept somewhere where rice was being threshed."

"Maybe he slept in a granary."

"If so, he was probably killed there. The husks have stuck to the lacerated flesh of his face. But there was really very little bleeding from those wounds, don't you think?"

Hitomaro frowned and scratched his head. "If he's no vagrant monk, then those are not his clothes. And if the killers changed his clothes after death, there wouldn't be much blood on them."

"Yes, you're quite right, but that still does not explain . . . Ah, there you are already!" Dr. Oyoshi had entered and was bowing politely. "You are more than prompt, my dear Doctor."

"I happened to be passing the tribunal on my way home from a patient, Excellency. I trust you are fully recovered?"

"Yes." Akitada smiled at the ugly little man. "I'm much obliged to you for your medicine. Both my wife and my secretary are knowledgeable about herbal remedies and most curious about the ingredients. My wife used to have a fine garden and raised many medicinal plants at her home in the capital. Now she wishes to learn about the medicines of this region."

"I shall write out the recipe for her, but I'm afraid some of the ingredients come from plants which grow only in remote mountain regions." Oyoshi cast a curious glance at the body on the table. "How may I serve you today?"

"As coroner. I just dismissed the incompetent sot who held that office."

Oyoshi bowed. "Thank you for your confidence, but I must warn you that Yasakichi has powerful friends. He was appointed by the high constable."

"I need competence, not influence. Have a look and tell me what you think."

Oyoshi set down his case and rolled up his sleeves. He stared at the wounds on the face and the stumps of the arms and legs, and shook his head. Reaching into his case, he took out a set of pincers and a sheet of paper, on which he carefully placed tiny bits of debris from the wounds. Next he checked the man's rags, even feeling and smelling them.

When he was done, he looked up at Akitada. "Would you like a preliminary report now before I remove the clothing and wash the body?"

"If you please."

"This man was about fifty years old and in poor health. In

fact," he said with a puzzled frown, "there is something oddly familiar about him. His head is shaven, so I assume he is a monk. Perhaps he belongs to our temple and I have had occasion to treat him in the past. But I don't think the clothes are his. They are too large and too dirty, for one thing, whereas the body seems quite clean. The wounds to his face and the mutilations were inflicted several hours after death. I cannot speak to the cause or time of death until I have made a more thorough study, and it is possible that the mutilation will make a definite diagnosis impossible."

"How do you know he was already dead when this was done to him, Doctor?" Hitomaro asked.

"There's hardly any blood in the wounds, Lieutenant. A dead man does not bleed. Most likely the mutilation happened in a place where rice is threshed or stored. There are husks in the wounds."

Hitomaro glanced at Akitada and was about to say something, but at that moment a loud clanging came from the tribunal gate.

"It's that bell again!" Akitada said. "And to think that only a short while ago I complained about a lack of official business." He told Oyoshi, "I must go. Please continue your examination. Later Hitomaro will show you another body. You may report when you have finished with both."

Oyoshi raised his brows, but said nothing and bowed.

Outside, Akitada and Hitomaro found a small group of people standing in the main courtyard. More people pressed curiously forward at the gate. The armed constables made a halfhearted effort to hold them back, while carrying on an exchange of crude jokes. The courtyard group stood around a stocky man who wore only a stained shirt and loincloth. A powerful odor of fish emanated from him.

Sergeant Chobei detached himself from the group and

greeted Akitada with a grin. "This man has a complaint, Excel-lency," he announced loudly. "A local fishmonger, name of Goto. His shop's at the western end of the market."

Goto spat, stuck out his chest, and glanced around impor-tantly. He said in a belligerent tone, "I want to see that dead man."

"Why?" Akitada looked the fishmonger and his supporters over. They appeared the type that scraped by with a minimum of work and a maximum of resentment for authority. As a rule they proved too cowardly to cause real trouble.

"My brother's missing and I'm thinking it may be him," the fishmonger said. "And if it's Ogai, you've got to arrest that bas-tard Kimura for his murder." He looked at his companions, who muttered in agreement.

Akitada frowned but decided not to make an issue of the man's disrespectful manner. "Is your brother a monk?"

"A monk? Not Ogai!" Goto and his companions burst into raucous laughter.

Akitada was about to send them away, when Goto said, "Ogai's a soldier. On leave from the garrison."

Akitada considered this. A soldier? True, not only monks shaved their heads. Soldiers did also, to prevent lice, a common plague in close barracks quarters.

"Come on then. Just you." Akitada strode off toward the jail, Hitomaro following.

In the jail cell, Dr. Oyoshi was just sponging the nude body. "Oh," he said, "you're back already." His eyes fell on Goto. "Is there a problem?"

"No. Just a matter of identification. Well, man? Is it your brother?"

The fishmonger peered, turned green, and slunk back, nod-ding. "Yes, that's him. P-poor Ogai! That bastard Kimura did that to him! It's terrible!" He wiped his eyes with filthy hands.

"Come outside. Hitomaro, a cup of water."

In the yard, the fishmonger took some deep breaths and drank. "Thanks," he said. "Made me sick, to see that. Ogai's been the best brother a man ever had. We were as close as a snail and his house, Ogai and me. But him and that Kimura—" He shook a fist. "May a hundred demons tear out his guts and scatter them on the mountaintops. They got into a fight over a dice game. Kimura said he'd kill him and he did. I can show your constables where Kimura lives so they can arrest him."

"When was that quarrel?" Akitada asked.

"Two weeks ago, and the very next day Ogai was gone. The garrison says he never signed in. They came to arrest him for desertion and searched my house and asked the neighbors questions. Only nobody's seen him." He jerked his head toward his companions. "They'll tell you."

"No doubt," Akitada said dryly. "Why did you not report your brother's disappearance earlier?"

Goto looked down at his bare feet. "Ogai was home on leave. I thought he'd just gone on a little trip before going back. But then the soldiers came for him and I got worried. Then I heard about the body at the tribunal gate . . . Holy Buddha! What that animal did to my poor brother!"

"Hmm. How did you recognize him? Any special marks?"

The man shook his head. "No, but I'd know my brother anywhere."

Akitada regarded the man through narrowed eyes. "How old was your brother?"

Goto suddenly looked nervous. "Thirty-five. But he looked older."

"I see. We will investigate your charge. Give my lieutenant the particulars."

"You'll arrest Kimura today?"

"You will be notified when your case comes up."

The fishmonger began to look belligerent again. "I won't be put off because I'm a poor man and Ogai's just a soldier."

"Come along!" Hitomaro growled, giving him a shove toward the main courtyard.

"Excellency?" Oyoshi met Akitada at the door of the jail. "Did that fellow say his brother was in his thirties and a soldier?"

"Yes. He was lying, I'm afraid."

"Even aside from the fact that the poor man in there never did any physical work, he must have been at least fifty years old. His shaven crown made me think he was a monk."

"I know. Soldiers shave their heads sometimes, but I suspect his deceitful identification was part of a plot to discredit me. No doubt once we arrest this Kimura and charge him, someone will produce the brother, hale and hearty. They'll have a good laugh and Kimura will charge me with false arrest."

"Ah!" Oyoshi nodded. "I was afraid there was something brewing in town. You may wonder that I did not warn you, but I am not universally trusted, in spite of my professional repute."

"I see. Well, as my coroner you may well find yourself completely ostracized. If you would prefer not to serve, I understand."

Oyoshi smiled a little sadly. "Not at all, Excellency. I was surprised and honored by your confidence. And," he added, pointing to the corpse inside the cell, "my professional curiosity is aroused. There is something odd about that one."

"Good!" Akitada said briskly. "But if the rest of your examination can wait a little, I think I would like your opinion on the other body first."

"Of course."

Tora and Hitomaro had put the dead Uesugi servant in the armory. This building, like the granary, was empty of its customary contents. The old man's body lay on the floor, covered with a straw mat. Akitada pulled the mat back.

Oyoshi sucked in his breath. "Hideo! What happened to him?" He fell to his knees beside the body. "Oh, dear. Does the boy know?"

"No. The youngster asked me to find his grandfather after the funeral yesterday, but Kaibara took the child away before I could ask questions. I remembered hearing a cry when I was in the west gallery during the banquet, so we went to Takata and had a look. The body was at the foot of the cliff below the north pavilion. I expect Uesugi will claim it was a suicide."

Oyoshi shook his head. "Hideo would never commit suicide. He dotes on his little grandson. Excuse me." He made a quick but thorough examination. When he was done, he rose.

"Poor Hideo," he murmured. "He died from the fall all right. Most of his bones are broken. But the injuries to the face suggest that he was beaten shortly—very shortly—before his death. I regret that there is no physical evidence of murder, but I would stake my life on it that it was not suicide."

Akitada nodded. "Thank you. It is as I thought. Please put your findings about both bodies in separate reports. I shall call you during this afternoon's hearing."

When they returned to the main courtyard, the fishmonger and his friends had gone, but Tora was back. He was talking to Hitomaro. They came up quickly, and Hitomaro said, "We'd like to follow that fellow Goto."

"What is on your minds?"

Tora said, "Hito thinks that bastard was lying."

Hitomaro explained, "That dead man's never been a soldier. And if Goto lied about the corpse, it follows that he's in on the plot, sir. He'll lead us to the person who composed the note."

"Possibly, but I doubt it," Akitada said. "He arrived here

rather late for that. Perhaps he just took advantage of the incident for his own purposes. But you had better go to the garrison and ask some questions about this Ogai. I can manage with Tora for the hearing this afternoon."

◆

Akitada was nervous about the hearing, his first official public duty. That in itself was miserable enough for a man who hated to attract attention to himself. But in this case, he also had to make a good impression in order to sway the local people to his side. He quaked at the thought of all those eyes on him, all those ears primed to catch him in some error of procedure or slip of the tongue. He had to remind himself of his duty, of his oath to serve the emperor to the best of his ability, of his education and training, of his good intentions.

At the sound of the great gong, he rose from behind his desk, straightened his dark blue court robe, adjusted his black cap of stiffened gauze, and put the flat wooden baton of office in his belt. Assuming what he hoped was a dignified mien, he walked down the corridor. A hum of voices greeted him when he stepped around the screen and onto the dais at the north end of the tribunal hall.

People filled the dim space to capacity, pushing, pressing, simmering with excitement, barely subdued by a pitifully small number of constables placed strategically around the room. Tora stood to his left, keeping an eye on things. His full suit of armor had been polished till it gleamed in the light of the candles and torches.

Akitada looked into the sullen or angry or merely avid faces of the citizens of Naoetsu and considered the irony of having wished for a modest turnout only yesterday. Now he had to contend with a hostile multitude.

He turned his mind to the task ahead. Best to forget about

impressing these people with the sacred power of justice and concentrate on business. Announce the discovery of two new bodies and then deal with the innkeeper's murder quickly before someone had time to start trouble.

Tora bellowed, "His Excellency, the governor. Bow!" Akitada watched as over a hundred men and women went down onto their hands and knees before him and put their foreheads on the floor.

The view of so many bent backs overwhelmed him. Shivering from the chill air and nerves, he arranged his face in an impassive mask and seated himself quickly on the cushion in the center of the dais, glancing first to his immediate left, where Hamaya and his assistants knelt behind three identical low desks with paper and writing implements, and then to his right, where Seimei, his own secretary, presided over the official seal and judicial mandates.

At Akitada's nod, Seimei began the reading of the Imperial Directive, composed more than three hundred years ago. It empowered the governor of a province to hear and decide difficult legal cases. As a young student at the university, Akitada had had to memorize this text, but today the beauty and propriety of the August Words struck him most forcibly.

A wide gulf separates the throne from the people, but a diligent governor is the bridge between them.

Let him ascertain and verify guilt, redress wrongs, discern lies, reveal evil, and disclose secret plots like a good physician who probes the body for the nature of the disease in order to heal the patient.

Let him be virtuous in pronouncing judgment on the guilty and showing compassion to the innocent, acting at all times like a father to his people.

How great then will be his happiness in having the respect of his people!

Seimei rolled up the document and reverently raised it above his head. The bent backs let out their breaths, and sat up. Akitada looked for respect in their faces and found none.

He tapped his wooden baton on the floor and announced, "The bodies of two men were brought to this tribunal during the night. An investigation into the manner of their deaths has begun. I will now hear the reports."

Tora brought Kaoru before the dais. The young woodcutter knelt, gave his name, and told of finding the body of the Uesugi servant: "I spent the day in the woods behind Takata manor, gathering fallen limbs for sale in the city, when my dog found a dead man in the snow. When I brushed the snow away, I recognized Hideo, who served the late lord of Takata. It being the day of the old lord's funeral, I thought it best not to disturb the family and to bring the body to the tribunal instead."

Akitada nodded and dismissed him. Tora stepped forward again and stated, "This morning the constable who opens the tribunal gate noticed something by the gatehouse and pointed it out to me. I investigated. It was the mutilated corpse of a middle-aged man. Subsequent identification by the fishmonger Goto says that the corpse may be that of his brother Ogai, a soldier."

"Thank you, Lieutenant. Has the coroner checked the causes for these deaths?"

"Yes, sir. Dr. Oyoshi is waiting to report."

When Oyoshi stepped forward, there was a murmur of astonishment from the crowd. Sergeant Chobei turned to stare at the new coroner with an expression of profound shock.

Oyoshi knelt. "This person is the pharmacist Oyoshi, coroner of this tribunal by order of his Excellency, the governor. I was called to the tribunal early this morning to inspect the corpse of a middle-aged male. His hands and feet had been severed and were missing and his face was badly damaged by a beating with a heavy blunt weapon. The cause of death may have been disease, possibly due to exposure and neglect, or from his wounds. Death occurred at least a day and two nights ago, and the mutilations were inflicted several hours later, possibly to hide a fatal wound."

Again there was a murmuring from the crowd, and Akitada rapped his baton. "The case will be investigated since there is a suspicion of murder. Continue!"

"The second man was much older. I immediately recognized him as Lord Maro's personal attendant Hideo. Death was due to multiple and severe injuries to the whole body. I am told the body was found near the foot of the cliff at Takata manor. The injuries are perfectly compatible with a fall from that height. Hideo had been dead for more than two days."

The doctor paused and looked at Akitada for instructions. Receiving a nod, he continued, "I have to report that, in addition to those injuries caused by the fall, the body also showed evidence of a beating about the face and head. These injuries were inflicted before death."

A buzz of interest rose in the crowd.

Akitada said, "Thank you, Dr. Oyoshi. This case will also remain under investigation." He paused briefly to gauge the mood of the audience. In vain. Taking a deep breath, he announced, "I shall now hear new evidence in the murder of the local innkeeper Sato."

A hush fell in the hall. Then the crowd parted to allow a veiled woman and two elderly people to approach the dais. With a sinking feeling, Akitada saw that Mrs. Sato and her parents had arrived. The widow wore modest hemp instead of silk on this occasion. He decided against calling her to testify before this hostile crowd. Ignoring her presence, he continued.

"I have studied the documents in the case carefully. Certain statements of the three suspects were left unverified, an oversight which had to be corrected before the case could be heard. Now witnesses have stepped forward to support parts of the prisoners' stories. That development, taken together with the fact that only two of the men have confessed and both have since recanted, could mean that the murder was committed by someone else."

The hall became noisy. Someone shouted, "Watch out! He's letting them get away with it." Someone else cried, "Where's our own judge?" In front, Mrs. Sato called on the Buddha and wrung her hands as her parents supported her on either side.

Akitada rapped his baton until some order was reestablished and then told Chobei, "Sergeant, bring in the prisoners."

Umehara, Okano, and Takagi were led in to cat calls, clenched fists, and spitting from the crowd. They wore chains that looped from their ankles to their wrists, and were made to kneel in front of the dais. Three constables moved in with whips at the ready and expressions of happy anticipation on their faces.

Umehara cast a frightened glance at Akitada, then stared at the floor. Next to him Okano twitched the skirt of his robe with a shaking hand and turned a tragic face toward the crowd. Only the slow-witted farmer looked unconcerned; he grinned and nodded to Akitada, Hamaya, and anyone else who looked familiar.

Akitada suppressed a sigh. At least Tora had made sure the prisoners were cleaned up and fed.

He took the three men through their testimony quickly, stressing their activities in town before the murder, and their explanations for the gold found on them. He had Okano speak twice about the unknown travelers who had called at the inn and left again while the actor was in the bath, and he asked Takagi about leaving his bundle unattended.

Twice there were jeers and laughter. The constables made

little effort to stop them. To judge from their broad grins, they shared the crowd's feelings.

When Akitada called for witnesses, the noise subsided a little. One by one, market vendors, shopkeepers, money changers, waitresses, and soup sellers, all familiar faces in the market, or neighbors and relatives of someone in the crowd, stepped forward and knelt. Their testimonies substantiated the three prisoners' claims.

An uneasy silence had fallen when Akitada dismissed the last witness and had Tora escort the prisoners out. He scanned the crowd. People looked puzzled, uncertain. He felt a stirring of hope.

He was thinking of releasing the three pathetic men as quickly as possible and began, "Today's testimony throws considerable doubt on the guilt of the three defendants . . ." when there was a cry of protest and the widow pushed past the constables to face him.

She threw back her veil and bowed. "This person is the widow Sato. As the widow of the slain man, I ask this court's permission to make a statement."

It was her right. Akitada compressed his lips and nodded.

She turned her head to look at the crowd. There was a murmur of admiration at her youth and beauty. "My husband was a humble man like most of you," she told them in a clear voice. "He worked as hard for his coppers as you do. Is it right that he should die for the greed of another man?"

"No," they muttered.

"Is it right that his killers—his *confessed* killers—should go unpunished to roam the streets and kill again?"

"No." There were shouts now.

"This," she cried, pointing at Akitada, "is not a proper court. You must not permit it to release my husband's murderers.

Where is our own judge? How can an official born and raised in the distant capital know our people and our laws? Our lawful judge would not let my husband's killers escape their just punishment. Our own judge would not permit my husband's restless spirit to cry for justice."

Akitada was using his baton to stop her harangue and point out a governor's duty to oversee the administration of justice in his province, but he saw the angry faces in the crowd and knew his words would make no difference.

Mrs. Sato shot him a triumphant glance. "We have all heard about the pardons given to murderers and robbers in the capital," she told him, "and we hear how those criminals repeat their crimes, yes, even in the very grounds of the emperor's palace. Injustice today brings more murder tomorrow. Already there are two more bodies in this tribunal. Is that the kind of justice you offer?"

"No," roared the crowd, shaking their fists in the air and surging forward.

Akitada had listened with a frozen expression. Not only was this woman, who had turned her back to him earlier so disrespectfully, calling people into open defiance of a duly appointed governor, but her arguments and her references to the deplorable conditions in the nation's capital proved her to be well-informed. Such knowledge went quite beyond the background of a mere innkeeper's wife. And why had she of all people stepped forward as the spokeswoman for the faceless threat to his administration?

Chaos reigned in the hall. The crowd moved against the restraining arms of the constables. Tora was back, his hand at his sword, looking up at him for an order, but Akitada shrank from committing public bloodshed. He scanned the crowd for some sign of support, however small.

Chobei, the insubordinate sergeant of constables, sneered at him openly. Next to him, the dismissed coroner smirked with satisfaction. Their thoughts were written on their faces: The fool from the capital was about to lose his position, perhaps even his life.

Glaring at Chobei and pointing his baton at him, Akitada raised his voice to be heard over the noise of the crowd. "Sergeant, give that woman ten lashes for inciting a riot."

There were gasps from the crowd and it became quiet. He scowled at their startled faces. "And if there is anymore trouble from anyone here, that number will be doubled—and given to each troublemaker."

Chobei gaped at him. Tora's sword hissed as he drew it from its scabbard. The crowd drew back and a tense silence suddenly filled the hall. Chobei shook his head and retreated.

And Mrs. Sato laughed softly.

Furious, Akitada rose to his feet. "Sergeant," he called out, "you will either carry out my order or my lieutenant will have your head."

Tora stepped up to Chobei, his sword in both hands.

Chobei turned white. Beads of sweat glistened on his face. After a moment, his shoulders slumped and he approached the widow. She cried out and tried to sidestep him, but he seized her arm. When he reached to strip her gown from her shoulders, Akitada snapped, "Leave her dressed." He had no wish to give the crowd a chance to ogle a half-naked woman as beautiful as this one. Besides, his stomach churned already at what was about to take place.

The widow twisted and screamed. With the practice of years of maltreating prisoners, Chobei flung her facedown on the floor. Her parents prostrated themselves, begging for mercy for her. Akitada ignored them. Two of his constables approached to hold her down, while Chobei pulled the leather whip from his belt and used it. He counted out ten strokes in a loud voice so he would be heard above the screams and sobs from the prisoner and her weeping parents. When he was done, he untied her ankles, and hauled her sagging figure back to her feet. The two constables dragged the whimpering woman past the crowd and out of the hall. Her parents hurried after her.

There was no more trouble, but Tora continued to stand with drawn sword, ready to cut down the first man or woman who stepped forward.

Akitada was sick. Aware that he was starting to shake from head to foot, he sat back down, rapped his baton, and said as steadily as he could, "The prisoners will remain in custody until the case is cleared up. This hearing is adjourned until further evidence has been collected."

He barely made it out to the back of the hall before vomiting.

TEN

RETURN TO TAKATA

The following day, Akitada rode back to Takata with an official cortege, scraped together from what was available. Two constables trotted ahead, their breaths steaming in the icy air as their chant—"Make way for the governor! Make way!"—scattered itinerant monks, old women, small children, and anyone else on the road. Tora followed on horseback, in armor and with sword and bow. Three more constables jogged behind him. The third carried the tribunal banner. Next came Akitada, trying to look impressive in formal attire on a horse with faded red silk tassels swinging from its harness. Dr. Oyoshi followed him and somewhat spoiled the effect by drooping on a sad-looking shaggy pony. The end of the cortege was made up of two more constables.

This pomp and circumstance hid discontent among the members. The constables were outraged by the forced march in the cold and had obeyed only because Chobei had been dismissed for insubordination and they were afraid to meet the same fate.

Tora shivered without his bearskins and missed Hitomaro, who had become very secretive, staying out late without explanations, and accepting with uncharacteristic eagerness their master's suggestion that he check out the fishmonger's tale. And he was gone again today. The doctor was in an abstracted mood, and Akitada had been seized by such a presentiment of looming disaster that his very soul felt as frozen as the wintry landscape around them.

Kaibara received them again in the main courtyard and led Akitada, Oyoshi, and Tora to the new lord and master of Takata.

News of the hearing must have reached Takata by now, but Uesugi pretended surprise. He was seated on his dais in the reception hall, wearing an ordinary house robe and an expression of petulant irritation. When Akitada came in, he bowed without rising and said with a tight smile, "An unexpected pleasure, Excellency. I hope you and your friends will join me in a cup of wine and a pleasant chat."

Akitada replied with equally cold politeness, "Though deeply honored by your generous hospitality, I cannot accept. Official business interferes."

"I am disconsolate. What official business might that be?"

"As you may have heard, a body was found below the north pavilion of your manor and delivered to the tribunal night before last. According to Dr. Oyoshi, my coroner, it belongs to a man called Hideo, your late honored father's personal attendant. It seems he died falling from the gallery."

Uesugi looked shocked. "Hideo? Oyoshi, you say it was Hideo? Are you certain?" He sighed deeply and closed his small eyes. "How sad! We all thought he had gone to the mountains to mourn my honorable father's death." He sighed again, more deeply, shaking his head. "A true servant, a rare man. How inspiring!"

"What do you mean, inspiring?" Akitada asked sharply.

Uesugi scowled at his tone. Kaibara explained smoothly, "His lordship means that Hideo made the final sacrifice by following his master into death, Excellency."

"Nonsense. The man was murdered."

There was a moment's silence. "Murdered?" Uesugi burst into forced laughter. "Someone has been pulling your leg, Governor. Not you, Oyoshi, I hope? Who would murder good old Hideo? No, no, he jumped. As Kaibara says, it was a very moving tribute by a loyal man."

Akitada said nothing and waited.

Uesugi cocked his round face. "I'm afraid you made this long journey for nothing, my dear Governor. Especially now, when you are needed in the city. There have been disturbing reports of unrest in Naoetsu. I hope it is nothing serious? We stand ready to assist you."

"Nothing I cannot handle," Akitada snapped. "I brought my assistants to investigate the site of the victim's fall and talk to the servants. I take it that neither you nor Kaibara saw the servant Hideo after your father's death?"

Uesugi and Kaibara exchanged a glance, then Uesugi said angrily, "You forget that this is a house of mourning."

"I regret, but the investigation of a crime takes precedence over such considerations."

Kaibara protested, "But even if a crime had been committed, it would come under the jurisdiction of his lordship. It occurred in his domain. You have no rights here."

Akitada looked at Uesugi. "Instruct your man in the proper respect due to my position!"

Uesugi's face was purple, but he hissed at Kaibara, "Apologize to his Excellency this instant!"

Kaibara looked murderous but he knelt and touched his

forehead to the floor, muttering, "I hope your Excellency will overlook a foolish soldier's bad manners. I spoke carelessly out of loyalty to my master."

Akitada ignored him and said to Uesugi, "The question of jurisdiction does not apply, since the crime was reported to me in Naoetsu and the victim's body was brought to the tribunal there."

"But even so, Excellency," Uesugi replied, "such matters have always been handled by us. The authority of the high constable rests with the lords of Takata."

"Not anymore. You recall that I have not requested a renewal of the appointment. I may reserve the position for myself."

Kaibara, who had remained in his abject posture, now popped up, his hand at his sword hilt. Uesugi shook his head at him. "I trust you will change your mind, Excellency," he said through clenched teeth. "It takes manpower to enforce the law here. For the moment, Kaibara will assist you in your investigation." He closed his eyes indicating that the interview was over.

"Thank you." Akitada turned to Kaibara. "Take us to the north pavilion!"

Kaibara led them out of the reception hall and down a long dim corridor. Rectangular patches of light fell through latticed windows high in one wall, illuminating family armor displayed on the other. Akitada slowed to look at swords, helmets, greaves, breastplates, battle fans, and batons. The collection was large, well-maintained, and of superb quality.

"Look at that," Tora murmured when they reached a magnificent suit of black-lacquered metal plates tied with scarlet silk cords. Golden chrysanthemum blossoms tangled with waving silver grasses on the breastplate. "It's like a painting."

Kaibara stopped. "You have good taste, Lieutenant." He did not disguise his pride. "The armor is of very superior workmanship. Yosai made it for the late lord's father who wore it in the battle of Kanagawa. A decisive victory. That's why we display it on the wall. Most of the other armor, very fine also, is stored in those chests." He gestured.

Akitada glanced down the corridor. For well over a hundred feet, wooden metal-banded chests stood side by side beneath wall displays bristling with spears, halberds, swords, bows, quivers, arrows, standards, and other battle gear.

Kaibara's smile broadened as he saw Akitada's amazement. "Your Excellency has noticed Lord Maro's swords?" He pointed to matching gold-hilted blades, one long, the other short. Taking down the long sword, he pulled it from the scabbard with a soft hissing sound. The blade emerged and flashed bluish silver in a shaft of light as Kaibara raised it with both hands above his head. His face turned into a snarl of such bloodthirsty ferocity that Akitada stepped back, out of reach of the long blade.

Dr. Oyoshi cleared his throat, and Kaibara chuckled.

Flushing with anger, Akitada stepped forward and took the sword from the steward's hand. "A fine blade" he commented. "A master made this."

There was a moment's pause, then Kaibara said harshly, "They say it drank the blood of a hundred warriors that day at Kanagawa. There's not a nick in the blade, though his lordship, fighting from a horse, was slashing through bone."

Returning the sword, Akitada said, "Forgive my ignorance. This battle, I take it, was fought many years ago?"

"Before my time. The late lord was a young man then. Both he and his brother were raised to a warrior's life." Kaibara replaced the sword and waited to move on. He seemed to have lost interest in the displays.

"There was a brother?"

"Yes. He was the older. When he died, Lord Maro succeeded. Shall we go on?"

They walked until Tora stopped to exclaim at an unusually

long, beautifully finished bow. A very long black arrow with a black-dyed eagle feather and a finely crafted steel tip was attached to its groove. "That bow must be at least one and a half times a man's height," Tora cried.

"That one's for archery contests only," Kaibara said with an impatient sigh. "We carry shorter ones into battle. The quiver of long arrows gets in the way of the sword arm, and the contest arrows are too expensive to waste on the enemy." He strode off down the corridor without waiting for more questions or comments.

They emerged onto a drafty outside gallery which took them to the north pavilion. Here Kaibara stopped and asked, "Where was the body found, Excellency?"

Tora and Akitada stepped to the railing and peered down.

"According to the fellow who brought it in," Akitada said, with a warning glance at Tora, "it must have been just about here."

"Who—?" began Kaibara.

"Look!" cried Tora. "There are scratches on the railing here. And there"—he pointed—"that looks like dried blood."

Akitada squinted at the brown streaks. "Doctor?" Oyoshi came and peered also. He nodded. Akitada turned to the steward. "Please unlock the pavilion."

Kaibara protested: He could not see the purpose of inspecting the pavilion. Hideo had jumped off the wall, not killed himself inside. Then there was the matter of sacrilege. The room was where Lord Maro had lived and died; his spirit was still there and should not be disturbed. And in any case, he had no authority to unlock the door.

Akitada said nothing but stepped to the door and waited.

Kaibara shook his head, fished a key from his sleeve, and admitted them to the late lord's death chamber.

The pavilion consisted of a single square room, empty except for a fine hanging scroll painting of an eagle on a twisted pine branch, two thick tatami mats, and a large leather trunk. The mats were near one of the windows, the only one whose blinds of speckled black bamboo were rolled up, revealing a view of distant snowcapped mountains. The view from here was magnificent.

Tora and Oyoshi looked around curiously, but Akitada went to the window. There was no gallery on this side; the outside wall of the pavilion joined the stone ramparts descending steeply to the rock gully far below.

Suddenly he staggered back, convulsed by a fit of coughing. They all looked at him in dismay. He choked and gagged, stumbling toward Tora who supported him anxiously. "Some water," he croaked, grasping his throat.

Oyoshi said sharply, "Lower your master to the ground against the wall there and loosen his robe at the neck. And you, Kaibara, fetch some water! Quick, man! There's no time to be lost! Do you want the governor's death on your hands?"

Kaibara hesitated only briefly, then ran out. Akitada stopped gasping, jumped up, and went to the trunk. "Let's have a look," he said to the gaping Tora.

The doctor chuckled. "I thought that did not sound quite natural." He joined them and watched as they removed several silk quilts and a rosewood headrest from the trunk. "Lord Maro's bedding," he said and, when they lifted out a large lacquered and gilded box at the bottom, "His writing box. What is it that you expect to find, sir?"

"I wish I knew." Akitada opened the box. Fitted cleverly inside were two carved ink stones, two porcelain water containers, four lacquer-handled brushes, and two cakes of the finest black ink. Akitada touched the ink cakes. "One is still moist," he said, holding up his black-tipped finger. "I suppose all those quilts kept the air from drying it out. I wonder . . ." He listened toward the door, then shut the box, putting it back into the trunk. "Quick, Tora! Put everything back and close it!" Tora obeyed while Akitada resumed his reclining position against the wall, coughing weakly as Kaibara ran in with a flask and cup.

Akitada drank, croaked "Thank you," and allowed himself to be helped to his feet again. "Sorry," he muttered, wiping his brow. "It must have been the way I breathed in when I looked out. What a nuisance!"

The doctor asked Kaibara, "Do you happen to know what Lord Maro's symptoms were before he died? I ask out of professional interest."

"I don't know. I expect it was his age. His mind went years ago, and he would not permit anyone, not even his son, near him. Only Hideo served him. This past summer his speech failed and finally his body followed." Kaibara paused and added piously, "The Buddha calls extraordinary men to him."

Akitada was listening with half an ear. He studied the room, its floor, walls, ceiling, windows, and door, without seeing anything out of the ordinary. Except for the crookedly fastened blind, the room was almost too neat. Someone had taken pains to clean up after the old lord's death. He was eyeing the thick tatami mats when Kaibara asked impatiently, "Whereto next, Excellency?"

Reluctantly Akitada abandoned his train of thought. "Oh, the servants, I think. Hideo's closest associates and anyone who might have been near the north pavilion the night of Lord Maro's death." He cast another glance about and followed the others out.

Kaibara ordered the manor's domestic staff to assemble in one of the courtyards.

"Bow to his Excellency, the governor," he told them. They fell to their knees. "He wishes to ask you some questions about poor Hideo's . . ."

Akitada interrupted him. "Thank you. This will do very well. We won't need to detain you any longer."

Kaibara opened his mouth but, meeting Akitada's eyes, he thought better of it, bowed, and departed.

Akitada scanned the gathering of young and old manservants and maids, guards, cooks, and runners. Some looked puzzled, others hostile. He addressed them in an informal manner.

"As you may already know, your fellow servant Hideo was found dead below the north pavilion. He must have fallen during the night Lord Maro died. I am here to find out how it happened. He served here all his life, and you all knew him. Some of you may have been his friends. Some may have seen him on the night of his death. And some of you may simply have seen or heard something unusual that night. They are the ones I would like to speak to. The rest of you may return to your work."

There was a buzz of excitement, and then the courtyard emptied quickly. Only four people remained: three maids and one old man. The old man looked painfully shy and was wringing his hands nervously. Two of the women were middle-aged and haggard, staring back stupidly, but without fear. Akitada thought they almost looked pleased to be questioned. The third maid was a stocky young girl with plain broad features, bright black eyes, and red cheeks. She was nervous, biting her lip and glancing over her shoulder as if she expected someone.

Proper protocol had to be followed, so Akitada addressed the male first. "What is your name?"

"This person is called Koreburo, your Excellency," the ancient quavered, bobbing several bows.

"Well, Koreburo, what do you know about this affair?"

"By the great Buddha, Excellency, I swear I know nothing. I've done nothing." His gnarled hands knotted and unknotted, and he breathed, "Amida."

Seeing that the man was inarticulate with awe or fear, Akitada gentled his voice. "Calm yourself. You have nothing to fear from me."

Koreburo took a breath and nodded.

"I see your hair has turned white in the service of your master. You must be of an age with Hideo."

"Ah," cried the old man, sitting up a little, and raising a hand, fingers extended. "I'm five years older and have served two years longer." He waved two fingers of his other hand at Akitada. "Hideo always said that he worked twice as hard, so he had really served one hundred years to my fifty. But it isn't so, Excellency. Hideo was a great liar sometimes."

Akitada smiled. "Only lifelong friends talk that way to each other."

The old man nodded, his eyes suddenly brimming with tears. "That's the truth. We played *go* together after work. I won mostly. When our old women were still alive, the four of us went on a pilgrimage to Ise. Oh, what a time we had! Now he's gone and there's only me." He hung his head. "Nobody to talk to anymore. The young ones, what do they know? They drink and gamble and chase the women. Hideo used to come to my room after he'd tucked in the master. I'd have the *go* board set out and we'd play, and all the time he'd worry about Lord Maro. He loved the master."

"Koreburo," cried one of the older women softly. "Remember what Master Kaibara said!"

The old man shot her an irritated glance. "Yes, yes. I'm not to talk of unimportant things, but this might be important. Because, Excellency, the night the master died, Hideo did not come. I waited a long time and wondered. His lordship was getting worse, and Hideo had said the end was near. And so it was, wasn't it?"

"Yes," said Akitada. He was intrigued by the maid's warning. Evidently Kaibara had anticipated his visit and cautioned the servants. He wondered what he had told them, but decided not to press the old man. "Thank you, Koreburo," he said. "If you remember anything else, you must come to the tribunal."

He turned next to the woman who had spoken, though he expected little from her or her companion. But precedence had to be followed here, too. "And who are you?" he asked.

"This person is called Chiyo, your Excellency." She bowed and pointed to her companion, "Mika and me, we were sweeping the corridor and we saw Hideo. He was running from the old master's room and then a little while later he was running back. That's all we saw of him that night, your Excellency."

"When was that?"

The two women exchanged puzzled glances. "I can't say, your Excellency," the first one stammered. "It was getting dark outside."

The second woman nodded. "The banquet was half over. They were taking in the pickled salmon and plums. We left then to lay out Lord Makio's bedding."

"Did Hideo speak to either of you as he passed?"

They shook their heads, and the second one said, "He looked so worried, I don't think he saw us. It wasn't his usual time to leave his master. Maybe he was sent for."

"No, Mika," chided the other one. "Don't be stupid. We'd been cleaning the end of that corridor. If somebody'd gone to fetch Hideo, we would've seen him. Nobody went down that corridor except Hideo."

Akitada looked at her attentively. "And later?"

They exchanged glances again. "We were in Lord Makio's room then," said the first woman.

"But," cried Mika, "the door was open. I heard footsteps, and then I saw Master Kaibara going past." She paused. "But I did wonder about the paper."

"Mika!" said her companion reproachfully. "Don't talk about unimportant things. Only about Hideo."

"Sorry." Mika put both hands over her mouth.

"Let her speak," said Akitada.

"It's stupid, really," stammered Mika. "I thought Hideo must have the runs. He had a sleeve full of paper and he was running back to the gallery and that leads to the latrines."

There was a stunned silence, and Mika put her hands over her face.

"You are very observant." Akitada remembered his own visit to the convenience that night. He had not seen the unfortunate Hideo, but that meant nothing. "If that is all, then perhaps this young woman has something to add?"

The red-cheeked girl cast another glance over her shoulder, then bowed and said quickly, almost as if she feared being interrupted, "This humble person is called Sumi and has served at Takata for five years. I look after the children when their parents are busy with their duties. Hideo's grandson Toneo has been in my charge since his parents died four years ago. The morning after Lord Maro died, very early, at dawn, Toneo came to my room and woke me. He said his grandfather had not slept in his bed and he couldn't find him. I got up, and we went to look for him. There was much confusion because the old lord had died during the night, but Hideo was nowhere and nobody had seen him. Finally in the afternoon we went to Master Kaibara. Master Kaibara said Hideo had been so sad that he had gone to the mountains to pray for the old lord's soul."

Akitada had hoped for more than this. "Thank you," he said. "I met Hideo's grandson at the funeral. The boy told me about it."

"Oh," she cried. "I didn't know if Toneo was telling the truth. He said the governor himself would help him find his grandfather." A gate slammed, and she tensed.

Akitada followed her eyes and saw that Kaibara was back. "Was there anything else on your mind?" he asked quickly.

"Yes, Excellency," she whispered, twisting her hands in her lap. Akitada bent forward to hear her. "I am worried about Toneo. He's gone."

ELEVEN

THE MERCHANT SUNADA

*H*itomaro found Genba in front of the Temple of the War God, amusing himself by taking on street urchins who wished to test their strength against the big wrestler. He had removed his bright red quilted jacket and was jumping about in shirt, knee-length pants, and wrapped legs.

"New clothes?" Hitomaro asked sourly. In his present mood, he felt neither admiration nor tolerance for Genba's unexpected rise to fame among the local people. He regarded Genba's occupation as a liability that interfered with his job.

Genba chuckled. "Presents from my fans." A new contender flung himself at him.

"Stop that and let's go!" Hitomaro pulled Genba's sleeve. "There's work to be done."

"Of course, brother." Genba removed the clutching arms of a skinny youngster from his massive thigh and swung him high into the air with a shout. The lad screeched with delight, his fellows waiting hopefully as Genba set him back on the ground. "Practice!" he told them, waving an admonishing finger, "and eat everything your mother gives you."

There was a chorus of protests when he snatched up his red jacket. Hitomaro strode off down the street.

"What's so urgent?" Genba, in spite of his bulk, caught up easily.

"We have work to do. What news do you have?"

"Not much. I think there's not much more to be had. The judge is said to be in Sunada's pay. That's why his thugs act the way they do. Every time they're in trouble, Hisamatsu dismisses the charges."

Hitomaro nodded. "Makes sense. I spent hours at the garrison yesterday, talking to Ogai's fellow recruits. Goto told the truth about his brother being absent without leave. The punishment is such a cruel caning that some don't survive, so his disappearance is either involuntary or he's deserted. I figured you could help me talk to some of the neighbors. People seem to open up to you. We need an unbiased account of that fight between Ogai and Kimura."

Genba glanced dubiously at Hitomaro's neat blue robe and official black cap. "You didn't wear your old clothes."

"Not much point in it. We're past that charade."

Genba gave him a startled glance but said only, "I'll try my best to help."

They passed through streets of modest dwellings. It was cold in spite of the sun that reflected blindingly from patches of snow that lingered on roofs and in yards where bare trees made traceries against the pale blue sky. Lines of frozen laundry hung stiffly and icicles dripped from the eaves. A skinny dog sniffed and licked the icy street where a woman had just emptied steaming kitchen slops.

But even on these side streets, business was transacted in the open air. Smoke curled from portable cookers and ovens, and tattered straw matting protected food stalls. These were of considerable interest to Genba, who stopped and peered periodically, much to the ill-concealed irritation of Hitomaro.

"Brother," Genba finally said with a worried look at his friend's face, "are you feeling quite well? I would've thought you'd be over that beating by now, but you look ill."

Hitomaro's "illness" had nothing to do with Boshu but he had no intention of discussing it with anyone. He glared. "Seeing you drooling into every pot since we left the Temple of the War God would turn anyone's stomach. Come on. We must be near that fishmonger's place."

They turned down a narrow, dirty backstreet. Across from them was a small wineshop. In spite of the cold weather, the owner had placed a rickety table and stools in the street. Three bare-legged laborers perched on them soaking up the feeble rays of the sun and the harsh and potent brew of the establishment.

Genba stopped. "Close enough. Let's talk to them."

"How do they stand this cold without shoes or leggings?" asked Hitomaro, shaking his head.

"Used to it. Also, they're very hairy people hereabouts. Some look more like monkeys than men." He sniffed the air. "Do you smell fried fish?"

"No time for food. We have work to do." Hitomaro crossed the street and asked the drinkers, "Anyone here know Kimura? He's a plasterer and lives around here."

The three men looked at his neat blue robe and black cap, then at each other. To a man, they shook their heads.

Hitomaro frowned. "I don't believe you. This is official business. It concerns a case before the governor. We need Kimura's testimony."

The hairy men stared back and shook their heads again.

Genba came and took a precarious seat on one of the stools. He nodded to the men and called for service. "Sit down!" he told Hitomaro. "I'm thirsty. Tagging along with you is hard on a man. Wish you were in some other business." Turning to the three men, he added, "He's with the tribunal, but he's not a bad fellow when you get to know him. Pay no attention to the official manner. I'm Genba, by the way. Wrestler by profession. I'm in the competition this year."

They broke into excited chatter, asking about his bouts, feeling his muscles, and offering to pay for his wine.

"Ho, ho!" laughed Genba. "I knew I'd like this town. Never met nicer people in my life. But this round's on me. And if one of you knows where that delicious smell is coming from, I'll buy the snacks, too."

Hitomaro sat down with a heavy sigh and waited while the owner carried out flasks of wine, and one of the guests disappeared around the corner, returning with a large basket filled with skewers of fried seafood.

While Hitomaro sat, arms folded across his chest and a pained expression on his face, Genba and the others ate, drank, exchanged simpleminded jokes and laughed uproariously at them.

Finally, when all the fish was gone and the flasks were empty, Genba patted his belly and said, "Well, it's too bad, but we must be on our way. My friend here has this assignment, and at his rate, it'll take all day and night to find this Kimura fellow."

A brief silence ensued. Then one of the men muttered, "That Goto's a big liar."

Hitomaro said quickly, "If you want to help Kimura, tell us what you know."

They looked at each other again. Then the man who had spoken asked, "How do we know we won't get in trouble?"

"Because I vouch for him," Genba announced grandly and belched.

"Well . . ."

"Go ahead. Tell him," said a skinny man who had been very impressed with Genba's muscles.

The first man said, "Kimura lives right around the corner. I was there when he and Goto's worthless brother were shooting dice and got into an argument. Ogai's a lazy soldier. He picked the fight on purpose. Kimura wouldn't raise a hand against anybody if he wasn't forced into it. Ogai kept pushing him against the wall till Kimura pushed back. Then they got into a slugging match. Mind you, Kimura's no slouch when he gets started. He got a black eye, but Ogai lost two teeth. Him"—he pointed to the skinny man—"and me, we stopped the fight and took Kimura home. We know Kimura doesn't hold a grudge. He told Ogai he was sorry about the teeth, but the bastard just made a fist and cursed him."

"What do you mean, Ogai picked the fight on purpose?" Hitomaro asked.

"Well, the dice weren't the real reason. It's a family thing. Goto has a quarrel with Kimura over a piece of land. It was Kimura's father's land, but the old man couldn't pay the taxes on it for a few years. When he died, nobody bothered Kimura for the taxes, so he forgot about them. Then, one day, Goto puts up a fence and the argument starts. Goto says Kimura's father sold the land to him. Kimura says Goto's a liar, that his father would never have sold that land, especially not to Goto. He didn't like him, and besides he'd had a better offer."

"That should be easy enough to prove," Hitomaro said. "Just have Kimura come to the tribunal and file a complaint against Goto. His Excellency, the governor, will untangle the matter fast enough."

There was a chorus of angry curses at that.

"Forget it," the spokesman sneered. "Kimura tried that. Poor people can't get justice at the tribunal. The judge gave the land to Goto. Seems the sneaky bastard's been paying the taxes. But Kimura had the last word. He dammed up his stream and diverted it. That's what made Goto so mad. Now he's got a piece of barren land." They all laughed.

Hitomaro opened his mouth to argue, but Genba touched his arm. "Well, thanks for clearing that up," he said. "We'd better be on our way, but it's been a real pleasure." He tossed a handful of coins on the table. "Have another flask on us, fellows."

"What do you think?" Genba asked when they were out of earshot. Hitomaro turned and walked rapidly toward the tribunal. "Hey, where are you going?"

"I want to pay that bastard Chobei a visit."

"But what about having a talk with the plasterer first?"

Hitomaro stopped and glowered at him. "Any fool knows that Kimura will tell the same story. I don't have time to waste, but you do as you please."

Genba's cheerful face fell. "What have I done, brother?" he called after Hitomaro, who was off again. Hitomaro did not answer, and Genba galloped after him and pulled his sleeve. "What's wrong, Hito?" he asked. "Why are you so angry? Has something happened?"

"You're wasting time on games when the master's in trouble—and we along with him."

"Is that what the master said?"

"No, it's what I say."

Genba looked unhappy. "All right. We'll do it your way."

They heard the sound of drums and gongs and the voices of street musicians long before they reached the market stalls. The market was crammed with crowds of shoppers clustering around acrobats and dancers or bargaining with shopkeepers.

"What's going on?" Hitomaro asked.

"Oh, didn't you know?" Genba tossed a coin to a vendor and took a steaming paper envelope of roasted chestnuts. "It's the last market day of the year. The farmers won't be coming to town again till the snows melt next summer. So everyone's having a party. Isn't it nice? Here, have some hot chestnuts. Put them in your sleeves and warm your hands on them."

Ignoring the offer, Hitomaro said, "If Chobei is in this crowd, he'll be about as easy to find as an ant in an ant hill." Cursing under his breath, he climbed on an empty basket to peer over the bobbing heads of the crowd. As far as he could see down the main street with its overhanging thatched roofs, people milled, eddying in streams past stalls and around groups of performers. The steam from a hundred cook pots hung in clouds about them, and the noise from laughter, chatter, and snatches of music was deafening.

He climbed down and found that Genba had attracted his own audience. A small group stood around him, admiring his enormous size and bulk and asking questions about the coming match. Men felt his muscles, and women held up their baby boys to touch him, hoping that his strength would pass from him to their sons.

A dumpling seller was offering his wares nearby, and an admirer pressed Genba to accept a small snack.

"What do you think you're doing now?" Hitomaro asked testily.

Genba chewed and smacked his lips. "Good. The bean paste might be sweeter. But," his round face split into a wide grin, "these dumplings are light as a feather and larger than any I've had. Hey," he called out to the dumpling man, "a couple more, if you please."

"We have to find Chobei, you mountain of lard!" Hitomaro gritted out.

Genba's fans glared at him. The dumpling man bobbed a

bow and passed over the dumplings. "Master Genba must keep up his strength," he said reprovingly to Hitomaro.

To Hitomaro's annoyance and the noisy approval of the by-standers, the dumpling man began to gyrate and chant, "Tie 'em into knots—ooh, ouch!—pick 'em up, and throw 'em down—whoosh!—kick 'em off their feet—whack!—knock 'em down and fall on 'em—splat!" He concluded with a brutal knockout punch into the air, followed by a comical pratfall. The crowd loved it, and when the dumpling man bounced back up, they cheered and bought dumplings. With a grin, he tended to his business.

Genba chuckled until Hitomaro cursed wrestling matches and bean paste dumplings roundly and eloquently. Shoving the rest of the dumpling in his mouth, Genba chewed and swallowed. "I'm sorry, brother," he said. "What would you have me do?"

But Hitomaro had turned his back and walked away.

When Hitomaro stopped to look after a well-dressed fe-male, Genba caught up. "Hey," he said. "You're not looking for Chobei. You're looking at pretty women."

Hitomaro snapped. "Don't be an idiot."

Genba peered into a large pot of soup in a noodle stall. The vendor reached for his ladle and a bowl. "Some nice fresh noo-dles in my special soup for the gentlemen?" he cried in a high singsong voice. "Best herbs and vegetables only! Gathered this very morning! Only two coppers."

"Come along," Hitomaro growled.

Genba sighed. "I suppose after the match, I'll be put on short rations anyway."

"Be good for you. The tribunal stairs won't take your weight." Hitomaro's arm shot out, pulling Genba behind the straw canopy of a stall. He hissed, "Duck! There's the bastard now."

Two men passed, walking purposefully. One was Chobei.

The former sergeant of the tribunal wore a new blue cotton robe, matching trousers, and straw boots. His companion was a short fat man in brown silk and a black sash with an official's black cap on his head. Chobei talked and waved his hands about. His companion looked haughty and kept shaking his head. They disappeared in the crowd.

Hitomaro stared after them. "Now I've seen everything!"

"Who was that with him?" Genba asked.

Someone giggled at their feet. A pretty girl with bright black eyes raised a hand to cover her mouth. She sat among her earthenware dishes and bowls, the owner of the stall they had ducked into.

"Please forgive the intrusion, miss," Genba said politely. "We didn't want to talk to those men and took advantage of your canopy."

Her eyes were on Hitomaro. "Maybe I can help. Which one are you interested in? That good-for-nothing Chobei or the judge?"

"That Chobei!" Hitomaro growled. "Where the hell did he get new clothes? And since when does that bastard keep company with the judge?"

She giggled again. "Since Judge Hisamatsu made him his overseer. That's how he got the new clothes, and a fine house besides. It's on the judge's property."

"How come that ignorant rascal had such luck?" Genba marveled.

She rolled her eyes. "The judge isn't right in the head."

Hitomaro gave a snort. "You can say that again. Chobei's worthless."

"No. Really. He thinks he's somebody else."

Hitomaro gave her his attention. She responded with a coy smile, and Hitomaro squatted and smiled back. "Who does he think he is? And how come you know these things?"

She brushed back her hair and smiled. "Easy. My mother works for the judge. She says he thinks he's really a grand minister."

Hitomaro frowned. "He didn't sound mad to me. What does he want Chobei for?"

A woman stopped at the stand and picked up one of the bowls. The girl hesitated. "I've got a customer."

Hitomaro grabbed her arm. "Answer me!"

She pouted and freed her arm. "The judge hired Chobei to run his estate," she snapped. "He said a nobleman needs retainers."

The customer cleared her throat and glared at Hitomaro, who glared back and stalked away. Genba muttered an apology and put down a handful of coins before following him.

"That's a really strange story," Genba said when he caught up. He got no answer, and chuckled. "Your mind's on other things. You're looking at girls again. I bet you've got a girlfriend."

Hitomaro turned on him. "What business of yours is my private life?"

"Sorry, brother. I meant nothing by it." Genba's eyes were large with shock and hurt. He muttered, "Maybe I'd better go."

Hitomaro slowly unclenched his fists. "No. It was nothing. Forget it."

But Genba's cheerful face had turned grave. "Hito, this isn't like you. Are you in some kind of trouble? We've been through too much together for you to act this way. Either you let me help, or we part company here and now."

Hitomaro stopped. He bit his lip. "The trouble is someone else's. I have promised not to tell." He paused. "Could you lend me some silver without asking what it's for?"

Genba's eyebrows shot up. "Silver? When you've been putting away every copper cash toward a piece of land. You've saved twenty bars of silver already."

"I . . . it's all gone. Please don't ask." Hitomaro made a helpless gesture.

"I have fifteen bars. They're yours."

"Thanks, brother. I swear, I'll pay you back as soon as I can."

"Keep it. I don't need it. If I win the contest, and I think I will, there's a prize of ten bars of silver and a new silk robe in it for me. Come, now that your problem's been solved, let's celebrate in that eating place over there. They make a very fine fish stew."

This time Hitomaro did not argue. They found a couple of empty spaces on a bench outside, ordered wine and two bowls of stew, and watched the passersby.

But before their food arrived, a commotion caused a general rush up the street. A woman screamed. Someone shouted for constables.

Hitomaro was on his feet. Genba heaved himself up, casting a despairing look toward the waitress who was coming with their order, and followed.

Hitomaro plunged into the press of people. Genba made his way by simply lifting people out of his path until he caught up with Hitomaro.

In an open space in the center of the market street, a tall well-dressed man was bending over the body of a young beggar. The crowd watched the scene, transfixed. A woman sobbed hysterically, but the rest looked merely shocked or curious. The well-dressed man wiped the blade of a slender knife on the man's rags, then straightened up. Looking about him with a frown, he tucked the knife into his sash. He was a very handsome man, yet Hitomaro felt an instant surge of hatred.

Genba made a growling noise in the back of his throat and moved forward, but Hitomaro held him back. "No, brother," he said in a low voice. "Stay out of this! If I'm not much mistaken, this is no ordinary brawl."

Hitomaro pushed aside the people in front of him and went to the body. Getting on one knee, he checked the victim. The beggar had been stabbed once in the chest and was quite dead. "What happened here?" he asked, getting to his feet.

The handsome gentleman raised his brows. "Who are you?" He took a paper tissue from his sleeve and wiped his fingers.

"Lieutenant Hitomaro, provincial tribunal. Who are you? And what happened?" Hitomaro gestured to the inert figure on the ground. "Did you kill him?"

"Ah, Lieutenant," said the elegant stranger. "So many questions. It is difficult to guess your rank without your uniform. Yes, I'm afraid I had to kill the villain. A drunken lout who attacked me. I'm Sunada."

The name rang a bell, and Hitomaro gave him a sharp glance before bending over the body again. The dead man had the look of a ruffian and had been knifed through the heart. Straightening up, Hitomaro extended his hand. "The weapon?"

Sunada sighed but handed over a dully gleaming blade with a beautifully made silver handle. Hitomaro ran his thumb over the blade. "A dangerous toy," he commented, tucking the knife into his own sash. "Yours or his?"

Sunada snorted. "Don't be ridiculous, man! Does he look like someone who can afford a fine blade like that?"

"Then the victim was unarmed?"

"How should I know? And if he was, so what?"

"I'm wondering why you stabbed an unarmed person."

Sunada rolled his eyes. "Oh, you would try the patience of the Buddha himself! Look here, Lieutenant—if you are a lieutenant—I told you, he attacked me. I simply defended myself. Now get on with your duties. Have someone take the body away and write up your report. I'll put my seal to it, and be on my way. I am already late for an important meeting. In case it is of interest, the governor has asked for my support with the local business leaders. He will not thank you if you delay me."

Hitomaro shook his head. "Sorry, sir. There are regulations. It will take more time than that."

Sunada snapped, "It is urgent. We are trying to find ways to avert open rebellion in this city. Clearly you people at the tribunal are unable to handle anything."

Hitomaro smiled through gritted teeth. "There are rules to be followed in a case of violent death. And questions to be answered. For example, why and how did this man attack you?"

"Dear heaven, what a thickheaded fellow! I'm a rich man, and Koichi's poor, as any idiot can see." Sunada clenched his fists in anger and turned to the crowd. "Tell him," he cried. "You all saw it, didn't you?"

The crowd began to inch away. Some people shook their heads.

"You there!" Sunada pointed to a tall laborer. "Come here and tell this officer what happened."

The laborer shuffled closer, bowing many times to both Sunada and Hitomaro. "It is true what Mr. Sunada says," he said humbly and attempted to slink back.

"Wait." Hitomaro stopped him. "What's your name?"

With an anxious glance at Sunada, the man muttered, "Rikio. A fisherman, sir, from Wild Swan village."

"All right. What did you see?"

The fisherman pointed at the body. "I saw him. Koichi. He was in front of Mr. Sunada. He looked angry. His hands were waving, and he cursed. Koichi is a very bad person. A jailbird."

"Did he hit Mr. Sunada? Put his hands around Mr. Sunada's throat? Throw stones? What did he do? What did he say?"

The fisherman looked at Sunada and twisted his hands together. "He may have been hitting. I couldn't hear the words."

At this point, another man in the dark brown ramie robe of a well-to-do merchant pushed through the crowd. After bowing to Sunada, he said to Hitomaro, "I am Tsuchiya, sake wholesaler. I live in the big house over there and saw everything from my upstairs window. Poor Mr. Sunada here was just walking along, when this dirty person stepped in his way. Mr. Sunada was trying to pass, speaking calmly, but the man was shouting and raising his arms. I myself thought he was mad and would kill Mr. Sunada. Thank heavens Mr. Sunada was quick. A great blessing to us all! What a loss Mr. Sunada's death would have been to this city! I will gladly testify to Mr. Sunada's total innocence and to his excellent reputation in this province."

Hitomaro regarded the sake merchant dubiously. Turning back to Sunada, he said, "What is your trade?"

Sunada flushed angrily. "Everybody knows I buy and sell rice and other goods here and in other provinces. My warehouses are in Flying Goose village near the harbor, and I keep a fleet of sailing ships at anchor there. Now are you satisfied that I'm an honest citizen?"

Hitomaro ignored the question. "Did you know the victim?"

"I don't keep company with criminals."

"If you have never seen the man before, how did you know his name? Koichi, I believe, you called him?"

"Of course I had seen him and knew he was called Koichi. Everyone in this town knew him as a dangerous criminal."

"Ah! Have you ever been attacked by him before?"

"No, but as you saw, I always carry a weapon."

Hitomaro nodded. "Very well. The rest can wait till later. You and your witnesses will follow me to the tribunal." He looked about, saw two brawny bearers mingling with the crowd and whistled to them. Before he could tell them where to take the body, Sunada seized his arm.

"Are you deaf or stupid? I told you that I don't have the time," he snapped. "If I can manage it, I shall stop by the tribunal sometime tomorrow." Looking over Hitomaro's shoulder at the sake merchant, he bowed slightly and said, "Good night, Tsuchiya. Give my best to your family."

"Hey, where do you think you're going?" Hitomaro caught Sunada's elbow just as the man was turning and spun him around roughly. Sunada's hand went to his empty sash. Hitomaro bared his teeth and said, "Not this time, my friend. So. Resisting an officer of the law and threatening him with bodily harm? I believe I shall put you in jail."

Sunada stepped back, his face pale with fury. He scanned the crowd, then raised his left hand, making a curious gesture with his thumb and forefinger.

The ones close to them fell silent and moved back. Their places were taken by men in rough working clothes, brawny men with the deep tans of life outdoors, men with bulging shoulders and sinewy arms, men with the stubborn, dangerous faces of hired thugs.

And there was Boshu, Sunada's overseer. Boshu had a large iron spike in one hand and was tapping the palm of the other with it. "Mr. Sunada, sir," he said to his master without taking his eyes off Hitomaro, "we wondered if there was any trouble."

TWELVE

THE TWISTED WAYS
OF LOVE

𝓣he early morning gathering in Akitada's icy private office
was subdued. Day was breaking outside, but the shutters were
closed against the cold and a candle flickered in the drafts. Akitada himself sat white-faced with fatigue, his shoulders hunched
against the chill, his shaking hands tucked into his wide sleeves.
Tora had been nodding off and jerking himself awake earlier
but was staring at Hitomaro now, who had just finished his report and was waiting with the rigid face of a man expecting a
reprimand.

When Akitada said nothing, Tora could not restrain himself.
"You mean you let that bastard walk away from a cold-blooded
murder? Committed in broad daylight in front of a large crowd?
By the same man who sent his thugs after you once before? I
can't believe you'd be afraid to teach him a lesson when you
caught him in the act!"

Hitomaro, who was seated stiffly next to him, compressed his lips but did not take his eyes from Akitada's tired face. "If I have acted improperly, sir," he said, "I offer my resignation."

Outside the wind splattered wet sleet against the shutters like fistfuls of small pebbles.

Akitada shivered again and blinked. "No, no. Pay no attention to Tora. He is half asleep with exhaustion. You did quite right. A confrontation would have availed nothing and innocent people would have been hurt. Sunada is not going to abscond." He gestured toward some documents on the desk. "I'll have a look at the depositions later." He sighed. "At the moment we have a more urgent problem. The Uesugi servant's grandson has disappeared. Tora and I spent the night turning Takata manor and the surrounding country upside down." In a weary voice he told Hitomaro of their investigation.

Hitomaro relaxed a little. "The boy must be dead or you would have picked up some trail."

Akitada clenched a hand. "I refuse to believe that. It's what they want us to think. Sooner or later there will be a clue."

"In that case," grumbled Tora, "I wish you'd gone home when the doctor did, instead of wasting a whole night searching that accursed foxes' den."

Hitomaro frowned his disapproval of such insolence, but Akitada said quite calmly, "It served its purpose. After we talked to everyone and searched everywhere, neither Uesugi nor his steward will dare punish the maid for reporting the disappearance. And it may have gained us some goodwill from the servants. They seemed genuinely fond of Toneo."

"Well," muttered Tora after a huge yawn, "I don't care what you two do next. I'm going to bed. Send for me later if you have any orders." He got up and stretched, yawning again.

"Tora!" hissed Hitomaro.

"Sit down, Tora. Hitomaro is not finished." Akitada's voice was flat with exhaustion. "Go ahead, Hitomaro. You met Genba later, after you had taken the depositions?"

"Yes, sir. Genba stayed in the crowd to watch and listen." Hitomaro smiled a little. "If there had been a confrontation, Sunada's thugs would've had their second surprise. You would not recognize Genba. He's huge and can toss a grown man farther than I can jump. He will win that match, I'm sure of it. After he saw that I was letting Sunada and his goons go, Genba went to Flying Goose village. The fisherman Rikio"—Hitomaro tapped the depositions on the desk—"is one of Sunada's men. He got in debt and Sunada helped him out. Now he's working off the debt in Sunada's warehouses when he's not fishing. A lot of fishermen are in the same . . . er . . . boat."

Nobody chuckled. Akitada was rummaging among the papers on his desk. "Yes, I thought so," he muttered, shivering. "No doubt the sake merchant is equally obligated to Sunada. Where is Seimei? Is there any hot tea? Wine will put me to sleep and there is too much work to be done."

Hitomaro rose to call for Seimei. The old man arrived quickly, bowing to Akitada, and placing the tea utensils on the desk. Coughing, he muttered something about hot water and left again.

"I wish there were even the smallest sign of support for imperial authority," Akitada said peevishly. "I dislike the idea of serving as high constable, although there is both precedent and cause for it. If I could count on just a small faction to oppose Uesugi, I would gladly forgo that dubious honor."

Seimei reappeared with a steaming pot and prepared the tea.

"Well, there's the doctor," Tora offered.

Akitada said, "Yes. Thank you for reminding me, Tora. Oyoshi is a good man and a loyal friend, I think."

Seimei poured water and offered Akitada a steaming cup. "Friendship is a rare jewel," he said, suppressing another cough. "It may take more than a year to make a friend, but only a moment to offend him. Remember that, Tora."

"Thank you, Seimei." Akitada drank, then warmed his stiff fingers on the cup. "Tell me about the victim, Hito."

"His name is Koichi. He was a porter when he could get work, but he had a bad reputation and several convictions for theft and robbery."

Akitada clapped his hands and shouted, "Hamaya!" When the senior clerk bustled in and knelt, he asked, "Do you remember a defendant by the name of Koichi?"

"Koichi the porter? Oh, yes. Theft, robbery, intimidation, assault, and rape. A familiar face in the courtroom and a man who does not seem to feel the pain of the bamboo. A hardened case, sir. Is he in trouble again?"

"He is the murdered man brought in yesterday. I suppose Sunada will claim to have performed a civic duty."

Hamaya looked astonished. "Koichi is the man Mr. Sunada killed? That is strange!"

"How so?"

"Mr. Sunada employed Koichi after his last jail term. I thought it most generous because Koichi's reputation is well known. And now he attacked his benefactor!" Hamaya shook his head in amazement.

"Thank you, Hamaya."

When the clerk had left, Akitada remarked sourly, "The reports of Sunada's good deeds multiply like flies on a dead rat."

Seimei, on his way out, paused at the door. "This Sunada sounds very suspicious to me. Best watch out for him. He is the kind they call a devil chanting prayers." He coughed again and left.

Silence fell. Akitada hunched more deeply into his robe and stared into space. Tora snored, began to topple sideways, and came awake. "Wha . . . ?"

"Tora," said Akitada, "go get some sleep. We're done for now."

Tora nodded groggily and staggered from the room.

"Sir, I am unworthy of your great trust," Hitomaro said, as soon as they were alone. He shifted to his knees and touched his forehead to the floor. "I have let a personal matter interfere with my duty."

Akitada smiled a little. "Do not look so worried. I have no doubt that you will rectify whatever troubles you."

"Thank you, sir. I shall try harder in the future." Hitomaro paused, then said, "What Seimei said about friendship, sir? I shall not forget it again."

"He meant it for Tora," Akitada said, surprised.

"I know, sir. But I almost hit Genba yesterday, and he was very kind . . ." Hitomaro broke off, overcome with the memory of his friend's generosity.

Akitada got up and touched his shoulder. "Never mind, Hito. These are difficult times for all of us." He sighed deeply. "That little boy asked my help. I cannot forget his eyes."

Hitomaro stood. "What can I do to help, sir?"

Akitada pulled his earlobe and frowned. "I wish I knew. There is Judge Hisamatsu. I am not sure he is mad—he struck me more as a fool—but what you told me about his association with Chobei is very strange. He is close to Uesugi and his home is on the road to Takata. You might see if you can find out anything."

Hitomaro nodded.

"But first there is the matter of the fishmonger and his missing brother. It is time that case was settled. Arrest the fishmonger, and ask Captain Takesuke for more information about the brother."

◆

Hitomaro glanced at the sky. The clouds were as low and thick as ever, and gusts of wind drove painfully sharp grains of sleet into his face and the backs of his hands. His armor was covered with a straw rain cape, and instead of a helmet he wore a straw hat which the wind would have torn off if he had not tied it on firmly. As it was, icy blasts pulled at the bow and quiver he had slung over his shoulder and blew wisps of straw into his eyes.

Back at the tribunal, Tora would be snoring in his warm quilts, and their master, no doubt, had also retired. Hitomaro did not begrudge them the rest after their night scouring Takata for the boy, but he, too, had lost sleep, though far more pleasantly. In fact, lost sleep had been a matter of both joy and shame to him for many days now.

He intended to do penance by working harder.

The garrison gates stood wide open in a welcoming manner. Hitomaro looked for guards and, finding them inexplicably absent, walked in.

Inside the palisades, among the wooden barracks and on the exercise fields, was more evidence of relaxed discipline, if that was the word for it. Garbage was stacked in corners, the courtyard was littered with horse droppings and dirty piles of snow, and the garrison flags, slapping wetly against their poles, were tattered and torn.

Hitomaro located the administrative building and entered. In the large hall, groups of soldiers were gathered about braziers, throwing dice, drinking, talking, or sleeping. After a casual glance at his bow and the sword protruding from under the straw cape, they paid no further attention to him, and Hitomaro walked past them to a corner that was screened off by makeshift stands covered with reed mats.

He had guessed that this must be the commander's office.

Pushing aside one of the screens, he found Captain Takesuke engaged in mutual fondling with a round-faced boy recruit. The youngster wore only a light robe and a loincloth, but the cold did not seem to bother him; he was flushed with wine or desire, and slow to disengage when both became aware of Hitomaro.

"What do you want?" snapped Takesuke. "Who sent you in here?"

Hitomaro suppressed his disapproval, snapped to attention, and saluted. "Sorry, sir. There was nobody at the gate, and the men outside seemed occupied. Lieutenant Hitomaro from the tribunal, on orders of the governor."

Takesuke pushed the half-naked youth away. "Well, Lieutenant," he growled, "what is it that you want?"

Hitomaro avoided eye contact and instead kept his gaze just above the captain's right shoulder. "You are missing a soldier by the name of Ogai, and we have a mutilated body at the tribunal. Goto, a local fishmonger, has identified it as that of his brother Ogai. This Goto has laid murder charges against a neighbor, but we have reason to believe that Goto lied about the body. His Excellency has sent me for Ogai's military documents."

"Ogai? That lazy bastard?" Takesuke glowered. "You mean he's not dead after all? By the Buddha, he'll wish he were when I get my hands on him. Absent without leave again! He's deserted, that's what he's done. And that sly weasel of a brother has made up the story to save his own skin." He slapped his hands on his knees. "If only there were some action. That would keep the men out of trouble. Don't you worry, Lieutenant. We'll take care of the matter for his Excellency."

"May I ask, sir, why Goto would tell such a lie?"

Takesuke stared. "Are you joking?"

Hitomaro shook his head. "Of course not, sir. I am puzzled why a man would lay a false murder charge against another man. That's an offense punishable with a hundred lashes."

Takesuke laughed. "What's a hundred lashes to a man who's about to lose his property? Goto stands surety for his brother. If Ogai deserts, his brother is a beggar."

"Ah," nodded Hitomaro. "Thank you, sir, and forgive the interruption."

The prospect of punishing both Ogai and his brother made Takesuke jovial. "Not at all, Lieutenant." He smiled. "Give my humble regards to the governor. He'll have his report this very afternoon."

From the garrison, Hitomaro walked to Goto's shop. It was empty of customers, and the fishmonger was leaning on his slimy counter, swatting at flies. Several large wooden tubs held fish—bonito and bream, tuna and eels packed in melting blood-flecked snow or swimming in filthy water. Fat flies crawled everywhere. Only the grossest stench from fish offal would attract flies in this cold, Hitomaro thought, and held his breath.

Goto recognized him and straightened up. "Lieutenant!" He bowed several times. "An honor. You bring me news about my poor brother's murder?"

"No. I'm here to arrest you for lying to the governor and accusing an innocent person of a capital offense."

Goto's jaw dropped. He tried a sickly smile. "You're joking. Ha, ha, ha. Soldiers will have their fun. My poor brother was just such a one."

Hitomaro slowly unwound a thin chain from his waist. "Put your arms behind your back!"

Goto backed away. His eyes measured the distance to the door, but Hitomaro's bulk blocked the way. "I didn't lie," he cried. "I could've made a mistake. The worry about my missing brother . . . we were like two beans in one pod. I was expecting the worst. You know how it is, Lieutenant."

"I know nothing." Hitomaro stretched the chain experimentally between his fists. "Turn around."

"If it was not my brother, what a relief! What good news! You must allow me to invite you to a celebration. Wine and dinner. In the best restaurant. Yes, and bring your friends. I am very grateful." Goto laughed too loudly.

Hitomaro sighed. Transferring the chain to his left hand, he stepped forward and gave the fishmonger's shoulder a quick jab, wrapped his other arm around the man's neck, and squeezed. Goto went limp. Hitomaro let him fall and rolled the inert body over to tie the man's wrists behind his back. Then he filled a bucket with icy water from the fish tub and poured it over Goto's head. Goto jerked up, coughing and spitting, small fish flapping in his shirt and sliding off his hair.

"Get up and march!" ordered Hitomaro, pointing him in the right direction with a kick to his posterior. Amid grins from neighbors and jeers from small boys, they walked to the tribunal, where one of the constables locked the half-frozen fishmonger into a cell.

This done, Hitomaro stopped by the main hall, fully expecting to be told by Hamaya that his Excellency was still sleeping. But Akitada was in the archives, bent over a map of the district. He was making notes on a slip of paper.

"Yes, what is it, Hitomaro?" he asked absently.

"Goto's in jail. Captain Takesuke told me that he stood surety for his brother Ogai."

Akitada straightened up. "Good work! That does explain his persistence in the face of the obvious age difference of the corpse."

"Surely it solves the murder, too, sir? He must have killed a vagrant to save his brother's skin and his own property. And he probably shaved the victim's head to make his identification more convincing."

"But why write the note? And I doubt he can write in any case. No, I believe Goto only took advantage of the incident at our gate."

Hitomaro's face fell.

"You did very well," Akitada said consolingly. "What did you think of the garrison?"

"Very lax discipline, sir. No guards at the gate, soldiers gambling and drinking, and I walked in on the commandant making love to one of his men in the middle of the day."

"I would not put too much importance on Takesuke's sexual preferences," Akitada said. "Such things are common amongst warriors. Garrison life breeds familiarity. But if Takesuke supports Uesugi, the lack of discipline may be good news for us."

Hitomaro nodded. "I thought I'd talk to the judge next. Undercover."

Akitada raised his brows. "I thought you had met."

"It was pretty dark and I don't think he bothered to look at me. Chobei, of course, could be a problem."

"Well, good luck. Be careful what you say to him. We don't want to alarm our enemy yet."

Hitomaro returned to his quarters to change. He put on a plain dark blue gown of the type any scribe or student might wear and tucked a small black cap in his sleeve. After a moment's thought, he removed a small package from a spare pair of boots and placed it in the other sleeve. Then he put on his straw cape, hat, and boots again, and went to saddle his horse.

◆

By the time he approached the thatched gate of the judge's country house, the weather had turned bitterly cold. The sleeting had stopped, but now a sharp wind pushed the gray clouds across the sky at great speed, tossing the bare branches of the willows beside Hisamatsu's villa and cutting like ice needles through Hitomaro's light clothes. He knocked at the gate with his fist.

It creaked open slowly. An old man peered out, grumbling irritably when he saw the horseman.

"Is your master at home?" Hitomaro asked.

"The maids are out, the boy's out, the groom and Mr. Chobei are visiting West village, but me and the master are in."

It could not be better. Hitomaro smiled at the grumpy servant, who opened the gate fractionally wider. Hitomaro rode into a dirt courtyard. The villa, a one-story house thatched in a rustic manner, had five or six outbuildings and storehouses. The old servant led the way to the main house where Hitomaro dismounted and tied his horse to a post. In the entryway, he shed his wet straw cape and boots and put on his black cap.

"Tell your master," he said, "that I'm a student and have come from afar to make the judge's acquaintance."

The old man grunted and took him to a spacious room. It was dark because the shutters had been closed against the weather, but he lit a few rush lights, which provided meager illumination. Shelves filled with books and papers sprang into being, but the light was too feeble to reach them. Hitomaro was about to take a closer look when a door squeaked behind him. He swung around and found himself facing the judge.

"I am Hisamatsu," the judge announced in a nasal voice, enunciating every syllable carefully. He blinked at his guest. "Who are you?"

Hitomaro bowed deeply and said, "It is a great pleasure to meet your Honor at long last. The fame of your accomplishments has reached far, and since I am visiting this province, I stopped to pay my respects and perhaps benefit from your wisdom. My name is Hitomaro."

The judge came a little closer and peered at him nearsightedly. "Family name?" he demanded.

"Saga, your Honor. From Izumi province."

"Really? A fine family." Hisamatsu thawed. His round face broke into a smile. "You have come to congratulate me, no doubt. Please sit down!"

Hitomaro obeyed.

The judge lowered his stout figure with a grimace, clapped his hands for the servant, and ordered wine and food. The old man glared at him, then shuffled out, muttering under his breath.

"Forgive these rustic manners and surroundings," Hisamatsu said, frowning after the servant. "I have not yet moved into my official residence."

Hitomaro looked around. "You are too modest. Surely this is a charming and delightful retreat for a scholar."

"Scholar?" His host glanced at the room vaguely. "Oh. You refer to my former work. I retired recently from a position as district judge. No time for that sort of thing now. As adviser to the Lord of Takata I can hardly worry about local crime. No, no."

"Advisor to the Lord of Takata? Surely your talents lie in the legal field, your Honor."

Hisamatsu pursed thin lips. "Young man, you cannot possibly know all my talents, as you call them. As a judge I am perfectly trained to formulate and administer laws, and for someone with vision there are no limits in government. The Lord of Takata is expanding his territories into Dewa province. In fact, the establishment of a northern empire is not out of the question. His Lordship relies on me for advice on the most confidential matters of state. Keep this to yourself, but I expect official appointment soon and will then take over the local administration." Fixing Hitomaro with a sudden suspicious stare, he asked, "Is this not what brought you here in the first place? News of our august leader has surely spread to Izumi province."

This sounded so patently mad it took Hitomaro's breath

away. The girl in the market had been right. He put on an apologetic expression and bowed deeply. "Forgive me, Excellency," he stammered. "We have indeed heard rumors. I should have offered my humble felicitations right away but thought it wiser not to speak of it. Besides, I have always aspired to be a great judge like you and could not help thinking that your elevation must be a great loss to jurisprudence. Your children must be very proud of their father."

"I have no children. Cannot abide them." Hisamatsu was appeased by the flattery. "So you wish to be a judge? Let me tell you, there's no advantage in it. Any upstart court official can order you about." He nodded for emphasis. "But true genius rises above the common run of things. I'm afraid my own nature is quite different from yours."

Hitomaro sincerely hoped so. "I could never compare myself to a great mind like yours," he said. "Indeed, I feel that I am in the presence of an intellect like that of . . . of Master Confucius. In your presence I am ashamed of my lack of education. I managed to qualify for the imperial university in the capital, but family matters prevented my going. Now the best I can hope for is to become a tutor to merchants' sons."

A brief silence fell. Hisamatsu continued to stare at him. "You qualified for the imperial university, you say?" he finally asked. "And you are looking for work?"

Hitomaro bowed humbly.

"People become rather touchingly dependent on someone like me," Hisamatsu said. "It pleases me to help them better their lot in life. Perhaps you could assist me. Mind you, I expect complete loyalty, and no doubt you have much to learn." He sighed. "But I suppose we must expect to train our future officials."

Hitomaro expressed himself overwhelmed with gratitude and then pointed to the books on the shelves. "Is that a complete set of the Chinese masters, I see?" he asked. "I'm afraid, Excellency, my Chinese is not fluent."

Hisamatsu waved the objection away with a pudgy hand. "Never mind that. I don't bother with Chinese. The locals are not able to grasp it. Those are translations."

"In that case, how soon may I start? I hope with your guidance . . ."

Hisamatsu interrupted, "I am a very busy man. But come tomorrow anyway. No sense in wasting time." He looked at the door.

Recognizing dismissal, Hitomaro made several deep bows and murmured, "Thank you, Excellency. I am most grateful for the opportunity," as he backed out of the room.

He almost fell over the old man crouching in the dark hallway.

"I'm leaving," he told the servant, unnecessarily since he had clearly been eavesdropping.

The servant scowled. "Your horse is in the stable. Get it yourself. Do you think I have nothing better to do than wait on every fellow who calls?"

"I suppose," Hitomaro said, "your master has many visitors since he has become such an important person."

"Pah," said the old man.

"Looking after all those important guests must be a chore for an elderly person like yourself. I assume they stay here? Perhaps even families with children?"

"Are you mad? He hates children, and nobody stays here. What is it to you?"

"I am to be his assistant."

The old man made a sound that might have been a grunt or another "pah" and shuffled off down a dark hallway.

◆

By this time, dusk had fallen. Hitomaro got on his horse and glanced back at the villa huddling under the bare willows. No sane man would conceive of the scheme Hisamatsu had proposed. Merely mentioning such matters was high treason. But here in the north, so close to the barbarians, many things were not as they should be. Hitomaro debated for a moment whether to return to the tribunal to make his report. But he had another promise to keep, and there was no longer any urgency. Toneo was certainly not hidden in Hisamatsu's house. The ill-tempered servant would have complained, had he been asked to look after a small boy. On the other hand, there might be other secrets, secrets connected with the mutilated corpse. How fortunate that the mad judge had offered him a job. All in all, it had been a very productive day, and Hitomaro felt he had earned a night of pleasure.

Spurring his horse, he hummed, "Ofumi, my love, loosen your sash and soothe my troubled heart."

The sharp-nosed woman—he knew by now her name was Mrs. Omeya and that she claimed to be a respectable lute teacher, though, in fact, she was a procuress who purchased the services of young women by paying money to their parents—opened to his knock and helped him off with his wet straw cape and boots.

"You are later than usual, Lieutenant," she gushed. "The pretty flower is waiting anxiously." She accepted her usual fee, gave him a coy wink, and led him to the customary room, closing the sliding doors after him.

After the cold and stormy darkness outside, the room embraced him with perfumed warmth, soft light, and the gentle chords of music. He stood for a moment and drank in the scene, feeling, as always, the hot blood starting to pound in his temples and groin.

Silken bedding had been spread on the mats. Ofumi reclined on it, idly moving an ivory plectrum over the strings of a lute. She wore only the thinnest white silk robe, and her thick, long hair fell over her shoulders, framing her beautiful face.

Her resemblance to his late wife always moved him profoundly. Lost in the momentary memory of the dead past, he whispered, "Mitsuko," then winced at the jarring sound from the lute.

She sat up, her beautiful face angry. "I have told you not to call me that." Her loose robe had slipped, revealing pink-tipped breasts and a softly rounded belly. Hitomaro's eyes greedily searched lower, but she snatched at the silk and covered herself.

He was instantly contrite. Falling to his knees beside her, he begged, "Forgive me, my beloved. Your beauty has bewitched me until I no longer know who or where I am."

"Tell me that I am more beautiful than that dead wife of yours," she demanded.

His heart rebelled, but his eyes wandered over her body, lingering where warm skin shimmered through the silk. "You are more beautiful than any woman living or dead," he murmured, lightly touching a breast and then cupping it in his hand.

She shuddered and moved away. "How cold your hands are. Where have you been?"

His eyes fell on the lute. Even to his inexperienced eye this was a rare instrument. It was made of sandalwood and the front and back of the oval body were covered with an intricate floral design of inlaid amber, mother-of-pearl, and tortoiseshell. Such an instrument was worth a fortune. The bitter bile of jealousy rose in his throat. She had another lover.

"Who gave you this?" he asked hoarsely.

"The lute? Oh, I borrowed it. Isn't it beautiful? An antique dealer saw me admiring it and let me try it out. When I told him how much I liked it, he insisted I take it home for a while. He said a beautiful lute must feel the touch of a beautiful woman to stay in tune. Wasn't that charming?" She smiled up at him. "Will you buy it for me, Hito?"

"Anything, my beloved." Hitomaro reached for her again.

"No, Hito! Your hands are like ice. I asked you where you have been."

"An assignment outside the city. The wind is very cold." He held his hands over the brazier of glowing coals and rubbed them briskly.

"Outside the city? Where?"

"The judge's place."

She cried, "You went to see Hisamatsu? Why?" Seeing his surprise, she added, "Surely a judge is beyond reproach."

Hitomaro saw a flask of warm wine and two cups, and went to pour himself some with the idea of speeding up the warming process. "Not this one. He hired our former sergeant, a thorough scoundrel if ever there was one. I was sent to check him out, and what do you think I found? His honor is plotting some mad scheme of rebellion against the emperor."

She stared. "You must be joking. Hisamatsu is a bit eccentric. Better not take it seriously or you'll look a fine fool." She held her breath, but when Hitomaro chuckled, she changed the subject. "There was some rumor about a murder in the market."

Hitomaro disrobed, folding his clothes neatly. "A merchant killed a vagrant. He claims the man attacked him. I had to let him go."

"What will happen in court tomorrow?" she asked as he stretched out beside her.

"Oh, I expect . . ."—he brushed back her hair, revealing a dainty ear and a soft white neck, and kissed both—"I expect his Excellency will announce the findings of this murder and report on the other pending cases." He bent to breathe in the warm scent of her body, caressing her neck and shoulder with his lips.

She purred softly and turned toward him. Nuzzling his ear,

she murmured, "What other cases?" Her fingers traced a design on his bare chest. "Is there new evidence? Will he pronounce any sentences?"

"Ofumi!" Hitomaro drew back. "What is the matter with you? Why all the questions? You know I come here to forget my work, and you want to do nothing but talk."

"Oh." She pouted. "How rude you are! You men are all the same. You only want to use our bodies. You care nothing for us as persons. I was trying to show you that I take an interest in what you do and that I think about you all day long." Her soft lower lip quivered and tears gathered in her eyes. "To you I am just another whore," she sobbed.

"No. Oh, no." Hitomaro flushed with contrition. "Please don't cry. You know how deeply I care for you. I want you to marry me, Ofumi."

"Truly? Oh, Hito! If only it were possible! If only we could be together day and night! All our lives! It would be paradise." She gave him a melting look, then turned away with a little sob. "It will never be. Too much money is owed to Mrs. Omeya. You said you did not have enough to buy me out."

He reached for her with a soft laugh and pulled her into his arms. "I have a surprise, little one. See!" Reaching into his bundle of clothes, he extracted the small package. "Take it! There is enough to buy your freedom."

She lifted the package. "It is small."

"I changed the silver bars into gold. Now will you marry me?"

She unwrapped the gold and sat looking at it with a rapt expression.

"Well?"

"Oh, Hito," she cried, throwing her arms around his neck. "You are the most generous, the kindest, the strongest of men."

Her arms slid over his muscular shoulders and her fingers

moved lightly across his chest and down to his loin cloth. Hitomaro drew a shuddering breath.

She smiled up at him, her pink tongue slowly licking her lips. Her practiced hands undid the cloth and, shaking with desire, Hitomaro pushed aside the folds of her robe. She sank back into the silken quilts and parted her thighs.

THIRTEEN

RAISING THE DEAD

*S*oon after Hitomaro left to visit Judge Hisamatsu, Akitada walked across the tribunal compound to the jail. He had explored in vain every conceivable step he could take to locate the boy without endangering the child's life. If Toneo knew something about his grandfather's murder, any further attempt to locate him might bring about his death.

If, indeed, Toneo was still alive.

Akitada was convinced by now that the answer to the servant's murder must lie in the master's death. And that made the demise of the late Lord of Takata suspicious.

Ducking through an icy blast of air which whipped the skirts of his quilted robe about his legs, he pushed open the door to the jail.

Five men sat around a large brazier on the dirt floor of the main room. Kaoru, his new sergeant of constables, and Dr. Oyoshi were bent over the black and white playing pieces on a *go* board, while the prisoners Takagi, Okano, and Umehara watched.

Seeing the three prisoners reminded Akitada that he had made no progress in the case of the innkeeper's murder. He was convinced of their innocence but could not let them go until he arrested the real killer, or at least had a notion of what had happened at the inn that day. Meanwhile Sato's widow was agitating against him. He consoled himself with the thought that getting to the bottom of the conspiracy would more than likely clear up the Sato case also, and both Genba and Hitomaro were working on that.

"Excellency!" Kaoru jumped up and stood to attention. The three prisoners knelt, their heads touching the floor.

"A very pleasant day," Oyoshi said, inclining his head. "Outside the wind howls, but here we are warm and at peace. Will you join us, Excellency?"

"Thank you." Akitada lowered himself to one of the thin straw mats and held his hands toward the brazier. "Please be seated again. I must move my office here. It is as drafty as a hermit's cave."

Kaoru chuckled. "I doubt that, sir. Those caves are actually quite comfortable. Rock keeps out the cold much better than wood and paper. Can I pour you a cup of wine?"

"No, thank you, Sergeant. You seem to know something about such religious retreats. I remember hearing in the capital about extraordinary feats of self-discipline. For example, *yamabushi* are said to stand for hours under icy waterfalls in the middle of winter. Is there any truth to such tales?"

Kaoru looked uncomfortable. "It has been known to happen. Would your Excellency like to inspect the cells? We have a new prisoner."

"Ah, yes. The fishmonger Goto." Akitada glanced at Takagi,

Umehara, and Okano, who were watching him nervously, and wondered why they had special privileges but decided not to ask. Instead he said, "No, Sergeant. I came to speak with the doctor, but will have a word with you also before I leave. I have an assignment for you."

Kaoru bowed and turned to the three prisoners. "Come, you fellows. To the kitchen with you. It's time to start the evening rice."

The three odd characters brightened instantly and jumped up to scramble after Kaoru.

Oyoshi chuckled. "Umehara makes a superb fish stew with cabbage and Okano has his mother's touch when it comes to tofu. It melts on your tongue. Takagi keeps the fire going."

Akitada hid his astonishment. "I see. They look well and contented. I had not expected such a change."

"No?" Oyoshi regarded him with a twinkle in his eyes. "You thought they were languishing in chains in freezing cells and blamed yourself for not having proved their innocence yet? Do not worry. Your new sergeant is a kind man, and I, too, am grateful. I know of no better place to relax and share an occasional meal."

Akitada smiled, but he disliked having his mind read so easily. "Have you had a look at the body from the market?"

Oyoshi nodded. "You keep your coroner busy. The person, a male about thirty years old, was healthy except for numerous old flogging scars on his back and legs."

"I am told he was a small-time crook called Koichi. He has been arrested for assorted crimes and usually punished with the customary number of lashes."

"I see. The calluses on his hands and shoulders suggest that he may have worked as a porter."

"You are right again. When he was not robbing people, that is. What about the cause of death?"

Oyoshi placed a finger on the left side of his chest. "A single stab wound here. Lieutenant Hitomaro showed me a silver-hilted knife. The blade is consistent with the wound. I understand Sunada did it in self-defense?"

"So he claims."

Oyoshi pondered this, then asked, "Any news about the boy?"

"No. I meant to speak to you about something else. Yesterday, in Lord Maro's room, you asked Kaibara about the old lord's symptoms before he died. Why?"

Oyoshi met Akitada's eyes and looked away. "Just professional curiosity," he said blandly. "Why?"

"I have an extraordinary favor to ask of you. You may wish to decline. I want you to accompany me to Takata after dark. The trip is likely to be uncomfortable in this weather, but there is another reason why you may decide to refuse." He hesitated. "You will need your instruments."

The older man tensed. "An unpleasant business involving sacrilege, I take it? I am at your service."

Akitada released his breath. "Thank you."

A door slammed and firm footsteps brought Kaoru back. "Will you stay for the evening meal, Doctor?" he asked. "A soup of rice, red beans, vegetables, and eggs, I'm told. Umehara says it's a specialty of the mountain villages in Shimosa province." He gave Akitada an uncertain look. "Perhaps your Excellency would also like to sample it?"

Akitada was hungry. "Thank you, Sergeant. Soup sounds excellent in this weather. I accept with gratitude."

"Oh." Kaoru looked both pleased and embarrassed. "It will take another hour or two. Will you eat here or . . . ?"

"Here. It's warmer. I will come back and tell you about your assignment. I'm afraid it will mean riding back to your village tonight to make an arrest."

Kaoru stiffened. "Sir?"

Akitada sighed, then said, "I am aware that your people have given shelter to fugitives and I do not approve. Still I am willing to overlook the matter for now, but this particular man has committed another crime against your people since you took him in, and his testimony is needed in tomorrow's hearing. Can I rely on you in this?"

Kaoru bowed. "I know the man, sir, and he shall be here."

◆

The darkness in the woods was so dense that the three men rode close together, trusting to the sure-footedness of Oyoshi's donkey to keep them on the narrow path. It was not safe to light lanterns, for even though the woods offered cover, there was always the chance that someone might be looking out across the landscape from the galleries, as Akitada had done on his first, ill-omened visit to the manor.

They emerged into a clearing. Fitful clouds scurried across the nearly full moon, which cast a gray light on the scene. The icy wind tore at their straw capes; the horses snorted, and the breaths of men and beasts hung in the air like ghostly exhalations. Akitada pulled back on his reins and stared at the wooded hillside ahead. The shapes of grave markers marched up among the trees like lines of ghostly soldiers. In their midst, he had been told, was the entrance to the tomb of the Uesugi chieftains.

"There it is," he said, controlling a shiver of nervousness. "Tora and I could not have found the place without you, Doctor."

"I gather ginseng root on top of the burial hill," replied Oyoshi. "It grows particularly well in these parts, with large, fleshy roots. My patients claim it helps them." They kept their voices low even though the graveyard was deserted.

Akitada glanced curiously at the huddled figure on the donkey. "Don't you believe in the curative powers of ginseng?"

Oyoshi chuckled. "It's enough if they do. If a sick person has faith in its efficacy, then that person will feel better shortly."

"I wish I had some of that special ginseng from China that makes you live forever," Tora muttered. "What if the old lord's ghost comes after us?"

"If he does, he'll save you a lot of hard work," Akitada said dryly.

Tora reached for his amulet inside the shaggy bearskin.

Oyoshi said with a sigh, "Living forever is a curse, not a blessing."

Tora shuddered visibly, and Akitada snapped, "Pull yourself together."

"Only the spirits of the dead make me nervous," Tora said defensively.

"Ssh!" Akitada raised his hand. He thought he heard sounds: dry branches cracking and small creaks. They held their breaths and calmed their mounts, but there was only the wind in the trees.

Akitada felt as tense as Tora, but for different reasons. In the murky grayness, the dim shapes of the grave markers stood in their patches of snow like a frozen army watching over the tomb in their midst. The image reminded him of their danger as they trespassed on the sacred land of ancient warlords. He took some consolation from the fact that the snow had been trampled by those who had attended the funeral. Their tracks would be lost among the old ones.

Pushing aside the sense of impending disaster, he said briskly, "Come. Let's get it over with. Bring your tools, Tora." They dismounted, and tied up their horses.

Walking across the clearing and climbing uphill past the silent markers, they found the entrance of the tomb. The large stone doorway, its moss and lichen scarred by the recent opening, was almost as wide and tall as a man. When Akitada went closer, he saw that it was inscribed with sacred texts and the Ue-sugi crest. Marks in the muddy ground showed that the stone pivoted outward.

"Come here, Tora, and see if you can lever it open." Aki-tada said.

"Amida!" prayed Tora, but he obeyed, selecting from among his tools an iron truncheon he had picked up in the constables' armory.

It took a while. Akitada and Oyoshi waited, stamping their icy feet and moving their arms to keep warm, while Tora mut-tered prayers and magic spells under his breath and probed the door to the burial chamber of the late Lord of Takata.

Around them the ancient pines and cedars stirred and creaked as the wind blew through them, and Akitada felt doubly like a trespasser. Not only was this Uesugi land, the final resting place of their dead, but it was a spirit world which should be in-habited at this hour only by shifting shadows and strange sighs of the wind.

"Hurry up!" His voice sounded unnaturally loud.

Tora grunted, leaning all his strength into the iron bar. The space between the stone doorway and its frame widened with a harsh grating sound. Tora muttered another prayer, then put his hand inside and pulled. Akitada went to help him, and with more jarring and scraping, the great stone moved outward. A dark tunnel gaped before them.

Tora backed away.

"Come on" snapped Akitada. "Surely you don't expect me to finish the job."

"Look!" Tora choked and pointed. "It leads straight to hell."

"Nonsense." But when Akitada peered down the tunnel, he saw faint firelight flickering deep inside. Behind him, Tora was shaking so badly that his teeth chattered.

"All right, stay here." Akitada took up the lantern, struck a flint and lit it, then ducked into the tunnel. The air was moist and cold, and it smelled of the earth. The tunnel was built of granite: Cut stones formed the walls and large slabs the low ceiling. He had to walk with his head bent. Under his feet were more stones. His lantern threw weird moving shapes against the wall beside him, as if shadowy creatures moved on either side.

The tunnel was not perfectly straight, but curved slightly to the left. After a few paces, Akitada found the source of the flickering light. The tunnel suddenly widened and arched up into a small chamber, and here rested a sarcophagus. Offerings of food for the dead lord had been placed at its foot between two burning oil lamps. The oil in the dishes was getting very low. Soon eternal darkness would descend on the tomb.

He heard steps behind him and turned. Dr. Oyoshi joined him with his case of instruments and looked around curiously. "I knew they built this," he said. "Years ago. They said Lord Maro requested it. Look at the paintings."

Akitada, having bent over the coffin to see how it opened, straightened up. The chamber was taller than the tunnel, and high on each wall and on the ceiling were panels of white plaster. Each panel was decorated with ancient directional symbols: the black tortoise of the north, the azure dragon of the east, the red bird of the south, and the white tiger of the west. The colors shone fresh in the light, and on the ceiling sparkled gold stars: astronomical constellations.

"I have heard tales of the ancient burials of the first emperors that must have been something like this," he said. "Uesugi thought highly of himself."

Oyoshi chuckled. "Maybe. Or maybe he wanted nothing to do with the Buddhist rites that insist on cremation because that's what the Buddha chose. Lord Maro was a strange man."

"I am told he went mad and had to be confined. We need help with this stone lid." Akitada called for Tora.

Tora slunk in, looking green and panicky, but he did as he was asked, and together they shifted the stone lid enough to reveal the corpse.

Tora clutched his amulet and recited a string of "Amidas."

"Go back and keep watch outside," Akitada snapped. "We can manage the rest."

Tora disappeared through the tunnel. Sounds of retching, interspersed with fervent calls upon the Buddha, reached them faintly.

The smell of death and decomposition was very slight. For once the season had favored them; the cold stone had kept the body fresh and pliable.

The doctor placed the lights. Together they lifted the wrapped corpse and stretched it out on the stone floor. Oyoshi unwound the silk wrappings. The emaciated form of a very old man appeared in the uncertain light. His protruding ribs resembled a bamboo cage, and the face, peaceful in death, was, with its sunken cheeks, toothless gums, and deeply recessed eyes, more skeletal than the body. Air currents surged through the tomb, stirring the thin wisps of beard, and for a moment it looked as if the dead man were about to speak.

Akitada crouched, watching as Oyoshi, on his knees next to the body, began his examination. In the flickering lights, the scene reminded him of gruesome paintings of the demons of hell in a Buddhist monastery.

Oyoshi was thorough but respectful of the dead man. After verifying that the body bore no obvious wounds, he began his inspection with the head, first feeling the skull for soft spots. These might mean that Lord Maro had been bludgeoned. Next he examined the eyes, ears, nostrils, and mouth for signs of bleeding. He inserted a silver probe into the dead man's mouth and studied it, and he looked closely at the thin neck. Then he went over the rest of the body, all the way to the old man's bony feet with their yellowed toenails.

Akitada, impatient and disappointed, asked, "Nothing?"

Oyoshi sat back on his heels and shook his head. "No wounds, no signs of poison, no evidence of strangulation or smothering. No bruising. The condition of the body is consistent with the disease of old age."

Akitada cried in frustration, "But there must be something. Everything points to murder. Why else kill Hideo? And why the suspicious behavior of Makio and Kaibara during the banquet, and now Toneo's disappearance? None of it makes any sense unless the old lord was murdered that night."

Oyoshi looked at Akitada. "You are worried about the boy, aren't you?"

"I am worried about a lot of things. One of them is this needless exhumation of a body. It is a sacrilege and a capital offense. You and I, Doctor, and Tora also, will lose our freedom and perhaps our lives if anyone finds out about this. Let's finish and leave."

Oyoshi nodded. "You took a great risk. You are a man with a soft heart. I knew it the first time I laid eyes on you. It is an admirable quality."

"And you are a foolish old man," snapped Akitada, turning away. "Go ahead and wrap him up again. If you say he died of natural causes, so be it. Tora, come help the doctor!"

Tora did not answer or appear. Faint sounds came from outside. The doctor's donkey brayed, and a horse gave a frightened whinny.

Akitada said, "I wonder what Tora is up to."

They listened, but all remained silent. Akitada regretted

having come unarmed on this excursion. Spurred by a sudden
sense of urgency, he helped Oyoshi wrap the body and then
bent to lift it into his arms.

A shout came from the tunnel entrance. "Come out! You are
surrounded." It echoed crazily among the stones. Akitada almost dropped the late Lord of Takata, but instead slid the body
back into the open coffin. Oyoshi helped him push the heavy lid
across, and Akitada extinguished the lights.

The voice came again. "Who are you and what are you doing
here? Come out."

They had little choice. There was no sign of Tora. Perhaps he
was dead. For all they knew a small army of Takata warriors
waited outside.

Akitada sighed. "Take your instruments, Doctor, and let's go
before they decide to close that stone door."

They emerged cautiously. There was no sign of Tora, but the
snowy woods held no army either. Looking around, Akitada felt
relief and wondered if—overwrought by thoughts of danger—
he had imagined the shouts.

When their ghostly visitor materialized it looked as if one of
the grave stones had come to life and started walking toward
them. The figure became vaguely human when it reached them:
an armed man, holding a sword, and pushing back his helmet.

Kaibara.

His eyes were on Oyoshi. "The good doctor," he sneered.
"What a surprise! Have you taken to robbing tombs now? And
the tombs of your betters, too. Tsk, tsk! A capital crime. You
should have been more careful."

Akitada stepped from the shadow.

Kaibara's jaw slackened.

"Let me explain, Kaibara," said Akitada, adopting a reasonable manner. They had been caught red-handed, and he was
desperately searching for an adequate reason for their presence.

"I wanted to spare the family's feelings, but there was a suspicion that your late master was murdered, and we had to investigate. It would be best if we kept the matter to ourselves."

Kaibara's eyes went from Akitada to the open tomb and Oyoshi's instrument case. A slow, crafty smile came into his face. "Is this so? A blasphemous insult to the late Lord of Takata. And a highly illegal proceeding, I believe. Loyalty to my master unfortunately makes it impossible to accede to your Excellency's request."

Oyoshi walked up to Kaibara angrily. "Listen here, Kaibara," he cried. "Don't be an infernal fool and—"

Kaibara was quick. With the flat side of his sword he dealt the older man a vicious blow across the face. Blood spurted briefly, and Oyoshi cried out and fell. Placing a foot on Oyoshi's chest, Kaibara raised his sword with both hands to strike down. "Pray to be reborn, pill peddler!" he cried.

"No!" Akitada leaped and grabbed for Kaibara's sword arm. Kaibara was hampered by his armor, but he twisted away and lashed out with his other arm to punch viciously at Akitada's chest. Akitada gasped for breath but held on, determined to protect Oyoshi. He shouted, "Drop that sword!" and twisted Kaibara's arm back. Kaibara grunted and turned. Akitada saw the murderous fury in the other man's eyes, knew that the next stroke would be for him, and suddenly the struggle for the sword had turned into a fight to the death.

It had not occurred to Akitada that he was in danger of being killed. He had feared charges of trespass, sacrilege, grave robbery, and other serious offences involving recall and trial, but not cold-blooded murder. He put all his strength into disarming Kaibara, but as he adjusted his stance to gain leverage, he slipped on a patch of ice and landed on his knees.

Kaibara laughed out loud. He stepped back and bared his teeth. "This is much the simplest way," he snarled. "Begging on your knees won't help you now, dog official." He raised the sword again. The blade flashed dull silver in the moonlight.

Oyoshi screamed for help, and the blade hissed as it cut through the air. Akitada flung himself aside, scrabbling desperately on the muddy ground. Kaibara followed, loomed above him again. Akitada's fingers closed around a dead branch. He parried the stroke as it came. The branch slowed the blade but it bit into Akitada's arm near the shoulder, and the pain, when it came, was paralyzing. Kaibara straddled him, his body monstrous in the heavy armor, the sword raised for the fatal stroke. Akitada thought of how he had failed Tamako and his unborn child and closed his eyes.

He felt a crushing blow to his chest. A giant hand compressed his rib cage and he could not breathe. And then the night was shot through by flames and stars and a suffocating blanket of fog. His last thought was, "So this is what it feels like to die."

But death was slow in coming. Sounds penetrated the fog. Someone was shouting and cursing. The crushing weight was lifted from his chest, and he tried a deep, shuddering breath, savoring the cold, fresh air, savoring even the sharp pain. He welcomed it, because it meant he was alive.

"Here, move him on his side and let me get a look at that shoulder."

Oyoshi sounded strangely tongue-tied. And he was making spitting noises.

"It's all my fault. I wish I was dead."

Akitada opened his eyes. Tora was peering down at him with a stricken expression. "Don't be an idiot," Akitada muttered. "You'll have to close the tomb."

Oyoshi snorted. "Good! You're conscious. Sit up, sir, so I can bandage your wound. Kaibara got you, I'm afraid."

With Tora's help, Akitada struggled up. He gritted his teeth as Tora and Oyoshi eased the gown from his shoulder. "Kaibara. Where is he?" Tora stepped out of the way, and Akitada saw the lifeless form of the steward on the ground nearby. "Did you kill him, Tora?"

"I got here too late." Tora sounded bitter.

"But who . . ." Akitada's eyes went to Oyoshi. The doctor's face was puffy and covered with blood. His eyes were almost swollen shut.

"Don't look at me," Oyoshi mumbled through cut lips. "He collapsed on top of you before he could strike again." He tied the last knot of the bandage and stood up. Tora helped Akitada put his arm back into his sleeve.

Wincing with pain and clutching Tora's arm, Akitada staggered to his feet. Kaibara lay prone, his arms and legs flung out, and his face turned sideways. His helmet had slipped and a dark puddle of blood was seeping from under his face.

When he bent closer, Akitada saw what had killed the man. From the narrow gap between the top of the armor and the helmet guard protruded the long shaft of a black arrow crowned with a black eagle's feather. It had hit Kaibara's neck in one of the few instantly fatal places on the human body.

FOURTEEN

THE FISHMONGER

*H*itomaro walked through the tribunal gate with a light step, returning the guard's brisk salute and smiling with satisfaction at the trim appearance of the constables sweeping the courtyard. Kaoru was doing a fine job with them.

After the stormy weather, the skies had cleared and the sun sparkled on many small icicles hanging from the eaves of buildings. Hitomaro glanced toward the far corner of the tribunal compound where a small wooden house stood. Private yet convenient, it would make a fine home for a tribunal officer and his spouse. Today he would ask permission to live there with Ofumi. The place was humble but in good repair, and in time they would furnish the two rooms to their liking. They would save their money and buy some land where they would build a larger house and raise a family.

Blinking into the sunlight, Hitomaro stretched, laughed out loud, and ran up the steps to the barracks room he shared with

Tora. He could hardly wait to see Tora's face when he told him the news.

Whistling happily, he pulled off his boots and placed them next to Tora's.

"Hey, Tora!" he shouted. "Wait till you hear! I'll take you out tonight and buy you the best meal in town and all the wine—" He walked in and came to an abrupt halt. "What—?"

Tora was seated cross-legged on a piece of white cloth. His torso was bare, because he had slipped his robe off his shoulders. In front of him lay a sheet of paper, covered with clumsy brush strokes, and on this rested his short sword. There was an expression of intense concentration on Tora's face.

"What are you doing?" Hitomaro asked, his heart skipping in his chest because he guessed at the significance of these preparations.

Tora bowed lightly. "I've been waiting for you," he said with uncharacteristic calm. "Will you assist me?" He reached for the other, longer sword beside him and extended it toward Hitomaro.

Hitomaro did not touch it. "Why? What happened?"

Tora laid the sword down again. "Last night we went to dig up the body of the old lord," he said tonelessly. "Kaibara surprised the master and almost killed him."

Comprehension began to dawn. "Where were you?"

For a moment, Tora's shoulders sagged. "Being sick with fear."

"Is the master badly hurt?"

"A cut near the shoulder." Tora added bitterly, "I wish Kaibara had carved out my heart instead."

"That's not too bad," Hitomaro said soothingly. "I expect Kaibara waited till you were out of the way."

"You don't understand. I should have hurried back, but I was afraid of the ghost and trembling like a foolish woman. The

master had no sword. Kaibara would have killed him, if someone else hadn't done my job for me and shot the bastard."

"Kaibara's dead? Who did it?"

"It was dark. We found no one."

"Does the master know about your . . . this?"

Tora reached for the piece of paper and handed it to Hitomaro. "He will when he reads this . . . if he can make out the
writing. I can't do anything right." He touched the short sword
and looked up at Hitomaro with earnest eyes. "Help me do this
one thing well, Hito. I am only the son of peasants, but you with
your fine upbringing know the proper way for a soldier to die.
I've bathed, shaved, put on clean clothes and tied up my hair.
I'm ready. I thought I would just sort of fall forward on my
short sword, but now that you're here, I might try shoving it in
my belly with both hands. Then, if I'm losing my strength before I'm done cutting across, you can cut off my head. That's the
way it's done, isn't it?"

Hitomaro dropped the paper and scowled. "Have you thought
what this will do to the master? How do you think he'll feel? Last
night you did not mean to desert him, but now you are. And he's
in much greater danger now. This whole province is in turmoil. If
you wish to die, at least die fighting against his enemies."

Tora stared at him. "But how can I show my face?" he asked
uneasily.

Hitomaro reached down and tore up Tora's suicide note.
"You will tell the master how you feel and that you owe him two
lives instead of one. What did you do with Kaibara's body?"

Tora looked blank. "I thought this would make it all right,"
he said, looking about the room helplessly.

"No!" Hitomaro's voice was sharp. "You can die later. For
now the master needs your help." He waited until Tora nodded
slowly. "Where is Kaibara?"

Tora scrambled up and rearranged his clothing. "We brought the body back. He's with the others."

"Come on then. I want to take a look at him. You can fill me in on the way."

"Hito?" Tora asked plaintively on the veranda as they put on their boots. "What would you have done in my place? I mean, if you had failed like I have?"

Hitomaro scowled at his boots. "I would've tried harder and complained less," he snapped. Getting up, he put his hand on Tora's shoulder and added more gently, "Come on now, brother. We're none of us perfect. All we can do is try. Now no more talk. We have work to do."

Four covered bodies awaited them in the icy storeroom, their temporary morgue. Hitomaro shook his head. "If this keeps up, we'll have to move them to a larger building. Thank heaven it's cold."

Tora drew back the reed mat from the nearest corpse. The dead man lay on his back, and the mat got caught on the tip of the arrow protruding from his neck. Tora untangled it carefully.

Hitomaro bent closer and peered at the face. "So that's Kaibara," he said. "Funny, I've never seen the bastard up close. He's in full armor. That means whoever got off that shot was either very lucky or very good." His eyes went to the arrow. "Isn't that one of yours?" he asked, astonished.

Tora nodded.

"But I thought you said—"

"There was another arrow. It looked unusual. The master had the doctor take it out and put one of mine in." Turning away abruptly, Tora cursed and flung the mat violently across the room. "To my shame!" he cried, burying his face in his hands. "His way of telling me that I should have shot the bastard."

"You know very well that was not why the master did it. He

would never shame you. Still, it was a strange thing to do. Did he explain?"

Tora did not answer. He had gone to pick up the reed mat he had thrown. It had fallen across another body, disarranging the mat covering it. Now he stood bent, staring down at the corpse's shaven head.

"Amida!" he muttered. "Hito, come here and look at this. I could swear that's the same scar on his ear as on the sick man at the Golden Carp. Remember, I told you about the poor bastard the widow was going to throw out in the street? I thought it looked like a mouse took a bite out of his earlobe. And this is just the same." He slammed his fist into his hand. "By the Buddha, I bet it's a secret sign. A gang mark. They both belonged to some secret society. Come on. We've got to tell the master." Flinging the reed mat back over Kaibara, he dashed out the door, leaving Hitomaro to lock up.

◆

When Tora burst in with his news, Akitada was seated behind his desk. Things had gone from worse to disastrous, and he had not slept. The wound in his shoulder caused a constant searing ache that he had hidden from his wife. Tamako was unaware of his injury and distracted by the fact that Seimei had taken to his bed with chills and a bad cough. She had dosed him with his own concoction and he had finally slept. Akitada, on the other hand, had lain awake, worrying about Seimei, about the danger they were in, about the missing boy Toneo, and about the next day's hearing. A vicious cycle of separate calamities kept him company until he rose at dawn.

But now he smiled at Tora. "Good," he said. "I wondered what had become of you. Matters seem to have reached a critical point. I need all of you to stand by."

Tora flushed. Falling to his knees, he bowed his head. "I was going to kill myself this morning, but Hito said you needed me." He did not see Akitada's astonishment nor his momentary amusement, and continued in a rush, "It's true you sent me to check the horses before Kaibara came, but I was taking my time because I was afraid to come back. Afraid of the ghost, I mean, not that bastard Kaibara. But it was cowardly and it's my fault you got hurt. Hito says I now owe you two lives instead of one and that you would need me to die fighting your enemies. So I decided not to kill myself." He knocked his head on the floor three times and sat up.

Akitada said, "I understand, and Hitomaro is right. I do need you."

Tora said fervently, "I'll remember next time, sir." He paused for a moment. "About that mutilated body. I just happened to look at it with Hito and I saw a mark on his ear. It's just like one on the dying man at the Golden Carp."

Akitada made a sharp move of surprise and gasped, reaching for his wounded shoulder. "Call Hamaya," he croaked.

Hamaya came in, followed by Hitomaro. "Hamaya," Akitada said through gritted teeth, "Send for Dr. Oyoshi." Three pairs of eyes widened with concern. "No, wait," he corrected himself. "Tell him it's about one of the bodies, and to meet us in the storehouse. Hitomaro, you can report on the way. Tora, help me up."

He staggered to his feet, holding Tora's arm to steady himself against a bout of dizziness. "It's nothing," he murmured, when he saw Tora's white face. "Remember, it was the same when I was wounded in the capital? They say losing blood leaves emptiness in the head. In time it will fill again."

Tora nodded but looked unhappy. While the three men walked slowly to the storeroom, Hitomaro reported on his visit to the judge's villa. Akitada listened without comment.

Dr. Oyoshi joined them at the storehouse door. His face was

colorfully bruised, but his eyes were bright. "How are you feeling this morning?" he asked Akitada.

"I shall be better when we get to the bottom of all these mysterious killings. In each case, it seems to me, we lack one crucial piece of information. Now perhaps Tora has found one for us. I want you to listen to what he has to say about the mutilated man, because it may jog your memory."

Hitomaro unlocked the door, and they stood around the corpse. Tora lifted the mat and explained about the ear, offering his theory about a secret society.

At Tora's first words, Oyoshi grunted and knelt, looking closely at the dead man's face, chest, and tongue. Straightening up with a sigh, he said, "Of course. I made a terrible mistake, sir. How could I have forgotten, when I saw the man myself just a few days earlier! Tora is quite right. It *is* the poor fellow at the inn. He was dying of lung disease." He shook his head. "I am getting old and incompetent. Please, forgive my carelessness, sir. I understand that I have caused you embarrassment and that this disqualifies me as coroner."

There was an awkward silence. Then Akitada said sharply, "Nonsense. You reminded us repeatedly that you were dissatisfied with the diagnosis."

"But how could it be the same man?" Tora asked, astonished. "The one at the inn was old. He had gray hair."

Oyoshi said, "Someone shaved his head. That can change a man's appearance amazingly."

"It explains why you didn't recognize him, Doctor," Hitomaro said. "Besides, his face is pretty much destroyed."

Oyoshi shook his head. "It is kind of you to make excuses for an old man, but in my profession we do not consider a patient's looks but the symptoms of his disease. Those I should have recognized."

"Come," said Akitada, touching his arm. "I have had enough

of this . . . this self-recrimination from all of you." He pointed to the four bodies stretched on the floor, almost filling the small room. "Look at them! The nameless guest from the inn. The old servant Hideo. The thug Koichi. And now Kaibara. If you add Sato, the innkeeper, we have five unsolved cases. And a missing child. Why should you blame yourselves for minor mistakes, when I have failed so grossly and completely in my duty?" For a moment he swayed on his feet, and Tora put out an arm to steady him.

"You should not be up, sir," scolded Oyoshi. "Come, back to your room with you. I insist on bed rest until tomorrow."

Akitada protested in vain. They walked him to his office, where Tora and Hitomaro spread some bedding and brought him tea.

Akitada drank it meekly and smiled. "I must be thankful that Seimei is too sick himself to concoct one of his vile brews," he joked feebly.

"I look forward to meeting him," said Oyoshi. "I may have just the medicine to make him better." He sat down next to Akitada and felt his forehead. "As for you, you're slightly warm, but that may be due to exertion. Rest is essential. You must avoid overheating yourself. By the way, you may be certain now that the man from the inn was not murdered. He was dying when I saw him. Even if Mrs. Sato threw him into the street after my visit, she could not properly be held responsible for his death."

"Yes." Akitada chewed on his lower lip. "I admit that's a disappointment. The woman is detestable. However, though she may not be responsible for his death, she knows something about the conspiracy and who mutilated the dead man. Let her try to talk her way out of that!" He glanced at Tora and Hitomaro, who were hovering nearby. "Sit down, both of you. It's time for a council of war."

When they had gathered around, Akitada said, "Hamaya,

Seimei, and I have drawn up the documents appointing me high constable. Notices will be posted all over the city. This step will allow me to assume command over the garrison and declare a state of emergency if necessary. It may also convince the people that Uesugi power can be broken. I checked the law carefully and studied similar cases and believe the action is unusual but perfectly legal. The circumstances certainly make it necessary. We are trying to foil a conspiracy against imperial authority in this province."

Hitomaro grunted. "That's where that judge fits in, sir. Remember his talk about a new ruler? And Chobei is up to his neck in the plot of the mutilated corpse. I saw his face when we found the body at the gate. He's working for Hisamatsu now, a man who has a whole library of Chinese texts and could have written the note that was pinned to the dead man. And that reminds me." He reached into his sleeve and pulled out a piece of paper. "I helped myself to a sample when I was in Hisamatsu's house."

Akitada took it and nodded. "It looks like the same paper. Have Hamaya compare it later. From what you told me about Hisamatsu it seems likely he wrote this, but he does not strike me as the sort of man who could organize a conspiracy of the complexity and seriousness of this one. There is more than a touch of madness here."

The possibility of an uprising against the emperor was frightening. Without military support, they were helpless to avert it. One thing seemed certain to Akitada: When he failed in his duties, he did so spectacularly. Freshly assigned to a post which had seemed an open door to rapid promotion, he was about to lose the province to the enemy. Unless they fled, they would also lose their lives, of course, but there was no point in dwelling on that detail.

Hiding his fears, he said, "Much depends on Captain Takesuke, of course, and on Uesugi himself. And let's not forget Sunada. I wonder what that rascal's part is in all of this, and what a small-time crook like Koichi wanted from him. A pity Kaibara is dead. He would have had answers. Who shot him? And why? His killer may have saved my life, but what if that was not his real purpose?" He frowned. "I wish there weren't so many pieces missing. Do you know what this situation reminds me of? The shell matching game my sisters used to play. I feel that it's my play and I don't know which piece to turn over."

Tora and Hitomaro looked blank, but Oyoshi nodded. "A very good comparison, sir." He explained, "The shells are plain on the outside but hide pictures on the inside. For each picture there is a matching one in only one other shell. The object is to find the match. Well, sir, we have just matched our first shell by identifying the mutilated corpse. Will you let the other players know?"

"Yes, perhaps that is the logical next move. There will be a court hearing later. Tora, go tell Hamaya to make the arrangements."

"But you are wounded," protested Hitomaro.

Akitada refrained from pointing out that his shoulder was a small matter compared to their all being slaughtered by the Uesugi. "Never mind," he said. "I shall rest till then. I'm perfectly capable of conducting a brief hearing. Tell Kaoru to have Mrs. Sato brought in."

Oyoshi poured some tea and added one of his powders. Stirring, he said, "This should dull the pain a little and let you rest."

Akitada smiled his thanks, swallowed the draft, and closed his eyes as the others stole from the room.

◆

The crowd in the hall was smaller and more subdued than last time, and they watched him intently. Akitada saw them through a haze. What Oyoshi had given him for the pain unfortunately made him see and hear everyone as if from a great distance. He also felt flushed and uncomfortably warm.

He began the session by announcing his new status. When the crowd began to buzz, he rapped his baton sharply, calling for the prisoners and the witnesses in the Sato case.

Kaoru knelt and reported that Mrs. Sato had claimed to be too ill to appear.

Akitada shifted irritably and winced. "Arrest her," he said. The crowd whispered like wind rustling through dry grasses. He pulled himself together. "We will start with the fishmonger's case."

When two constables dragged in Goto, a new wave of excitement rippled through the onlookers. Goto was in chains but drew courage from them.

"This person," he cried when he faced Akitada, "wishes to complain about the cruel treatment he's received. I'm an honest citizen and pay my taxes, but I was beaten and chained, and then thrown in jail like a criminal. Me, a poor shopkeeper who's never been in trouble with the law! Meanwhile my brother's body lies someplace, cut to pieces, without a proper burial, and his killer is smiling while I suffer. Is that justice?"

The crowd buzzed their support. One of the constables kicked Goto in the back of the legs, shouting, "Kneel!"

Goto fell to his knees with a loud wail. The crowd became noisy.

"Silence!" Akitada shouted, rapping his baton again. He felt unaccountably weak and languid. He looked for Kaoru and saw that constables moved among the people to control them. Gradually it became quiet. Akitada turned his attention back to the fishmonger. "State the case against this man, Sergeant."

Kaoro announced, "This man is called Goto and is a fishmonger in this city. He stands accused of having lied to this tribunal and of having falsely accused one Kimura of murder."

"What? I never lied . . ." Goto's outraged protest died with a kick from his guard.

Kaoru continued impassively, "He identified a body found outside the tribunal gate three days ago as that of his brother Ogai, a soldier absent without leave from the local garrison."

Akitada asked the prisoner, "Do you persist in your identification?"

Goto cried, "It's my brother, I swear it."

"Have the maid brought in!" Akitada commanded.

The maid of the Golden Carp marched past the crowd with a smile of self-assurance. Akitada saw that she was a sturdy, plain woman with a knowing look on her face. Near the dais she passed Tora and stopped with a gasp. Tora kept his eyes carefully fixed on a corner of the hall. The maid looked outraged. Putting her hands on her hips, she cried, "So this is where you've been hiding out, you lying dog! If I'd known that you were a stinking spy for the tribunal, I'd have made you wish you were bedding a rabid monkey instead."

There was a moment of stunned silence, then a ripple of laughter started and crude jokes flew back and forth. Akitada bit his lip and rapped his baton on the boards while Kaoru started for the girl.

Tora was crimson. Satisfied with the scene she had created, the maid spat on his boots and walked to the dais.

There she knelt, bowed deeply, and said, "This humble person is called Kiyo. She works as a maid at the Golden Carp. She apologizes for having lost her temper with a lying dog."

In view of the provocation, Akitada decided to ignore her outburst. "You were shown the corpse of a mutilated man," he said. "Did you recognize him?"

"Aiih!" she cried. "It was horrible! It turned my stomach what they did to poor Mr. Kato."

"Answer the question."

"I recognized him. May the Buddha comfort his soul! It was Mr. Kato, one of our guests. He died last week. Someone must've stolen the body. They cut off his feet and hands. And shaved his head. Who'd do a nasty thing like that to a dead man? I hardly knew him except for that ear of his. I nursed the poor man till he died. The doctor and my mistress saw him, too."

"Dr. Oyoshi has already identified the body. Where is your mistress?"

Kiyo spread her hands. "Who knows? She says she's sick but she stays away a lot. I bet she's meeting some man." She turned to shoot a venomous glance in Tora's direction and shook her fist at him. "She's a fool."

Akitada snapped, "Stop that! Did this Kato die from his illness?"

"Yes, sir. The night after the doctor came. The mistress sent for someone to take his body away."

Akitada said, "Let the record show that the maid Kiyo has identified the body left at the tribunal gate as that of one Kato, a guest who died of an illness at the Golden Carp." Turning to Goto, he asked, "What do you say now?"

The fishmonger was trembling. He prostrated himself, knocking his head on the floor, and cried, "Forgive this ignorant person, your Honor! My brother had disappeared and I . . . my eyes are weak. Heaven be praised it is not my brother! But the rest was true. Kimura did fight with Ogai, and now Ogai has disappeared."

Akitada said, "Bring in the other prisoner."

The constables dragged in a burly man in chains. He was quite ugly, with the straggly beginnings of a beard surrounding a slack mouth which lacked most of its front teeth. One of his arms was bandaged to a piece of wood.

The moment he appeared there was a cry from the crowd. A

thin man in a hemp jacket and short pants pushed his way to the dais and fell on his knees.

Akitada rapped for order, and waited impatiently until the constables had made their prisoner kneel next to Goto, whose mouth fell open in surprised horror. The resemblance between the two men was apparent.

Akitada nodded to the thin man and said, "State your name and purpose here."

"This insignificant person is called Kimura. I'm a plasterer and a neighbor of that lying piece of dung Goto. Goto told everyone I murdered his brother Ogai, but there is Ogai, safe and sound." Kimura pointed at the ugly fellow with the bandaged arm. "Goto lied because I built a dam across the creek that waters the land he stole from us, so now the land's no good to him. Please, your Honor, tell him to stop making trouble for me."

Akitada frowned. "I am glad that you have finally come forward with your complaint. Let it be a lesson to you next time to have the court settle your disputes. I have reviewed the documents of your case since they had some bearing on Goto's charges. The court gave the land to your neighbor on the evidence of a bill of sale and tax receipts for more than ten years. Why do you claim he took your land?"

"I have no proof, your Honor," Kimura said sadly, "except that my father did not like Goto and would never have sold him the land."

"Was it not customary ten years ago to have a sale witnessed by two neighbors of the owner?"

Kimura looked blank, but someone in the crowd shouted, "That's true. They changed the law later."

Akitada turned to Goto. "Why does your bill of sale not have the signatures of both witnesses?" he asked.

Goto paled. "A small oversight," he pleaded.

"You lie," said Akitada, nodding to one of the constables who stepped behind the fishmonger with his whip.

Goto shrank from him in horror. "No! Not another beating! I'll tell the truth. Old man Kimura agreed to the deal, but he died before he could put his mark on the papers, so I did it for him. I didn't know about other witnesses." He prostrated himself, crying, "Please have mercy. Please forgive an ignorant person."

Akitada snapped, "Why should this court believe you? You lied when you falsely identified the body. Who put you up to that?"

Goto wiped sweat and tears from his face. "Nobody," he wailed. "I was trying to save my brother's life. That's why I said the dead man was him. So the soldiers would stop looking for him."

The crowd had fallen silent, caught up in the proceedings, but now someone in the back shouted, "Don't listen to the dirty bastard, Governor. He's always been a liar."

The constables made a show of glaring at the offender, and Akitada turned to the fishmonger's brother. "State your name and profession."

"Ogai," the man muttered sullenly. "I'm a corporal in the provincial guard."

"Not much longer," shouted a jokester from the crowd.

Akitada frowned at the audience. He hoped the sweat beading his face was not visible. "I am told," he said to the prisoner, "that you deserted and were discovered hiding in the outcast village. What part did you play in your brother's false accusation of Kimura?"

"None." Ogai avoided looking at Goto. "I know nothing about that. It was all Goto's idea. Just like the land deal. He made me pick a quarrel with Kimura."

"You lying bastard!" Goto grabbed for his brother, but a constable struck his hand with the butt of his whip.

Ogai growled, "I'm not getting anything out of this. You are!

You're the one stole the land. So don't pin your troubles on me. I've got enough of my own."

"You do indeed," said Akitada. "I am glad you understand the seriousness of your position. You are not only a deserter, but you have proven your bad character by committing a rape in the outlaw village that offered you protection and hospitality. I have no qualms about turning you over to your captain for military trial."

Ogai wailed.

Akitada ignored him and turned to his brother. "You, Goto, shall receive fifty lashes and do six months of conscript labor for the government. The disputed land shall be returned to Kimura, the tax payments you made serving in lieu of rent that you owe him. In addition, your own property shall be confiscated and sold. The proceeds will go to Kimura in compensation for the false murder charge. Constables, remove the prisoners."

The crowd broke into noisy cheering. Akitada, aware only of a mind-paralyzing tiredness, raised his eyes and lifted his baton to rap for order before closing the hearing when he saw that Seimei's startled attention was on the side door nearest him.

Akitada turned to look, and there, in the light of a small oil lamp, stood the slender figure of his wife, Tamako, her face tearful and pale with anxiety.

FIFTEEN

THE WRESTLING MATCH

Tora and Hitomaro were sitting in their quarters, their noses in their morning rice bowls, shoveling the steaming food down with the help of chopsticks, when the first eerie sound reached their ears from across the tribunal compound. Both lowered their bowls simultaneously and looked at each other. And both started to laugh.

"That infernal flute!" cried Hitomaro, shaking his head. "It's worse than ever."

Tora set down his bowl and slapped his knees in glee. "It means he's feeling better. I was worried. There's that nasty cut. And then his fretting about the little boy. That has been eating away at him like a hungry rat at a rice cake."

Hitomaro snorted. "Considering our other troubles, what's so special about the child?"

Tora looked at him in feigned surprise. "I don't mean to offend you, Hito," he said, "but any moron can see our master is fond of children. You shouldn't have told him the boy was probably dead. That was not a kind thing to do to him."

Hitomaro flushed. "So that's why he got so angry." A particularly discordant note sounded from the main hall, and he flinched.

"Well," said Tora magnanimously, "we all make mistakes. The main thing is that his wife has taken him in hand. I knew he'd be all right when she looked for him at the hearing yesterday. Did you see his face?"

Hitomaro smiled. "He was embarrassed. Who wants to be checked up on by his wife? Imagine, he never told her about being wounded. She had to find out from Hamaya. I bet she had a few things to say to him."

"Nothing like a good argument with a pretty wife to give a husband ideas about settling the matter without words," Tora said with a grin.

In the distance, the flute started over with the same exercise. They sat and listened to its wailing and shrieking for a moment, then shook their heads and burst out laughing.

"Especially," chortled Tora, "a man who's really fond of children."

The door opened and Akitada's elderly secretary came in. "And what is so funny?" Seimei asked, seating himself.

"Seimei, my wise old bird," Tora greeted him. "Glad to see you up and around again. Why didn't you manage to lose that infernal flute?"

Seimei gave Tora a cold look.

"Welcome," said Hitomaro with a bow. "We are honored by your visit."

Seimei smiled graciously and bowed back. "Thank you, Hitomaro. It's a pleasure to see you well."

"So how's the master today?" Tora asked, undaunted. "Did

222 I. J. Parker

his lady's special touch put things right with him?" He winked broadly at Hitomaro.

Seimei shuddered. "There is no medicine against your foolishness, Tora. As Master Kung Fu said, 'Rotten wood cannot be carved, nor a wall of dried dung troweled.'"

Hitomaro grinned. "What did his lady say about the master's injury?"

"When she found out, she couldn't wait for the end of the hearing. She came to see him for herself." Seimei shook his head. "So impulsive!"

"I like spirit in a woman," observed Tora. "What a day! First the master solves the case of that mutilated body and locates a missing deserter when a whole garrison of soldiers could not find the bastard, and then the master's wife makes him send everyone home so she can take care of him. He went like a kitten, too. And now listen to him." He laughed again.

Across the yard the flute performed a series of elaborate but jarring trills before rising to a climactic shriek and falling silent. They held their breaths, but all remained quiet. Seimei said in a tone of reproof, "You should have looked after your master better, Tora. It's lucky only the master and I knew she was there."

Tora flushed and hung his head.

Seimei was pleased with this reaction and added for good measure, "He was extremely feverish. It was all he could do to walk to his room."

"Oh, come on," said Hitomaro with a glance at Tora. "You know how he is when he thinks it's his duty."

Seimei sniffed. "Her ladyship made him comfortable and sent for Dr. Oyoshi. The doctor's face still looks very bad, but I must say I was glad to make his acquaintance. A very knowledgeable man. His medicine eased my cough right away. We consulted together and made up a special tea from some of my herbs for the master—it was ginseng and mint, with a touch of gardenia and a pinch each of willow bark and cinnamon, so soothing to a weakened constitution—and added an interesting powder the doctor brought with him. The medicine soon produced a sound sleep, and the master awoke this morning feeling much better. This is what I came to tell you. Also that he wants both of you in his office now."

"Well, why didn't you say so right away?" Tora was up and out the door, before Hitomaro and Seimei could get to their feet to follow.

The scene they found in the courtyard stopped them.

A group of about twenty armed and mounted warriors, with Uesugi emblems on their clothes and on the flying banners, waited in the wintry sun in front of the tribunal hall. There were several riderless horses, one of them with a gold-lacquered saddle and crimson silk tassels fluttering from its shining tail and halter.

"Surely not the Emperor of the North himself?" Tora said. "Do you suppose Uesugi's found the boy?"

"Let's go find out," said Hitomaro.

◆

For Akitada, the Lord of Takata was an unexpected and, at the moment, unwelcome visitor.

After a restful night covered with scented silken quilts and protected from the cold drafts by carefully placed screens, he had woken to the tender ministrations of his wife. Greeted with fragrant hot tea and Tamako's soft eyes and sweet smile, he had dressed and started his day in a very pleasant frame of mind in spite of his worries. His morning gruel was subtly flavored with herbs, and a new, much larger brazier made his office very comfortable. And then he had played his flute.

The Lord of Takata and two senior retainers were announced by Hamaya just when Akitada had felt near success with a particularly tricky passage. He reluctantly put down the flute. His visitors looked slightly taken aback by Akitada's scowl.

Now Uesugi was seated on a silk cushion on the other side of the broad desk, while his companions knelt behind him. Akitada watched sourly as his wife poured some wine for his visitors.

Hitomaro and Tora came in, glowered at Uesugi's men, and took up position at the door. Tora said, "I hope it's good news for a change, sir." He received a frown from Akitada and looked sheepish. Tamako smiled and poured more wine, but her husband looked grim.

"I had not expected to meet your noble lady," Uesugi remarked to Akitada, bowing graciously to Tamako and ignoring the others. "I am afraid the tribunal is not a fit place for a refined person in her delicate condition."

Akitada felt a surge of anger followed by fear. Uesugi kept himself too well informed about them. Controlling his voice, he said, "My wife is understandably concerned after the attack on me."

Uesugi looked solicitous. "An attack? I heard a rumor that you sustained an injury. My dear Governor, you should have sent for me instantly. I had no idea that things had gone so far in this city. Too bad that Kaibara has disappeared. He was checking on some trespassers and has not returned. I think I should move my troops into the tribunal compound. That will straighten matters out fast enough. I wonder if the attack on you had something to do with your recent activities? I trust you are recovering?"

Akitada regarded him coldly. "Yes. No thanks to your man Kaibara, however. It was he who attacked me while I was out taking some exercise. I was unarmed and he fell upon me with his sword."

Uesugi jumped up, pretending an almost comical surprise.

"Kaibara attacked you? Impossible. Kaibara would never do such a thing. He had no orders."

Akitada raised his eyebrows. "Then perhaps he anticipated them?"

Uesugi tried to cover his slip. "No, of course not. That is not what I . . . if it happened as you say, it must have been a mistake."

"Are you calling me a liar or a fool?" Akitada asked.

Uesugi reddened. "Neither," he ground out. Then he sat down again heavily and muttered, "It will be best to discuss this calmly. I was referring to a mistake Kaibara made. He must have thought you someone else."

"Who?" Akitada asked interestedly.

Uesugi snapped, "I don't know. No doubt you arrested and questioned him. What does he say?"

Akitada ignored the question. "What is your relationship with Judge Hisamatsu?"

"Hisamatsu?" Uesugi shot a glance at his retainers. "I see the judge rarely. Why change the subject? Where is Kaibara?"

"You surprise me. I recall that Hisamatsu was a guest at the banquet you gave in my honor. He seems to admire you."

The Lord of Takata clenched his fists. "A mere courtesy to you," he said with ill-concealed impatience. "I also asked the garrison commander, a city merchant, the abbot of the Buddhist temple, and your new coroner, Oyoshi. Surely you don't think I have a special . . . relationship, as you call it, with all of them?"

"Ah, no," Akitada said dryly. "Not all of them."

There was a brief silence. Uesugi shifted. "Let me speak to Kaibara," he finally demanded. "I'll have this matter cleared up fast enough. He will be punished for his carelessness."

"I'm afraid that is not possible. He died in the attempt."

"What?" Uesugi stiffened. His retainers reached for swords

that were not there because they had been left outside, and Tora and Hitomaro walked around them to stand on either side of Akitada.

Uesugi unclenched his fists and some of the tension left his body.

Akitada thought that he seemed relieved by the news that Kaibara could no longer be interrogated. And that was interesting. He went on, "Kaibara's extraordinary behavior throws a new light on the murder of your late father's servant and the disappearance of his grandson. I shall have to pay another visit to Takata."

There was a brief silence, then Uesugi smiled. "Of course," he said smoothly. "I shall do everything in my power to assist you!" He reached for his cup, and drained it. "What a thing! Kaibara of all people. And you suspect him of murdering the servant and the boy? He must have gone mad." He paused, cocked his head, and said, "Perhaps not. Perhaps it was a plot. If he really killed my father, I would have been next, no doubt. What a thing!" He shook his head at the monstrosity of such a thought, then added, "I shall certainly be in your debt if you can discover the truth, Excellency."

Akitada looked grim. "I doubt that, but I do intend to investigate the irregularities in this province, both as its governor and its high constable."

Uesugi cried, "So it's true! You have assumed the powers which rest with my family. That is illegal."

"Do not presume to lecture me about the law, Uesugi. It is what I am trained in, and I assure you that I am quite within my rights. When there is evidence of conspiracy against the emperor or his lawfully appointed representatives, extraordinary powers may be used at the discretion of the governor."

They looked at each other. Uesugi's fury faltered, but only for a moment. Akitada caught something in the man's eyes—it certainly was neither nervousness nor fear. He rose to depart with stiff expressions of regret. Akitada barely nodded.

"Pah," said Tora, when he had gone. "The bastard lied. It's easy to accuse a dead horse of eating the missing bale of straw."

Hamaya put his head in. "The doctor, sir."

Oyoshi came in, made a small bow to Tamako, nodded to the others, and then approached Akitada. "You look better, sir," he said and touched Akitada's forehead.

Akitada looked at Oyoshi's discolored face and the scabs left by Kaibara's blade. "Thank you. I wish I could say the same for you. Sit down and have a cup of wine."

Oyoshi smiled. "I'm not a vain man and this will heal. It might have been much worse."

"Surely you will not travel to Takata soon?" Tamako asked her husband anxiously as she poured the doctor's wine.

"Now that the battle lines have been drawn, the sooner, the better," Akitada said in a tone which brooked no argument. "There is no time to be lost. Uesugi did not make any threats, but that does not mean he won't take up arms."

"But it sounds dangerous. And you are far from well," she protested. "Remember what happened yesterday. If not for Dr. Oyoshi's powder, your fever might have moved to the wound, and then you might have died." Her voice trembled over the final word, and tears filled her eyes.

Akitada was embarrassed but softened. "Well, perhaps it can wait until tomorrow." He added more firmly, "You may leave us now."

His wife bowed formally to her husband and inclined her head to the others before slipping from the room with a soft rustle of silk robes and a faint trace of orange blossom scent.

Akitada motioned everyone closer. While they found cushions, he put away his flute, tying the silk cord into a neat bow on top of the oblong box.

"Where did you learn to play?" Oyoshi asked.

"In the capital." Akitada paused with the box in his hands. "I taught myself. The first instrument was a gift from a kind and noble man. I took it as a reminder that a part of my education had been sadly neglected. You see, as a boy I never received any musical instruction. I am quite determined to make up for it now." He was puzzled by the expressions of alarm on the faces of his lieutenants.

The doctor smiled. "How extraordinary!"

"Yes, wasn't it?" Akitada agreed eagerly. "At first it seemed impossibly difficult. But with persistence I may prevail. I realize how important a musical skill is for a man's ability to think clearly. It requires concentration to play certain sequences and it purifies the mind amazingly. Would you like me to demonstrate?" He started to undo the box again.

"No, please don't trouble," Oyoshi said, raising a hand. "You were just about to give us your instructions. Perhaps some other time?"

Akitada put the box away with a small sigh. "Of course." Pulling forward a stack of official papers, he risked another glance at the flute and said, "This is not the same instrument, you know. The first one got broken. It saved my life when I was attacked by a murderer. Remind me to tell you the story sometime."

"I remember. That killer was also a doctor," Tora said with a nod.

Oyoshi stared at him and turned quite pale.

Akitada thought his reaction odd. He said, "Never mind that now, Tora. The most troubling problem facing us is still the missing boy. I am afraid we made no progress at all. I am thinking of returning to Takata to ask more questions. And then there is Hisamatsu. Hitomaro has been invited to work for the judge. He will try to find more information about Uesugi's plans and accomplices. Hitomaro's place at the tribunal will be filled by Genba. Genba's disguise has served its purpose. Inform him before you leave the city, Hitomaro. As for Tora . . ." He broke off when he saw his lieutenants' expressions. "What is the matter now?"

"The wrestling match is this afternoon," said Hitomaro.

"What wrestling match?"

"Genba's match. He's a top contender, sir," pleaded Tora.

Akitada snapped, "Do you mean to tell me that he, and both of you, consider some wrestling bout more important than your duties in the present crisis?"

Oyoshi cleared his throat. "Perhaps I can explain. The wrestling match is a most significant event in this province. In a remote place like ours the citizens follow wrestling with an almost religious devotion since they have little else to look forward to but a long and hard winter."

"Really?" Akitada thought about it. If Genba was a favorite, then his participation would go a long way to create goodwill for the tribunal later on. "I suppose I should have kept myself better informed," he said. "Is Genba really good enough?"

"Oh, yes," said Hitomaro. "You would not recognize him, sir."

"Then I have been remiss," Akitada said with a nod. "We shall all attend. I should have planned to do so from the start. It cannot hurt to reinforce the good impression we made on the local people yesterday."

"You cannot go, sir." Seimei, who had been a quiet observer until now, was adamant. "Not only are you not well enough, but by going out to a public event of this type you invite another attack. Neither Tora nor Hitomaro can protect you against an assassin in a crowd."

Dismayed, they all looked at Akitada.

He frowned. "You exaggerate the danger, Seimei, but to satisfy everyone I shall wear ordinary clothes and watch with the crowd. I feel much stronger. This is only a small excursion, the weather is pleasant, and I need fresh air." He raised his hand to stop further remonstrance. "Enough! I have made up my mind."

◆

In order to attract no undue attention, Akitada wore no cap and only a plain dark gray jacket over his old blue lined silk robe. Oyoshi had calmed everyone's worries about his health by offering to accompany him.

They left the tribunal by the back gate. The street outside was empty except for a few stragglers hurrying ahead of them. The shops were closed and shuttered, and the town seemed deserted. From the distance came the muffled sound of drums.

"Extraordinary," muttered Akitada, striding along and looking about him. "Not even the Kamo festival in the capital attracts such total support."

Oyoshi, being shorter and older, had trouble keeping pace. "You have much to learn about the customs hereabouts," he gasped.

"Yes, and going about like an ordinary person seems a good way to keep myself informed," Akitada said. "I must do this more often." He was enjoying himself.

They had almost reached the end of the street. The curving roofs of the temple loomed ahead through the branches of bare trees. A shrill whistle sounded in the distance, followed by a roar of applause and more drumbeats. The sweet sound of zither music came from the door of a small curio shop. It mingled pleasantly with the drumbeats from the temple. Akitada stopped.

"Ah. Shikata is playing," said Oyoshi.

Akitada listened for a moment, then entered the shop. Oyoshi followed, mopping his face with a sleeve.

The shop was very small, consisting only of a four-mat platform normally open to the street entrance on one side, with shelves on two other walls and a shuttered window on the fourth. The shelves held a collection of musical instruments, lacquer ware, carved figures, games, and dolls. An ancient man sat on the platform with a beautifully decorated *koto* zither before him. He looked at them, then stopped playing and bowed deeply.

"Welcome." His voice was very soft and sounded as if it came from far away.

"I heard your music," Akitada said, slipping off his shoes and stepping up on the platform. "It is very fine, but why aren't you at the wrestling match?"

The old man smiled. "My legs won't carry me any longer. And what is your reason?"

Akitada was pleased with the old-timer's lack of ceremony. Apparently his disguise was good. "I'm in no hurry," he said, looking at the zither curiously. "When I heard you playing this fine instrument, I decided to have a look."

"Do you play?"

"I play the flute. Do you have any good ones in stock?"

"See for yourself." The curio dealer pointed a clawlike hand toward the shelves. "I'm alone here. The boy's at the match."

Akitada went to look.

Behind him, the curio dealer said to Oyoshi, "Sit down, Doctor. Have you been in a fight?"

"It's nothing. I slipped on the ice."

"Ah. I thought it was your new job. Your master is younger than I expected. Do you find him a sensible man?"

Akitada turned. Surely he could not have been recognized by this old relic.

Oyoshi shot him a glance and cleared his throat. "Oh, yes."

"Well, that makes a change," chuckled the dealer. "A flute player, eh? They are either fools or wise men. Not like zither players. Zither players like to show off. Never offend a zither player. His sense of his own importance won't bear it."

Akitada flushed and pretended to examine the wares on the shelves. He recognized fine craftsmanship in every item on display. Shops in the capital had a larger selection, but hardly finer than Shikata's. Incense guessing games, several versions of the shell-matching game, a backgammon board made of several kinds of rare woods, two sets of lacquered writing implements, a handsome silver mirror, several lutes, another zither, assorted figures of Buddhist and Shinto divinities—they were all, in their own way, quite beautiful.

Meanwhile, Shikata played another tune with three picks worn on the fingers of his right hand. When he was done, he said, "Lutes are different. They are for lovers and beautiful women. One of my best lutes is being played by a local beauty. Her protector is a very wealthy man. It is so rare, he was the only man in the province who could afford my price."

Oyoshi said, "Then you have become a wealthy man yourself, Shikata. No wonder you are rude to your friends and betters."

The curio dealer thought this funny and heaved with wheezing laughter.

Akitada said loudly, "There are no flutes here, only games and a few other instruments."

"Never mind," said the old man, turning a toothless grin his way. "You don't want a flute anyway. Better get something for your wife instead."

"A lute?" Akitada smiled.

"Hah," cried the curio dealer with another wheezing chuckle. "For your sake, I hope not. Beauties are all very well, but they make terrible wives." For a moment, his face became serious. "*Terrible* wives!" he repeated, and shoved the zither aside. "Better give her a shell game. A suitable gift from a young husband to a faithful wife."

The old one had no manners, but he was amusing and the idea appealed to Akitada. The game had been on his mind only recently. It was a traditional gift to brides because only two shells made a perfect match, like a husband and wife. But Akitada had thought of it as a symbol of the hidden relationships between people in this province. Still, the game would give Tamako pleasure during the coming months of a long winter and the waiting for the birth of their child.

He looked at the elegant sets and the hand-painted shells inside them and then chose the older one for its special beauty. Finely detailed golden chrysanthemums bloomed among silver grasses on the container's brilliant red lacquer background.

Shikata nodded when he saw Akitada's choice. "You have good taste. I ordered that forty years ago as a gift for one of the Uesugi ladies. It was specially made, very fine work, very costly. It took all my savings then, and I've kept it as a warning to myself not to rely on young men's promises nor on young women's lives, but you shall have it."

"Oh." Akitada hesitated. Their finances were still severely strained after the expensive journey here. "How much is it?" he asked anxiously.

"A silver bar? It is worth much more, but I wish to be rid of it. It depresses me."

Akitada agreed quickly and arranged to have the game delivered to the tribunal as soon as Shikata's boy returned from the wrestling tournament.

"For which we are very late," urged Oyoshi, getting to his feet. "If I am not mistaken, those drumrolls mark the beginning of the final matches."

◆

The contest was staged in the main courtyard of the temple. Brown-robed monks greeted them and directed them to a space where the crowd was not as dense as elsewhere.

Akitada was familiar with the annual wrestling tournament

at the imperial palace and liked the elaborate ritual. It involved musical performances, religious rites to the ancient gods, and colorful decorations, but he had not expected anything like it in this remote northern province. To his surprise, there was little difference in the arrangements.

In spite of the cold, the abbot, surrounded by assistant priests and guests, watched from the broad veranda of the great hall, much as the emperor did in the capital. Below the abbot sat the orchestra members with two great drums, two gongs, and assorted smaller instruments. Across from him, the provincial guard stood at attention under gaily fluttering banners. To one side, the contestants sat on cushions. Each man had stripped to his loincloth and placed his outer clothing neatly folded beside him. The referees, in formal white robes and black hats, quivers slung across their backs and bows in their hands, stood near them, watching the ongoing match. It all looked quite proper and professional.

Akitada, who was taller than those in front of him, saw that two contenders had just entered the ring, marked out by thick straw ropes buried in a thick layer of white beach sand. Their loincloths formed short aprons in the front and disappeared between their huge haunches in the back to emerge in an elaborate bow at the waistband. Steam rose from their bodies in spite of the chilly air. When the closest referee raised his hand, they stamped their feet, raised their arms to show they had no concealed weapons, clapped their hands, rinsed their mouths with a sip from a dipper on the water barrel, and spat. Then they took their places on either side of the dividing line in the center of the ring. At another signal from the referee, they began to circle, then grasped each other, striving mightily to push each other across the ropes of straw and out of the ring.

The crowd began to stir, at first only muttering, but soon moaning or shouting their distress or triumph.

One of the wrestlers was as hairy as an animal, with a shaggy mane and ragged beard; the other, by comparison, looked like a very large pale baby. Man against beast, thought Akitada, amused, and what a weak, naked, and vulnerable creature man was! A clearly uneven match. Only, suddenly the baby seized the animal by his hairy middle and tossed him out of the ring with one mighty heave. A tremendous cheer went up from the crowd, and the big baby bowed, grinning from ear to ear.

Akitada blinked. The baby was Genba. When he had last laid eyes on his third lieutenant, they had parted company outside the city. Genba had always been tall and broad. With his healthy appetite, he had gained weight rapidly after his lean years in the capital, but this clean-shaven mountain of rosy flesh looked nothing like the thick-haired, bearded man he had parted from.

A drumroll marked another match, but Akitada paid little attention to it. His eyes were on Genba, now seated again by his bundle of clothes, waiting for his next, and final turn. The winner of the remaining contests would face Genba for the top prize.

"Good heavens," muttered Akitada to Oyoshi. "You don't suppose Genba will win and be sent to the capital?"

"Certainly not," snapped a bald fellow near him. "Nobody beats Tsuneya. He rips out full-grown pines with his bare arms. He's from my village and I've seen him do this myself."

"Tsuneya's strong and he's a local boy, but he has no technique," cried a pockmarked man with a fierce mustache. "Genba will only have to use his foot to trip him, and when he's off balance, he'll push him across the ropes. I've seen him use that move and many others besides. He's a master at technique because he was a wrestling teacher in the capital."

"You know nothing, fool," cried the bald man, raising a fist, and shouts broke out all around. For a moment it looked as though a separate match would be fought in the crowd, but the whistle of the scorekeeper recalled attention to the official bout, and peace returned.

Akitada felt a touch on his sleeve. One of the young monks was bowing to him. "His Reverence asks the gentlemen to join him," he said.

Akitada glanced across the broad courtyard at the raised veranda of the main hall where Abbot Hokko was seated with other dignitaries before brilliant red silk hangings. The abbot looked back and smiled.

So much for remaining an anonymous observer. Not only had the curio dealer guessed who he was, but now Hokko had seen him and was about to display him to the crowd.

They followed the monk to a rear staircase and then walked to the front of the great veranda. Hokko gestured to two cushions. Akitada sat beside the abbot, and Oyoshi farther back. Mercifully, the crowd below seemed too preoccupied with the contest to pay attention.

"You must forgive me, Excellency," murmured the abbot. "I think you wished to remain unrecognized, but I have an urgent message for you."

Akitada was irritated. "Here and at this time?"

Hokko pointed down into the courtyard. "None better," he said. "All eyes are on the final match."

Below Genba had reentered the ring. His opponent stood already waiting. Akitada had never seen a human being of that size. He towered even over Genba by more than a head and he was all muscle.

"Is that the man they call Tsuneya?" Akitada asked, momentarily distracted.

"Yes. And he will win," remarked Hokko. "Still, his opponent, a stranger to me, has been very good, and that means nobody will pay attention to us."

Akitada resented Hokko's calm assurance about the outcome. He frowned and kept his eyes on the contestants who had
begun to circle, crouching low, looking for an opening to grap-
ple with the opponent or trip him. Genba's adversary was huge.
Bulging muscles rippled across his back and shoulders as he
moved. He was also quick and tricky. Akitada saw him dodge,
feint, and seize Genba several times. But again and again Genba
managed to break his hold or step aside to seek his own opening. It promised to be an extraordinary match.

The confrontation took on a symbolic relevance for Akitada
that far exceeded a mere exercise of skill and sportsmanship. In
his imagination, Tsuneya, the local champion, stood for the
forces pitted against Akitada in this mysterious and hostile land;
Genba, the outsider, was the champion of distant imperial authority. The outcome of the match would spell Akitada's success
or failure.

"How can you be so sure Tsuneya will win?" he asked the abbot without taking his eyes off the wrestlers.

"I know the boy well. His mind is pure," said Hokko simply.
Then he lowered his voice. "The message I have for you was
given to me by an unimpeachable source, so you may rely on its
accuracy. You are to guard against an attack on the tribunal
tonight or early tomorrow morning."

Akitada tore his eyes from the contest just as Genba nar-
rowly avoided being pushed across the rope in a mighty and
roaring charge by his opponent. "What? Who sent this message?" he demanded angrily.

Hokko smiled and shook his head. "I cannot tell."

"Then the warning is worthless."

Hokko sighed. "You will be well advised to prepare a defense, or you and yours will be lost."

Akitada searched the other's face. How could he trust this

man? A Buddhist abbot? His last experience with provincial clergy had taught him that pure evil could lurk behind the mask of saintliness. And why should he find an anonymous benefactor in a province where he had met with nothing but treachery? "How strong a force?" he asked.

Hokko responded with a question. "How many serve at Takata?"

Silence fell between them. Then Akitada nodded. "Thank you," he said. "I will take your advice."

"Look, over there is Captain Takesuke." The abbot pointed to a small group of officers watching from the eastern gallery. "He has been most accommodating in helping with crowd control today. A very useful young man when one needs to keep peace and order."

Akitada looked toward Takesuke, then at the abbot. Hokko nodded.

Thoughts racing, Akitada wondered about the size of the provincial guard and about the Uesugi forces. His information about the strength of either was sadly inadequate. The crisis he had feared was at hand, and he was unprepared. Dazedly he turned his eyes to the courtyard again.

In the ring, Genba feinted, ducked under Tsuneya's arms and grasped the waistband of his opponent's loincloth. He gave a mighty heave upward to lift Tsuneya off the ground, but the other man hooked a leg around Genba's thigh. The two contestants strained in the thin winter sun, their bodies locked together, steaming, their muscles bulging with effort.

And Akitada felt sick at his helplessness. He had brought them all to this: Genba, Tora, Hitomaro, and old Seimei. And worst of all: What was to become of Tamako and his unborn child?

The two wrestlers broke apart, and Akitada clung desperately to the hope that fate would be with them.

Hokko touched Akitada's sleeve. "I almost forgot. There was another part to the message. I am to tell you that the boy is safe."

Akitada blinked. He had forgotten the missing boy over his own danger. For a moment, he did not know what to say. When he found the words to ask about Toneo, a great roar went up from the crowd: "Tsuneya! Tsuneya! Tsuneya!"

Genba had lost the match.

SIXTEEN

THE SHELL GAME

It was only late afternoon, but lanterns swaying from the rafters of the restaurant already cast a smoky golden light over the flushed and shining faces of men; old and young, poor and well-to-do, laborers and merchants were celebrating with the champions of the wrestling contest. Harried waitresses moved among the guests, pouring warm wine and carrying heaping trays of pickled vegetables and fried fish. Someone was singing along with the folk tunes played by an old zither player, and Tsuneya, the champion, was giving a solo performance of a local dance on a sake barrel.

Genba was there also, surrounded by his own circle of supporters. It mattered little to Genba's fans that he had lost the final match; he had come very close to winning, and that was reason enough for them to celebrate. And there was always next year.

Akitada, a stranger to all but Genba, stayed well in the background. He had come to congratulate Genba and because he wanted to gauge the mood of the local people. Their light-hearted revels reassured him, but his thoughts were on the coming night and his attention on the door to the restaurant.

Genba did not look at all unhappy with his loss to Tsuneya and was soaking up compliments, food, and wine in enormous portions. Akitada had put aside his fanciful notions about the contest somehow forecasting his future and felt relieved that Genba had not won. Winning the title would have meant his departure for the capital to perform before the emperor.

Thinking of this, Akitada leaned toward Genba and asked, "Will you continue with your wrestling?"

Genba put down his cup and burped softly behind his hand. Then he grinned, patting his huge midriff. "Sorry, sir. I've had no wine during training and now it seems to put wind in my belly. As for the wrestling, well, I guess it's in my blood. I was amazed how easily it all came back to me. And that was a good match today, sir. Never think they are yokels fresh from the farm or mountain men who live in caves the rest of the year. No, people honor the art hereabouts. Tsuneya has a very good chance of becoming national champion."

"I could see that." Akitada's heart sank at the thought that he was losing Genba after all. But he added bravely, "I had no idea that you were so good. I was very proud of you."

"Thank you, sir." Genba lowered his eyes and scratched his shiny scalp, overcome with embarrassment.

The zither player struck up another tune, and Akitada's eyes wandered to the door again. Nothing. "So, I suppose," he persisted, "you will not wish to take up your duties at the tribunal now?"

Genba stared at Akitada, his smile fading. "Why not? Don't you want me anymore?"

"Don't be foolish!" snapped his master, his nerves stretched as tight as the old man's zither strings. "Of course I want you. I even need you. But you cannot serve as my lieutenant in the tribunal and at the same time engage in wrestling as a profession."

"Oh!" The grin returned to Genba's face. "In that case, don't worry. I was afraid you were angry with me for spending so much time away. I'll be going back to the tribunal with Hito and Tora as soon as this party is over. My landlord's already paid off, and my things are over there in that bundle by the door. Some more wine, sir?"

"Thank you," said Akitada with feeling and held out his cup. His eyes went to the door again. He noted the bundle, then tried to control the sick panic that had been forming in his belly ever since the abbot's warning. But the door finally opened and Hitomaro slipped in, brushing a dusting of snow from his jacket.

Akitada put down his cup and got up to meet him. "Well?" he asked, his heart beating faster.

"No difficulties at all, sir." Hitomaro took a tightly folded and sealed paper from his sleeve and handed it over. "The weather is changing," he added. "The captain seems to think that will make it easier to hold the tribunal."

Akitada felt almost dizzy with relief. He scanned the letter and nodded. "The abbot was right. Takesuke will help us. One hundred men. He expresses his eagerness to uphold imperial authority in this province. Very proper." He gave Hitomaro the letter with a twisted smile. "Perhaps his fervent wish to 'sacrifice his own life and that of all his soldiers in this stand against the military might of traitorous warlords' is a little unsettling, but I am grateful for his support. It seems we are not friendless after all. Come, join us for a quick bite and a cup of wine. I expect we have a long night ahead of us."

◆

Much later that night, past the hour of the tiger, Tora and Hitomaro, in partial armor, sat dozing in Akitada's office. They had spent several hours helping to prepare for the defense of the tribunal. Now there was nothing left but the waiting. Akitada had sent Seimei, who was still weak from his recent illness, to bed.

The smell of wood smoke was in the air, and a faint red glimmering showed through the closed shutters where metal cressets filled with oil-soaked kindling lit the courtyard. Now and then one of the guards outside pulled his bowstring with a loud twang to show that all was safe. Their master slept, wrapped in quilts and protected from the pervasive drafts by low screens. Genba snored in a corner.

"Go turn him over," muttered Hitomaro, "before he wakes the master."

Tora stumbled up, shook Genba, who grunted and rolled onto his side. From the courtyard came the muffled shouts of the sentries. Tora stretched and yawned. "I'll take a look around," he whispered to Hitomaro and slipped out.

Behind the screen Akitada said, "Hitomaro?"

"Yes, sir." Hitomaro got up and walked around the screen.

"Any news?" Akitada was propped on his good elbow and looked wide awake.

"Nothing, sir. It's been quiet as a grave."

"Not an apt comparison, I hope," Akitada said dryly and threw back his cover. He was fully dressed under the *yoroi* which protected his torso and thighs, but the rest of the equipment—shin guards, neck guard, left shoulder plates, and helmet—lay in a corner of the room, where he hoped they would stay. "Is there any tea?" he asked, getting up with some difficulty and sitting down behind his desk.

"I'll get hot water, sir." Hitomaro headed out the door, as Tora came in with Captain Takesuke.

Takesuke, in full armor, light gleaming on the lacquered scales and the round helmet, saluted smartly. He looked tense and excited. "I just received a report from my reconnaissance troop, sir."

"Yes?"

"A force of mounted warriors has left Takata. Most of their banners have the Uesugi crest, but there are also some strange banners with dragons and an unknown crest among them. We have counted at least a hundred and fifty warriors. They are moving slowly, but should get here in less than two hours."

"Thank you, Captain. You have done exceptionally well so far, and I have no doubt that you will hold the tribunal in spite of the lack of fortifications."

Takesuke flushed and bowed snappily.

Tora said with a grin, "The cowardly bastards will turn tail when they see your flags flying over the tribunal, Captain. And if not, we'll give Uesugi something to think about."

"Those banners," Akitada mused. "The dragon is a symbol of imperial power in China. I suppose the judge must have suggested it to Uesugi as appropriate to the status of a ruler of the northern empire. But what is the other crest? Did you get a description, Captain?"

Takesuke handed over a scrap of paper. "It's not very good, I'm afraid. My man was some distance away and it's snowing."

Akitada spread out the scrap and looked at it. The brush strokes looked like something a very small child might make for a tree, a heavy vertical central stroke which sprouted three or four dashes angling upward on each side. "What is it, do you suppose?"

"A tree?" suggested Takesuke. "That's what my man thought it was."

Hitomaro came in with a steaming teapot. He and Tora both peered at the strange symbol.

"Some plant," Tora said. "Seimei might know it."

"If the lines were neater, I'd say a feather," Hitomaro offered, pouring Akitada's tea.

"A feather? Part of an arrow?" Staring at the sketch, Akitada raised the cup to his mouth, then remembered his manners. "Some tea, gentlemen?"

They shook their heads. Tea was bitter medicine to most people.

Akitada clapped his hands for Hamaya and woke up Genba, who yawned, blinked at them, and went back to sleep. Hamaya came in, but shook his head when he was shown the sketch. "If you will wait just a moment . . . ," he muttered, and scurried from the room. When he returned, he carried a document box which contained carefully drawn lists of family crests for all recorded landowners in Echigo and its neighboring provinces. None matched the unknown crest.

"It means nothing," snorted Hitomaro. "The sketch must be wrong."

Takesuke protested, "He's a good man, sir. And he swore that it looked like that."

Akitada nodded. "Curious. Perhaps, like the dragon symbol, it is a new crest. Clearly Uesugi has someone's support, and it is not one of the registered families. Thank you, Hamaya." He watched as the elderly man gathered the documents and left. Hamaya had proved another staunch supporter during this trying time, refusing to return to the safety of his house in town. With a sigh, Akitada said to the others, "Well, we have two hours to find out if Uesugi will attack or withdraw. If he withdraws, tomorrow will be a day like any other. For the sake of reassuring the people, matters must appear as nearly normal as possible. Your soldiers, Captain, had best conduct a military exercise outside the city within view of the road to Takata. It will allow you to keep an eye on things."

Takesuke nodded. "Yes, sir. Tomorrow, sir. But now, if you don't need me, I shall prepare for battle. In case there's an attack tonight."

When the door had closed after him, Akitada said, "A surprisingly good man. He wasted no words. But I am afraid he hopes for hostilities tonight."

"Well, I'd rather have some action myself," snorted Tora. "This sitting around on our haunches is hard on an old campaigner like me. Why don't the three of us get up some plan to defend this hall? With the help of Kaoru and his constables, we could hold this building for days even if Takesuke fails."

Akitada suppressed a shudder. Should the enemy reach the hall, they would set fire to it. That would leave those inside the choice of being burned alive or falling to the swords and arrows of the waiting Uesugi warriors. He said, "No. Unlike you and the captain, I'm betting on a withdrawal. Meanwhile there is unfinished business." When Hitomaro and Tora looked blank, he reminded them, "We still have three prisoners, Umehara, Okano, and Takagi, and the unsolved murder of the innkeeper Sato to take care of."

"We shouldn't be wasting time on that now," protested Tora.

Hitomaro added, "Those three are happy in jail. They are warm and get three fine meals a day. Besides, they've made friends with the sergeant and the constables. Umehara has them running for new ingredients for his soups and stews. The farmer's boy does their cleaning chores in return for a game of dice. And Okano puts on a show every night. Our jail seems like paradise to them, and the constables treat them like their pets."

"Good heavens." Akitada shook his head in wonder. Then he said dryly, "Nevertheless. Winter is coming and their families are waiting. Once the heavy snows start, they will have to stay in Naoetsu till summer. I must remind you that the tribunal budget does not allow us to provide comfortable lodging for extended periods."

"But what can be done when that Mrs. Sato has disappeared?" asked Tora. "Her people haven't seen her, and her parents are worried sick. For all we know, she's been killed, too, and lies buried somewhere. We may never find her."

"Hmm." Akitada frowned and tugged on one of the armor's silk cords that pressed on his injured shoulder. "There is another matter that has been worrying me. I noticed a very peculiar reaction by Oyoshi when he misunderstood something you said. It almost looked as if he thought he was suspected of murder. Perhaps we should have asked some questions about his background. He visited the Satos frequently to care for the husband. And it was curious that he did not recognize his own patient."

"You can't suspect the doctor," cried Hitomaro after a moment's stunned silence. "Why, if we cannot trust him, whom can we trust?"

"That is true." Akitada sighed. He pulled a brocade-wrapped bundle closer and untied the silk cord. Inside was the lacquer box he had bought from the curio dealer. He opened it and poured a pile of shells onto the desk. Akitada stirred them idly with a long, slender finger, then picked out two, holding them up. "In the shell-matching game," he said, "you may pick a shell from the pile and, at first glance, it is a perfect match to one of yours, like these two zither players. But when you look more closely, you see a slight difference. The pictures are identical except for one small detail. One lady is performing on the thirteen-string zither, the other on an older type with only six strings. A careless player may forfeit the whole game by jumping to conclusions."

"I don't like such tricky games," muttered Tora.

Hitomaro picked up the picture of a woman playing a lute

and stared at it before laying it back down. He cleared his throat nervously. "Sir?"

Akitada looked up.

"I, er, met someone. Er, a female." Hitomaro stopped, flushing to the roots of his hair.

Akitada raised his brows. "Am I to congratulate you on this feat?"

"No, sir. That is, we thought we would get married, if . . . if it is all right, sir."

Mildly startled, then pleased, Akitada said warmly, "This is a serious matter, indeed! If she has captured your heart, my friend, she must be a very special woman. But you certainly don't need my permission." He paused, then asked anxiously, "You are not planning to leave, are you?"

"Oh, no, sir. Quite the reverse. I was wondering if we might have the empty storehouse in the far corner of the compound?"

"The empty . . . ?" Akitada began to laugh. "Of course. But please settle your affairs quickly, for I can see that your mind is not on business. My wife will be of assistance. What is the charming lady's name?"

Hitomaro bit his lip, then said defiantly, "Her name is Ofumi. She is wellborn, but misfortune has forced her to earn her living as an entertainer. She is very talented, a fine lute player, and wellspoken, sir."

"A lute player, eh?" Akitada studied Hitomaro's flushed face. Then he nodded. "I am sure that you have chosen wisely. Ofumi shall be welcome in our family."

Hitomaro knelt and touched his forehead to the floor. When he straightened up, he was completely businesslike. "What is my assignment tomorrow, sir?"

Outside footsteps crunched through the gravel. Male voices spoke in rapid exchange. Hitomaro and Tora tensed and looked toward the closed shutters.

Akitada frowned and adjusted the leather-covered plate over his left shoulder. He was not used to wearing armor and found it cursed uncomfortable, especially with the recent shoulder wound. He hoped there would be no fight tonight.

When all became silent again outside, Tora asked, "Should I wake Genba, sir?"

"No. Let him sleep. He has had a hard day."

They all looked at the gently snoring mountain and smiled.

Akitada thought. "There is still Judge Hisamatsu. But I think you are right, Hitomaro; he is merely mad, more of a liability to his fellow conspirators than a threat to us."

"What about the child?" asked Hitomaro. "I could search Hisamatu's place in his absence."

Distractedly Akitada ran a hand over his hair. "Heavens! I forgot to tell you. The abbot says the boy is safe."

"Safe where?" Tora's disbelief was plain on his face.

"He did not say, but . . ."

"Then how do we know it's true?" interrupted the normally courteous Hitomaro.

"The abbot has proved our friend. Besides, I believe Hokko because I think I know who has the boy. No, I cannot tell you. There are still a number of unanswered questions." Akitada moved restlessly again. "If only I could find a way to get into Takata manor again. I know part of the answer is there."

Hitomaro and Tora looked at each other and shook their heads. There was a small army between them and Takata.

"But there is still the dead Koichi," said Akitada.

"What is puzzling about that case?" asked Hitomaro. "Sunada admitted to killing the man, and a whole crowd says it was self-defense."

Akitada shook his head. "I don't care what they say. I don't like it. There was something far too pat about the whole affair. I should have paid Sunada a visit long ago. He wields a great deal of power in the province, as evidenced by his support among the leading merchants."

"Not to mention Boshu and his henchmen," Hitomaro agreed. "Sunada has certainly turned the shipping business to good account. Half the fishermen in Flying Goose village are in his pay, and he controls all the shipping along the coast."

Akitada frowned. "Shipping. It may have some significance in all this. There are our empty granaries, for example. Inadequately explained by Uesugi as a matter of moving the rice to more convenient storage or using it in provisioning the troops fighting in the north." He moved his shoulder and grimaced. "I have not had time to inspect Uesugi's granaries. What if the rice is gone? If there is a bad crop next year, people will starve by the thousands, and I shall be blamed." Suddenly he stiffened and picked up the sketch Takesuke had given him. "Hmm," he muttered, frowning at it, then said, "Wake Genba for a moment."

When Tora shook him, the big man grunted, then sat up and rubbed his eyes. "Are they here?" he asked.

"No, no," Akitada said. "It will be another hour or so. This concerns Sunada. I have the feeling it was a mistake not to investigate him fully. We have had two warnings that all is not as it seems with that gentleman. Did you hear any gossip in town about his personal affairs?"

"Oh, him. After his people attacked Hito, I checked out Sunada, but there was no proof that he knew about it."

"That is not what I meant. What about his private life, his family, friends, his closest associates?"

"Well, he's said to be the wealthiest man in the northern provinces. But he's a loner. No family, no friends. He lives in a large manor in Flying Goose village, near the harbor where his ships and warehouses are, but there's nobody with him apart from his servants. People say he was married once, but his wife died in childbirth. After that he took his pleasures elsewhere."

"Right," Hitomaro said. "One of your friends made a comment about that." Seeing Akitada's questioning look, Hitomaro flushed and looked uncomfortable. "Something about Sunada being a regular at one of the houses of assignation."

Genba nodded. "The current gossip is that he's taken a concubine from outside the pleasure quarter, being tired of the local ware."

Akitada considered this. "Strange that there is no family, no heir to a business of that size," he said. "A son has a sacred obligation to his parents and to his ancestors to provide sons in his turn. The man is either an irresponsible fool or he has been bewitched by some female he cannot take to wife. And that amounts to the same."

Tora grinned. Akitada's own marriage was still quite recent.

Hitomaro shifted in his seat. "If a man has character and loves such a woman, he makes her his wife anyway," he said so fervently that the others stared at him in surprise.

An embarrassed silence fell. Akitada busied himself with putting the shells back into their container and wrapping it again. Genba got up and poured himself some lukewarm tea.

From outside came the sudden sound of shouted commands and then the trotting of men's feet across gravel. They tensed and listened.

"It's just a changing of the guard," said Hitomaro after a moment, and everyone relaxed. Akitada reached for a batch of documents and began reading. Another heavy stretch of waiting began.

"Sir?" Tora interrupted the silence after a while. "I've been meaning to ask you. How did you figure out where that fellow Ogai deserted to? The fishmonger's brother. I've been racking my brains to understand that."

Akitada had already given up making sense of the erratic bookkeeping of his predecessor. He slowly came back from a nagging worry that he should have recognized the significance of the strange crest worn by some of Uesugi's men and focused on Tora's question. "Oh," he said. "Hitomaro told me about him."

"Me?" Hitomaro looked flabbergasted.

"Yes. When you reported your stay in the outcast village, you told me that they habitually took in fugitives on the say-so of the old *yamabushi*. By the way, he is another questionable presence in this province who bears looking into. But to get back to the soldier: You mentioned one man, a rowdy fellow who had lost his front teeth. That fit Ogai, who was on the run from his military duty and recently toothless after a fight with Kimura."

Hitomaro slapped his knees. "How could I have been so stupid! Of course, that's it. Well, at least that's one case solved."

"Not quite. Someone placed the dead Mr. Kato at our gate, and it was not the fishmonger. Whoever did is involved in the Uesugi rebellion."

"Hisamatsu," said Hitomaro confidently. "He wrote the note."

"No, the widow Sato," cried Tora. "She's the one who had a dead man to get rid of."

Akitada nodded. "Yes. They are both suspects. Perhaps when we find the widow, we shall get some answers."

"But where is she?" asked Genba. "We've looked everywhere. That female has vanished into thin air. The constables have searched both the inn and her parents' farm."

Akitada rubbed his shoulder and thought. Suddenly he smiled. "We will set a trap for her," he said. "Yes, that's it. Tomorrow Tora will bring that maid to the tribunal for more questioning—"

"Oh, no!" cried Tora, "I'm not tangling with that wildcat again."

"Ho, ho." Genba laughed, his belly shaking. "The girl's made for you. A wildcat for the tiger. The fur will fly."

Tora shook a fist at Genba.

"Pay attention!" Akitada frowned at them. "Tora, you will keep the girl waiting outside my office for a few hours. Then I shall ask her some unimportant questions and let her go. Genba or Kaoru will follow her. I want anyone who speaks to her brought to me."

Tora shook his head and was about to protest again, but Genba cried, "It's a good plan. The widow has friends we don't know about, and they'll take an interest in what is happening in her case. They'll want to know why you kept the maid so long and what she told you."

"Can't Genba fetch the maid?" asked Tora. "I'll follow her."

"No, you would be recognized," said Akitada, and turned his head to listen.

Someone was running in the hall outside, and they all tensed. Hitomaro got up and went to the door. He was just in time to admit the captain.

Takesuke was out of breath, but his eyes sparkled. "They're here, sir," he said. "An advance troop of eight mounted warriors. They rode up to within a hundred yards and stopped to look at our banners and the burning fires. Then they turned around." He wiped some melting snow off his face and added, "I've sent a good man after them, but I have no doubt that Uesugi is close by with his whole force."

Instantly Akitada's three lieutenants were up and running out the door. Takesuke remained standing. Akitada looked up at the captain. "Was there something else?"

"Er," said Takesuke, "can I give you a hand with the rest of your armor? They will be here very shortly."

Akitada glanced at the pile of heavy leather-and-metal pieces missing from his costume and made a face. "Thank you, no. I don't think that will be necessary, Captain. Keep me informed."

Takesuke stared at him for a moment. Then he compressed his lips, saluted, and withdrew so abruptly that he left the door ajar.

Akitada shivered and stared down at his hands. It was difficult to meet people's expectations and yet that was his duty here. He was no soldier and hoped to avoid bloodshed. As a youth, he had received the customary training in archery and sword fighting, but he had never fought a battle. In fact, his performance with bow and arrow had been distinctly mediocre, though he had always done well with a sword. But Hitomaro, the only skillful swordsman among his retainers, had pointed out that fighting a battle was very different from the practice bouts they had engaged in.

Akitada sighed. The soldier Takesuke had reason to disdain the official from the capital, but he was surely not the coward Takesuke thought him.

A soft rustle alerted him to the presence of his wife. She had thrown a deep crimson brocade mantle over her thin white underrobe, but her hair was loose, sweeping the floor behind her. In the light of the oil lamp she looked like one of the fairies of the western paradise.

"Are you in pain?" she asked softly.

"No," he lied. "We have been discussing the schedule for the coming day. And Captain Takesuke was just here with a report."

Her eyes searched his face. "All is well?"

"Yes. All is well." He reached for the brocade bundle. "I have a gift for you."

She came quickly and knelt by his side to undo the ties. Her hands shook a little. "Ah," she cried when she saw the lacquered box. "A shell game! And how beautiful!"

He watched her excitement, the way she touched the box and opened it, then lifted and looked at each shell with little cries of pleasure, her slender hands graceful. She was trying very hard to be strong and filled him with pride. There was a touch of color in her cheeks, and her silken hair slipped charmingly over her shoulder. Suddenly he felt enormously wealthy and, like any rich man, he was afraid.

"Come," he said. "Keep me company for a little while and play a game with me."

Outside there was the silence of the cold predawn. Here, in the soft light of the lamp, Tamako, who bore his child, placed shells on his lacquered desk with little clicking sounds, and smiled at him, murmuring, "It is the most exquisite present."

SEVENTEEN

THE TRAP

"There!" said Tamako, pushing the pair of shells toward him. "I won again. A perfect match!"

Akitada glanced at the lute players depicted on the shells and then at his wife. Her slender face was flushed and her eyes shone with pleasure. He thought her quite beautiful.

"You did indeed." He sighed with mock chagrin. "This game turns out to be unlucky for me. Twice I was quite close to winning, but you beat me each time."

"Oh," she cried, dismayed, "you won't take a dislike to the game? It is merely chance, you know. The next time it will be your turn to win."

Before he could answer, the door opened and Captain Takesuke entered. He looked tired and glum. The sight of Akitada playing a game with his wife seemed to anger him.

"The enemy has withdrawn," he announced.

"Oh! That *is* good news, Captain," cried Akitada's wife, rising to her feet, her eyes bright with relief. "You will take a cup of warm wine after your cold vigil?"

Takesuke seemed on the verge of declining, but changed his mind. "Thank you, Lady Sugawara." On Akitada's invitation, he sat down, holding himself stiffly erect and meeting Akitada's eyes stonily.

Akitada gave an inward sigh but waited until Tamako had served them and withdrawn to her own room. Then he said, "You wished for an armed encounter, I think."

Takesuke's eyes flashed. "Any man of courage must regret a missed opportunity."

Akitada managed not to flinch at the implied insult. He studied the other man's face and noted the faint tinge of pink, the compressed lips, the defiant eyes. Yes, Takesuke despised him for a coward and had the courage to say so to his face. For such open insubordination, he might well be ordered to die. But Akitada had no intention of losing the service of a good officer and of one who had just saved their lives. Should he explain himself? Tell the man that he wished to avoid the loss of even a single innocent life in this struggle for power? He discarded the thought immediately. There was only one thing a man like Takesuke understood and respected, and that was higher authority.

"Captain," he said coldly, "it would be best if you guarded your temper in the future. Only the fact that you have performed your duties so well restrains me from issuing an official reproof."

Takesuke flushed more deeply and bowed, but the defiance did not leave his eyes.

"It is not," Akitada continued in the same cold voice, "in any case, for you to judge matters which do not concern you. I arrived here with specific mandates and the authority to carry them out. Only his Imperial Majesty himself can change these mandates. You and I merely obey."

He watched as the other man's eyes widened with respect. Takesuke prostrated himself and cried, "This stupid soldier regrets extremely his careless words. They were spoken out of a fervent wish to offer up my life to his Majesty."

"Very well," Akitada said, grudgingly and with a deep scowl. "I suppose you were tired. You may go."

Takesuke scrambled up.

"You may return to the garrison today but keep your men in readiness. I want a continuous watch put on Takata manor. All movements of Lord Uesugi, military or otherwise, are to be reported to me instantly."

Takesuke saluted and left so rapidly that the door slipped out of his shaking hand. Akitada sighed with relief. The night was past and they were safe.

His eyes fell on the desk. The shells still lay scattered. He touched the pair Tamako had so proudly pushed forward and smiled again. It had been a mismatch. The two lutes were not the same, but he had not had the heart to tell her. He started to scoop them back into their containers, when a thought struck him. For several minutes he sat transfixed, staring into space. The lute. Surely it was only a coincidence. But the thought made him so uneasy that he decided he would pay the curio dealer Shikata a visit as soon as the sun was up.

◆

Akitada expected his trap to catch its prey. He took no pleasure in it, but watched wearily and with a sense of impending disaster as events unraveled. The curio dealer had confirmed his suspicion and raised new ones.

Right after his return from Shikata's shop, Tora brought in the maid Kiyo and left her outside Akitada's office to cool her heels and pour vituperations on him and the clerks. Akitada sat with Seimei, immersed in the ongoing chore of checking Hamaya's roster of rice tax payments against the provincial register and old reports from granary masters. They could hear her angry voice wishing all officials to the devil for a wide range of depraved actions.

Seimei made a face and said, "That woman's voice will pierce a rock."

There was a time when Akitada had been amused by the girl's lack of respect for authority, but the persistence of her tirades made him thoughtful. When she was eventually admitted to his office toward noon, he looked at her with fresh interest. Tora, red-faced and white-knuckled, pushed her into a kneeling position, but she immediately raised her head again and glared defiantly at Akitada.

"Lieutenant," growled Akitada, "what is the meaning of the infernal racket this female has been making?"

"Sorry, your Excellency. She seems to think she and unspecified others have been treated unjustly by this administration."

Akitada stared at her with wrinkled brows. "Unjustly? What is your complaint, woman?"

"This is unjust," she cried, waving an accusing arm at Akitada's office and herself. "I've got a living to earn. I can't be spending all day sitting around the tribunal when I've already told everything over and over again. People say there'll never be an end to injustice now."

That phrase rang a bell. The widow Sato had used it, too. "It is of no concern to this court what you or others may think," Akitada said coldly. "Your duty is to cooperate in the investigation of a crime. But I have no time to explain this to you. Answer quickly! Who sent the inn's stable boy away the day before Sato's murder?"

For a moment she clamped her lips together stubbornly.

Then she muttered, "The mistress, I suppose. Or maybe the master. What difference does it make?"

"Just answer the questions," warned Tora, raising his fist.

Akitada asked, "Did the Satos treat their servants well?"

She looked at him blankly. "They were all right."

"That's not what you told me," Tora said. "You called the wife a bitch and said she had lovers and treated you like dirt."

"I did not," the girl snapped.

Before Tora could contradict her, Akitada said quickly, "Very well. You may go for now, but there may be more questions tomorrow."

She got up and walked out with a sniff.

"She's lying," Tora said, outraged.

"Yes. Let's hope Hitomaro has something to report. I am beginning to share your opinion of the girl."

Seimei shook a finger at Tora. "That woman is a she-devil. Let it be a lesson to you not to run after every skirt you see. Not all pockmarks are dimples, you know."

Tora muttered something under his breath and left.

When Hitomaro walked in a little later he was accompanied by a middle-aged female with sharp features and quick eyes. She twitched a silk scarf on her head into place and gave Akitada an ingratiating smile.

"This is Mrs. Omeya, sir." Hitomaro's voice was clipped, his face expressionless. "She stopped the maid Kiyo outside the tribunal and engaged her in conversation." He paused and swallowed. "I happen to know Mrs. Omeya. She runs a house of assignation behind the Fox Shrine."

Akitada gave him a sharp look, but Hitomaro would not meet his eyes.

The woman raised a protest. "A house of assignation? No! The honorable lieutenant is making a mistake." She knelt and bowed several times, bobbing up and down before Akitada.

"I'm a poor widow," she said, "and the house, which my late husband left me, is my only source of income. I rent rooms to respectable single women. One of them has, it appears, fallen in love with this handsome officer and somehow caused him to make such a mistake. I assure your Excellency that I was not aware of improprieties between them till recently, and that I will not permit his visits any longer."

Akitada saw panic on Hitomaro's face. He bit his lip and asked the woman, "Why did you stop the maid Kiyo on the street?"

"The girl works for an acquaintance of mine. I merely passed the time of day."

Akitada raised his eyebrows but did not comment. He told Hitomaro to take Mrs. Omeya away and make her comfortable and to bring Tora and Kaoru back with him.

Hitomaro saluted.

When he returned with Tora and their new sergeant, Akitada sent Hitomaro to find Judge Hisamatsu and bring him in for questioning. He hoped that the errand would keep him away until nightfall.

"Our trap worked," Akitada informed the other two when Hitomaro had left. "Hitomaro brought in a Mrs. Omeya who keeps a house of assignation. It's behind the Fox Shrine and I have no doubt that you will find our elusive widow installed there. Go and arrest her."

"Sir," said Tora, "isn't that where Hito's . . . ?" He faltered unhappily.

Akitada compressed his lips. He said pointedly, "Hitomaro has left for another assignment. Be quick about this. I intend to wrap up the Sato case during this afternoon's session."

The reports from Takata were that all was quiet, but Akitada had new worries to add to his fears of another Uesugi attack. When he entered the tribunal hall, he glanced nervously about. The session was well attended, and this time the crowd was respectful and orderly. Again, Hitomaro was absent, but this time Akitada had sent him on an errand because he wanted him out of the way. But Tora stood by and Kaoru awaited his signal. Akitada rapped his baton and started proceedings.

"Bring in the prisoner, Sergeant!" he called out.

An anticipatory hush fell. When Kaoru reappeared, leading the widow Sato by a chain which tied her wrists behind her back, whispers passed through the crowd. Mrs. Sato looked pale and wild, her silk gown torn and her long black hair disheveled, but she was, if anything, more beautiful than before. When she reached the dais, she stumbled and began to weep loudly.

Akitada had decided to handle the woman with the greatest care. He relied heavily, and perhaps unreasonably, on her wish to appear cooperative. "Untie the prisoner!" he ordered.

Kaoru obeyed and announced in a loud voice, "The widow Sato, wanted for questioning in the murder of her husband. She was found hiding in a house of assignation behind the Fox Shrine. The owner of the premises was not home."

"No, oh, no," wailed the widow, dropping to her knees and wringing her hands, "I wasn't hiding. I'm not a fugitive. I was a prisoner held against my will by that evil woman. I have suffered unspeakable things there."

What now? An excited buzz went though the crowd. Those in front pressed forward to see and hear better. Akitada frowned. "Explain yourself!"

The widow sat back on her feet and dabbed at her face with a torn sleeve. "Forgive this poor, foolish female, sir," she said, giving him a pitiable glance before lowering her lashes. "I'm ashamed to come before you like this—dishonored, dirty, unclean, foul." She suddenly slipped her gown off her shoulders, revealing white breasts covered with bloody scratches. "Look!" she cried. The crowd pressed forward.

Though common sense told him that this was another act and the scratches were most likely self-inflicted, Akitada recoiled.

Kaoru stepped forward and smacked her sharply across the face with the back of his hand. She gasped and collapsed sobbing. The crowd muttered.

Akitada, feeling his ears burn with embarrassment, growled, "Make yourself decent. You are in a tribunal. You will either speak calmly and keep your clothes on or be removed for another flogging."

She sat and pulled up her gown. "Forgive me, your Excellency," she murmured. "I am not myself. First my poor husband is murdered, and then that demon Omeya let her accomplice torture me. Knowing well that I was alone and without protection, she lured me into her brothel by offering me free music lessons. I thought they would ease my grief and accepted. I studied the lute with her, always in the daytime, until one day a man accosted me as I was leaving." She looked around the room as if she expected to see him there. "Mrs. Omeya suggested a meeting, but I refused. Then, three days ago, after a lesson, she offered me a cup of wine. I accepted out of courtesy." She shuddered a little. "The wine must have been drugged because, when I woke up, I was lying naked on the floor, and the man who had accosted me was raping me." She covered her face with her sleeve and burst into fresh tears.

Akitada saw the avid faces of the crowd and rapped his baton. He knew now that she was blackmailing him, but he was helpless to prevent it.

She raised her head and continued in a trembling voice, "After that night I was locked up. The same man returned again and again and she forced me to submit to him for unspeakable and painful acts. If I refused, they beat me or held a candle to my face or feet till I screamed and submitted. He enjoyed hurting me. Each time he came, the old woman greeted him and took money from him. When I called her a devil, she laughed in my face, saying, 'Better be polite, or worse things will happen to you.'" She bowed. "That is my story, your Excellency. I suffered the true torments of hell until your men released me. I ask for justice."

Akitada did not speak immediately. Whatever he had expected, it was not this. The woman was fiendishly clever. Since her charge must be investigated, another public hearing would have to be called. On that occasion, Akitada had no doubt, she would manage to identify Hitomaro as the man who had raped and tortured her. This would, in turn, cause the maid Kiyo to come forward and bring rape charges against Tora. Thus the two women would effectively discredit not only his staff and administration, but his investigation into her late husband's murder and, by extension, his authority in this province.

"I regret extremely," he finally announced, "that any decent woman in our city should have suffered such an outrage. A full investigation will begin immediately. But, difficult as this must be at the present time, Mrs. Sato, you must answer a few questions first."

"Oh," she wailed, to a sympathetic murmur from the crowd.

"Pour the prisoner a cup of water," Akitada instructed Kaoru. A reminder of her present status proved salutary. She pulled herself together and the crowd grew quiet again.

"You recently had a guest die at your inn?"

"Yes, your Excellency. The poor man died of a fever."

"What did you do with the body?"

"Why, the usual. I sent my stable boy to the temple to tell the monks to get it for the funeral. They did."

"You saw them take it away?"

"No. I had much business to take care of after my husband's death. They must have come in my absence."

"How do you know this? Is there a servant who had instructions to turn over the corpse?"

She made a show of confusion. "I . . . I don't really know what happened. We sent the message and left the body outside the gate to be picked up. Later it was gone. Naturally I assumed—"

"What do you mean, you assumed?" demanded Akitada. "It is illegal to dump corpses on the street as if they were so much garbage. It offends against every law of this nation. It offends our gods and the Buddha himself."

She bowed her head. Then she prostrated herself, crying, "This poor widow admits her fault. Having lost a dear husband so recently and being burdened by grief and business worries and ignorant of legal matters, she has gravely offended. I beg your Excellency's mercy."

A sense of defeat settled into Akitada's stomach and sickened him. She had outsmarted him again. He had no evidence that she had plotted with another person to make use of Kato's corpse. He also knew better now than to call her servants to testify against her. The key witness in the murder case, the maid Kiyo, had changed her story. There was only one other move available to him. Though it might well turn out disastrous by involving Hitomaro, it could no longer be avoided.

He said, "You will pay a fine of five bars of silver to the court clerk and make an equal contribution to the local shrines and the Buddhist temple to appease the divine powers and give rest to the dead man's soul."

She murmured her thanks, then asked humbly, "May I go home now?"

"In a moment. I have some preliminary questions concerning your ordeal. Sergeant?" Kaoru stepped up and bowed. "Bring in the woman who is waiting outside."

Mrs. Omeya, the perfect image of a respectable middle-aged matron in her black gown and patterned silk scarf, approached the dais calmly. She ignored curious stares from the crowd, but was visibly startled to see the widow there on her knees.

Kneeling next to the younger woman, she bowed and announced, "This insignificant person is called Omeya, widow and landlady in this city."

Mrs. Sato gasped and turned. She pointed a trembling finger. "That's the one! She's the demon. She held me prisoner in her house."

Mrs. Omeya's mouth fell open.

"Please, Excellency," cried the beauty, "make her tell you about the man who tortured and raped me at her house. She knows who he is."

Mrs. Omeya looked at Akitada. He held his breath. She said, "What is she talking about? I don't understand. What man? I thought you wanted to know about the maid."

"The widow Sato," Akitada informed her, "has accused you of forcing her to prostitute herself to a customer with a perverse taste for cruelty."

"What?" cried Mrs. Omeya. "She has gone mad! Several months ago, a local gentleman of the highest reputation arranged to rent one of my rooms so he could meet her in private. But recently she took another lover. I warned her that she was playing a dangerous game, but she wouldn't listen. Her regular patron is as normal in his tastes as you and me. And as for the other one . . ."

The rest of her words were drowned out by Akitada's baton and the young woman's shrill cries, "Liar! Demon!"

Akitada could not proceed further without bringing Hitomaro into it. He announced, "The woman Omeya, having been accused of abduction and pandering, will remain jailed. The woman Sato will be released after paying her fines but is to appear again in court when called." He rapped his baton three times to close the hearing, rose, and left the hall.

◆

Back at his desk, Akitada attempted to think through the shambles of this situation. He had accomplished nothing. The Sato woman, as deceitful a female as he had ever known, was aware of his intentions and fighting back. She had also once again won public sympathy.

Meanwhile, Uesugi continued to threaten with his troops, and Akitada was no closer to knowing the identity of all the conspirators, nor the precise extent of the conspiracy against the emperor or himself. He was nearly certain that it was not Uesugi who was pulling the strings. An undertaking of this magnitude required intelligence and careful planning, and his estimate of Uesugi was of a small local tyrant without enough brains or energy for such a task. Hisamatsu was somehow involved but seemed mentally even less equipped than Uesugi.

Akitada had already considered Abbot Hokko. Years ago, Akitada had encountered just such a conspiracy. That time, a corrupt Buddhist abbot had used his spiritual powers to recruit and train an army of soldier monks. Hokko was a very different type from Master Joto, but he was trusted and treated with respect by Uesugi and, as abbot of the largest temple and monastery in the province, he wielded great influence. However, in the meantime Hokko had warned him of the attack planned by Uesugi and suggested that Takesuke and the garrison would be loyal to the emperor.

He thought of the others who had been present at Uesugi's banquet. Kaibara was dead, but there was still the troublesome merchant Sunada. He also wielded influence, though with the merchant class. From what Genba had reported, Sunada used thugs to guard his property and spent a good deal of his time in houses of assignation. There was the incident in which he had stabbed his alleged attacker and Akitada suspected him of being connected with local criminals, but neither fact linked him to Uesugi. True, the most recent developments had thrown a new light on Sunada, but Akitada was not ready to accept a mere merchant as the mastermind of such a plot.

There was another guest that night who qualified by both his intelligence and contact with the local community, but Akitada was even less happy with that thought. The trouble was, Akitada had taken him into his confidence without knowing his background. Oyoshi had cured his stomach trouble, but he was knowledgeable about herbs which could cause such complaints in the first place. What better way to win Akitada's trust? Since then Oyoshi had raised serious suspicions. How, for instance, could he have failed to recognize the mutilated corpse of his former patient? And he could have told Kaibara about the secret exhumation of the late lord. For that matter, could his diagnosis be trusted? Akitada recalled vividly how Oyoshi had paled when Tora had mentioned a murderous physician.

He needed time and proof. The Omeya woman was his only hope at present. She was a witness against the widow—or Ofumi, as she had called herself there—and she also knew Ofumi's patron. And Mrs. Omeya, at least, was safe and sound in Akitada's jail.

In less than an hour, he learned differently. Tora burst into his office, crying, "The prisoner has hanged herself."

When Akitada got to the jail, he was met by Oyoshi, who confirmed Mrs. Omeya's death.

Akitada pushed past him and strode to the cell. The three other prisoners, Takagi, Okano, and Umehara, huddled fearfully in a corner of the main room. Kaoru was in the cell, bent over the inert body.

Mrs. Omeya looked much frailer in death. She was lying near the cell door, the cut pieces of her patterned silk scarf beside her.

"Kaoru found her and cut her down," said Oyoshi, who had followed him. "Since I was in the kitchen with the others, I came at once. She must have hanged herself with her own scarf from one of those bars." He pointed to a metal grille in the wooden cell door. Part of the scarf was still tied to the topmost bar.

Akitada said nothing. He tasted sour bile on his tongue, and his blood thrummed in his head like a large temple bell. He did not believe that she had committed suicide. She was innocent of the charges laid against her. He had meant to protect this woman—for purely selfish reasons, to be sure—but had instead hastened her death. His every action seemed to turn to disaster, not only for himself, but for those he came in contact with. If he could not guarantee the life of this one female for more than a few hours, how was he to govern a province? How, for that matter, was he to save himself and his wife and unborn child?

Oyoshi cleared his throat, and Akitada made an effort to pull himself together. Turning to Kaoru, he demanded, "How could this happen? Was she not being watched?"

The young sergeant looked wretched. "She seemed to calm down quickly, and after eating a bowl of soup, she lay down to sleep. So we all had our own dinner."

Akitada looked from the cell of the dead woman to the outer room. The three prisoners stared back with pale faces. He noted absently that Okano was wrapped in some trailing purple stuff and clutched a large paper lantern. "Someone must have been close enough to see or hear what was happening," he pointed out.

Kaoru shook his head. "We ate in the kitchen, sir."

Akitada stared at him. "What? Everybody? There was no one in this jail except Mrs. Omeya and the prisoners?"

There was a pause. Then the sergeant said, "Just Mrs. Omeya, sir. Takagi, Okano, and Umehara were eating with us."

Akitada clutched his head. This, too, was his fault, of course. He had known of the liberties the three had been given since Kaoru had taken over the administration of the jail. It had seemed humane at the time. Now it was one more example of his own unfitness for his office.

Kaoru was distraught. "You see, sir," he tried to explain, "Umehara is the cook, and Takagi said it was his birthday today. So Okano offered to put on a little show. To celebrate Takagi's birthday." When Akitada said nothing, Kaoru muttered, "I know it was against the rules, but we all thought the woman was asleep."

"Did anyone leave the kitchen during your celebration?" Akitada asked tiredly.

A look of understanding flashed in Kaoru's eyes. He paled, thought a moment, and said, "I cannot be certain. At one point, Okano wanted the lights out to do a lantern dance."

Akitada turned to Oyoshi almost ferociously. "Well, Doctor? Was it suicide?"

Oyoshi winced. "Possibly," he said.

"Are you just being mysterious or is something wrong?" Akitada snapped.

Oyoshi seemed to shrink within himself. "What I meant is that one can hang oneself in just this manner with the help of a thin garment and a handy hook or bar."

Akitada went to look at the knot, then turned abruptly to kneel by the dead woman. He checked her face and throat. "There is a small bruise here," he said, pointing.

"When she dropped, her temple may have hit the door," Oyoshi suggested.

Akitada measured the distance between the grate and the floor with his eyes. "She is very short. Were her feet touching the floor when you found her, Kaoru?"

"Not quite, sir."

"Why didn't she use that stool over there?"

There was no answer.

Akitada picked up the cut scarf. He recalled how proudly she had worn it and sighed. "Hand me that chain over there, Kaoru, and help me measure." Between them, they straightened the body and measured it. Then they held the marked piece of chain against the door. Akitada nodded. "As I thought. She could not have reached high enough to tie that knot, which is in any case on the outside of the grate." He looked at Oyoshi. "Do you still think it likely that she committed suicide?"

Oyoshi regarded Akitada warily. "I thought it was possible."

Akitada bent to spread the scarf over the dead woman's distorted face. "I see," he said. "Thank you."

◆

After a cursory meal of rice and pickled vegetables shared with Tamako who, after one glance at her husband's face, refrained from making conversation, Akitada sat alone in his office, sipping lukewarm wine and glumly considering his situation. Someone had murdered the Omeya woman in his own jail. The murderer had come into the jail, called the prisoner to the door, reached through to strangle her, and then hanged her from the grate. It had taken remarkable nerve, but this person had taken such risks before. Hitomaro's testimony against the widow was now useless, and Akitada had lost his gamble. Neither an orderly retreat after resigning his office nor precipitate flight was possible, even had he been able to resort to such shameful solutions.

At that moment in his ruminations, Hitomaro himself appeared. He walked in abruptly, accompanied by a dazed-looking constable, and sat down across from Akitada without a greeting.

Akitada frowned at the constable. "You may wait outside," he said, wondering what the man was doing here. The constable hesitated just a fraction of a moment, then left and closed the door behind him.

Akitada's first impression was that Hitomaro was ill. He was perfectly white, and his eyes met Akitada's with the blank fixity of a corpse's stare. His voice, when he spoke, was flat and emotionless.

"She's dead."

Akitada jumped a little. "What? Who is dead? Are you feeling all right?"

One of Hitomaro's hands moved slightly in a dismissive gesture. "Ofumi. The woman you know as Mrs. Sato," he said in the same remote manner.

Akitada's eyes went from Hitomaro's hand to his robe. There were dark splotches on the deep blue cotton. They spread across the chest and down the front. Hitomaro's right sleeve was stained all the way to the wrist. It dawned on Akitada that Hitomaro wore no sword. He controlled a wave of fear.

"Report."

At first there was no answer. Then Hitomaro's shoulders straightened. Looking past Akitada, he recited in the official manner, "I proceeded to Hisamatsu's villa as ordered and found it deserted. Making inquiries of the servant, I found out that Hisamatsu and Chobei had left during the night, taking a pack horse with them. The servant claims he does not know where they went. I returned to the tribunal to make my report. When I heard from Tora what happened at the court session, I was seized by anger and shame that my foolish indiscretions should have warned Hisamatsu and compromised the case against the widow Sato. I immediately went to the Omeya house. She— the Sato woman was there." He stopped and looked Akitada squarely in the eyes. "I'm under arrest for her murder, sir. The constable brought me here."

EIGHTEEN

THE BROKEN LUTE

Akitada found it nearly impossible to raise his eyes from the blood-soaked sleeve. "Hitomaro . . . ?" he began and faltered.

Hitomaro's voice was abject and his tone oddly detached. "Forgive the trouble I have caused. You saved my life once, but I should have known it was forfeit. I'll make it easy for you. Once a killer, always a killer, they'll say."

A furious anger seized Akitada, and his voice shook. "Make it easy for me? Like Tora, you mean? You think that will make it easy? Why did you do it? You had your life before you. The other time you killed to avenge your wife's honor. And I . . . I thought I had found a man I could trust with my life, a friend, and I counted myself lucky. I would have done anything, faced anything in this godforsaken place to avoid this." He struck the desk with both fists. "Why, Hitomaro?"

Hitomaro lowered his eyes and shook his head mutely.

"Did you think to save me by killing the woman?"

"I thought of it. Also because I was angry that she had lied to me and used me to get to you."

Akitada put his face in his hands and groaned.

After a moment, Hitomaro continued in the same dreamy tone, "I was so angry I could've killed her, perhaps I would've killed her . . . but when I saw her, she looked asleep. Her head was turned away and I couldn't see at first. She wore that white robe—she must have changed into it after she got back from the tribunal—and I thought she was covered with a piece of crimson silk. Strange, I wanted to kill her, but I also felt desire. She was so beautiful . . . lying there."

Slowly Akitada raised his face from his hands and stared at Hitomaro. "You did not do it? She was dead? When you found her, she was already dead?"

Hitomaro nodded very slowly. His eyes were unfocused, staring past Akitada as if at a memory indelibly etched on his brain. "I could see what was wrong when I came closer," he said in the same terrifyingly detached voice. His right hand touched his neck. "Her head was almost cut off. She was lying there in her own blood. It was still flowing . . . and warm. It was her blood that had turned the white silk red."

"Dear heaven."

The toneless voice went on. "I drew my sword and went to look for her killer. In every room. There was no one there, not even the maid servant. Then I went back to her. I . . . I tried to hold her, but her head . . . I thought, perhaps she's not quite dead. So I tried to tie up the wound. I cut some of the fabric of her gown with my sword. That's when they found me. The maidservant and the constables."

"But you did not kill her," Akitada confirmed again, relief washing over him like a warm spring shower.

Hitomaro shook his head mutely.

276   I. J. Parker

"Have you any idea who did?"

Hitomaro plucked at his blood-soaked sleeve. The glazed look was still with him.

"Hitomaro." Akitada leaned forward. "Think! We must find the killer to clear you. Anything may help. Did she complain about anyone? Who were her friends? Was she worried about anything?"

Hitomaro shook his head to every question. He frowned, seemed to make an effort to think. "She asked a lot of questions about the murder investigation. But she also asked other questions, once about the judge." His voice turned bitter. "I was the last man she would have confided in. She used me to get information." His eyes met Akitada's for a moment. "Let it go, sir. This way she cannot make any more trouble. If you start looking for her killer, the enemy will take other action. Now it will just be seen as a lover's quarrel."

"And you will die for it. Even the most lenient court in the capital will balk at passing over a second murder."

Hitomaro's mouth quirked into a ghost of a smile. "Do not worry so. I am done with life."

"What?" With that angry shout, Akitada rose. "Well, then, go to jail, for I cannot save you from that, but do not think that your friends will rest while you submit to trial, sentence, and execution because you are tired of living." He strode to a clothes chest and threw it open, rummaging until he found his quilted hunting robe, heavy leggings, and an old fur-lined cap. Hitomaro watched without comment as Akitada put those on, snatched his sword from its stand, slung it over his shoulder, and then clapped his hands.

The constable peered in.

For so big and strong a man, Hitomaro looked oddly shrunken and helpless, sitting there slumped, his head bowed, and his broad hands resting limply on his knees.

"Take the lieutenant to the jail and lock him up," snapped Akitada.

◆

There was the usual crowd of ghouls when Akitada got off his horse in front of the Omeya house. Only Tora and Genba, both grim-faced, accompanied him. In his hurry, Akitada had dispensed with the usual runners, banner bearers, and scribes, but he was recognized nevertheless, and the people parted before him silently.

Akitada glanced at them, then looked up and down the street, at the neighboring houses, and at the rear garden of the Fox Shrine across the road. When he had an idea of the surroundings, he entered the Omeya house.

A thin girl with a grotesquely large head and thin, greasy hair twisted into a bun tried to fade into the wall of the hallway leading to the rear of the house. Behind her, steep steps led up to the second floor.

"You there!" Akitada called to the girl. "Come here!"

She shook her head violently and turned to scramble up the steps with the agility of a monkey.

"Get her!" Akitada snapped to Tora and walked into the first room. It was furnished as a reception room and empty. He continued down the corridor, opening doors and closing them again on unoccupied rooms. Upstairs he heard Tora's pounding footsteps and the squeals of the girl.

At the end of the corridor a constable suddenly appeared from one of the doors. "Out!" he shouted, waving both hands. "No one is allowed! How many times do I have to tell you bastards . . . ?" As Akitada stepped from the shadows, the constable fell abruptly silent and dropped to his knees. Akitada walked around him and into the room the man had come from.

The murder scene was as Hitomaro had described. Genba,

who came in behind him, gasped audibly, then went to feel for a pulse behind the dead woman's ear. A heavy, sweet smell of blood mingled with an exotic blend of incense. The bloodied gown, which had seemed like crimson satin to Hitomaro, was now a dark rust color, and the puddle the woman lay in had partly congealed and partly soaked into the grass mat.

Akitada bent to undo the blood-soaked bandages Hitomaro had wrapped around the severed neck. Both neck and chest looked like a single massive wound, but the pale face and glossy black hair were untouched and still achingly beautiful. Akitada stood looking down at the woman he had known as Mrs. Sato, but who had also been Hitomaro's Ofumi.

Tora walked in, dragging along the maidservant. "She won't talk, sir. Doesn't make a sound. Maybe the shock has addled her brain." He glanced at the body and whistled. "Merciful Amida! I can see how it would." He released the girl.

She scuttled into a corner, where she cowered on her knees and bobbed up and down in silent obeisance.

Akitada approached her cautiously. "Don't be frightened, girl," he said. "Nobody is going to harm you."

She bobbed more violently.

"Stop that!" Akitada ordered, stamping his foot. "Look at me!"

She became still and raised small, anxious eyes to his face. Her bony, work-reddened hands hovered before her face and then touched her ears.

"Were you here during the day?" Akitada asked.

She only looked at him with wide, frightened eyes.

"Did you see anyone in this house after the midday rice?"

Still no answer.

"Were you here when this woman returned? Speak, girl! You won't be punished."

"Sir?" Genba joined him. "I think she's a deaf-mute. I've

seen them make that sign with their hands. You know, pointing to their mouth and ears."

"Good heavens, what next?" said Akitada in disgust. "A witness who may have seen the killer and can't speak."

"She may read lips. Let me try, sir," Genba offered and crouched down next to the girl.

Akitada turned away. The room's luxury and good taste astonished him. Even the mat on which the body lay was at least two inches thick and woven of the finest grass, its edges bound in purple brocade. He bent to touch its surface. The mat was smooth, soft, and springy and must have cost a great deal. Around it stood curtain rails of painted lacquer draped with robes embroidered in silk and gold threads with a design of cherry blossoms, birds, and pine branches. The brazier, its coals barely glimmering under a thick layer of ashes, was a finely chased bronze replica of a pair of mandarin ducks, symbol of faithful lovers. The four clothing boxes of gold-dusted lacquer, each decorated with symbols of the season—plum blossoms for spring, wisteria for summer, chrysanthemums for autumn, and snow-covered grasses for winter—stood stacked against a wall. He flung them open one by one. Each contained a rich wardrobe of women's robes for that time of year.

"She lived pretty well for a whore," Tora commented.

"What?" Akitada was still looking about for an object that should have been there but was not.

"It's clear where Hito's money went," Tora said, pointing at the clothes chests.

"Not Hitomaro's money. Someone else's," said Akitada. "All of these things are of extraordinary quality and consummate taste. The innkeeper's widow, though apparently a woman of many talents, did not have the education to select such treasures. Neither would she have found them in this city."

Genba scrambled to his feet and joined them. "Sorry," he said. "The girl's not just deaf and dumb, but a bit slow. She kept shaking her head when I asked if Ofumi had had any visitors. It seems she found the body when she came to turn down the bedding and she ran to get the constables. When they returned, they found a man, covered with blood, and with a bloodstained sword in his hand, crouching over the dead woman. I think it must've been Hito. She believes he was the killer. She kept pointing to the curtain stands. Apparently she thinks that he was hiding behind them when she came the first time."

"That is no help at all!" Akitada snapped. He caught a glimpse of the girl's pale, frightened face as she slunk from the room.

"If it wasn't Hito, then who?" asked Tora. "I mean who else would want her dead? The bastard who hanged the Omeya woman in jail so she wouldn't testify against this one wouldn't turn around and kill her, too. It doesn't make sense."

"Maybe not," Genba said hotly, "but it wasn't Hito. I'd bet my life on it. He loved that fox of a woman. And besides, he would never kill a defenseless female."

"Hmm," muttered Akitada. "Genba? When you asked that servant if anyone had come to see Ofumi, did you use the word 'visitor'?"

"Yes. Why?"

"Look around you. Someone may have called who was not, in the servant's eyes, a visitor but had a right to be here. Come on, both of you. We are going to Flying Goose village."

◆

The road to the coast was wide and lined with stands and road-side eateries, among them the shrimp shack where Hitomaro had first tangled with Sunada's henchman Boshu. The wind carried the tangy smell of the ocean. Now, in this icy weather and at this time of day, the road was deserted. The gusts buffeted them and tossed the horses' manes and tails. They were thankful when the gray eastern sea came into sight beyond a forlorn cluster of fishermen's wooden shacks and more substantial warehouses. There were only traces of dirty snow about here, but the sky was an ominous gray and the waves roared and crashed onto the rocky shore. Far out, a fleet of three merchant vessels tossed and bucked on their anchor ropes. All the smaller fishing boats, hundreds of them, lay pulled up on the beach, weighted down with heavy nets and rocks.

Barely glancing at the whitecapped sea, Akitada rode straight through Flying Goose village toward the only buildings important enough to be Sunada's residence. The large compound was enclosed by dirt walls and shaded by windswept pines.

Its main gate was made of heavy beams and boards, studded with big iron nails which had left bloody trails of rust on wood grayed by the wet and salty sea air.

Tora pulled his sword from the scabbard and delivered a series of resounding knocks with its hilt. "Open up in the name of the governor!" he bellowed.

The right side of the gate opened soundlessly on well-oiled hinges. An elderly one-legged man on a crutch stared up at them. "What is it?" he croaked in the local dialect. "The master's resting."

"Out of the way!" Tora urged his horse forward and the man twisted aside, grabbing in vain for Tora's bridle before he fell.

They galloped past large storehouses, stables, and servants' quarters to the main residence. There they dismounted, pushed past another gaping servant, this one missing an arm, and into the interior of the house.

Akitada saw with one glance that the mansion was spacious and built from the finest woods but in the style of well-to-do merchants' houses. He turned to the servant who had fallen to his knees before him and seemed to be objecting in his heavy dialect.

"What is he saying?" Akitada growled to Genba, who was more likely than Tora to have picked up the local patois.

"I think he says that his master's sick." Genba sounded dubious and added, "The fishermen hereabout talk differently from the townspeople."

"Sick? Ask him if Sunada has been out today?"

Genba did so, but the man kept shaking his head and repeating the same phrase while wringing his hands.

Akitada grumbled, "Come on! We'll find the patient ourselves."

The anteroom opened into a large, gloomy reception hall where heavy pillars rose to the high rafters. The tatami mats looked thick and springy, and on the walls paintings on silk— courtiers and ladies moving among willow trees and graceful villas—glimmered in the dim half-light. At the far end, a long dais stretched the entire width of the room. It held only a single red silk cushion in its center.

Genba muttered, "If this is how a merchant lives, sir, Takata manor cannot be much better."

"Not much more impressive anyway, " said Akitada. With a glance at the paintings, he added, "And less richly furnished, I think."

"Come on," cried Tora from a corner behind the dais. "Here's a door to the private quarters."

They entered a smaller room, a sort of study. A lacquered desk with elegant ivory writing utensils stood in the center. Handsomely covered document boxes lined one wall, and doors opened onto a small garden. But this room, too, was quite empty and had the tidiness of disuse: a new ink cake, an empty water container, new brushes, and neat stacks of fine writing paper.

"Let's look in those boxes," said Genba. "I bet that's where he keeps all his business accounts."

"Later!"

In the dim hall, the servant still hovered near the other end of the dais. When he saw them coming back, he ducked behind one of the pillars and was gone.

Tora cursed. "Where did that sneaky bastard go? We'd better catch him before he warns Sunada."

"After him, Tora," Akitada said. "Genba and I will check the rooms."

They opened door after door on empty room after empty room. The roar of wind and tide was faint here; only the soft hiss of the sliding doors on their well-oiled tracks and the sound of their breathing accompanied them through luxurious, unlived-in spaces. There were more paintings, carved and gilded statues, pristine silk cushions precisely positioned and unmarked by human limbs, lacquered armrests, bronze incense burners without a trace of ash, copper braziers without coals, innumerable fine carvings, and containers of wood, ivory, jade, or gold.

"It's like he's emptied out a treasure house to furnish this place for a bride," said Genba in one room, looking into brocade-covered boxes of picture scrolls and illustrated books which filled the shelves of one wall.

They reached the end of the hallway without seeing anyone. Heavy double doors led outside to a broad veranda that extended across the back of the villa and continued along two wings on either side. Below was a large garden. Pines tossed in the wind and large shrubs hid paths leading off in all directions. Roofs of other buildings, large and small, were half-hidden by the trees.

"Which way now?" asked Genba, looking from side to side. "Should I shout for Tora?"

"No. Listen! I thought I heard music."

But the rhythmic boom of the sea and creaking and rustling of the trees covered all human noise.

Akitada shook his head. "It must have been the wind. You take the right wing! I'll go left."

"What about the garden?"

"When you're done. We'll meet by that bridge over there."

Akitada strode down the gallery, flinging open doors, checking more empty rooms. One of them contained a large painting of three ships at sea, the same ships, unless he was mistaken, as those in the harbor. Some odd-sized document rolls lay stacked on a large chest and he quickly unrolled the top one. It was a map, carefully prepared, of an unidentified shoreline. Strange symbols marked the land, and lines separated provinces and districts. On the water tiny fleets approached harbors. He was about to roll it up again, when he noticed one of the symbols. It was the emblem drawn by Takesuke's soldier, from the mysterious banner carried by some of Uesugi's troops. Proof that Sunada was at the heart of the conspiracy.

Akitada ran down the steps at the corner of the building and joined Genba on the bridge.

"Well?" he asked, seeing Genba's face.

"The whole wing's one huge room, sir. But I couldn't get in. It's locked."

"Come," cried Akitada running ahead. "That must be where he is. Couldn't you force the door?"—this last in a tone of frustration. Genba was, after all, immensely strong. If he could lift and toss a trained giant from the ring, why could he not break open a mere door?

The answer became obvious. This was no ordinary door. Its hinged, double-sided panels were made of thick slabs of oiled wood and embossed with bronze plates incised with gilded ornamentation. The locking mechanism was hidden in a bronze plate decorated with the same emblem as on the banners and the maps, only here there was no doubt what it represented: an ear of rice. And now Akitada understood the large warehouses outside. No doubt they held a good part of the province's rice harvests. The crest was that of a rice merchant. Sunada.

Akitada listened at the door. Nothing. Inside all was as silent as a grave. He turned away when he heard a cry of pain in the garden. They rushed down the stairs and along a path that led into the shrubberies. At a fork, they separated. Akitada found a rustic garden house, little more than a tiled roof supported by slender wooden columns. A heavy layer of dead vines curtained it. He thought he saw the vines move and flung the brittle tangle aside. Nothing. He turned to leave when someone flung himself on him, knocking him down.

"Got you, bastard!" snarled Tora, yanking Akitada's arms back. Akitada shouted at the pain in his shoulder, and the rest was confusion, because Genba arrived next and swung at Tora, knocking him across the narrow space and against one of the pillars. With a crash, the pillar gave and the garden house collapsed.

They disentangled themselves. Tora rubbed his back. "Sorry, sir. When I saw someone slipping into the garden house, I . . ."

"And I heard the master cry out," Genba said, "and thought some scoundrel had got hold of him. This is a very strange place. Where are all of Sunada's people? There is nobody here but us and two old cripples. Why surround yourself with cripples when you're as rich as Sunada?"

Akitada massaged his throbbing shoulder. "Sunada is a strange character. I remember he behaved with the utmost humility at Takata, but in the city he swaggered among the merchants and attempted to control my staff. Apparently he lives alone here, in a house which is large and empty—for we have seen neither bedding nor clothes boxes for a family—yet in the city he keeps women and indulges in lavish and luxurious parties. He hires cutthroats to intimidate the little people outside, but employs injured fishermen who can no longer make a living on the sea."

"Fishermen?" Genba asked, surprised.

"The two servants. Both of them are local men by their dialect and both are maimed."

"No wonder they wouldn't help us."

"Yes. But I wonder why the houseman looked so worried." Akitada turned to Tora. "Did you see anything unusual?"

Tora grumbled, "This whole place is haunted. There are ghosts in the trees playing lutes."

Genba laughed. "You've got to stop seeing ghosts all the time, Tora. It's addling your brains."

"Playing lutes?" said Akitada, grasping Tora's arm. "Where did you hear that? Show me!"

Tora retraced his steps. Suddenly, faintly, through the whistling of the wind in the boughs, they heard it. Someone was playing a lute.

Tora froze. "There. That's what I heard."

Akitada pursued the sound, followed by Genba and, reluctantly, Tora. They broke through a thicket at the end of the property and stood before a small pavilion. Beyond, the dunes began and sere grasses grew all around and up to its bleached wooden steps. The wind was loud here, but so was the sound of a lute, inexpertly plucked, but hauntingly sad in this desolate place.

Akitada's face was grim. He turned and said, "Both of you wait here till I call you."

He walked quickly up the steps of the small veranda, almost stumbling over the huddled shape of the one-armed servant who was cowering there, and flung open the door.

The room was tiny. All it contained were a pristine grass mat and the owner of the estate. If he had noticed Akitada's abrupt entrance, he gave no sign.

Sunada sat hunched over a beautiful lute, muttering to himself as he picked out a vaguely familiar tune. "The snows will come, and the snows will go," he sang softly, "and then my heart will melt into a flood of tears."

"A famous old tune," Akitada remarked, closing the door behind him. "Where did you learn it?"

Sunada did not look up. "She used to sing it." His voice was brittle, like the dried leaves of the summerhouse. "She sang beautifully. Astounding in someone of her class. I fell in love with her when I first heard her. Of course, there was also her physical beauty, but other girls had that." He paused to pluck more notes, random ones, and smiled. "I have traveled far and had many women. She was like none of them."

Akitada quietly lowered himself to the floor.

"How did you find me?" Sunada asked almost casually.

"The lute. The curio dealer told me that the woman Ofumi had one that was so rare and expensive that it could only be purchased by you."

"Ah. I did not plan this. One does not plan an obsession. Imagine. The daughter of peasants and wife of a doss-house keeper on the post road! She could not speak properly when I first met her."

"How did you meet?"

He waved a dismissive hand. "Pure chance. The Omeya woman used to find entertainment for me. One day I came to make arrangements for a small party and found her giving lute lessons to a perfect goddess. I canceled the party and spent the night with my goddess instead."

"She was willing?" Akitada thought of the widow's claims that she had been forced to submit to Mrs. Omeya's customer.

Sunada finally looked at him, surprised. With a cynical grimace, he said, "Naturally—eager even, as soon as the old one explained who I was. Oh, I always knew Ofumi for what she was, but I wanted her, needed her . . ." He grimaced again and broke off. Raising the lute with both hands above his head, he brought it down violently, smashing the delicate inlaid woods into splinters, and tearing at the strings with frantic fingers until the wires parted with a sound that hung in the room like a scream, and blood ran from his hands.

"It was you who killed her, wasn't it?" Akitada said softly.

"Dear heaven!" Sunada looked at his bleeding hands and began to weep. "This woman whom I raised from the gutter to become my consort, for whom I built and furnished this house, for whom I did unimaginable things—she betrayed me. Betrayed *me* with an oaf of a soldier. One of yours, Governor." He clutched his head and rocked back and forth in his grief.

"You did not answer my question," Akitada persisted.

Sunada lowered his hands and looked at Akitada. "Come, Governor, don't plague me with questions. Nothing matters any longer."

"What about Mrs. Omeya? Did you kill her?"

Sunada frowned. "That woman! You know what she whispered to me? That your lieutenant had been spending his nights with my future wife. She thought I could use the information against you." Sunada laughed. "The fool!"

Silence fell.

Akitada said, "I am arresting you for the murders of the woman Ofumi, her landlady, Mrs. Omeya, and the vagrant Koichi."

Sunada ignored him. He fingered the broken lute. "Music fades . . ." He raised his eyes to Akitada's. "You know," he said with a crooked smile, "Uesugi underestimated you, but I never made that mistake. A worthy adversary is preferable in a contest for power, don't you think? And I was winning, too. Wasn't I?"

Yes, thought Akitada, Sunada had been winning all along. Had it not been for the merchant's fatal obsession with that arch seductress, Akitada would have been powerless to prevent a disastrous uprising. Aloud he said, "No. The gods do not permit the destruction of divine harmony. You raised your hand against the Son of Heaven."

Sunada sighed. "Always the official view."

"It is over, Sunada."

The other man nodded. "I no longer care. You will find what you seek in my library, the large room in the west wing. Behind the dragon curtain are documents, plans for the insurrection . . . it will be enough to end my life . . . and the lives of others."

NINETEEN

THE TURNING WHEEL

"*W*ell done!" grunted Hitomaro, parrying Akitada's long sword and stepping back.

Both men were stripped to the waist, their bare skin covered with the sheen of perspiration on this gray and cold morning outside the tribunal hall. Akitada smiled briefly and checked the bandage on his left shoulder. "I think it's coming back to me," he said. "I was afraid my arm had stiffened."

"One rarely forgets the right moves."

Hitomaro's face did not lose its gravity. Akitada had hoped that the workout would lift his lieutenant's spirits, but he had not once lost his detachment. Akitada did not like that faraway look in Hitomaro's eyes; he seemed to be gazing into an unseen world, listening for an unheard sound.

"I would not wish to disgrace myself before Takesuke," Akitada joked lamely. "He already has a very poor opinion of me." They all thought that a battle was unavoidable. Men would die and, unlike Sun Tzu, Akitada did not believe that men ever died gladly. The responsibility frightened him more than his own death, but he could not falter now.

Hitomaro resumed his position. They reengaged and continued their practice until the nearby monastery bell sounded the call for the monks' morning rice. When Captain Takesuke arrived, they were bent over the well bucket, sluicing off their sweat.

Takesuke smiled when he took in the significance of the sword practice. "I'm happy to see you quite recovered, Excellency," he said with a smart salute. "I also have made preparations. You will be proud of the troops. In fact, I came for your Excellency's banner so we can make copies to carry into battle."

The feeling of well-being after the exercise evaporated with the water on Akitada's skin. Here was a man after Sun Tzu's heart. He shivered and reached for a towel. "Hitomaro will supply you with what you need. The problem is getting Uesugi out of Takata. That manor is too strongly fortified."

Takesuke said confidently, "He will fight. How can he refuse and retain his honor now that he has openly declared himself ruler of the northern provinces and demanded our formal submission?"

Akitada shot him a sharp glance as he tossed away the towel and reached for his gown. "Just how do you know that, Captain?"

Takesuke pulled a folded, bloodstained sheet of paper from under his shoulder guard. "One of my men brought this from Takata. When it got light enough, they noticed two posts that hadn't been there before. They sent a man to investigate. He found two fresh corpses tied to the posts. They had been disemboweled and one had this attached to his chest with a dagger."

Sickened, Akitada unfolded the paper. The writing was large and crude, the characters in the middle obliterated by the blood-soaked hole left by the dagger, but the content was clear:

"The traitor Hisamatsu sends this greeting to Sugawara and Takesuke: Bow to the new Lord of the North or suffer as I did."

"Hisamatsu is dead," Akitada said tonelessly, handing Hitomaro the message.

Hitomaro read and nodded. "He had no chance. What good is a raving lunatic to Uesugi? I suppose the other one is Chobei?"

Takesuke nodded.

Akitada said, "They were probably killed last night, a whole day and night after Hisamatsu went to Takata. That means Uesugi did not act until he got news of Sunada's arrest."

Hitomaro looked surprised. "You mean he blamed them for that?"

"Perhaps." Akitada refolded the paper and put it in his sleeve. "Or perhaps he had been waiting for Sunada's instructions. In any case, he keeps himself informed about developments in the city."

"The faster we move on him the better," Takesuke said eagerly. "When will your Excellency give the order to march?"

The man's eagerness to sacrifice himself and untold numbers of other humans on the battlefield was too much for Akitada. He swung around angrily. "Have you not been listening, man? We cannot take the manor. It is inaccessible—as you should have realized long ago. And I doubt that Uesugi will accommodate us by coming out. Get it into your thick skull and stop badgering me!"

Takesuke blanched. He bowed. "My apology."

Akitada bit his lip. He was ashamed of his outburst and tempted to leave the awkward scene for the safety of his office. Eventually he said grudgingly, "There is still a great deal of paperwork to be done before we can bring formal charges against Uesugi, but I suppose we must make ready to attack."

Takesuke got up and stood to attention. "Yes, Excellency. Thank you, Excellency."

Akitada sighed. He could not afford to antagonize this man. "Perhaps tomorrow, Captain," he said and walked away.

◆

The tribunal archives had lost their dusty, musty air of disuse. On a closer inspection of Sunada's house, the warehouses had held much of the province's rice stores, and the locked room had guarded the secrets of a planned uprising.

Now everywhere in the tribunal piles of document boxes covered the floor. The two clerks were bent over papers, reading, making notes, and sorting Sunada's records into neat stacks. Seimei bustled about, checking and labeling the stacks and making notes. A harassed but happy Hamaya greeted Akitada.

"Excellency, I am amazed," he cried. "You have uncovered an enormous conspiracy! Nobody could have dreamed of such a thing. And it is all here. Lists of conspirators' names, contacts in other provinces . . ." He snatched up one of the piles and followed Akitada into his office. "Look! These are the rice records for the last year. This is the Uesugi seal. Sunada paid Uesugi for eight thousand bales of the provincial fall harvest, and the amount is less than half of its value. According to Uesugi, that rice went to the troops in the north."

Akitada suppressed his impatience. Hamaya had worked hard and accounted for part of the missing governmental rice stores. He peered at the figures, nodded, and said, "Excellent work, Hamaya. You and your clerks are to be congratulated. We can charge Uesugi with diverting government property to his own uses. Start drawing up the paperwork."

Hamaya bowed, pink with pleasure. "Immediately, sir. Oh, I almost forgot . . . look at this. It's a letter from someone in the capital, I think. Stuck in the pages of the merchant's personal accounts. It must be a hoax. Surely it couldn't be . . . treason?"

Akitada snatched the letter from Hamaya's hand, glanced at

it, and felt his heart stop. "Someone's private joke, no doubt," he told the head clerk and tossed the paper carelessly on his desk. "Let me know when the charges are ready."

He waited until Hamaya had left his office, then read the letter again. It was addressed to Sunada and encouraged him in his plan to establish a separate northern rule with promises of high appointment in the capital if his endeavor could influence imperial succession. The letter was unsigned, but Akitada had recognized the seal. It belonged to one of the sons of the retired emperor. This young man had briefly served as crown prince, but had been replaced in the succession by a child, the son of the present empress and grandson of the Fujiwara chancellor.

Because of Fujiwara marriage politics, intrigue within the imperial family was always a danger, and punishment usually fell heavily on the innocent, on loyal servants and dutiful officials along with their families, rather than the highly placed principals.

Therefore Akitada stared at the elegant paper with particular horror. It lay on his desk between the black arrow which had killed Kaibara and saved Akitada's life and the lacquered box of Tamako's shell-matching game. Men played deadly games everywhere. Not only was he about to risk his life to secure this province, but the letter represented a bloody upheaval about to happen in the capital, and on his, Akitada's, report. Yet duty required him to make this report. By a twist of fate, he was forced to destroy lives, careers, and families, perhaps his own included, when he had struggled all along to avoid bloodshed.

Akitada knew that another man would burn the letter and forget its contents. Echigo was a remote province. If the insurrection collapsed here, the disaffected prince in the capital might well give up his aspirations.

But weighed against the present and future danger to the emperor, this was not an option open to Akitada. What if the news of the collapse of the northern uprising prompted desperate action in the capital? And what guarantee was there that an ambitious prince might not plot again, and again?

He raised his hands to his face and groaned.

"What is the matter, husband?" Tamako had entered silently, wide-eyed with concern. She looked frail in the morning light, her hands resting protectively on her swelling body.

Akitada smiled bleakly. "I am afraid I may have failed both of us," he said. "I no longer know what is to be done." He closed his eyes. "And I think I am about to fail the emperor no matter how I choose to act."

He heard the rustle of her silk gown as she sank down next to him, then felt the warmth of her body pressed to his. "You cannot fail me," she whispered, "no matter what you do. It is not in you." She withdrew a little. "You will fail yourself only if you shirk your duty. And how can you fail the emperor if you obey his laws and perform your duty?"

He shook his head and smiled a little at her fervor. "Here," he said, pushing the letter toward her. "This affects you and our unborn child as well. Read it!"

She read. "Whose is this?" she asked.

"It is Prince Okisada's seal."

She drew in her breath sharply. "I see." Her eye fell on the arrow on his desk. "Would you aim an arrow into a dark cave because you thought a bear was moving inside?"

A bear? A cave? What did she mean? Perversely, Tamako's words conjured up another memory: White Bear, Kaoru's dog. Kaoru's long bow. Akitada's hand went to the arrow. By its length and rare feather it was a contest arrow, not an ordinary soldier's issue. He recalled Hitomaro's amazement at Kaoru's bow, his skill with it. Like his coroner, his new sergeant of constables was an enigma.

The more he thought about it, Kaoru's education and his

difference from the other outcasts were mysteries he had not pursued because there were more urgent problems to be solved. Was this just a minor puzzle, or was it at the heart of the Uesugi stranglehold on this province? And how was it connected to Kaibara's death?

"Akitada?"

He was snatched back to the present. "What?"

"I only meant that you cannot know the situation in the capital. If you release the arrow, it may merely wound the bear, or kill its cub. Then you may be hurt instead."

How astute she was. "Yes. I know. That is the problem." He turned his attention to the arrow again, twisting it this way and that.

Tamako frowned. "A hunter might wait for another opportunity," she remarked anxiously.

"Yes. You are quite right. Thank you." He smiled at her, noting that the protective hand rested on her softly rounded belly again. Women played by their own rules, followed their own concept of honor, he thought and was surprised at the discovery.

She blushed as if she had read his mind. "Forgive me. It was not my place to advise you."

"On the contrary. I think you have helped me solve another mystery."

"Oh?" Her pale face lit up, then looked puzzled. "Again?"

"Yes. Your final match in our shell game led me to Sunada."

"The ladies with the lutes!" She clapped her hands. "But how?"

"The murdered woman owned a lute, a very expensive, rare one. After the murder, that lute was gone. I realized that only Sunada could have bought it, or had the taste to do so. And he would have taken it away with him."

"How horrible!" Tamako's eyes were large with shock. Then she added quickly, "But he must have loved her very much to have spoiled her so," and her eyes lit up as if a thought had crossed her mind. She glanced at the shell-matching game. "Did the game . . . cost very much?" she asked, half hopeful, half afraid.

Akitada did not know how to answer. He had paid much less than it was worth. Had not the curio dealer said the shell-matching game had been ordered as a gift for an Uesugi lady years ago? He had a dim memory of those same flowers and grasses among the decorations on a suit of armor in the Takata armory.

Would Tamako think he did not love her? The female mind drew the most astonishing conclusions sometimes. He said, joking though his heart was afraid, "However you might rate my affection, I certainly would never entertain any murderous thoughts."

Puzzlement, then comprehension and embarrassment passed quickly over her face. But to Akitada's relief, she burst into laughter. Tamako laughed like a child, eyes sparkling, head thrown back, pink lips revealing perfect white teeth. She rarely practiced the custom of blackening her teeth as ladies in the capital did. And this was not ladylike laughter either. It was wholly infectious, and Akitada joined in.

The door opened, and Tora looked in curiously. Behind him Hamaya and the two clerks craned their necks.

Akitada glanced back at his wife. Her hand now covered her mouth in the prescribed manner, but above it her eyes sparkled with mirth.

"Come in, Tora," said Akitada, smiling at his wife, who rose and, bowing to him, left the room. "What is it?"

"Kaoru sent me. Sunada wants to talk to you. Kaoru doesn't dare leave, not after what happened with the Omeya woman. He's afraid Sunada might kill himself."

"Thank you," Akitada said, jumping up, "this could be important. Anything I can use to avoid open war with Uesugi would be heaven-sent."

◆

The atmosphere around the jail was tense. Guards manned the entrance to keep away the curious. In spite of this, two cripples had taken up position near the steps and raised sad faces to Akitada. He could not understand their piteous cries and was about to toss them some coppers, when Tora said, "Sunada's servants. They followed him and have sat here ever since."

In the common room more constables snapped to attention. Kaoru was seated outside Sunada's cell door. He looked tired, but rose immediately and bowed to Akitada.

"Sergeant," said Akitada, "I want you to send one of the constables to Captain Takesuke and request five of his best men to carry a dispatch to the capital." His eyes fell on the barred window of a cell door which was suddenly crowded with three familiar faces.

Only Takagi's wore the usual vacant smile. Umehara looked pale and frightened, and Okano had been weeping.

"Why are they locked up again?" Akitada asked.

"I did not want to take any chances this time, sir," Kaoru said in a low voice. "Not after my recent negligence."

"Let them out."

The three men tumbled out hurriedly to express their gratitude. Okano, who had a flowered scarf tied about his face, looked more like a farmer's wife than ever. He insisted on kissing the hem of Akitada's gown. Umehara was gabbling something about salmon stew, and Takagi asked for his gold coins again.

The confused scene was an unwelcome reminder to Akitada that he must close their case officially. Their freedom depended on Sunada's testimony in court.

"Get everybody out," Akitada snapped to Kaoru, "and take care of that message. Immediately! It's urgent. Then come back here."

When they were alone, Akitada had Tora unlock Sunada's cell and went in.

The change in the man was shocking. The once smooth, shining face of the wealthy merchant was gray, and the skin sagged. He looked up at Akitada from heavy-lidded eyes without bothering to rise or bow. "I could not sleep," he said.

Akitada wondered whether this was a complaint about jail conditions or more expressions of his grief and despair. To his surprise, it was another matter altogether.

"Those three men." Sunada's eyes went to the wall that separated the two cells. "All night they talked. There is one—his words are those of a child, but he speaks with a man's voice. He talked of his father and mother. And he wept for them like a homesick child. It was terrible to hear his weeping. Another fellow wept with him. This one cried like a woman. And the old man talked about food all night. He was worried his salmon would go bad. Are they the men accused of Sato's murder?"

Akitada nodded.

Sunada sighed. "They are innocent. I expect they have gone mad expecting to be executed. Why do some men fear death so much? I welcome it."

"They are not mad," said Akitada. "Until recently they moved freely about the jail. Being locked up again has frightened them. But even when I first met them, they were not concerned about dying because they knew they were innocent. Their worries concern the problems of life. Takagi is a slow-witted farmer's son who is homesick. Okano is an actor who is out of work and alone in the world. And Umehara has discovered the joys and frustrations of cooking." Akitada paused. Sunada had surprised

him again. He said tentatively, "I had hoped to prove their innocence and release them this week."

"And now you cannot do so?"

"Not without your help." Sunada's words had given Akitada
new hope. Perhaps he had misjudged the man. Whatever his
crimes, he was not without pity. But was it reasonable to expect
a favor from someone he was about to sentence to death?
Sunada was guilty of triple murder and treason. Why should he
care about justice in the abstract? Why would a criminal who
faced execution in its most cruel form—treason against the emperor was punishable by disemboweling before decapitation or
by being beaten to death—care about three poor men? Takagi,
Okada, and Umehara had neither ambition nor potential. They
were the dregs of a society Sunada had risen from through lifelong effort and relentless pursuit of power.

But Sunada nodded. "That is why I sent for you. I am prepared to help you."

Akitada was astonished and relieved. They were alone, but
outside in the common room he could hear Kaoru in subdued
conversation with Tora.

He said, "As you know, Mrs. Sato was about to be arrested
for the murder of her husband. Now her death makes it impossible to charge her with the crime."

Sunada nodded again and asked, "How did you find out?"

"Her alibi for the day of the murder was unshakable. It was
that which led me to suspect her in the first place. It occurred to
me that she must have arranged to have her husband killed while
she was safely away visiting her parents. I assume you knew?"

"More than that, Governor. Ofumi was a remarkable woman
and perfectly capable of devising the plan on her own, but she
lacked the necessary contacts."

"So you found Koichi for her."

"That was clever of you. I rather suspected that you did not quite believe my story of self-defense when I killed him in the market the other day." Sunada grimaced. "It was a public service, though I was protecting myself. Unfortunately assassins are unreliable associates. When you refused to believe the three travelers guilty and started looking for another killer, he demanded money. I could afford to pay, but a man of his background and reputation cannot be trusted. I decided to act while I had witnesses. Then one of your men happened along—" Sunada broke off and clenched his fists. "Of course," he muttered. "The lieutenant who attempted to arrest me—he was the one who seduced her." He glowered at Akitada. "Wasn't he?"

Akitada was taken aback. How could this matter now? In justice to Hitomaro, he said sharply, "You are quite wrong. She seduced him."

For a moment their eyes held in a contest of wills, then Sunada lowered his head. "Perhaps she could not help what she was, what she made men do."

"A woman who plots to have her husband killed deserves no pity," snapped Akitada.

"What would you know of a woman's life?" Sunada asked wearily. "That girl—beautiful beyond belief, full of grace, endowed with talent, clever, lively, and filled with dreams—she was born into a peasant family and sold in marriage to an old man, a desiccated dotard so close to death that he stank of decomposition! What chance had she by your laws?"

"Not my laws. The laws of the gods. She was not mistreated. By all accounts Sato doted on her."

Sunada moved impatiently. "She was made for better things. He had no right to possess her."

This was absurd—as any good Confucian scholar knew. The ancients taught that a woman had no right to choose for herself.

Her duty was first to her parents, then to her husband, and last to her son. And if she was unfortunate enough to survive her immediate family, another male relative would direct her life.

But there was no point in arguing with this man. Akitada said, "So you 'contacted,' as you put it, Koichi, a man with a long record of crimes. In fact, you had him released from his latest jail term the day before Sato's death. Employing the unemployable had always worked well for you. Such men are grateful. Did Koichi balk at all at murder?"

"He was eager to do it and bragged about it afterwards. I found him repulsive."

"Ah, so he reported to you after the murder." Akitada was pleased. The case would be resolved more smoothly than he had hoped. "Koichi entered the Golden Carp in midafternoon, at a time when Mrs. Sato would have reached her parents' village and been seen there by as many people as possible. It was a sunny day, and the inn's hallway dim. Koichi stumbled over a packsaddle and damaged it. Okano, one of the three travelers, was taking a bath and heard the clatter but assumed it was made by customers who left again when no one greeted them. I do not know whether Koichi brought a weapon, but I think he saw a large knife lying in the kitchen and decided to use it. After killing the sick old man, Koichi emptied the money box, replaced the knife where he had found it, and left again as unobserved as he had come."

"I did not know about the packsaddle, and he certainly did not tell me about the money box," Sunada said. "Otherwise your deductions are correct."

"Sato had saved up some gold. His widow testified that there were seven pieces, but she provided that information after the three fugitives had been searched and seven gold pieces were found in their possession. Still, it is surprising that Koichi blackmailed you after having helped himself to all of Sato's savings."

Sunada laughed mirthlessly. "Come, Governor! Not even you can be that unworldly! Gold begets greed. He was to keep what he found as payment. Clearly it was not enough."

Akitada knew there was a loose end still, but it had nothing to do with Sunada. He asked, "Will you sign a statement and testify in court that Koichi killed Sato on your instructions and at Mrs. Sato's request?"

"Yes. But there is a condition."

"No." Akitada rose abruptly. The disappointment stung, though he should have expected it. "Even if I wished to grant you leniency, your fate is not in my power. Neither your culpability in the Sato case, nor the three murders you committed yourself signify when compared to a case of insurrection against his august Majesty."

Sunada smiled a little. "I know. My request is not for me."

Akitada hesitated. "The same applies to all your associates and includes your henchman, Boshu, and his villainous gang. They have terrorized the local people at your behest. I look forward to sentencing them to long terms at hard labor. Besides, your people had a hand in placing the mutilated body at the tribunal gate."

Sunada looked astonished. "For what it is worth, we had nothing to do with that. That was done by that animal Chobei, your former sergeant, on instructions from Hisamatsu. No one else could have misused a corpse in such a repulsive fashion."

"The corpse showed evidence of having been stored in a rice warehouse."

Sunada hunched his shoulders. "By all means add it to my charges. It does not matter. And do as you wish with Boshu and his men. I'm asking you to spare the two crippled servants you saw in my house. They are simple fishermen who lost the ability to go to sea. They neither read nor write and only took care of my simplest needs in my home. I never asked more of them."

Akitada remembered the two cripples. Again Sunada had surprised him, almost shamed him. "They have been outside this jail since you were brought here."

Sunada lowered his head, then brushed a hand across his eyes. "I plead with you," he said brokenly. "They must not suffer for their loyalty, for their love . . ." He choked on the word.

"Very well. If they are as innocent as you say, they may return to their families."

"Thank you." Sunada bowed deeply, his face wet with tears.

Back in the common room, Kaoru and Tora greeted Akitada with broad grins.

"We heard," cried Tora. "You solved the Sato case. It was brilliant. From little things like Umehara's backpack and a noise Okano heard, you put the whole thing together."

"And from Koichi's jail records, when no one knew he had been near the inn," added Kaoru. "Such wisdom is worthy of the famous judge Ch'eng-Lin."

Akitada looked at him for a moment, then smiled and shook his head. "I don't deserve any credit. From the beginning, Tora was closer to the answer than I was."

"Me?" Tora gaped.

"Yes. We should have arrested the maid. It would have saved trouble and lives. She was an accessory before and after the fact and should have been questioned rigorously."

"Kiyo? Why?"

"The bloody knife. Someone had to put it in Takagi's pack. Koichi knew nothing of the three travelers. I think we will find that Kiyo not only knew of the planned murder, but that she and Koichi split Sato's savings."

Tora stared at him. "But she hated her mistress."

"Probably. She also hated old Sato. When she thought you were a stranger passing through, she carelessly revealed her motive. It is to your credit that you recognized and reported it. Later she changed her story, but by then she knew that you worked for me, and that Sunada had killed Koichi. She was afraid."

"Well," Tora said with great satisfaction, "would you believe it? I have the instinct for it after all."

Akitada nodded. "Oh, yes. It is your case now. Go arrest the girl and get her confession. We also need a statement from Sunada." He paused and gave the sergeant a considering look. "All the clerks are busy with Sunada's papers . . ."

Kaoru said eagerly, "I can write well enough, sir," and gestured at a sheaf of reports on his desk.

Akitada looked and raised his eyebrows at the neat script, then smiled. "Very well, Sergeant, go ahead. But first tell your three prisoners that they are free to go. Hamaya will return their money and property to them. There should be additional compensation from Sunada's confiscated estate after both cases are settled."

◆

Someone, Tamako or Seimei, had brought hot tea and placed it on the brazier in his office. He poured some and drank greedily before sitting down at his desk.

The prince's letter still awaited his attention. Tamako had understood immediately that an official report to the chancellor would set wheels in motion which might well put Akitada and his family in personal danger. She had wanted him to wait. But this could not wait. The emperor himself was in danger.

Akitada reached for his writing utensils. His cover letter was very brief. He enclosed it and the prince's letter in another sheet of paper, sealed this, and addressed both to a man whose wisdom and kindness were well known to him, the retired emperor's brother who was a Buddhist bishop. Then he clapped his hands.

The young soldiers selected by Takesuke looked eager and

intelligent. Akitada gave his instructions and turned his letter over to them. This accomplished, he had another cup of tea and relaxed.

There was little left to do. The tangled web of murder and mayhem had resolved itself with Sunada's confession. Akitada took no pleasure in it. There had been many deaths and there would be many more, public executions which he must attend in his official role. Besides, it had not been his own effort which had brought justice to the three unfortunate travelers, or revealed and broken the conspiracy against the emperor. No, it had all been due to chance encounters between one woman and two men.

He considered the destruction Mrs. Sato had wrought in the lives of others. The good abbot Hokko had his own symbol to explain the inexplicable. Buddhist scripture taught that man occupied a precarious position midway between the angels and the demons on the wheel of life. A turn of the wheel propelled him either upward, toward righteousness, good fortune, and happiness, or it dragged him into the filth of evil and crushed him underneath. The wheel had crushed Sunada.

He sniffed. There was a strange fishy smell in the air. Then he became aware of a peculiar noise coming from the wooden shutters behind him. It sounded like the gnawing of a rat. A soft hissing followed, then a scrabbling noise. Akitada turned on his cushion so that he faced the shutters. As he watched, a narrow line of light widened into a crack and a pudgy hand appeared in the opening. More hissing followed—whispering, Akitada decided—and then a round red face topped with short black horns appeared and leered in at him from bulging eyes.

Both Akitada and the goblin jerked back in surprise. The goblin squealed, and the shutter slammed shut. Akitada opened his mouth to shout for a guard, when the shutter flew open again, revealing two human backs, bowed abjectly on the narrow veranda outside.

"Who are you and what do you want?" barked Akitada, his heart pounding.

One of the creatures, the horned goblin, visibly trembled, but the other one raised his gray head. Akitada recognized Umehara.

"Forgive us, Excellency," Umehara said, wringing his hands and sniffling. "We asked your clerk to let us see you, but it was strictly forbidden, so we came this way."

"Ah." Akitada regarded the shaking figure. A certain plumpness suggested Okano, but the horns? "Is that Okano?" he asked.

The spiked head nodded violently.

"What happened to your head, Okano? Are you playing a goblin?"

"Oh!" The actor wailed and covered the spikes with both hands. "See, Umehara? Okano should have worn his scarf! He is so ugly!"

"His hair is growing back," explained Umehara.

Akitada suppressed a smile. "Sit up and look at me, Okano."

The actor sat up slowly, pudgy hands fluttering from hair to face and finally dropping in despair. With great difficulty, Akitada kept a straight face. Above Okano's red face with its bulging, tear-filled eyes and quivering lips, black tufts rose into the air. Poor Okano needed no costume to play the part of a goblin. "Can you not comb it back?" he suggested.

"It's too short. See?" Okano slapped at the horns with both hands. "Umehara gave Okano some fish oil. But it made it worse."

That explained the strange smell.

"Ah. No doubt it will improve in time. You did not wish to consult me about your hair, I trust," Akitada remarked.

"Oh, no," they chorused, exchanging doleful looks.

Umehara was wringing his hands, "It's about the sergeant telling us to leave."

Okano wailed, "Where will Okano go? What will he do? He has no friends in the whole wide world. Okano will kill himself!"

"Holy heavens," cried Akitada. "Stop that nonsense at once. Umehara, can't you explain to him that he is a free man, cleared of all charges, and that he will receive some money for his suffering? Why, in heaven's name is he carrying on like this?"

Umehara began to weep also. "He understands," he sobbed. "It's all very well for Takagi." He wiped his streaming face and nose on his sleeve. "Takagi wants to go home to his village. But Okano and me . . ."—he sniffed—". . . we've got nobody and . . . we've never been as happy as we've been here. We don't want to leave your jail, sir."

Akitada was taken aback. After a moment, he said in a choking voice, "Well, if you are sure, I'll put in a good word for you with the sergeant."

TWENTY

THE WAY OF WAR

𝒯wo hours before sunrise Akitada still sat at his desk, staring now at the feathered arrow, now at the shell-matching game. The tea in his cup had long since been drunk and the brazier was filled with ashes. It had grown cold, but he felt neither the chill nor thirst or tiredness.

All night he had turned over in his mind the problem of the impregnable manor. Hamaya had searched the archives for information about its construction but found nothing of interest. Akitada's memory from his visits discouraged hope. The natural defenses were just too good. Each time, he had approached the mountaintop manor by its main gate—was there another access?—and found it could be defended against an army by a handful of bowmen on the watchtower above. A battering ram was out of the question, and so were ladders. The rocky hillside, topped with walls, was too high and steep to be climbed against defending archers.

Of course, a bonfire laid against the wooden main gate

would eventually consume it, but at what cost to those carrying and stacking the faggots and bundles of wood? Still, some cover might be constructed for them.

Even then, the big problem remained: When the gate was breached, the narrow entrance would only allow a small number of soldiers at a time to penetrate to the interior courts, and each of those was separately walled and defended. Uesugi had more than enough men to hold Takesuke off. Too many would die in such a gamble.

Akitada took up the arrow and fingered it thoughtfully. There was someone who might know a way.

He heard a sound in the archives outside his office, and clapped his hands.

Hamaya stuck his head in. "Your Excellency is up already?"

Akitada did not bother to correct him. "Send for Sergeant Kaoru. And get someone to bring more coals and some hot tea."

Kaoru was prompt. It had been a while since he had had occasion to come to Akitada's office. When he sat down, he saw the arrow and flinched. His eyes flew to Akitada's face.

"One of yours?" Akitada asked, watching him.

"What? Oh." He shook his head.

"It is the arrow that shot Kaibara. It occurred to me that it might have been you who shot him. Hitomaro told me of your skill with the bow."

Kaoru blinked. "No, sir, not me, though I wish it had been. You remember I was here at the tribunal that night."

"Ah, yes. Do you have any idea who might have done it?"

Silence. A servant entered quietly, bringing a fresh brazier of coals and a steaming pot of tea. Akitada waited until he was gone. Then he said, "Come! You recognized the arrow. Whose is it?"

Kaoru was pale now, but he answered in a steady voice. "It belongs to a dead man, sir. That arrow is part of a set of contest arrows used by the late Lord of Takata's elder brother."

"Ah. I was sure I had seen some like it in the Uesugi armory. It suggests that one of Uesugi's own people shot Kaibara."

"No!"

Akitada raised his brows. "No? How else could this arrow get out of the armory?"

Kaoru looked at it as if mesmerized. "The servants attach magic powers to . . . to these arrows and . . . there is much coming and going of servants at Takata. No doubt someone took it from the armory."

"No doubt," Akitada said dryly. "You seem well informed about the household. Have you spent much time there?"

A flush slowly rose on the other man's face. "I did not steal the arrow, sir," he said stiffly.

Akitada smiled. "Of course not," he said affably. "I ask because I had hoped for information about the manor. We will move on Takata and demand Uesugi's surrender today."

"You will?" Relief gave way to excitement. "Then the rumors are true. He will refuse to surrender and you will have to attack the manor. May I join you, sir?"

Akitada felt depressed by the other man's eagerness. "The bloodshed will be terrible. You would almost certainly be killed. Besides, you are needed here."

Kaoru bit his lip. His eyes searched Akitada's face. Finally he said, "I could be of use. I know the manor very well, having carried wood there all my life, ever since I was a small boy and went with my father." He added, almost as an afterthought, "He was a woodcutter also."

"A woodcutter, eh?" Akitada studied the other man. "Tell me," he asked casually, "where did you learn to read and write Chinese characters?"

"Chinese characters? I don't . . . oh, you mean the jail records. I know just a few, for brevity."

Akitada nodded. "Quite correct and appropriate for official

documents. Our native tongue is more useful for poetry and the ladies' romances. However, few people are adept at Chinese, especially at legal terminology, and I would guess your style is as good as Hamaya's. Where did you learn it?"

Kaoru fidgeted. "A Buddhist priest taught me when I was young," he finally said.

Akitada smiled. "Really? A Buddhist priest? I see. You have a gentleman's education and are a very talented young man, Sergeant."

Kaoru flushed more deeply. "I do not lie either, sir," he snapped.

"No, I can see that." Akitada paused a moment. Having enjoyed Kaoru's discomfiture, he decided he had tormented the young man enough. "Perhaps you would not mind drawing me a plan of the manor. I am particularly interested to know if there is access by means other than the main gate."

Kaoru brightened. "There is one way, sir. A hidden door and secret passage. But it will admit only a few men." He reached for Akitada's ink cake, poured a few drops of water in the dish and began to rub ink. "It's in the northeast wall and leads to a narrow passage inside the wall. You come out in one of the closed galleries. Its purpose is to allow the lord and his family to escape, or to send out messengers if the manor is under siege." Pulling over some paper with one hand, he dipped a brush into the ink and began to sketch rapidly. "Here, sir. That's where the exit is."

Akitada bent over the plan and nodded. "Hmm. It could be just what we need. What about guards?"

"I doubt many know about it. Besides, only one man at a time can use it. There is a movable panel that can be barred from inside." Kaoru paused and then asked hesitantly, "Will you have to tell many people about this, sir?"

"Don't worry, your secret is safe. Only Tora and Hitomaro will know."

Kaoru stared at him, but Akitada kept his face impassive. After a moment, Kaoru said, "I take it they are to go in and then open the main gate for Takesuke's men? I don't think that will work, sir. The secret passage may not be guarded, but it is a long way from the gate, and they do not know their way about. Please allow me to accompany them."

Akitada thought about it and nodded. "You may be right, and I suppose you are the only man for the job at that."

The other man blinked but said nothing.

"Very well," Akitada said, folding up the plan. "The four of us then."

"Surely not you, sir? What about Genba?"

"Genba has great strength and courage, but he has never learned to use a sword. Besides, someone has to stay here."

"But what if something goes wrong . . . the place is crawling with warriors. Think of your lady."

Akitada had looked in on Tamako during the night and watched her sleeping peacefully. The thought that they might not meet again, and worse, that his decision would destroy her also, perhaps as soon as the following day, had sickened him. Now he glared at Kaoru and snapped, "I'm going." Seeing Kaoru's dismay, he added more calmly, "We will need something to distract the soldiers' attention."

They sank into a glum silence.

"I think I have an idea," Kaoru suddenly said, "but it will mean withdrawing the siege troops a little."

"That can be arranged. Go on."

"My grandmother is a *miko,* a medium who foretells the future by going to sleep and letting the gods speak through her. You know what I mean?"

Akitada nodded, but his heart sank. Hitomaro's madwoman from the outcast village. He had little respect for such practices, and in this case their lives would depend on Kaoru's senile grandmother.

Kaoru saw his expression and said, "My grandmother is well known at the manor. She used to serve as a lady's maid there many years ago when she was a young girl, and she still has friends among the servants."

"Surely Uesugi will not admit her at the present time."

"On the contrary. He will welcome her because he is superstitious. If Takesuke withdraws and she shows up, he will ask for a prediction about his chances."

"Ah." Akitada considered it, then shook his head. "No, I cannot permit it. It would put your grandmother into extreme danger."

"She won't stay long. Besides, they will be afraid to harm her."

"But how will she be able to create a disturbance, yet leave before the alarm is given?"

"She will have help. She will only tell Uesugi his future and leave a message with one of the servants. Koreburo will take care of everything else. He could set a small fire perhaps?"

Akitada considered the drawing again and nodded slowly. "Yes, it might work. A small conflagration with much smoke, easily put out. Just here, I think. Where the southern gallery makes a turn." He pointed, then looked up. "Did you say Koreburo? Isn't that the old man who used to play *go* with Hideo?"

Kaoru nodded. "He will be eager to help. He blames Makio and Kaibara for Hideo's death."

"Does he indeed? He did not say so to me."

Kaoru shrugged. "He's a strange old fellow, but he could have picked up something from the other servants. In any case, he can be trusted."

Akitada gave the other man a long look, then nodded. "Very well. I will give detailed instructions to Takesuke before we meet. Meanwhile, you can make your arrangements."

Kaoru rose and bowed. "You honor me with your confidence, sir. Allow me." He stepped to the shutters and threw them open, letting in a gust of cold air. There was a full moon, fitfully revealed by dark clouds, but in the east the darkness grew faintly lighter. "It will be dawn in an hour. If I leave for my village immediately and carry my grandmother part of the way to Takata on my horse, Koreburo should be ready before the noon rice. Shall we meet below the manor at the start of the hour of the horse?"

"Yes." Akitada came and looked at the driving clouds. "When will the great snow start? I have been expecting it for weeks."

"Perhaps today, perhaps later." Kaoru spoke with the indifference of a local man. "The snows will come in their own time." He smiled suddenly. "It will still be possible to send the news to the capital that we have taken Takata."

Akitada raised his brows but said only, "We will need a signal from inside the manor."

"When all is ready, Koreburo will give the cry of the snow goose. If that is all, sir, I shall be on my way."

After Kaoru had gone, Akitada stood for a few more moments at the open shutters. The idea of war was foreign to him. This day would decide life or death for many. Uesugi, Takesuke, and Kaoru, perhaps even the fate of an emperor along with that of an old servant who risked his life for the memory of a dead friend. His own also, and that of Tamako and their unborn child. There were no more choices, no options of escape. He had accepted this charge and offered up the lives of his family and his friends along with his own. Tamako's warning about the letter to the capital came to his mind. Uesugi was not his only worry. Did any man have the right to gamble with the lives of others?

He sighed, hating this harsh northern land with its superstitions, its violence, its people's predilection for secrets and plots.

There was a scratching at the door. He called, "Enter!" and closed the shutters. Oyoshi came in hesitantly.

"Do I disturb you, sir?"

"No. You are very welcome." Afraid that his fears and self-doubts were written large on his face, Akitada was effusive, inviting Oyoshi to sit and pouring him a cup of tea.

Oyoshi looked strained, but Akitada's fussing seemed to reassure him. "I have waited anxiously to speak to you since we found Mrs. Omeya's body," he said after a sip of tea. "You have been very busy, and this has been my first opportunity. How are things going, sir?"

"I will leave for Takata later today," said Akitada, "to settle the Uesugi matter."

"Oh, dear. Forgive me. I have chosen a bad time. Let me be brief then. I wish to resign my office as your coroner."

"But why?" Akitada's heart sank. He had expected something, but he pretended surprised shock.

Oyoshi smiled a little. "There is no need to spare my feelings, sir. Even before Mrs. Omeya's death, I felt that you regretted my appointment. I made a foolish mistake with the mutilated body, and that certainly proved me incompetent. Since then, I'm afraid, there have been more serious suspicions. I won't embarrass you or myself by asking what they are, but I wanted to tell you that I will leave as soon as you have found a replacement."

Akitada sighed. "My friend," he said, "and I hope I may still call you that—I have made many mistakes since I arrived. Perhaps some of my mistakes have cost lives and will cost more. Not the least of my mistakes was to doubt you. I should have known that a man who would risk his life to perform an illegal exhumation at my request would not at the same time plot against me." He bowed to Oyoshi. "I apologize humbly for my foolishness."

The doctor became so agitated that he spilled his tea. "Oh, no," he cried. "Please don't. You were quite right to suspect everyone, and who more than myself? What could you know about me, who had hidden his past from everyone? What should you think when I gave the wrong testimony in court? Why should you trust me when I was so conveniently on the premises when Mrs. Omeya was killed? You did quite right and have behaved with the greatest justice and patience towards me."

"You will stay then?"

Oyoshi did not answer right away. He put down his teacup and wiped his fingers. "There is another thing. I killed someone," he said softly. "I had a very bad moment when Tora said something about murderous doctors and looked at me in a very knowing way. May I tell you about it?"

Akitada said quickly, "There is no need. I am quite satisfied."

"Allow me, sir. Many years ago, in another province, I served as personal physician to . . . a powerful man. I caused my patient's death after I discovered that my wife had spent more time in his bed than in mine. It was wrong to love her more than my duty." He broke off and raised a hand to hide his face in shame.

"You were not found out?"

Oyoshi lowered his hand and smiled bleakly. "No. He was ill and I attended him. Once I was a very good physician. I could have saved his life, but I let him die. Afterwards I divorced my wife and left the area. I spent the next ten years traveling, working at fairs and treating the poor, earning a few coppers as a barber now and then to buy medicines. For another fifteen years after that I tried the religious life. I entered a monastery, but in the end the guilt would not leave me and it grated on my ears to be called a holy man. So I took to the road again and ended up here, where I hoped to end my life in obscurity." He gave a hollow laugh and shook his head.

Akitada was relieved. "Legally you are not guilty of murder," he said. "This will not prevent you from serving as coroner."

"I must confess to yet another offense," Oyoshi said sadly. "When I saw you at Takata, ill, outnumbered, outmanipulated, and surrounded by forces you seemed neither by background nor by personality equipped to handle, you seemed lost. Then, when you asked me to serve as your coroner, I formed the somewhat confused idea of throwing in my lot with you. Circumstances favored this, and the more I learned about you, the more convinced I became that joining your downfall would be my personal atonement. I planned to end my life with you and thus make amends for my past. But I was quite wrong. You have fought the evil in this province successfully and you will prevail, while I must continue to bear my guilt."

For a moment Akitada was so taken aback by this that he did not know whether to laugh or be angry. Then he remembered the coming battle and said, "I suppose both my arrogance and my ignorance, obvious to everyone but me, blinded me to the local problems in the beginning. You were not wrong about me. I have little to be proud of, and had I known how badly I would bungle, I would have fled in panic. Let us hope that some good may still come of our most foolish actions. I want you to stay."

Oyoshi brushed at his eyes. "If you truly wish it, sir," he murmured. He rose awkwardly and stumbled from the room.

◆

Heavy gray clouds swirled above and sleet stung their faces. Below them, the forest enclosing the frozen fields looked funereal, like a black stole draped across a pallid hempen gown. It was past midday. Hours ago, Akitada and Takesuke had ridden up to the Takata gate and demanded Makio's surrender. A hail of arrows had been their answer. After that, Takesuke had withdrawn his troops, and Akitada, along with Hitomaro and Tora, had gone to meet Kaoru.

The four would make the dangerous attempt to get inside the fortified manor. They wore straw rain capes over light armor and waited hidden among trees where they could see part of the road leading up to the manor. A quarter of the hour passed before the old woman appeared, walking slowly and leaning on the arm of a girl.

"Isn't that your sister?" Hitomaro asked Kaoru. "Why risk her life?"

"My cousin. She usually goes along and I could not stop her."

They waited again, nervously now, until the two women returned. The girl loosened the shawl around her head and let it blow in the wind for a moment before she retied it.

"Good girl! All is ready," said Kaoru, adding grimly, "Let's hope we do our part as well."

Akitada looked up at the sky to gauge the time. There was no sun. The icy wind pushed angry gray clouds before it, clouds so low that they hid the snowy tops of the distant mountains. Wisps of cloud drifted across the dark roofs of Takata manor—shredded silk gauze from a mourner's train.

They left the trees at a run and dashed across the road. Up the hill, still at a run, they kept mostly to a gully, a jagged scar which ran up the barren hillside. The gully gave them some cover, but then they were in the open again and close enough to the manor that a single archer on one of the galleries could pick them off one by one, like running deer.

As they ran uphill, the low clouds finally released the first heavy drops. They congealed into sleet in the cold wind and stung their faces. Akitada clasped his heavy sword to his side so it would not get between his legs and trip him. His armor was also heavy and cumbersome, and the rain-soaked straw cape flapped wetly against him. His breath soon came in hoarse gasps, his chest hurt, and his leg muscles ached, but he was ashamed to fall back behind the others. When they reached the steep outcropping under the eastern wall, he sagged against the rock, drenched in sweat despite the bitter cold.

They huddled there for a little, in a blind spot where an

overhanging gallery hid them from watching eyes above, and waited for the signal. The icy wind cut through the straw coats and turned the metal scales of their armor into ice against their wet bodies. Akitada's teeth chattered from cold and nerves.

Below the land stretched away, empty sere fields traversed by the darker line of the road. They had come from the forest to the north and followed a path so narrow and overgrown that only Kaoru had known how to find it. He had kept an eye on the ramparts above them, but they had seen no watchers. Takesuke and his men were on the other side, below the approach to the manor's gate, and that was where Uesugi expected the attack to come from.

Here immense slabs of rock rose to an outer wall and to the black timbers of a gallery jutting into the stormy gray sky above them. Dry shrubs and stunted trees grew from cracks in the rocks. Kaoru moved along the path to one of the slabs of rock and felt it. He grunted and gave a push, and Akitada saw a crack widen into a thin black fissure.

Like the tomb entrance, Akitada thought with a shiver. He said aloud, "What about the signal?"

Kaoru nodded. "We wait a little longer, but there isn't much time left."

So they stood, shivering in the sleeting rain with their sword grips freezing to their perspiring palms, wondering if Koreburo had been caught. Akitada heard distant drumbeats carried on the wind in snatches. Takesuke was following instructions and exercising his troops. Akitada wished himself a common foot soldier, trotting briskly and unencumbered by heavy armor to the command of an officer. He was impatient to get this over with, to confront what lay in wait behind the stone door. Action, any kind of action, was preferable to this agonizing process of congealing in the freezing blasts.

When it finally came, that cry of the snow goose, once, and

quickly again, they exchanged glances, then tossed off their straw wraps and gripped their swords more tightly. Kaoru and Tora together pushed the stone aside. A dark and narrow stone stairway ascended inside.

Suddenly, before Kaoru could take the lead, Hitomaro pushed past Akitada and disappeared into the darkness. Tora muttered a curse, and Akitada drew his sword and went after Hitomaro into the murky shaft leading upward. Hitomaro's rapid steps sounded ahead, but it was too dark to see. What was the fool doing? At any moment he might run into danger and give them away. More steps shuffled behind, but Akitada was bent on catching up with Hitomaro.

The climb through a tight black space, only occasionally lit by air holes in the outer walls, seemed to last forever. The steps twisted, turned, and switched back. Akitada's sword once clattered against the wall and he caught it. Someone behind him slipped and cursed softly. Sweat trickled down Akitada's temples, and his fingers cramped around the sword hilt. He tried to listen, but his breathing and the blood pounding in his ears muffled all other sounds. If Hitomaro had encountered a guard, he was already a dead man. And so were they all.

Then he caught a faint whiff of burning oil. Wood scraped on wood and, as he turned a corner, faint light came through a grate just large enough for a man to get through. Hitomaro cowered there, a hulking black shadow, until Akitada saw his face flushed by the light as he removed the grate and slipped through the opening.

"Come, sir," he said softly, holding out a hand to Akitada. "It's safe."

"That was a very foolish trick," Akitada hissed angrily. "You might have ruined everything by rushing ahead when Kaoru knows the way."

Hitomaro's face was expressionless. "Sorry, sir."

Akitada climbed out into an empty enclosed gallery. The corridor was a little over a hundred feet long, its narrow shutters closed tight against the weather, and the dim space lit at each end by large metal oil lamps attached to beams. It was silent and deserted, but they could hear men shouting outside. No doubt Uesugi's warriors were getting ready for Takesuke's attack.

The other two joined them. Akitada said, "Very well. Let's see about finding Uesugi and opening that gate." It sounded ridiculously simple to his ears and, standing there in the enemy's stronghold, he half believed it would be.

"Come and see," Kaoru grunted and opened one of the shutters a crack.

When Akitada joined him, he looked through a loophole from which an archer could shoot arrows into the lower entrance courtyard. Armed soldiers sat about in small groups. Black-and-white Uesugi banners were everywhere. One man carried equipment to the tower above the gate. Akitada's heart sank. They could not reach the gate without being cut down in the attempt. Even if the men in the courtyard could be distracted long enough, the watchtower above bristled with archers.

Kaoru closed the shutter and went to put the grate back into place. "We cannot stay here," he said softly. "Someone might come any moment. Follow me, but remember the place in case you have to run for your life." They ran down the corridor away from the main house. Akitada chafed at this and at the fact that Kaoru had taken over and was giving the orders, but he submitted. He felt badly out of his depth.

The gallery adjoined another, equally empty, and this led to one of the service areas. Kaoru peered out cautiously. It was the kitchen yard, and deserted. No smoke came from the kitchen hearth. The cooking fires had been extinguished prior to battle.

Kaoru crossed the yard, headed for a storage shed. They followed, slipped in behind him, and he closed the door.

"You'll be safe here for the moment," he said.

They stood in a small space filled with baskets and brooms, kettles and pails, faggots and oil jars, all the paraphernalia to keep a large household stocked. Akitada's heart was pounding. He said, "The gate. We must reach that gate. How many men does it take to open it?"

"One, at the most two."

Kaoru still sounded confident, but Akitada had become all too aware of his own lack of planning. "You're sure?" he persisted, wondering if two of them could engage the soldiers he had seen, some fifteen or twenty, long enough to let the other two slip past to the gate. With the archers above, it wasn't likely.

"There's a counterweight. I can do it by myself."

"We need to draw some of the soldiers away. What about that fire Koreburo was to start?"

Kaoru opened the shed door and peered out. He closed it again. "No sign of it. He should have done so already. If you'll wait here, I'll try to find him." Before Akitada could protest, Kaoru had slipped out.

Akitada suppressed a sudden panic and motioned to the other two to sit down. They sat, each caught in his own thoughts, and waited in the murky semidarkness of the small shed. The smell of wood and dried grasses hung in the chill air.

Tora's eyes were wide open and his hands twitched occasionally with suppressed excitement. Hitomaro leaned back against the wall, perfectly still, his eyes closed, his chin on his chest. Looking at them, Akitada reflected how close these two men were to him, and how danger affected them all differently. He remembered Takesuke's fervent wish that Uesugi would attack the tribunal, while he himself had been weighed down with fears for his family and his people. Takesuke's high spirits had struck him as irresponsible and bloodthirsty then. Now he wondered if he was the one who was inadequate to his duty. Takesuke, Tora, and Hitomaro were all trained soldiers, while he was an official. What did he know of war? Yet, by accepting this appointment, he had also accepted the possibility of having to fight.

Here he was, in unaccustomed armor and uncomfortable, feeling ambivalent about the violence he was about to face and—worse—to commit. They had gained entrance to the stronghold without being discovered, but the real test still lay ahead, and Akitada doubted that he could pass it.

If Kaoru was caught, he would be questioned under torture. Whether he revealed their presence or not, a subsequent search would find them, and then they would die ignobly here, slaughtered among brooms and braziers. There was no defense against the odds, even if it were possible to swing a sword in these cramped quarters.

It wasn't going to be easy at all.

TWENTY-ONE

TO THE DEATH

*A*kitada did not want to wait for death.

Neither did the others. Tora broke into his thoughts impatiently. "Where in hell is Kaoru? He has nerve, telling us to sit here and wait for him. Who does he think he is? I don't like it. We're stuck here like rats in a box." He stood up and walked to the door, opening it a crack.

Hitomaro went to join him. "It's too quiet," he said.

Tora asked, "What if it's a trap, sir? To my mind the fellow's just too well informed about this place for a mere woodsman."

Akitada hated the inactivity, but he shook his head. "No, we must trust Kaoru. He'll be back any moment."

Hitomaro closed the door and paced. Tora grunted and sat down.

Akitada thought he could find the way to the gate from what he remembered of his earlier visits. They had been taken from the gate to an inner courtyard. From there, Akitada had gone into the main house. The trouble was, he was not sure where they were now. He closed his eyes and pictured Kaoru's sketch of the secret entrance. He must somehow get back to the main house. The gallery from which he had seen the north pavilion had been on the west side, but they had gone there through another gallery that served as an armory.

Never mind. They were not headed to the north pavilion but to the gate. They had to open the gate to let Takesuke in before they did anything else. The problem was how to get there from here. He had spoken to the servants in a courtyard not unlike the one they were in. For that matter, where were the servants? Some must be in the kitchen, even with the fires out. Had they all been pressed into defending the manor?

"Tora," he said, opening his eyes, "where did they take you during the banquet?"

"One of their barracks. They fed me. Seemed decent fellows." Tora grimaced.

Akitada guessed that Tora did not like the thought of killing such hospitable men, or being killed by them. "But where were the barracks? In relation to the gate and the main house?"

"Between the house and the gate. Why?"

That accounted for one of the courtyards. "I'm wondering if we can find our way to the gate without Kaoru. Takesuke's men are preparing to attack. We cannot wait much longer."

"Then let's go, sir." Hitomaro was on his feet. "I have a bad feeling about this."

Akitada sighed and rose. "Yes. Something must have gone wrong. We have waited long enough. Take another look outside and tell me if you see any smoke anywhere in the compound."

Hitomaro reported, "Nothing, sir. They must've caught both of them."

Akitada looked around the shed. "Very well. Since the materials are at hand, we'll make the fire here. Pile up all the baskets, brooms, and kindling against that wall over there. Then we'll pour the lamp oil over it and light it."

Tora grinned. "Good idea. The kitchen next door has a thatched roof. That should get their attention."

Hitomaro nodded, and they fell to work. Akitada emptied baskets and tossed them on the pile. "We are going back the way we came," he said as he worked. "That gallery should take us to the main house, and from there we'll get to the gate."

"They'll be coming that way when they see the fire," Hitomaro muttered.

"We'll just have to be fast," said Tora happily.

Akitada thought it likely that they would be seen even before the smoke attracted notice. He dragged one of the huge earthenware jars full of oil across the dirt floor. Hitomaro came to give him a hand. Together they lifted and emptied the dark, viscous liquid over the pile. Their enemies had thoughtfully supplied an assortment of flints, wicks, and spills to keep the manor's oil lamps lit, and in a moment eager flames licked upward, joining others with a cheerful crackle, and cast a flickering red light on their faces. Smoke rose.

They looked at each other. Tora's grin looked more like a demon's snarl in the firelight. Akitada tried to shed the image of hell, and said, "Good. Let's go."

Just as they burst from the shed, Akitada in front, a woman cried out. The kitchen door stood open, and two maids goggled at them and at the inferno behind them. Ignoring the maids, they crossed the courtyard at a run and entered the enclosed gallery. Miraculously, it was still empty. Midway, Akitada checked his speed and opened one of the loophole shutters. The scene below had changed. The watchtower, almost on a level with the gallery, now bristled with archers and the men in the courtyard were on their feet, swords and halberds at the ready. Judging from the sounds of high-pitched whinnies and scuffling of hooves, there were horses, too. Akitada estimated thirty men below and twenty on the tower, and more were probably out of sight or waiting in other courtyards. Those he could see had their backs to him, their attention on what was going on outside the gate. And now he heard it, the sound of approaching battle drums.

Takesuke had arrived, and they must move, but attempting to open the gate would be certain suicide. When would the enemy notice the fire? And would they care enough about a fire in a kitchen yard to abandon their watch on the gate? But fires spread. They could not ignore this. At least some of the men in the courtyard would rush to put it out.

One of the archers on the watchtower finally turned his head and saw it. "Fire!" he screamed, and again, "Fire!" his arm pointing. Akitada stepped back from the shutter. The men in the courtyard turned, cried out, and after a moment's consternation, an officer shouted orders, and they began to run in all directions. Tora came to look and laughed out loud.

Akitada slammed the shutter. "Come on."

They ran to the end of the corridor and into an open gallery crossing a walled interior garden. Sleet had driven in to gather against the walls and whiten the few shrubs and rocks. A gate led from the garden. Akitada found the stairs, and they ran down. Just as they reached the small gate, it burst open and a warrior came rushing through. He saw them, cried, "Tell his Lordship there's a big fire in the kitchens. Lieutenant Imazu has gone to put it out." He turned, then paused and swung back, puzzled. "Who are you?"

Hitomaro's blade flashed. There was a sickening sound, and the man's head rolled into the shrubbery, his blood spurting over Hitomaro and Akitada as the body sagged at the knees and

fell across their path. Hitomaro stepped over it to the gate. Akitada gulped and wiped at the warm wetness on his face.

"Go on, sir," urged Tora behind him, and Akitada gripped
his sword, stepped over the fallen man, and followed Hitomaro
through the gate and down more steps. He saw that they were in
the barracks courtyard now and no longer alone. Soldiers ran
this way and that, shouting to each other. Nobody paid attention to three armed men coming from the direction of the main
house.

They moved quickly and purposefully and passed unhin-
dered through the inner gate, down more steps and into the
gate courtyard.

Here there were fewer soldiers than before, though the
watchtower was still fully manned with archers who sent volley
after volley of arrows down at Takesuke's men outside. The arrows found their targets. Screams came from outside, and triumphant shouts from above. Akitada thought of the narrow
space outside and how any attempt on the closed gate meant almost certain death.

He hurried, trying to remember what Kaoru had said about
the gate—something about its being counterbalanced so that
one man could open it. There was another bloodcurdling
scream, and he broke into a run. Tora and Hitomaro followed.
Someone shouted at them, but all three made it under the gateway, and there, in the shadows, Akitada saw the ropes and pul-
leys. Huge stones hung suspended by ropes that ran over wheels.
The gate itself was massive, iron-studded, and barred with
an enormous horizontal timber. He could faintly hear the
sound of battle-axes against the many layers of wood—Takesuke's
brave men dying in a shower of arrows from above—and
felt defeated by the massiveness of the structure. Where was
Kaoru? Tora was already pushing at the bar, and Hitomaro ran
to give him a hand. The bar did not budge. Akitada turned to

look up at the ropes and stones, trying to trace their path, hoping to understand the crude but effective mechanism. Three of Uesugi's men rushed in, shouting questions. Akitada grunted something in answer, but it was no good. They had realized the truth and attacked. One of them, a big, bearded man, ran at Akitada with the wicked steel blade of the halberd aimed at his belly. Akitada moved aside, felt the blade slice through his trousers, took his sword in both hands and swung down, severing the halberd's wooden handle—a foolish move, because his attacker simply dropped it and drew a short sword instead. For a moment they grappled. The other was bigger and stronger and forced Akitada back against the wall. Another soldier appeared behind him, grinning too soon, because suddenly Kaoru was there beside Akitada and slashed at the man's legs. As he fell screaming, Akitada managed to break free and shove his sword into the man's chest with such force that it disappeared nearly to the hilt. An almost comical expression of surprise passed over the bearded face, then he sagged, skewered, a dead weight on the sword. Akitada had to put his foot on the dead man's body to pull out his weapon. He turned away, dazed by the violence.

"Get back, sir. Get outside!" Kaoru shouted to him and jumped for the largest of the suspended stones.

"Where have you been?" demanded Akitada.

Kaoru missed and jumped again. "Not now," he gasped. This time he grasped the stone and brought it down with him. The wheels spun, ropes creaked—

"Sir!" shouted Tora.

Akitada swung around and looked into another halberd coming at his chest. Uesugi's people had finally grasped what was happening, and the fight was on. Akitada brought up his sword instinctively and deflected the halberd. Equally instinctively—for nowhere had his past training involved fighting with swords against these vicious long-handled weapons carried by most foot soldiers—he drove forward and was mildly astonished how easily his blade slid into the other man's belly.

"Sir—watch out!"

Tora again, and Akitada jerked back, bringing the sword with him followed by a gush of blood and his victim's scream. The gate enclosure had filled with men. There was no time to think, just to fend off the attack and kill. His lessons forgotten, Akitada slashed and swung, two-handed, at wild-eyed shouting men, making a path to the outside, dimly aware of Tora's curses and Hitomaro's broad shoulders and flashing blade. They beat them back, one by one, into the courtyard.

Others came running, but a loud clanking and grinding signaled the opening of the gate, and then came the triumphant din of shouting men as Takesuke's soldiers streamed into Takata manor. They carried the Sugawara insignia of the white plum blossom on their red banners, and Akitada felt a moment's dizzy pride—until the slaughter began.

The passage was narrow, and as the men emerged in groups of three or four at a time, a hail of arrows from above greeted them. The archers felled every second man. Akitada saw one of the arrows pass through a banner and into the man's unprotected skull. As he watched the soldier topple forward, another arrow glanced off his own helmet, making his ears ring, and Hitomaro pulled him into the shadow of the wall.

"Stay here, sir. Tora and I are going up."

Akitada gulped some air and glanced up. Stairs led to the tower platform above him. From there, the Uesugi's archers were taking out Takesuke's men as easily as the courtiers back in the capital used to shoot the deer driven into an enclosure by beaters. He cried, "Come on!" and made for the stairs.

"Wait, sir." Tora caught his sleeve.

Akitada wanted to tear away angrily, but then he remembered his place and stepped aside. A retainer's duty was to protect his master. Shame attached to him if he failed to do so. Hitomaro was already running up the steps, Tora at his heels, when Akitada followed.

The first steps were of stone but where the tower began, they changed to wood and the space narrowed so that only one man could climb. Akitada could see the gray sky ahead. Then a face appeared against it. Tora flung himself against the wall, and Hitomaro ducked. An arrow hissed past Akitada's ear, hit the wooden wall behind him with a sharp *thwack*. The shaft hummed as it vibrated from the impact.

Tora jumped forward. With a roar, he seized the archer's leg and pulled him down through the opening. As the man fell, Hitomaro ran his sword through him, pulled it out, and pushed the body down toward Akitada.

Akitada ducked aside, then ran up the rest of the steps. The top of the watchtower was becoming a scene of carnage. In the dreary light of the winter day, Tora and Hitomaro slashed right and left at the archers who dropped their bows but had only short swords against their long ones.

He took a deep breath, gagged on the smell of fresh blood in his nostrils, and flung himself into the fray of clashing blades and grunting, screaming men. He lunged and slashed, lunged again, parried, felt his sword bite, and dove under a raised weapon. He partially decapitated one man who was about to stab Tora in the back, then turned and slashed at another who was coming at him. With his longer blade, he caught him across the belly, laying open pale intestines quickly covered with blood. The man dropped his sword and clutched at himself, his eyes wide with pleading. But Akitada was already moving past him, pursuing another man, his mouth opened in terror as he backed away. Before Akitada could kill him, the man screamed and flung himself over the railing to his death below.

It became quiet on the watchtower. Outside the clouds

moved slowly in the wind and gusts of sleet blew in. A few of the archers had escaped down the stairs, another had jumped, the rest lay dead or wounded. The wooden boards were slick with blood. Only the three of them were left standing. Tora wiped blood from his face and bellowed a cheer. Then he grinned at Akitada. "We got them, sir."

Akitada grinned back, feeling an enormous surge of exultation. He had fought and survived. One of the wounded wept noisily. Akitada slipped in a puddle of blood oozing from a dead man. This was war and it was more exciting than anything he had ever done before. He wanted more of it. Leaning over the side of the tower, he looked down into the courtyard. Frightened horses ran among the scattered bodies. Here and there, a wounded man was dragging himself to safety. Takesuke's soldiers were everywhere, their red banners with the Sugawara crest fluttering where Uesugi's black and white ones had been before. From the barracks courtyard he could hear more sounds of fierce fighting—screaming men and clashing metal. To the east, the dense cloud of smoke over the kitchen area had doubled in size and flames licked through the blackness.

Time to look for Uesugi. Why had he not joined his men? The main house lay as yet untouched.

Hitomaro was already running down the stairs. Tora checked the wounded and tossed their weapons over the balustrade.

"Have you seen Kaoru?" Akitada asked.

"Who cares about him," Tora growled. "I couldn't believe my ears when he started giving the orders."

Akitada, still filled with joy, chuckled and wiped his bloody blade on the jacket of one of the dead. "It's in his blood, Tora."

Tora paused to stare. "What?"

Akitada made for the stairs. "Never mind. Come, there's more work to be done. You don't want Takesuke to have all the glory, do you?"

They ran down the stairs and across the entrance courtyard, dodging horses and Takesuke's men. Tora snatched one of the Sugawara banners from a fallen man and carried it. No point in getting killed by their own. Up the next set of stairs and into the barracks enclosure. They caught up with Hitomaro, and together again they skirted the vicious fighting. More Uesugi archers were shooting arrows from the loopholes of the gallery they had been in earlier, and below foot soldiers slashed and lunged at each other with halberds. Neither Uesugi nor his senior retainers were in sight.

They made for the small door that led to the main house.

"Wait!" Kaoru, bloodied but determined, joined them. They went through the door and into the small garden where the headless corpse still lay across the path.

"What took you so long?" Akitada demanded, stopping just inside and glaring at Kaoru. "We waited in that shed until we were sure you had been captured."

Kaoru grimaced. "I couldn't find Koreburo right away. They caught him setting his fire. He was still alive when I found him and . . . I could not leave him right away. Sorry, sir."

Akitada was sobered. "Poor old man. Very well, let's go get Makio and stop this killing."

There was no more need for caution now. The archers at their loopholes were too intent on the foe outside to turn around. The four of them ran past and into the main house, their boots thumping up stairways and across the glossy boards. They slammed through doorways and flung back sliding doors. The armory had served its purpose. Weapons chests stood open and empty, some of their contents gone or scattered about. Helmets, parts of armor, long swords, discarded halberds, and an upended quiver of short arrows lay abandoned like the toys of giant children.

In the reception area, four senior Uesugi officers, older men with lined faces and grizzled beards, guarded the doors to the ceremonial hall. They drew their swords. Hitomaro instantly flung himself at them, and Kaoru and Tora joined him. There were four of the enemy, seasoned fighters and rested, but Akitada could not wait. His bloody sword in hand, he moved past them and flung open the great double doors to the hall.

"Takata has fallen. In the name of the emperor, surrender!"

Time seemed to pause as startled faces turned toward him. Uesugi sat, straddling a campaign stool on the dais. He wore white silk robes under black lacquered armor and his black horned helmet was on his head. Seated on the floor in a semicircle before him were seven or eight armed men, their helmets held respectfully against their bodies. Akitada almost laughed out loud: the general at a council of war after the battle was already lost.

But then, of one accord, the warriors were up, dropping their helmets, drawing their swords and charging. There was no time left to prepare. Like the four outside, these were older men, but they were desperate and duty-bound to die for their lord. Akitada knew he could not fight them all and survive, and suddenly the icy clutch of fear twisted inside him again. He slashed out wildly at the first man and, with more luck than skill, severed his sword hand, but two more were on him. He lunged, parried a hard stroke, took a step forward and lunged again, slashing at one man's thighs, then brought up his blade to sweep the other man's sword aside. The Uesugi warrior screamed and fell, and suddenly he was no longer alone. Tora was beside him, shouting, "Kill the bastards!" as he cut off a man's head in a spray of blood. Akitada's blade scraped across a breastplate, driving another fighter back. He followed, aiming for the unprotected neck of his helmetless adversary. The other twisted away, and the blade missed, slicing deeply into his arm instead. Akitada's sword became entangled in the cords of the other man's armor. He kneed him in the groin and jerked it free. And then he saw his way clear and made for the dais, dodging one blade, and slashing at another, his eyes on Uesugi.

The Lord of Takata had jumped up, sword in hand, his round face as white as his robe. The small eyes bulged and his mouth was open. He saw Akitada coming for him, but he stood, sword dangling, frozen and speechless.

So it was going to be easy after all, thought Akitada, surprised—almost disappointed. He simply stepped up on the dais and placed the tip of his sword against Uesugi's throat. "Stop the fighting!" he shouted over the noise of clashing swords and the cries of the wounded. He told Uesugi, "It's over. Tell your men to surrender!"

It became quiet in the hall.

Uesugi swallowed, then nodded his head violently, causing the tip of Akitada's sword to nick his throat. A few red drops fell on the white silk of his robe. He looked down, whimpered, then sat, muttering, "Blood. She said blood on snow. Blood on the snow!" Raising his hands to Akitada, he cried, "I surrender, I surrender! Don't kill me! I will serve the emperor. I have many men, much influence. A treaty. We can make a treaty. I guarantee protection against the northern barbarians in exchange for my life." Behind Akitada someone cursed loudly—one of Uesugi's men.

Akitada put up his sword and turned away in disgust. Two of the Takata warriors, both wounded, had lowered their swords at Uesugi's cry of surrender. Tora was leaning against a pillar. He bled from several wounds. Akitada looked for the others. Kaoru, also bloody, pulled his sword from the belly of a fallen Uesugi fighter and released a red tide. His victim died with a shout and convulsion, and Kaoru gave Akitada a nod.

Hitomaro, miraculously unscathed, stood in a pool of blood above a fallen warrior, sword gripped in both hands, on his face the fierce snarl of one of the guardian spirits at temple gates. He was looking around for more butchery, but the last two Uesugi officers dropped their swords with grim faces and knelt. It was over.

"Who is second in command here?" Akitada snapped.

One warrior looked around at the bodies, then rose.

"You heard your master. Go outside and order your men to lay down their arms. This stronghold has fallen and Lord Uesugi is my prisoner." As an afterthought, he added, "In the name of his most august Majesty."

At that moment, Akitada savored the intoxicating taste of victory. His hands and knees trembled with the emotion. But he reminded himself that the credit for their success must be shared and turned to Kaoru. "You may take charge of Takata manor."

Then, with hideous irony, fortune turned.

Akitada had shifted his attention from Kaoru to Tora, to ask about his wounds. As their eyes met, Akitada saw Tora's widen in sudden horror. What happened next would always remain a blur in his memory. He heard a hoarse, almost inhuman roar, and saw Hitomaro rush at Uesugi with a drawn sword.

Instinctively Akitada stepped in front of his prisoner and into Hitomaro's path. The force of their collision cost them both their balance. Akitada was flung aside and half fell. He saw his burly lieutenant falter and change the grip on his sword, saw Uesugi up and moving forward with his sword, saw Hitomaro stagger back, then swing his blade in a wide arc.

It was all over in a breath, but compressed into that moment were sounds as well as sights, the stamping of feet, the clatter of the toppled campaign stool, the rustle of Uesugi's silks and hiss of Hitomaro's sword, human grunts, and then the heavy thud of bodies falling onto the wooden dais. And silence.

He was sickened. A single mistake, a wrong move, and triumph had turned to despair.

Uesugi and Hitomaro lay sprawled across the dais in a parody of embracing lovers. The Lord of Takata was dead. His head, partially severed, rested oddly next to his right shoulder in a quickly widening pool of gore; the piggish eyes had rolled upward, showing their whites, and his teeth were bared in a final snarl. The horned helmet lay near Akitada's feet, which were speckled with blood. And Uesugi's snowy silk robe now bore the crimson blossoms of his violent death.

Hitomaro, who had fallen partly across Uesugi's body, slowly rolled onto his back. His left hand was at his chest, clutching the blade of Uesugi's sword which protruded from his ribs. He grimaced with pain. The fingers of his right hand relaxed around the grip of his own bloodstained blade.

Tora came and bent over his friend. When he straightened up, he had a strange, hurt look on his face. "Sir?"

The blood bubbling up between the sword and Hitomaro's hand was bright red and foamy. There was no surviving such a wound to the lungs. Akitada fell to his knees beside him.

"My friend," he pleaded, putting his hand on the one that still gripped the deadly blade. "Please forgive me."

Hitomaro looked up at him and shook his head. "Nothing to forgive . . . I wanted death," he mouthed, half-choking. Then, making a great effort, he added, "Sorry about . . ." and coughed once, blood trickling from the corner of his mouth into his beard. "Too much . . ." He raised himself up a little, coughed again, then vomited a crimson flood and fell back.

Akitada got up. He looked about the room blindly. "How did this happen? Why did Hitomaro attack Uesugi? There was no need. Uesugi had surrendered. It was all so easy. Why?"

Tora said, "Uesugi drew his sword, sir. While you had your

back to him. The slimy coward was going to cut you down. Hitomaro stopped him."

A grim-faced Kaoru walked up and stood staring down at the two corpses. "A warrior's death for Hitomaro," he said. "No man could die better than this."

Without a word, Akitada turned and strode from the hall. Out in the gallery, he stepped over the dead warriors and threw wide a shutter to gulp in the frigid air. Sleet had gathered like grains of rice on the sill. Below, the land lay dark and forbidding under the heavy clouds. Faintly, the sound of temple bells came on the wind from the distant city.

The icy air settled his stomach a little. His face tingled with cold and when he touched it, he found it wet with tears. Ashamed, he rubbed the moisture away. From the courtyard below rose the victorious shouts of Takesuke's men. He leaned forward and looked down. The Sugawara family crest blazed on the banners. This day he had taken an impregnable fortification for the emperor but lost a loyal friend.

Looking down at his hands he saw that they were stained with blood—Hitomaro's along with that of too many other men he had killed. How was he to live with his friend's blood on his hands? Hitomaro had saved his life, and he had stupidly stepped in his way and caused his death as surely as if he had held Uesugi's sword himself. He clenched his fists until his nails bit deeply into his palms.

Something soft and white drifted in. A snowflake. For him this snow country would always be tinged with blood. He sighed deeply and glanced toward the north pavilion overhanging the ramparts, site of the death of the previous Lord of Takata and the murder of his faithful servant Hideo. It reminded him that he had one more errand to perform.

Hunching his shoulders against the icy air, he walked quickly down corridors. A maid peered from an open doorway, paled at the sight of his blood-smeared face and hands, and ran. When he reached the open gallery, he found that the wind had died down, but the snow still fell softly and silently. There was very little smoke now, and he realized that they must have extinguished the fire.

The door to the north pavilion was unlocked, and inside everything looked the same. He had worried that Uesugi would order a thorough cleaning, but either respect or superstition had caused him to leave the room untouched.

He went to the window above the thick mat where the old lord had died. The crooked blind of speckled bamboo was as he remembered it, and beside the mat was the chest which held the dead man's bedding and his writing set, the single clue to what had happened that night.

Stepping on the mat, he untied the bamboo shade, half afraid that his guess had been wrong. But it unrolled with a rush and clatter, releasing a sheet of paper which fluttered to his feet. The thick mulberry paper was covered with spidery script and bore a crimson seal.

Picking it up, Akitada noted both signature and seal, glanced at the content, then rolled up the document and put it in his sleeve.

TWENTY-TWO

CHRYSANTHEMUM
AND GRASSES

When they returned to the tribunal late that night, Akitada was exhausted in mind and body from the business of settling affairs at Takata—he had left Kaoru and Takesuke in control—and emotionally drained. The long ride back with Hitomaro's corpse slung over the horse beside him had given him unwanted time to brood on his actions. Takesuke had congratulated him on his courage, and Akitada had wanted to wipe the look of admiration from his face. At least Tora, who had lost a lot of blood, would heal. Akitada felt profoundly guilty that, of the four of them, he had come out of the fight unscathed.

Genba wept like a child when he carried the body of his friend to a temporary bier in the tribunal hall. There he and Tora would keep watch over Hito's corpse.

Akitada entered his private quarters only briefly. Seimei tried to fuss over him, but the small amount of bleeding from his old shoulder wound and assorted bruises where his body armor had deflected sword blows amounted to nothing. When Akitada saw the joyous relief on Tamako's face, it seemed so inappropriate to him that he was sickened and turned from her without a word to seek the solitude of his office. He wanted nothing so much as sleep, oblivion, a few hours of escape from himself—from a man he never knew, from the blood lust that had lain hidden inside him all his life, from the death of a friend.

But it was not to be. By the flickering light of the oil lamp, he saw a strange figure sitting at his desk. A very old man was hunched over the lacquered box of the shell game, turning it slowly in gnarled hands, absorbed in the pattern of the decoration. He raised his eyes unhurriedly to Akitada and nodded a greeting. The *yamabushi* had returned.

He looked at Akitada for a long moment. Then he gently set down the game and indicated the other cushion. "Please be seated, Governor," he said courteously in a deep, restful voice. "You look very tired."

Dazed, Akitada obeyed. He tucked his hands into his sleeves and shivered, but it was not from cold, for it was almost cozy in the light of the single oil lamp casting a warm glow on the desk between the two men.

The old priest pushed the brazier a little closer to Akitada. Steam and a curious fragrance rose from the small iron tea kettle on it. The master reached for a cup, poured, and stirred. "Drink this," he ordered, sharp black eyes watching from a face as wrinkled and dark brown as a nut.

Akitada tasted, then slowly emptied the cup.

"An infusion of dried berries, herbs, and certain tree barks," the master said, answering an unspoken question. "You will feel refreshed in a moment and later you will sleep."

"Thank you. It has a pleasant taste." The visitor's solicitude was comforting. Akitada became aware of a welcome warmth. He frowned with the effort to remember. "You're right. I have had a long and difficult day." Even the soreness in his shoulder seemed to ease. His eyes strayed to the desk where the *yamabushi*'s conch shell had joined the black-feathered arrow and the shell game.

"Tell me what happened at Takata," the priest encouraged.

"We took the manor. Makio is dead . . . and so is Hitomaro." And no medicine or spell would make that right again.

"Ah!" A long pause ensued, then the *yamabushi* shook his head regretfully. "It's a pity about Hitomaro. I liked that young man." His silver hair and beard shimmered in the light of the oil lamp. He looked at Akitada and said, "But you, you are alive. You must learn to forgive yourself for what is merely a manifestation of fate. It is a hard lesson, but death is right in its time."

Empty platitudes, Akitada thought. He felt shame like the thrust of a knife to his belly and turned his head away.

"Come, I did not think you a fool, Governor," the *yamabushi* said more sharply.

Angered, Akitada swung back. "I am not a fool. But neither am I a saint or a martyr like you, my Lord. When I lose a friend through my own carelessness, I cannot shrug it off and busy myself with good deeds and prayers instead."

The old man sighed. With his gnarled finger he traced the design on the lacquer box. "The chrysanthemum is the last flower to bloom," he murmured. "Its petals fall and the young grasses shrivel and die when the storm of winter touches their brief lives. Death, Governor, is a wide gate no one can close."

Akitada clenched his fists. "Never mind! You cannot understand."

The priest laughed very softly. "On the contrary. I, of all people, understand very well. If you know who I am, you should also know that."

The man's complete detachment filled Akitada with fury. He leaned forward and stabbed an accusing finger toward him. "I know that you are the late Lord Maro's older brother, the uncle of Makio," he growled. "I know that you have a grandson, Kaoru, who has played various roles—among them those of a humble woodcutter from the outcast village and my sergeant of constables. I know about the crime of which you stood accused. I know that you fled, giving up your birthright and hiding among the outcasts as a mountain priest." He paused and pulled from his sleeve the document he had found at Takata and tossed it on the desk. "And now I also know that you were innocent of the murder of that woman and child. Read your brother's confession."

The old man ignored the paper. "Did my foolish grandson reveal so much?"

"No. Kaoru did everything he could to protect your secret. Every time I asked questions about you or his background, he became evasive. But I noticed that he was as familiar with a hermit's life in a mountain cave as with the secret passages in Takata manor."

The white head nodded. "He likes you, too," he said, seemingly inconsequentially.

This was getting them nowhere. Akitada pointed at the paper on the desk. "Your brother wrote this on his deathbed. Forty years ago he used one of your black arrows to murder your father's young wife and son because he wanted to rid himself of both you and your father's favorite. But the deed haunted him. I have no doubt he eventually spoke to his son about it, and that Makio kept him a virtual prisoner after that. When your brother felt death approaching, he asked a trusted servant to smuggle paper to him during the banquet Makio gave in my honor. Today I retrieved his confession from the place where the two old men had hidden it."

Akitada fell silent.

Today! Was it still the same day? The memory of the blood, of the tangled bodies of Makio and Hitomaro rose vividly before his eyes. Hitomaro's last words had been about his wish to die. He had rushed toward death from the moment they had entered the secret passage. Life was too short for some, and much too long for others. The old man across from him had held the key to a deadly mystery for forty years. It could be argued that all the suffering in this province had been caused by the wrong son seizing power in Takata forty years ago. Now the true heir was sitting across from him, apparently unmoved and unsurprised, not even curious enough to pick up the scroll for which the faithful Hideo had died.

As if he had read his thoughts, his visitor asked, "What happened to Hideo?"

Akitada said coldly, "He was tortured and then thrown off the mountain when he would not reveal the hiding place of your brother's confession. No doubt he would have died in either case, since he knew the truth."

To Akitada's satisfaction, the old man finally reacted. He put a hand over his eyes. "Makio did this?" he asked in a tight voice.

"Kaibara. I was there that night. Kaibara was the only one who left the banquet at the right time. He was seen going to the old lord's pavilion by the same two maids who had watched Hideo taking writing paper to your brother earlier."

"Ah." His visitor lowered his hand, and nodded. His face was calm again.

"However, since Kaibara had not been summoned from your brother's pavilion, it means almost certainly that he was carrying out Makio's instructions."

The white head nodded. "Yes. It may well have been so."

Without disguising his contempt, Akitada said, "Many people have died as a consequence of that false accusation, my Lord. You knew it was false, yet you chose to run and hide among the outcasts when you should have faced your troubles and fought for justice. Not doing so has plunged this province and its inhabitants into misery and bloodshed. It cost Hideo his life. And today I lost a friend because of it."

The old man looked back at him calmly. "That is very true."

"Just now you lectured me about fate," Akitada cried angrily, "but you understand nothing of duty. If you had done your duty by your people and defended yourself against the charges, fate would have taken a different course. Your religious life with all its sacrifices, your service to the poor, and your sentimental protection of every criminal in the area do not absolve you from the guilt of having abandoned your duty."

"When it comes to duty," said the old man with a gentle smile, "I hope that you will think my offense somewhat mitigated by the fact that I found a suitable substitute in you." He took the arrow and held it up. "I can still bend a bow and hit a target when it is required."

Akitada tensed. Of course. How could he have forgotten? This old man was the Uesugi heir who had been a champion archer in his youth. It was he who had killed Kaibara and saved his life that night among the graves. "Yes," he said. "I should have known it was you." Miserably, he added, "I suppose I must be grateful, though I cannot take much pleasure in my life at the moment." Hitomaro's death would not have happened, if Kaibara had been successful that night.

"No need to thank me." The old man took the arrow and put it into his rope belt. "It was not a personal matter. I merely mention it, because you doubted my sense of duty to my people. Fate also follows the dutiful action. Kaibara's is the only life I have ever taken, and I broke my Buddhist vows when I decided that your life was more valuable to my people than his." He sighed. "I suppose I must add another sin, the satisfaction of having avenged my old friend Hideo."

Suddenly Akitada felt overwhelmed by sadness. So many wasted lives. And now all was over and done with. What remained was the future. He looked at his visitor uncertainly. Even the ravages of decades spent exposed to the harsh elements of the cold north could not altogether hide the grace and charisma of the strange creature across from him. His skin was blackened, and his hair and beard flowed wildly about his shoulders and chest, but his eyes were alive with intelligence. He wore fewer clothes than the poorest beggar and looked more like a goblin than a rational man, but his speech and manners were those of a man born to rank. Moreover, he seemed to have gained the respect, even reverence, of the local people.

With a sigh, Akitada said, "It is late. You must spend the night. We will meet again in the morning to discuss your reinstatement. It will please the people and bring harmony back to the province."

The rightful Lord of Takata raised his hand. "No. I am a Buddhist priest and have no desire to resume my title."

"What?" Akitada was dumbfounded.

The old man stroked his beard, smiled, and nodded. "My grandson will do very well instead," he said complacently.

"Kaoru?" Akitada opened his mouth to argue, but thought better of it. The capture of Takata manor would have been impossible without that remarkable young man's ruse, and he had proven his courage and military skill not only in combat but also on the occasion of Boshu's attack on Hitomaro. Hitomaro!

"Dew and tears are equally transient," remarked the old man with a sympathetic nod.

Akitada flushed. The way the other man seemed to read his mind was uncanny. "It is true that your grandson Kaoru has some superior qualities," he said stiffly. "I assume it was you who taught him archery and to read and write Chinese? He told me the arrow that killed Kaibara belonged to a dead man and that a Buddhist priest instructed him in Chinese."

The proud grandfather chuckled. "A quick learner, that boy! His father did not do as well."

And that raised the problem of legitimacy. Akitada hesitated, then asked bluntly, "You say you are a priest. Did you take one of the outcast women to wife?"

For the first time, the old man looked uncomfortable. His dark, leathery hand reached out to the box of shells and touched it almost apologetically. "No," he said, "not an outcast, though we both became untouchable. Masako was a young woman of good family who had the bad karma to be sent to Takata for training in household matters. She became fond of me. When I had to flee, she followed me into exile. It seemed right that I should make her my wife. I took priestly vows after her death."

"Ah!" At least she was not the madwoman of the outcast village, the one through whom the gods spoke. That one must be the mother of the dead son's wife. "You married in exile? And you had a son soon after?"

The old man nodded.

Akitada stared at him. "Good heavens, man! You were the older son, the heir; you were the pride of the Uesugi clan. More importantly, you were innocent of the murders. Why did you not stay and fight for your birthright, for the birthright of your son?"

"Because I was guilty."

"No." Akitada tapped the old lord's confession on the desk between them. "It was your brother who committed those murders."

The priest said sadly, "Poor Maro. We met in the forest one day, you know. At first he didn't recognize me. I was greatly changed, you see." He gestured at his clothes and beard. "But I spoke to him, and he fainted. Perhaps he took me for a demon or thought I was seeking vengeance, I don't know. When I saw what I had done, I went away. They say he went mad after that."

"Not mad. He went home and told his son that you were alive. Makio locked him up in the north pavilion." Akitada reached for the rolled paper and pressed it in the old man's hand. "Read what your brother wrote before he died," he urged.

The priest put the paper back on the desk. "It changes nothing. What is written is of things long past. Only the heart knows all the gains and losses."

Baffled, Akitada ran his hand through his hair. He was getting drowsy. "I don't understand," he complained. "Why should your brother confess to a lie on his deathbed? How could you have been guilty? Nothing makes sense."

The *yamabushi* picked up the conch shell, and rose. He fastened the conch to his belt, took up his staff, gave a last tender touch to the box on the desk, and said, "Farewell, Governor! You should be able to sleep now."

Akitada stumbled to his feet and barred the way. "Wait! You cannot leave like this! I must know the truth. How could I have been so wrong? After all that I learned of your past, both before and after the murder of the young woman and her child, I cannot believe you capable of such a heinous crime."

The old man looked at him, and something in the black depths of his eyes made Akitada back away. "All men," the master said, "are naked under their loincloths. Remember that. I did not bend my bow nor aim my arrow on that golden autumn afternoon, but they died for my offense. The boy was not my father's son. He was mine. That is my guilt, and it caused their deaths." He gestured toward the game on the desk. "That shell game was my gift for her. I ordered it before her death. The chrysanthemums and grasses of our forbidden love. She was named for that flower, and our child was the young green blade of grass growing up in her arms. When my brother found out, he killed both of them—out of respect for our father and for our family honor."

That Akitada did not believe, but the enormity of the other man's tragic transgression and loss left him speechless. He stumbled to his desk and picked up the box. "Here," he said, offering it.

The priest raised both hands in refusal. "No." He smiled a little and said, "I have met your lady and saw that she is with child. When you become downcast again over what cannot be changed, remember: To have her is like having the sun and the moon in your sleeve and holding the universe in your hand. You will need to think of that often in the future."

Barefoot and bare-headed, his lean black frame covered by the rough hemp and skins, the *yamabushi* bowed with a nobleman's grace and softly padded out of the room.

Akitada sank down on his pillow still holding the box. Weariness overwhelmed him, and he looked toward the bedding Tamako had spread for him in the corner. The blankets looked strangely tangled and lumpy. He put the game down and went to investigate.

When he peeled back the layers of quilted silk, he uncovered two soft brushes of glossy black hair, each tied with red silk cord, and a small boy's rosy cheek and silken lashes. Toneo was fast asleep, his round childish hand curled about Akitada's flute.

He covered the child again, and looked about the room. Where was he to sleep? Then his eyes fell on the game.

When he slipped into Tamako's room, she was huddled under the bedding. But he knew she was awake and sighed. She sat bolt upright, looking at him, her eyes large and tragic in the light of his candle.

"Tamako?" His voice encompassed all his grief, and guilt, and pain, and utter, utter weariness.

Wordlessly she reached out to him, the paleness of her skin touched by the golden candlelight—and he went into her arms.

HISTORICAL NOTE

In the eleventh century, Japan was ruled by court nobles under an emperor who was often a minor and retired by the time he reached his thirties. The government was centralized in Heian-Kyo (modern Kyoto) and kept an increasingly tenuous control over the various provinces by assigning court nobles to serve as provincial governors for four years at a time. The more unpleasant assignments were often filled by minor nobles while the actual appointees remained at court and collected part of the stipend.

Both Japanese culture and political structure were based on those of the Chinese T'ang dynasty, but many of these customs were only loosely followed by this time. Contemporary historical sources pertain mostly to the pursuits of the aristocracy in the capital, and for purposes of this novel considerable license was necessary to project what life was probably like in the more distant provinces.

The historical province Echigo is the modern Niigata prefecture, known as "Snow Country" because of its unusually long winters and heavy snowfalls. Little is known of its early history. Naoetsu (or Naoenotsu) was near the coast and is listed as the provincial government post in the twelfth century. By that time, Takata was a local stronghold, though the Uesugi family rose to power later. The description of Takata manor is fictional. However, references to the continuous warfare against the Ezo (Ainu) people of the north, the existence of military garrisons in both Echigo and the adjoining Dewa province, and the ascendancy of local hereditary warlords over the appointed governors are all historical facts for the eleventh century.

References to outcasts require explanation, since Western readers rarely associate either caste or slavery with the Japanese. But from earliest times a separate group of people existed who were shunned by most Japanese and tolerated only for the most menial labors. These outcasts were probably descendants of slaves (taken during wars) or of exiled criminals. More than likely in the northern province of Echigo such outcasts could have had mixed Ainu and Japanese blood by this time, partially because many exiles were sent there from other parts of the country.

The issue of exile brings up law enforcement as it was practiced in eleventh century Japan. Originally based on the Chinese system of local wardens, constables, tribunals, and judges, the harsh punishments meted out in China soon became unacceptable to the Japanese because Buddhism forbids the taking of life. Any crime which would have demanded the death penalty was therefore punished by exile with or without hard labor. Criminals were generally arrested either by local constables working under a headman, or by the police (*kebiishi*), under an officer.

The police system had been established early in the ninth century in the capital and gradually extended throughout the provinces. As in China, confessions were necessary for conviction, and these could be obtained through flogging.

Two religions coexisted in Japan: the native Shinto faith, an animistic belief tied to Japanese gods and agricultural matters, and Buddhism, which was imported from China via Korea and dominated the aristocracy and therefore the government. Occasionally the two faiths merge, as in the strange mountain priests, the *yamabushi*. They are Buddhist ascetics, or hermits, who grow their hair long, practice healing and shamanistic rituals like exorcism, and sometimes marry their female mediums. Shinto is responsible for the belief in spirit possession and many taboos, including those against contact with the dead and directional taboos. Buddhism brought faith in relics and miracles, the concepts of heaven and hell, and the belief in rebirth and karma. Monsters, ghosts, and demons abounded in popular superstitions, and the souls of the dead were thought to dwell among the living for forty-nine days, occasionally haunting their enemies.

The calendar of ancient Japan is complicated, being based on the Chinese hexagenary cycle. It has named eras, designated periodically and irregularly by the government. Greatly simplified, there were twelve months and four seasons as in the West, but the lunar year begins later (in early spring). A work week lasted six days, started at dawn, and was followed by a day of leisure. By the Chinese system, the day was divided into twelve two-hour segments. Time was kept by official water clocks and announced by guardsmen, watchmen, and temple bells.

Food and drink in the eleventh century differed little from later times, although tea drinking had not yet become a custom. (Tea was known but expensive and used primarily for medicinal purposes.) The common drink was water or rice wine (sake).

Meat was not consumed because of Buddhist strictures against the killing of animals, though the nobles did eat the wild fowl they hunted, and everyone ate fish. Generally the wealthy ate a diet of rice, fish, and fruit, while the poor and Buddhist monks consumed millet, beans, and vegetables.

Two plots, the story of the deserter and the murder of the innkeeper, are based on brief accounts in the ancient Chinese collection of famous criminal cases (*T'ang-Yin-Pi-Shih*, 23 and 33). The collection was known in Japan at an early date.